THE MODERN LIBRARY
OF THE WORLD'S BEST BOOKS

Selected Stories of Sholom Aleichem

Selected Stories of

Sholom Aleichem

with an introduction by
ALFRED KAZIN

THE MODERN LIBRARY · NEW YORK

c. 1

Library of Congress Catalog Card Number: 56–8836

"On Account of a Hat," translated by Isaac Rosenfeld, and "The Pair," translated by Shlomo Katz, in *A Treasury of Yiddish Stories*, edited by Irving Howe and Eliezer Greenberg, copyright, 1954, by The Viking Press, Inc., and reprinted by permission of The Viking Press, Inc., New York. The remaining stories in this book were translated by Julius and Frances Butwin in *The Old Country*, copyright, 1946, by Crown Publishers, Inc., and reprinted by arrangement with Crown Publishers, Inc.

Random House IS THE PUBLISHER OF *The Modern Library*

BENNETT CERF • DONALD S. KLOPFER

Manufactured in the United States of America by H. Wolff

CONTENTS

INTRODUCTION

by Alfred Kazin

The way to read Sholom Aleichem is to remember from the outset that he is writing about a people, a folk, the Yiddish-speaking Jews of Eastern Europe. There are a great many Jews and non-Jews who resent the idea that the Jews are a people, for they think that this requires all Jews to speak the same language and to live in the same territory. But the characters in this book already are a people. They are a people not merely because they speak the same language, Yiddish, or because they live in the Pale of Settlement that the Czarist government kept Jews in. They are a people because they think of themselves as a people. And what is most important, they are a people because they enjoy thinking of themselves as a people.

This is the great thing about the Jews in this book. They enjoy being Jews, they enjoy the idea of belonging to the people who are called Jews—and "their" Sholom Aleichem, perhaps more than any other Jewish writer who has ever lived, writes about Jewishness as if it were a gift, a marvel, an unending theme of wonder and delight. He is one of those writers whose subject is an actual national character, a specific type—the Jew as embodied in the poor Jew of Eastern Europe. In a way he does remind us of Mark Twain, who was so entranced with a new character, the Western American, that he was always trying to weigh him, to describe him, as if he, Mark Twain, had discovered a new chemical element. When Mark Twain writes of "the calm confidence of a Christian with four aces," we know that the pleasure he gets in writing that is, in part, the satisfaction of knowing that no one but an American could have written that sentence. It is an artistic pleasure, not a chauvinistic affirmation or a defensive maneuver; it is the pleasure of presenting certain local traits, feelings, habits, jokes, even certain biological characteristics, as a physical *substance,* a living addition to the world of nature—something that you can smell and taste and enjoy. You find this kind of artistic substance in Shakespeare's presentation of a lower-class character like Pistol; in Dickens' Cockneys, who walk off the streets of London, delighting us with their pleasure in being Londoners, in their physical relish of their identity as people of that place and time (and who are proud that they spring straight from the imagination of Charles Dickens). Americans, in their attempt to endow a new country with a specific national type, have contributed very largely to this art of national character. But, generally, this kind of pleasure in one's own national being is, I should say, more European than it is American. I have often noticed the difference in the greater pride with which Europeans tend to project their own language, as opposed to our more functional and careless use of English. I have seen it particularly in the Neapolitan dialect theater of Eduardo de Filippo, and in Italian movies, where a type will appear that instantly captivates the audience because he is recognizable, a symbol of the country's human wealth, a tangible re-creation of the life of ordinary experience.

It is this kind of European, seasoned, familiar pleasure in the national circle of one's own people, that lies behind Sholom Aleichem's stories. But what kind of enjoyment can these people derive from being Jews, since they are incessantly harassed by the Russian government, and are surrounded by peasants who are usually anti-Semitic and can easily be goaded, with the help of the usual encouragement from the government itself and a lot of vodka, into making pogroms? What is it, in short, that makes for *enjoyment* in these local terms? The answer is that one enjoys being a member of a people because one shares in the feast of their common experience. You share in something that is *given* to you instead of having to make every institution and every habit for yourself, out of nothing, in loneliness and with exertion. The secret of this enjoyment consists not so much in physical solidarity and "togetherness," in the absence of loneliness, as in the fact that a deep part of your life is lived below the usual level of strain, of the struggle for values, of the pressing and harrowing need—so often felt in America—to define your values all over again in each situation, where you may have even to insist on values themselves in the teeth of a brutish materialism. We enjoy things only when we can commit some part of our daily life to tradition, when we can act ceremonially, ritualistically, artistically, instead of having to decide in each case which act to perform and how to go about it and what we are likely to get out of it. What we enjoy is, in fact, nothing less than the unconscious wealth of humanity, which is its memory.

This is the fabled strength of "the old country," which deprived the Jews of Eastern Europe of every decency that we take for granted, but allowed them to feast unendingly on their own tradition—and even to enjoy, as an unconscious work of art, their projection of their fiercely cherished identity. The very pen name, "Sholom Aleichem," is an instance of this. (His real name was Solomon Rabinowitz; he was born near Kiev in 1859 and died in the Bronx in 1916.) "Sholom Aleichem" is the Hebrew greeting, "Peace Be Unto You," that is exchanged between Jews. It is said with more lightness and playfulness than you would guess from the literal translation. Its chief characteristic, as a greeting, is the evidence it gives of relatedness. Now Solomon Rabinowitz, who actually belonged to the prosperous and more "emancipated" middle class of Russian Jewry (he even married into its landed gentry), took this pen name precisely because he found, in the phrase, an image of the sweet familiarity, the informality, the utter lack of side, that is associated with the Yiddish-speaking masses of Eastern Europe. A Yiddish writer who calls himself *Mister* Sholom Aleichem tells us by this that he has chosen cannily to picture himself as one of the people—and modestly to be a register or listening post for his people. Sholom Aleichem! The name's as light as a feather, as "common" as daylight, as porous to life as good Yiddish talk: it is the very antithesis of the literary, the mannered, the ornate. If you didn't know anything else about Mister Sholom Aleichem (several of his characters address him so when they bring their stories to him) you should be able to guess, from the name, the role that he has chosen to play in his own work. He is the passer-by, the informal correspondent, the post office into which Jews drop their communications to the world. All he does, you understand, is to write down stories people bring him. He invents nothing. And need one say—with that name, with that indescribably dear, puckish, wrinkled face of his—that you will never learn from him what he has invented, that he has all Yiddish stories in his head, that any one story people bring him will always be capped with another?

In the world of Sholom Aleichem, nothing has to be made up, for the life of the Jews, to say nothing of the Jewish character, is an unending drama. Nor can it be said of *anything* that it's never been seen or heard of before. The Jews have lived with each other for a very long time, and they know each other through and through—and this, often enough, is what they enjoy. Their history, alas, has too often been the same, and everything that you see in Kasrilevka (the little Jewish town which is all little Jewish towns) or Yehupetz (Kiev, the big city) can be matched from something in Mazeppa's time, which is late seventeenth century, or Haman's, who tried to kill all the Jews in Persia in the fifth century B.C. Nor, indeed, is anything ever said just *once*. Everything is real, everything is typical, and everything is repeated.

You must understand, first, that the characters in this book possess almost nothing except the word—the Holy word, which is Hebrew, and the word of everyday life, which is Yiddish. They are "little" people not in the sense that they are poor little victims, but in the sense that they are unarmed, defenseless, exiled, not in the world, not in *their* kind of world. All they have is the word. They talk as poor people always talk—because poor people live near each other, and so have a lot of opportunity to talk. They talk the way the European poor always talk—Cockneys or Neapolitans or Provençals: they talk from the belly; they roar, they bellow, they grunt, they scream. They imitate the actual sounds that life makes, and they are rough and blunt. But most of all, they are poor Jews talking, i.e., they find an irony in language itself. Their words strive after the reality, but can never adequately express the human situation.

This sense that the letter strives after the spirit, but can never fully capture it—this seems to me the essence of the historic Jewish consciousness, with its devout and awestruck yet faithful obedience to some overmastering reality. We are all familiar enough with the Hebrew psalmist's despair that he can find the word, the deep, deep word still lacking to human speech, that will convey the bounty of God. But Yiddish, which is particularly the language of the exile, of the long Jewish wandering, is identified by these poor Jews with the contrast between the Jewish situation in the world and the large and inextinguishable hope of another world which they profess. They do not "despise" Yiddish because it is the tongue of everyday life, and one which they themselves call a vernacular; they love it; it is theirs. But by identifying it with their reduced situation, with their exile, with their isolation, they embody in it an historical moment, the present and its desolation, rather than the world of eternity which is mirrored in Hebrew. Yiddish is the poor Jew's everyday clothes rather than his Sabbath garment. But in the Jewish consciousness it is precisely the life of everyday that is contrasted with the divine gift of the Sabbath, and it is this awareness of what life is actually like (seen always against the everlasting history of this people and the eternal promise) that makes the very use of Yiddish an endless commentary on the world as found.

And it is a commentary on the spirit of language itself. One of the things you get from Sholom Aleichem is this mockery of language, a mockery which—need I say it?—carries a boundless pleasure in language and a sense of the positive strength that goes with mighty talk. The mockery may indicate the inadequacy of words when describing the vastness and strangeness of Russia in which Yiddish-speaking Jews felt lost: ". . . They all began to tell each other stories about spirits and ghosts, incidents that had occurred right here in Zolodievka, in Kozodoievka, in Yampoli, in Pischi-Yaboda, in Haplapovitch, in Petchi-Hvost, and other places." It conveys, over and over, a mild, loving, but positive irony toward the Creator. "How cleverly the Eternal One has created this little world of His, so that every living thing, from man to a simple cow, must earn its food. Nothing is free." The mockery may indicate despair at reproducing a really odd face: "In appearance Shimmen-Eli was short and homely, with pins and needles sticking out all over him and bits of cotton batting clinging to his curly black hair. He had a short beard like a goat's, a flattened nose, a split lower lip and large black eyes that were always smiling. His walk was a little dance all his own and he was always humming to himself. His favorite saying was, 'That's life—but don't worry.'" Sholom Aleichem leaves the rest to the imagination. Only the imagination can do justice to the rest.

Or the mockery may, as in a familiarly shrewish tirade by a wife or mother-in-law, mean not only the opposite of what it seems to mean (i.e., it may actually hide affection, though no one but the husband-victim should be expected to know this), but, even more, it will be a commentary—to put it gently!—on the world which a woman cannot always act in, but which, with tongue and blazing eyes, she implacably judges. The husband is always in a direct line of fire, since he is a ne'er-do-well, a *shlemiel,* a genius at bad luck, a *shlimazl.* But it is not the husband's failures alone that are scorned; it is the folly of the world itself—for daring to think of it as *the* world (i.e., a place where human beings can live). Thus Menachem-Mendel ("In Haste"), who tries his hand at everything in the big city and succeeds at nothing, and who, precisely because his ambition is exceeded by his innocence, illustrates the cruelty of the great world in which he naïvely tries to get a living. The particular joke just now is that he has become a professional matchmaker. Home for Passover, he sees, first off, his mother-in-law in the yard, who is engaged in furious housecleaning for Passover:

When she saw me, she managed to control her joy. She kept right on with her work, muttering to herself:

"Well, well! You mention the Messiah—and look who comes! Here he is, my bird of Paradise . . . If he doesn't spoil, he'll find his way home. Goats run away, chickens get lost, but men always come back . . . The only place they don't return from is the Other World. Now I know why the cat was washing herself yesterday, and the dog was eating entrails . . . Oh, Sheine-Sheindel, daughter, come here! Welcome your ornament, your jewel, your crown of gold and diamonds! Your holy of holies . . . Quick, take the garbage away!"

At this point my wife runs out, frightened, and sees me. Her welcome is more direct.

"Tfui!" she spat out. "You picked just the right time to come. All year long you roam around that dirty city, lying around in all the attics, engage in every idolatry—and here you come fluttering in on Passover Eve, when we're busy cleaning up and there is not time to say a word to each other . . ." Etc. Etc.

An irate man says of a stranger he doesn't like: ". . . comes all the way from Zolodievka and fastens himself to us like a grease spot." Sholom Aleichem says of Kasrilevka itself (the very embodiment of all little Jewish towns, the poor man's town): "From a distance it looks—how shall I say it?—like a loaf of bread thickly studded with poppy seed." He remarks, in passing, that "the real pride of Kasrilevka is her cemeteries." The wonderful, the lovable Tevye, Tevye the dairyman, the poorest and most faithful and most touching of all Sholom Aleichem's poor Jews, remarks in passing: ". . . with God's help I starved to death." And when he comes through the woods from Boiberik to Kasrilevka, late, so very late, that he has to say his evening prayers on the spot, the horse runs off, and Tevye runs after his wagon— saying his prayers as he runs. Characteristically, he regrets that he cannot, now, *enjoy* saying his prayers. "A fine way to say *Shmin-esra!* And just my luck, at a moment when I was in the mood to pray with feeling, out of the depth of my heart, hoping it would lift my spirits."

In this world, the extreme is a matter of course—and yet, from a Jewish point of view, an understatement. For these people have much to think about, much to live with, much, much, to live through. In the lovely lyric story, "A Page from the Song of Songs," which portrays the closeness to nature, to ordinary sensuous enjoyments, that these Jews so rarely experienced, the boy cries out, in the rapture of Passover, of spring: "What delights the Lord has provided for his Jewish children." But Tevye the dairyman, who loves God with all his might, can still remember, as he runs after his horse, "chanting at the top of my voice, as if I were a cantor in a synagogue," he can still remember to add private comments on his prayer. *"Thou sustainest the living with loving kindness* (and sometimes with a little food) *and keepest thy faith with them that sleep in the dust.* (The dead are not the only ones who lie in the dust; Oh, how low we the living are laid, what hells we go through, and I don't mean the rich people of Yehupetz who spend their summers at the *datchas* of Boiberik, eating and drinking and living off the fat of the land . . . Oh, Heavenly Father, why does this happen to me?) . . ." And coming to the part of the evening prayer which asks, "*Heal us, O Lord, and we shall be healed,*" he cannot help adding under his breath: "Send us the cure, we have the ailment already."

For Tevye and his people the word is not the beginning of things, the foundation of the world; it is a response to the overmastering reality—to the world and the everlasting creation, the eternal struggle and the inestimable privilege of being a Jew.

ALFRED KAZIN

Selected Stories of Sholom Aleichem

ON ACCOUNT OF A HAT

"Did I hear you say absent-minded? Now, in our town, that is, in Kasrilevka, we've really got someone for you—do you hear what I say? His name is Sholem Shachnah, but we call him Sholem Shachnah Rattlebrain, and is he absent-minded, is this a distracted creature, Lord have mercy on us! The stories they tell about him, about this Sholem Shachnah— bushels and baskets of stories—I tell you, whole crates full of stories and anecdotes! It's too bad you're in such a hurry on account of the Passover, because what I could tell you, Mr. Sholom Aleichem—do you hear what I say?—you could go on writing it down forever. But if you can spare a moment I'll tell you a story about what happened to Sholem Shachnah on a Passover Eve—a story about a hat, a true story, I should live so, even if it does sound like someone made it up."

These were the words of a Kasrilevka merchant, a dealer in stationery, that is to say, snips of paper. He smoothed out his beard, folded it down over his neck, and went on smoking his thin little cigarettes, one after the other.

I must confess that this true story, which he related to me, does indeed sound like a concocted one, and for a long time I couldn't make up my mind whether or not I should pass it on to you. But I thought it over and decided that if a respectable merchant and dignitary of Kasrilevka, who deals in stationery and is surely no *litterateur*—if he vouches for a story, it must be true. What would he be doing with fiction? Here it is in his own words. I had nothing to do with it.

This Sholem Shachnah I'm telling you about, whom we call Sholem Shachnah Rattlebrain, is a real-estate broker—you hear what I say? He's always with landowners, negotiating transactions. Transactions? Well, at least he hangs around the landowners. So what's the point? I'll tell you. Since he hangs around the landed gentry, naturally some of their manner has rubbed off on him, and he always has a mouth full of farms, homesteads, plots, acreage, soil, threshing machines, renovations, woods, timber, and other such terms having to do with estates.

One day God took pity on Sholem Shachnah, and for the first time in his career as a real-estate broker—are you listening?—he actually worked out a deal. That is to say, the work itself, as you can imagine, was done by others, and when the time came to collect the fee, the big rattler turned out to be not Sholem Shachnah Rattlebrain, but Drobkin, a Jew from Minsk province, a great big fearsome rattler, a real-estate broker from way back—he and his two brothers, also brokers and also big rattlers. So you can take my word for it, there was quite a to-do. A Jew has contrived and connived and has finally, with God's help, managed to cut himself in—so what do they do but come along and cut him out! Where's Justice? Sholem Shachnah wouldn't stand for it—are you listening to me? He set up such a holler and an outcry—"Look what they've done to me!"—that at last they gave in to shut him up, and good riddance it was too.

When he got his few cents Sholem Shachnah sent the greater part of it home to his wife, so she could pay off some debts, shoo the wolf from the door, fix up new outfits for the children, and make ready for the Passover holidays. And as for himself, he also needed a few things, and besides he had to buy presents for his family, as was the custom.

Meanwhile the time flew by, and before he knew it, it

was almost Passover. So Sholem Shachnah—now listen to this
—ran to the telegraph office and sent home a wire: *Arriving
home Passover without fail.* It's easy to say "arriving" and
"without fail" at that. But you just try it! Just try riding out
our way on the new train and see how fast you'll arrive. Ah,
what a pleasure! Did they do us a favor! I tell you, Mr.
Sholom Aleichem, for a taste of Paradise such as this you'd
gladly forsake your own grandchildren! You see how it
is: until you get to Zolodievka there isn't much you can do
about it, so you just lean back and ride. But at Zolodievka
the fun begins, because that's where you have to change, to
get onto the new train, which they did us such a favor by
running out to Kasrilevka. But not so fast. First, there's the
little matter of several hours' wait, exactly as announced in
the schedule—provided, of course, that you don't pull in
after the Kasrilevka train has left. And at what time of night
may you look forward to this treat? The very middle, thank
you, when you're dead tired and disgusted, without a friend
in the world except sleep—and there's not one single place
in the whole station where you can lay your head, not one.
When the wise men of Kasrilevka quote the passage from
the Holy Book, *"Tov shem meshemon tov,"* they know what
they're doing. I'll translate it for you: We were better off
without the train.

To make a long story short, when our Sholem Shachnah
arrived in Zolodievka with his carpetbag he was half dead;
he had already spent two nights without sleep. But that was
nothing at all to what was facing him—he still had to spend
the whole night waiting in the station. What shall he do?
Naturally he looked around for a place to sit down. Whoever heard of such a thing? Nowhere. Nothing. No place to
sit. The walls of the station were covered with soot, the floor
was covered with spit. It was dark, it was terrible. He finally
discovered one miserable spot on a bench where he had just
room enough to squeeze in, and no more than that, because
the bench was occupied by an official of some sort in a uniform full of buttons, who was lying there all stretched out

and snoring away to beat the band. Who this Buttons was, whether he was coming or going, he hadn't the vaguest idea, Sholem Shachnah, that is. But he could tell that Buttons was no dime-a-dozen official. This was plain by his cap, a military cap with a red band and a visor. He could have been an officer or a police official. Who knows? But surely he had drawn up to the station with a ringing of bells, had staggered in, full to the ears with meat and drink, laid himself out on the bench, as in his father's vineyard, and worked up a glorious snoring.

It's not such a bad life to be a gentile, and an official one at that, with buttons, thinks he, Sholem Shachnah, that is, and he wonders, dare he sit next to this Buttons, or hadn't he better keep his distance? Nowadays you never can tell whom you're sitting next to. If he's no more than a plain inspector, that's still all right. But what if he turns out to be a district inspector? Or a provincial commander? Or even higher than that? And supposing this is even Purishkevitch himself, the famous anti-Semite, may his name perish? Let someone else deal with him—Sholem Shachnah turns cold at the mere thought of falling into such a fellow's hands. But then he says to himself—now listen to this—Buttons, he says, who the hell is Buttons? And who gives a hang for Purishkevitch? Don't I pay my fare the same as Purishkevitch? So why should he have all the comforts of life and I none? If Buttons is entitled to a delicious night's sleep, then doesn't he, Sholem Shachnah that is, at least have a nap coming? After all, he's human too, and besides, he's already gone two nights without a wink. And so he sits down, on a corner of the bench, and leans his head back, not, God forbid, to sleep, but just like that, to snooze. But all of a sudden he remembers—he's supposed to be home for Passover, and to-morrow is Passover Eve! What if, God have mercy, he should fall asleep and miss his train? But that's why he's got a Jewish head on his shoulders—are you listening to me or not?— so he figures out the answer to that one too, Sholem Shachnah, that is, and goes looking for the porter, a certain

Yeremei, he knows him well, to make a deal with him.
Whereas he, Sholem Shachnah, is already on his third sleepless
night and is afraid, God forbid, that he may miss his train,
therefore let him, Yeremei, that is, in God's name, be sure
to wake him, Sholem Shachnah, because tomorrow night is
a holiday, Passover. "Easter," he says to him in Russian
and lays a coin in Yeremei's mitt. "Easter, Yeremei, do
you understand, *goyisher kop?* Our Easter." The peasant
pockets the coin, no doubt about that, and promises to wake
him at the first sign of the train—he can sleep soundly and
put his mind at rest. So Sholem Shachnah sits down in his
corner of the bench, gingerly, pressed up against the wall,
with his carpetbag curled around him so that no one should
steal it. Little by little he sinks back, makes himself comfortable, and half shuts his eyes—no more than forty winks, you
understand. But before long he's got one foot propped up
on the bench and then the other; he stretches out and drifts
off to sleep. Sleep? I'll say sleep, like God commanded us:
with his head thrown back and his hat rolling away on the
floor, Sholem Shachnah is snoring like an eight-day wonder.
After all, a human being, up two nights in a row—
what would you have him do?

He had a strange dream. He tells this himself, that is,
Sholem Shachnah does. He dreamed that he was riding home
for Passover—are you listening to me?—but not on the
train, in a wagon, driven by a thievish peasant, Ivan Zlodi
we call him. The horses were terribly slow, they barely
dragged along. Sholem Shachnah was impatient, and he
poked the peasant between the shoulders and cried, "May
you only drop dead, Ivan darling! Hurry up, you lout! Passover is coming, our Jewish Easter!" Once he called out to
him, twice, three times. The thief paid him no mind. But all
of a sudden he whipped his horses to a gallop and they went
whirling away, up hill and down, like demons. Sholem Shachnah lost his hat. Another minute of this and he would have
lost God knows what. "Whoa, there, Ivan old boy! Where's
the fire? Not so fast!" cried Sholem Shachnah. He covered

his head with his hands—he was worried, you see, over his lost hat. How can he drive into town bareheaded? But for all the good it did him, he could have been hollering at a post. Ivan the Thief was racing the horses as if forty devils were after him. All of a sudden—tppprrru!—they came to a dead stop, right in the middle of the field—you hear me? —a dead stop. What's the matter? Nothing. "Get up," said Ivan, "time to get up."

Time? What time? Sholem Shachnah is all confused. He wakes up, rubs his eyes, and is all set to step out of the wagon when he realizes he has lost his hat. Is he dreaming or not? And what's he doing here? Sholem Shachnah finally comes to his senses and recognizes the peasant—this isn't Ivan Zlodi at all but Yeremei the porter. So he concludes that he isn't on the high road after all, but in the station at Zolodievka, on the way home for Passover, and that if he means to get there he'd better run to the window for a ticket, but fast. Now what? No hat. The carpetbag is right where he left it, but his hat? He pokes around under the bench, reaching all over, until he comes up with a hat—not his own, to be sure, but the official's, with the red band and the visor. But Sholem Shachnah has no time for details and he rushes off to buy a ticket. The ticket window is jammed, everybody and his cousins are crowding in. Sholem Shachnah thinks he won't get to the window in time, perish the thought, and he starts pushing forward, carpetbag and all. The people see the red band and the visor and they make way for him. "Where to, Your Excellency?" asks the ticket agent. What's this Excellency, all of a sudden? wonders Sholem Shachnah, and he rather resents it. Some joke, a gentile poking fun at a Jew. All the same he says, Sholem Shachnah, that is, "Kasrilevka." "Which class, Your Excellency?" The ticket agent is looking straight at the red band and the visor. Sholem Shachnah is angrier than ever. I'll give him an Excellency, so he'll know how to make fun of a poor Jew! But then he thinks, Oh, well, we Jews are in Diaspora—do you hear what I say?— let it pass. And he asks for a ticket third class. "Which class?"

The agent blinks at him, very much surprised. This time Sholem Shachnah gets good and sore and he really tells him off. "Third!" says he. All right, thinks the agent, third is third.

In short, Sholem Shachnah buys his ticket, takes up his carpetbag, runs out onto the platform, plunges into the crowd of Jews and gentiles, no comparison intended, and goes looking for the third-class carriage. Again the red band and the visor work like a charm, everyone makes way for the official. Sholem Shachnah is wondering, What goes on here? But he runs along the platform till he meets a conductor carrying a lantern. "Is this third class?" asks Sholem Shachnah, putting one foot on the stairs and shoving his bag into the door of the compartment. "Yes, Your Excellency," says the conductor, but he holds him back. "If you please, sir, it's packed full, as tight as your fist. You couldn't squeeze a needle into that crowd." And he takes Sholem Shachnah's carpetbag—you hear what I'm saying?—and sings out, "Right this way, Your Excellency, I'll find you a seat." "What the devil!" cries Sholem Shachnah. "Your Excellency and Your Excellency!" But he hasn't much time for the fine points; he's worried about his carpetbag. He's afraid, you see, that with all these Excellencies he'll be swindled out of his belongings. So he runs after the conductor with the lantern, who leads him into a second-class carriage. This is also packed to the rafters, no room even to yawn in there. "This way please, Your Excellency!" And again the conductor grabs the bag and Sholem Shachnah lights out after him. "Where in blazes is he taking me?" Sholem Shachnah is racking his brains over this Excellency business, but meanwhile he keeps his eye on the main thing—the carpetbag. They enter the first-class carriage, the conductor sets down the bag, salutes, and backs away, bowing. Sholem Shachnah bows right back. And there he is, alone at last.

Left alone in the carriage, Sholem Shachnah looks around to get his bearings—you hear what I say? He has no idea why all these honors have suddenly been heaped on him—first class, salutes, Your Excellency. Can it be on account

of the real-estate deal he just closed? That's it! But wait a
minute. If his own people, Jews, that is, honored him for
this, it would be understandable. But gentiles! The conductor! The ticket agent! What's it to them? Maybe he's dreaming. Sholem Shachnah rubs his forehead, and while passing
down the corridor glances into the mirror on the wall. It
nearly knocks him over! He sees not himself but the
official with the red band. That's who it is! "All my bad
dreams on Yeremei's head and on his hands and feet, that
lug! Twenty times I tell him to wake me and I even give
him a tip, and what does he do, that dumb ox, may he catch
cholera in his face, but wake the official instead! And me
he leaves asleep on the bench! Tough luck, Sholem Shachnah
old boy, but this year you'll spend Passover in Zolodievka,
not at home."

Now get a load of this. Sholem Shachnah scoops up his
carpetbag and rushes off once more, right back to the station
where he is sleeping on the bench. He's going to wake himself up before the locomotive, God forbid, lets out a blast
and blasts his Passover to pieces. And so it was. No sooner
had Sholem Shachnah leaped out of the carriage with his
carpetbag than the locomotive did let go with a blast—do
you hear me?—one followed by another, and then, good
night!

The paper dealer smiled as he lit a fresh cigarette, thin as
a straw. "And would you like to hear the rest of the story?
The rest isn't so nice. On account of being such a rattlebrain, our dizzy Sholem Shachnah had a miserable Passover,
spending both Seders among strangers in the house of a Jew
in Zolodievka. But this was nothing—listen to what happened afterward. First of all, he has a wife, Sholem Shachnah,
that is, and his wife—how shall I describe her to you? *I* have
a wife, *you* have a wife, we all have wives, we've had a taste
of Paradise, we know what it means to be married. All I can
say about Sholem Shachnah's wife is that she's A Number
One. And did she give him a royal welcome! Did she lay

into him! Mind you, she didn't complain about his spending the holiday away from home, and she said nothing about
the red band and the visor. She let that stand for the time
being; she'd take it up with him later. The only thing she
complained about was—the telegram! And not so much
the telegram—you hear what I say?—as the one short phrase,
without fail. What possessed him to put that into the wire:
Arriving home Passover without fail. Was he trying to make
the telegraph company rich? And besides, how dare a human being say 'without fail' in the first place? It did him no
good to answer and explain. She buried him alive. Oh, well,
that's what wives are for. And not that she was altogether
wrong—after all, she had been waiting so anxiously. But this
was nothing compared with what he caught from the town,
Kasrilevka, that is. Even before he returned the whole town
—you hear what I say?—knew all about Yeremei and the
official and the red band and the visor and the conductor's
Your Excellency—the whole show. He himself, Sholem
Shachnah, that is, denied everything and swore up and down
that the Kasrilevka smart-alecks had invented the entire story
for lack of anything better to do. It was all very simple—the
reason he came home late, after the holidays, was that he had
made a special trip to inspect a wooded estate. Woods? Estate? Not a chance—no one bought *that!* They pointed him
out in the streets and held their sides, laughing. And everybody asked him, 'How does it feel, Reb Sholem Shachnah,
to wear a cap with a red band and a visor?' 'And tell us,' said
others, 'what's it like to travel first class?' As for the children,
this was made to order for them—you hear what I say?
Wherever he went they trooped after him, shouting, 'Your
Excellency! Your excellent Excellency! Your most excellent
Excellency!'

"You think it's so easy to put one over on Kasrilevka?"

THE PAIR

It was a damp and dreary spring night. The world slept in darkness and in silence. It was a night for weird dreams.

The dreams that troubled our hero were violent. All night long his mind was disturbed by chickens, geese, and ducks. And in his dream one rooster figured with special prominence, a red bird, young and insolent, who refused to fade away. Persistently he remained in the foreground and provokingly chanted a nonsensical ditty:

> *Cockadoodledo-o-o-o . . .*
> *They will catch you too-oo;*
> *They will beat you,*
> *They will eat you,*
> *They will slit your throat too-oo-oo.*

And each time the red rooster concluded his chant, all the chickens, geese, and ducks would make an unbearable noise.

Our hero was preparing to teach this audacious young rooster a lesson when suddenly there was heard a stamping of feet. A light appeared. Wild unfamiliar voices shouted in unearthly tones, "Not this one—the other—grab him—don't let him get away—tie him—careful with his legs, don't break them—ready?—get a move on—into the wagon with him—"

A pair of powerful hands seized our hero, bound him, twisted his legs, and thrust him into a roomy wagon. In the dark he could discern another creature, apparently female, crouching in the corner and trembling. Two people were puttering about the wagon. One was a savage-looking individual with head bare, the other equally savage but with his head covered by a fur cap. The bareheaded one carefully examined the wagon and the horses. The one with the fur cap leaped savagely onto the wagon and landed on the feet of the prisoners with such force that their heads reeled.

"Be careful now that they don't get untied and escape. Hear me?"

The admonition came from the bareheaded one, but the other did not trouble to answer. He merely lashed the horses and they were off.

2

That they survived the night was itself a miracle. They had no idea where they were, to whom they were being taken, or why.

Because of the darkness they could not see each other very well. Only after dawn could they make each other out and converse quietly.

"Good morning, madam."

"Good morning."

"I could swear you're one of our kind—"

"There's no need to swear. You'll be believed without an oath."

"I recognized you at once, by your beads."

"That shows you have a good eye."

Some minutes passed and he spoke again. "How do you feel?"

"I could wish my feelings on my worst enemies."

Another pause, and then he whispered into her ear, "I want to ask you something."

"Yes."

"What are you accused of?"

"The same as you."

"I mean, what have you done wrong?"

"The same as you."

"It strikes me that you're annoyed about something."

"Annoyed! The boor! He plants himself on my feet and then complains that I'm annoyed."

"What are you saying? I, on your feet?"

"Who else?"

"It's he, that savage with the fur cap, may the devil take him!"

"Really? And I thought it was you. Forgive me if I hurt your feelings."

They could say no more, for the man in the fur cap roused himself and began whipping the horse furiously. The wagon leaped forward. The two prisoners listened to the quivering of their vitals. Suddenly the wagon came to a halt, and they beheld something they had never seen before.

3

For the first time in their lives they saw a tremendous gathering of horses, cows, calves, pigs, and people. There were wagons with hoods raised, filled with goods, loaves of bread, and living creatures—chickens, geese, and ducks piled on top of one another. To one side a bound pig lay on a wagon, and his screeches of protest were deafening, yet no one paid any attention to him. Everyone was excited, everyone talked at once, everyone bustled about—it was a regular fair.

It was to this place that the fur-capped savage brought them. He lowered himself from the wagon and began puttering around with his prisoners. They awoke, strangely excited. What would be done with them now? Would they be untied? Or would he free them and let them go at will?

But their joy was short-lived. He merely moved them

somewhat higher on the wagon, probably so that they could
be seen better. A terrible humiliation! And yet one could
think of it in another way. Perhaps it would be better if
everyone could see them. Let the world see! Some kind soul
might take their part and demand an explanation from the
savage: Why? For what?

Thus the innocent prisoners reasoned, and it seemed that
they reasoned well, for a kind soul did appear, a thickset
woman in a Turkish shawl. She approached, felt around in
the wagon, and asked the fur cap, "Your pair?"

"Any of your business?"

"How much do you want?"

"Where will you get so much money?"

"If I had no money would I talk to a lout like you?"

Such was the conversation between the Turkish shawl and
the fur cap. They haggled for a long time. The savage in the
fur cap remained cold and indifferent. The woman in the
Turkish shawl grew excited. She turned away as if to leave,
but came back at once and the bargaining resumed. This
went on so long that the fur cap grew angry and the two
started cursing each other. Meanwhile the prisoners exchanged
a few words.

"Do you hear, madam?"

"Of course. Why shouldn't I?"

"Is it likely we are about to be ransomed?"

"It certainly looks that way."

"Then why does she bargain over us as if we were geese?"

"The humiliation!"

"Well, let them quarrel, just as long as we go free."

"Amen! I hope so."

The Lord be praised! The Turkish shawl dipped her hand
into her pocket and took out the money.

"You won't let the price down?"

"No."

"Perhaps—all right, all right, just look at him rage. Here's
your money."

And the pair passed from the savage in the fur cap to the

fat woman in the Turkish shawl—that is, from one bondage to another.

4

At the new place the prisoners were untied. Joyfully they felt the ground beneath them. They stretched and paced back and forth to make sure their feet still served them. In their happiness, however, they neglected to notice they were still far from free. Indeed, it took them a while to realize that they remained prisoners. They found themselves in a dark corner, with a warm oven on one side, a cold wall on the other, and an overturned ladder barring the exit. Food and drink had been left for them, and they were now alone, at God's mercy, so to speak. After examining their new dwelling they stood eying each other for a long time, as strangers will, and then they turned each to his own corner, where each surrendered to his own thoughts.

But they were not allowed to think for long. The door of their prison opened, and a crowd of women headed by the Turkish shawl came in. The Turkish shawl led the women to the prisoners, pointed at them, and, her face aglow, asked, "How do you like these two?"

"How much did you pay for them?"

"Guess."

All of them guessed and all were wrong. When the Turkish shawl named the price they clapped their hands in amazement.

Envy crept into their faces. Their cheeks grew flushed, their eyes gleamed, but from their mouths flowed a stream of well wishing.

"Use them in good health! May you enjoy them! May you be as lucky all year! Together with your husband and children!"

"Amen! The same to you. The same to you."

The women left, and a moment later the Turkish shawl

returned, leading in tow a man, a strange creature whose face was matted with red hair. Her face beamed with pride as she led him up to the prisoners.

"Now, *you* are a man of understanding, what do *you* think of this pair?"

The hairy person stared wildly. "I, an expert? What do I know of such things?"

"You're a scholar, and where there is learning there must be wisdom. Shouldn't God grant us a kosher Passover? Isn't it all for the sake of His precious name?"

The hairy person passed his hand over his beard, gazed heavenward, and intoned piously, "May the Almighty grant a kosher Passover to all Jews!"

The Turkish shawl and the hairy man departed, leaving the pair alone. For a moment they stood speechless, still wary of each other. Then she uttered a strange cry that was a cross between a cough and a scream.

He turned toward her. "What ails you, madam?"

"Nothing. I was thinking of home."

"Nonsense. You must forget that. We'd do better to get our bearings and consider what to do."

"Get our bearings? It's clear enough. We're in trouble, great trouble."

"For instance?"

"Don't you see we've been sold to savages just as one sells domestic beasts?"

"What will they do to us?"

"Plenty. When I was still a little bit of a thing I heard a lot of stories about what these savages do to those of our kind who fall into their hands."

"Nonsense! You mustn't believe in fairy tales."

"These aren't fairy tales. I heard it from my own sister. She said they are worse than wild beasts. When one of us is caught by a beast he is devoured, and that's all there is to it, but if—"

"There, there, my friend, it seems to me that you take too pessimistic a view of the world."

"Too which?"

"Too pessimistic."

"What does that mean, pessimistic?"

"It means, well, that you look through dark glasses."

"I don't wear glasses."

"Ha-ha."

"Why do you laugh?"

"Madam, you are a—"

"A what?"

He wanted to tell her, but the door suddenly opened and—

Better read on.

5

The door opened wide, and a mob of small fry charged in like a whirlwind. Their cheeks flushed and their black eyes eager, they dashed toward the oven.

"Where are they? Where? Here they are, right here. Yankel! Berel! Velvel! Elie! Getzel! Quick! Over here!"

Only now did the pair discover what hell really meant: torment, suffering, endless humiliation. The small fry fell upon them like savages in the jungle. They skipped around them, examining them from all sides and loudly ridiculing them.

"Yosel, just look at that nose!"

"A schnozzle, Berel, a real schnozzola."

"Velvel! Pull his nose."

"No, by the mouth, Elie, like this!"

"Pull harder, Getzel! Make him holler!"

"You're all crazy. They holler only when you whistle at them. They can't stand whistling. Want to see? I'll whistle: Pheeeeeeee."

Ruffled, the prisoners blushed, lowered their heads, and exclaimed in unison, *Halder! Halder! Halder!*

The small fry picked it up and savagely mocked them. "Hold him! Hold her! Hold 'em."

Further enraged, the prisoners shouted louder. The youngsters were delighted. Convulsed with laughter, they mocked still louder. "Hold him! Hold her! Hold 'em!"

This competition resulted in such a racket that the Turkish shawl, God bless her, came charging in, grabbed the small fry, and tossed them out one by one, giving each a few sound slaps. This procedure she concluded with an all-round curse. "May a stroke descend on you, O Lord of the World, a fire and a plague and a cholera. May it seize you and shake you one by one, together with all the apostates, dear God, and may not one of you remain to see the Passover, dear merciful God."

Once rid of this torment, the prisoners did not regain their composure for some time. The savage outcries, the whistling, the laughter of the little barbarians rang in their ears. Later our hero came gradually to realize that it was pointless to continue grieving on an empty stomach, and he slowly approached the food.

"Madam," he said to his companion, "how long will you keep worrying? It's time to eat. The heavens haven't caved in, believe me, and we haven't had a bite all day."

"Eat well. I don't care for any."

"Why not? Are you fasting?"

"No. It's just that I don't care for any."

"Perhaps you want to teach them a lesson? Go on a hunger strike? You'll only succeed in doing yourself harm —that's all the good it will do."

"I don't see how one can possibly eat anything. It just won't go down."

"It'll go down, it'll go down. The first bite acts like a drill."

"A what?"

"A drill."

"You do use such strange words."

"Ha-ha!"

"Laughing again? What's the occasion?"

"I remembered the small fry."

"That's no laughing matter."

"What do you want me to do? Cry?"

"Why didn't you laugh when they were here?"

"What did I do?"

"It seemed to me you screamed."

"I screamed? I?"

"Who else? Maybe I did?"

"You were the first to start crying *halder, halder, halder.*"

"Excuse me, but it was you who first cried *halder, halder.*"

"So what is there to be ashamed of if I was the first?"

"And why should I feel ashamed if I was the first?"

"If there is nothing to be ashamed of, why have you lowered your nose?"

"I lowered my nose?"

"Who else?"

"Oh, it's so easy to notice someone else's nose!"

It was a pity that this interesting conversation could not be continued, but they were interrupted by the Turkish shawl, the mistress of their prison—as will be related in the next chapter.

6

The Turkish shawl, as it turned out, was not their only mistress. They were fated to make the acquaintance of still another strange creature, a girl with a greenish complexion and a red kerchief. The two entered with arms full of good things: a bowl of rice mixed with beans and peas, a plate of boiled potatoes, chopped eggs, and an apronful of sliced apples and nuts.

As soon as they came in the greenish maid with the red kerchief pointed to the pair and addressed the Turkish shawl. "Look, they haven't even touched the food."

"Let's feed them now. I'll hold them and you put it in their mouths. Well? Why are you standing there like a dummy, with your teeth hanging out?"

"Why do they scream so when they look at me?"

"Silly girl! Take off that kerchief—they can't stand red."

"May all my troubles descend on their heads!"

"On your own head, silly—you come first. Why don't you put some rice and beans into his mouth?"

"Mistress dear, may you live long! I don't like the way he stares. Be careful that he shouldn't, God forbid, choke."

"You choke—you come first! All of a sudden she talks of choking, as if it were the first time I've done this. Stuff it down his throat—this way! I've been a housekeeper for twenty-one years, thank God. Now put a piece of apple and a nut in his mouth. More, more, don't be stingy!"

"I begrudge him? Why should I? It isn't mine. It's simply a pity, the way he suffers!"

"What do you say to this girl! A pity, she says. Am I doing him any harm? I'm only feeding him. And for whose sake? For the sake of God! For the sake of the holy Passover! The Almighty help me, I have fattened more than one pair for Passover. Let's have another nut and make an end of it. He's had enough for now. Now her. Begin with rice and beans."

"Good health to you, mistress, but how can you tell which is he and which is she?"

"May all my evil dreams descend on your head! She's asked to do one thing and her mind is the devil knows where! Wait till you get married, silly girl, and become a housekeeper, then you'll ask. Meantime do as you are told. More, more, don't be stingy! It's for the sake of nobody, except His Precious Name. For Passover! For Passover!"

Finished with their task, the women went off and the tortured prisoners remained alone. They staggered into a corner, rested their mournful heads upon each other, and surrendered themselves to thoughts of sadness, such as come very rarely, perhaps only a few minutes before death.

7

Nothing begets friendship so readily as trouble. The two unfortunate prisoners are the best proof of this. During the
brief term of their imprisonment they became as one, they
began to understand each other at a mere hint, they were no
longer bashful before each other, and they gave up address-
ing each other with the formal "you." They became, indeed,
like one soul. She would address him as "My dear," and he
would counter with "My soul."

Whenever the Turkish shawl and the red kerchief came
with the food they could not admire the pair enough.

"What do you say to my pair?"

"A delight."

"Just feel them. Now what do you say? Some flesh, eh?
Now shouldn't God help me because of the pair I fattened
for Passover?"

When their work was done the wild women left, and the
couple pondered the meaning of the Turkish shawl's remarks
that she "fattens them for Passover" and that God should
help her. Why should He? They thought hard and discussed
the matter.

"Dearest, what is Passover?"

"Passover, my soul, is a sort of holiday among them, a
holiday of freedom, of liberation."

"What does that mean—liberation?"

"Let me explain it to you. They consider it a great good
deed to catch one of our kind and fatten him until this holiday Passover comes around, and then they let him free. Now
do you understand?"

"Is it long till this Passover?"

"According to what I overheard the Turkish shawl say, it
shouldn't be more than about three days."

"Three days!"

"What scared you so, you silly? The three days will pass
like a dream, and when the dear Passover comes, they will

open the doors for us and, 'Out you go, back where you came from.' Will we make tracks!"

"Dearest, you say such wonderful things. If only it were as you say, but I am afraid of one thing—"

"Sweetheart, you are always afraid."

"My dear, you don't know these savages."

"And where did you learn about them?"

"I heard plenty about them, dearest; when still at home I heard tell such stories about them! My sister told me she saw it herself."

"Again your sister's stories? Forget them."

"I would gladly forget them, but I can't. I can't get them out of my head by day or out of my dreams by night."

"And what are these stories that bother you day and night?"

"Darling, you won't laugh at me?"

"Why should I laugh?"

"Because you are like that. Whenever I tell you something you laugh and call me a silly goose or a foolish turkey or some other name."

"I promise not to laugh. Now tell me what you heard from your sister."

"My sister told me that people are worse than beasts. When a wild beast catches one of us it devours him and that's all, but when people catch one of us they imprison him and feed him well until he gets fat."

"And then?"

"And then they slaughter him and skin him and cut him to pieces and sprinkle salt on him and soak him."

"And then?"

"And then they make a fire and fry him in his own fat and eat him, meat, bones, and everything."

"Fairy tales, nothing to it, a cow flew over the moon. And you, you silly, you believe all this? Ha-ha-ha!"

"Well? What did I say? Didn't I say you'd laugh at me?"

"What else did you expect me to do, when you don't understand anything at all? It seems to me you must have

heard a hundred times that the Turkish shawl said she was
feeding us for the sake of no one but God."

"So what of it?"

"Just this, darling, that you are a silly goose."

"That is your nature! Right away you become insulting."

"Who do you mean by 'you'?"

"I mean all of you men!"

"All men? I am curious to know how many men you have
known."

"I know only one, and that's quite enough for me."

"Oh no, you said 'men,' and that means you knew others
besides me."

"What will you think of next?"

"Now you are angry again. Come here, I want to whisper
something to you."

This loving scene was suddenly interrupted by the gang of
small fry outside the window. They were not permitted inside, so they came each day to the window, and there they
made strange gestures, stuck out their tongues, and shouted
halder, halder, halder. The two would naturally respond, not
as angrily as they had the first time, but more in the way of a
greeting.

There is nothing in the world to which God's creatures
can't become accustomed. Our prisoners had grown so used
to their troubles that they now thought things were as they
should be, just like the proverbial worm that has made its
home in horseradish and thinks it sweet.

8

There came a foggy morning. Inside it was still dark. The
pair was immersed in deep sleep. They dreamed of their old
home—a broad, unfenced out-of-doors, a blue sky, green
grass, a shining brook, a mill that turned around, made noise,
and splashed water. Ducks and geese splashed near the bank.
Hens scratched, roosters crowed, birds flew about. What a

beautiful world God had made for them. For them? Of course. For whom else were the tall, broad-branched trees under which one could stroll? For whom else was the mill where their entire family fed without letting anyone else near? For whom the round light in the sky that dipped into the river each evening? What wouldn't they give now for just one more look at the beautiful warm sun! at the big, free, light out-of-doors! at the mill and everything near it!

In the very midst of these sweet dreams they were seized and carried out. The fresh air of the foggy morning hit them full force. Another instant and they would take off and fly away over roofs and gardens and forests to where their home had been. There they would meet their own kind. "Welcome home, where have you been?" "Among wild people." "What did they do with you?" "They fed us for Passover." "What is Passover?" "It's a sort of holiday among people, a fine, dear holiday of freedom and liberation."

This is how they dreamed as they were taken to a narrow, dank alley where they were dropped in the mud. The wall was spattered with blood and many bound fowl lay on the ground in pairs and even in threes. Alongside stood young women and girls chatting and giggling. The pair looked about. Why had they been brought there? What were all the bound fowl doing there? What were the women and girls giggling about? And what was the meaning of the blood-stained wall? Was this the dear, good holiday of Passover? And what about freedom? And liberation?

Thus did the pair reason as they examined the bound fowl that lay quietly without asking any questions, as if this were the natural order of events. Only one loud-mouthed hen did not rest. Straining with all her strength, she flapped her wings in the mud and raved insanely. "Let me go! Let me go! I don't want to lie here! I want to run! Let me go!"

"Cockadoodledooo," a red rooster bound to two hens responded. "What do you say to this smarty? She doesn't want to lie here! She wants to go, she wants to run. Ha-ha!"

Our hero raised his head, carefully examined the insolent

red rooster, and felt the blood rushing to his head. He could
have sworn that he knew the fellow; he had seen him somewhere, had heard him before, but where? He couldn't remember. Yet wasn't there something hauntingly familiar
about him? In heaven's name, where had he seen him? He
raised his head a little higher, and the rooster noticed him
and intoned in his high soprano:

> *Cockadoodledooo . . .*
> *You were led*
> *And you were fed,*
> *Now you're tied,*
> *Soon you'll be fried—*

The red poet had no chance to finish. Someone's hand
grabbed him with such force and so unexpectedly that he
suddenly lost his voice.

The one who grabbed the rooster was an uncouth fellow
with sleepy eyes, tall, thin, with long earlocks, his sleeves
rolled up and his coat tails tucked in. In his hand he held a
black shiny knife. Without delay he drew the rooster to himself, pulled up his head, looked briefly into his eyes, plucked
three small feathers from his neck, and, *fft*, he passed the
knife over his throat and tossed him back into the mud. For
a moment the rooster lay motionless, as if stunned, then he
got up and started running and turning his head back and
forth as if looking for someone, or as if he had lost something. Our hero looked at the rooster and recognized him; it
was the same one he had seen in his dream, and he recalled
the song the rooster had sung. Now he could not say a word
to his beloved, who lay close to him, trembling in all her
limbs.

Meanwhile the savage with the shining knife proceeded
with his work, unconcerned, like a true executioner. One
after another the fowl flew from his hands, each first being
tickled on the throat with the knife before being tossed into
the mud. Some stretched out their legs, trembled, and kicked
as they lost blood. Others flapped their wings. And every

minute more victims joined them with cut throats. The women and girls observed all this yet did not seem to mind. On the contrary, some of them seized upon the still living fowl and started plucking their feathers, meantime chatting and joking and giggling as if it were water that flowed instead of the blood of living creatures. Where were their eyes? Where were their ears? And their hearts? And their sense of justice? And their God?

Our two bound prisoners watched the terrible scene, the horrible carnage at daybreak. Could it be that they too had been brought here for the same purpose as the chickens, ducks, and geese? Could it be that aristocrats, who hailed from among the Indians, would share this terrible end with ordinary beings? Was it really true, what they had been told about these savages? And the prophecy of the red rooster, was that also true?

They began to understand the cold, bare truth and to comprehend everything they had seen and heard. One thing only they could not fathom. Why had the Turkish shawl boasted that God would reward her for fattening such a pair for Passover? Was that what their God wanted?

A few minutes later our loving pair, the prisoners, lay on the ground. Their still warm throats rested on each other, and from a distance it might have seemed they were asleep and dreaming beautiful dreams.

THE TOWN OF THE
LITTLE PEOPLE

The town of the little people into which I shall now take you, dear reader, is exactly in the middle of that blessed Pale into which Jews have been packed as closely as herring in a barrel and told to increase and multiply. The name of the town is Kasrilevka. How did this name originate? I'll tell you:

Among us Jews poverty has many faces and many aspects. A poor man is an unlucky man, he is a pauper, a beggar, a *schnorrer*, a starveling, a tramp, or a plain failure. A different tone is used in speaking of each one, but all these names express human wretchedness. However, there is still another name—*kasril,* or *kasrilik*. That name is spoken in a different tone altogether, almost a bragging tone. For instance, "Oh, am I ever a *kasrilik!*" A *kasrilik* is not just an ordinary pauper, a failure in life. On the contrary, he is a man who has not allowed poverty to degrade him. He laughs at it. He is poor, but cheerful.

Stuck away in a corner of the world, isolated from the surrounding country, the town stands, orphaned, dreaming, bewitched, immersed in itself and remote from the noise and bustle, the confusion and tumult and greed, which men have created about them and have dignified with high-sounding names like Culture, Progress, Civilization. A proper person may take off his hat with respect to these things, but not these little people! Not only do they know nothing of automobiles, modern travel, airplanes—for a long time they refused to believe in the existence of the old, ordinary railroad train. "Such a thing could not be," they said. "Why," they said, "it's a dream, a fairy tale. You might just as well talk of merry-go-rounds in heaven!"

But it happened once that a householder of Kasrilevka had to go to Moscow. When he came back he swore with many oaths that it was true. He himself had ridden in a train to Moscow, and it had taken him—he shrugged his shoulders—less than an hour. This the little people interpreted to mean that he had ridden less than an hour and then walked the rest of the way. But still the fact of the train remained. If a Jew and a householder of Kasrilevka swore to it, they could not deny that there was such a thing as a train. It had to be true. He could not have invented it out of thin air. He even explained to them the whole miracle of the train, and drew a diagram on paper. He showed them how the wheels turned, the smokestack whistled, the carriages flew, and people rode to Moscow. The little people of Kasrilevka listened and listened, nodded their heads solemnly, and deep in their hearts they laughed at him. "What a story! The wheels turn, the smokestack whistles, the carriages fly and people ride to Moscow—and then come back again!"

That's how they all are, these little people. None of them are gloomy, none of them are worried little men of affairs, but on the contrary they are known everywhere as jesters, story-tellers, a cheerful, light-hearted breed of men. Poor but cheerful. It is hard to say what makes them so happy. Nothing—just sheer joy of living. Living? If you ask them, "How do you live?" they will answer, with a shrug and a laugh. "How do we live? Who knows? We live!" A remarkable thing—whenever you meet them they are scurrying like rabbits, this one here, that one there. They never have time to stop. "What are you hurrying for?" "What am I hurrying for? Well, it's like this. If we hurry we think we might run into something—earn a few pennies—provide for the Sabbath."

To provide for the Sabbath—that is their goal in life. All week they labor and sweat, wear themselves out, live without food or drink, just so there is something for the Sabbath. And when the holy Sabbath arrives, let Yehupetz perish, let Odessa be razed, let Paris itself sink into the earth! Kasrilevka lives! And this is a fact, that since Kasrilevka was founded, no Jew has gone hungry there on the Sabbath. Is it possible that there is a Jew who does not have fish for the Sabbath? If he has no fish, then he has meat. If he has no meat, then he has herring. If he has no herring, then he has white bread. If he has no white bread, then he has black bread and onions. If he has no black bread and onions, then he borrows some from his neighbor. Next week, the neighbor will borrow from him. "The world is a wheel and it keeps turning." The Kasrilevkite repeats this maxim and shows you with his hand how it turns. To him a maxim, a witty remark, is everything. For an apt remark he will forsake his mother and father, as the saying goes. The tales you hear about these little people sound fabulous, but you may be sure they are all true.

For instance, there is the story of the Kasrilevkite who got tired of starving in Kasrilevka and went out into the wide world to seek his fortune. He left the country, wandered far and wide, and finally reached Paris. There, naturally, he wanted to see Rothschild. For how can a Jew come to Paris and not visit Rothschild? But they didn't let him in. "What's the trouble?" he wants to know. "Your coat is torn," they tell him.

"You fool," says the Jew. "If I had a good coat, would I have gone to Paris?"

It looked hopeless. But a Kasrilevkite never gives up. He thought a while and said to the doorman: "Tell your master that it isn't an ordinary beggar who has come to his door, but a Jewish merchant, who has brought him a piece of goods such as you can't find in Paris for any amount of money."

Hearing this, Rothschild became curious and asked that the merchant be brought to him.

"Sholom aleichem," said Rothschild.

"Aleichem sholom," said the merchant.

"Take a seat. And where do you come from?"

"I come from Kasrilevka."

"What good news do you bring?"

"Well, Mr. Rothschild, they say in our town that you are not so badly off. If I had only half of what you own, or only a third, you would still have enough left. And honors, I imagine, you don't lack either, for people always look up to a man of riches. Then what do you lack? One thing only— eternal life. That is what I have to sell you."

When Rothschild heard this he said, "Well, let's get down to business. What will it cost me?"

"It will cost you"—here the man stopped to consider—"it will cost you—three hundred *rubles.*"

"Is that your best price?"

"My very best. I could have said a lot more than three hundred. But I said it, so it's final."

Rothschild said no more, but counted out three hundred *rubles,* one by one.

Our Kasrilevkite slipped the money into his pocket, and said to Rothschild: "If you want to live for ever, my advice to you is to leave this noisy, busy Paris, and move to our town of Kasrilevka. There you can never die, because since Kasrilevka has been a town, no rich man has ever died there."

And then there is the story of the man who got as far as America . . . But if I started to tell all the tales of these little people I'd have to sit with you for three days and three nights and talk and talk and talk. Instead, let us pass on to a description of the little town itself.

Shall I call it a beautiful little town? From a distance it looks—how shall I say it?—like a loaf of bread thickly studded with poppy seed. Some of the houses are built on the slope of a hill, and the rest are huddled together at the

base, one on top of the other, like the gravestones in an
ancient cemetery. There are no streets to speak of because
the houses are not built according to any plan, and besides,
where is there room for such a thing? Why should there be
vacant space when you can build something on it? It is written that the earth is to be inhabited, not merely to be gazed
at.

Yet, don't be upset. There are some streets—big streets,
little streets, back streets and alleys. What if they happen to
twist and turn uphill and downhill and suddenly end up in a
house or a cellar or just a hole in the ground? If you are a
stranger, never go out alone at night without a lantern. As
for the little people who live there, don't worry about them.
A Kasrilevkite in Kasrilevka, among Kasrilevkites, will never
get lost. Each one finds the way to his own house, to his wife
and children, like a bird to its own nest.

And then in the center of the city there is a wide half-
circle, or perhaps it is a square, where you find the stores,
shops, market stands, stalls and tables. There every morning
the peasants from the surrounding countryside congregate
with their produce—fish and onions, horseradish, parsnips
and other vegetables. They sell these things and buy from
the little people other necessities of life, and from this the
Kasrilevkites draw their livelihood. A meager one, but better
than nothing. And in the square also lie all the town's goats,
warming themselves in the sun.

There also stand the synagogues, the meeting houses, the
chapels and schools of the town where Jewish children study
the Holy Writ. The noise they and the rabbis make with
their chanting is enough to deafen one. The baths where the
women go to bathe are also there, and the poorhouse where
the old men die, and other such public institutions. No, the
Kasrilevkites have never heard of canals or water works or
electricity or other such luxuries. But what does that matter?
Everywhere people die the same death, and they are placed
in the same earth, and are beaten down with the same
spades. Thus my Rabbi, Reb Israel, used to say—when he

was happiest, at a wedding or other celebration, after he had
had a few glasses of wine and was ready to lift up the skirts
of his long coat and dance a *kazatsky* . . .

But the real pride of Kasrilevka is her cemeteries. This
lucky town has two rich cemeteries, the old and the new.
The new one is old enough and rich enough in graves. Soon
there will be no place to put anyone, especially if a pogrom
should break out or any of the other misfortunes which be-
fall us in these times.

But it is of the old cemetery that the people of Kasrilevka
are especially proud. This old cemetery, though it is overgrown with grass and with bushes and has practically no upright headstones, they still value as they might a treasure, a
rare gem, a piece of wealth, and guard it like the apple of
their eye. For this is not only the place where their ancestors
lie, rabbis, men of piety, learned ones, scholars and famous
people, including the dead from the ancient massacres of
Chmelnitski's time—but also the only piece of land of which
they are the masters, the only bit of earth they own where a
blade of grass can sprout and a tree can grow and the air is
fresh and one can breathe freely.

You should see what goes on in this old cemetery a month
before the New Year, during the "days of weeping." Men
and women—mainly women—swarm up and down the paths
to their ancestors' graves. From all the surrounding country
they come to weep and to pour their hearts out at the holy
graves. Believe me, there is no place where one can weep so
freely and with such abandon as in "the field" of Kasrilevka.
In the synagogue a person can weep pretty freely too, but
the synagogue doesn't come up to the cemetery. The cemetery is a source of income for the Kasrilevkite stonecutters,
innkeepers, cantors and sextons, and the month before the
New Year is, for the paupers thereabouts and the old women
and the cripples, the real harvest time.

"Have you been in 'our field' yet?" a Kasrilevkite will ask
you cheerfully, as though he were asking if you had been in
his father's vineyard. If you haven't been there, do him a

kindness, and go down into "the field," read the old, half-obliterated inscriptions on the leaning tombstones and you will find in them the story of a whole people. And if you happen to be a man of feeling and imagination then you will look upon this poor little town with its rich cemeteries and repeat the old verses:

"How beautiful are your tents, O Jacob; how good are your resting places, O Israel."

THE INHERITORS

The Maiers and the Schnaiers . . .

Actually there was only one Maier and one Schnaier. They were twins and they looked so much alike that there were times when it was impossible to tell which of the two was Maier and which was Schnaier. As babies, the story goes, a queer thing happened to them. They were almost exchanged —and it is possible that they really were exchanged. This is how it happened.

Their mother, you may know, was a tiny woman and quite frail, but very fruitful. Every year without fail she gave birth to a child, but the sickly infant barely lingered through its first twelve months and then died. This went on until she finally stopped having children and thought she would never have another. But in the end a miracle happened. In her old age the Lord blessed her again, and this time with twins. And since it was too hard for her to suckle two babies, she had to hire a wet nurse. What else was there to do? A Kasrilevkite —no matter how poor he may be—will never throw a child of his into the streets or give it to a stranger to raise, unless, God forbid, the child be an orphan.

Having hired the nurse, the mother took Maier for herself (he was older than Schnaier by half an hour) and she gave Schnaier to the nurse. But since the nurse was herself not such a healthy woman, neither Maier nor Schnaier got too much milk. Both babies were equally starved; they screamed all night long; tore the house apart with their noise. It happened one day that the women were bathing the babies, naturally in one basin. They undressed them and put them into the hot water. Then, adding fresh water to the basin, they watched the children, red and bloated, splashing their little hands and feet, rolling about like beetles, enjoying themselves hugely. When they were through bathing them they took the babies out, wrapped them in a sheet (naturally one sheet) and put them to bed (naturally one bed) to dry. But when they started to dress them again, they couldn't tell which was Maier and which was Schnaier. And an argument took place between the two women.

"Look here, I could swear that this is Maier and this is Schnaier."

"How could you say that? This one is Maier and that one is Schnaier. Can't you see?"

"Do you think I'm dreaming? Either you're crazy, or just out of your head!"

"Good Lord! Can't you tell by their eyes that this is Maier and that is Schnaier? Look at those two eyes of his!"

"A fine argument! What do you want him to have—three eyes?"

Well, one of them kept insisting that Maier was Schnaier and Schnaier was Maier, and the other that Schnaier was Maier and Maier was Schnaier. Until at last the men came in and offered a solution. After all, they were men, with superior brains.

"Do you know what?" they suggested. "Try nursing the babies and we shall see. The one who takes his mother's breast must be Maier and the one who takes the nurse's must be Schnaier. That's simple enough."

And so it happened. As soon as the babies snuggled up to the breast, they each began to suck hungrily, smacked their lips, kicked their legs and made sounds like hungry puppies.

"A miracle of God!" said the men, with tears in their eyes. "See how the Almighty has created His world!"

And as a final test they decided to change the babies and see what would happen. The poor infants were torn away from their breasts and changed about, Schnaier taking Maier's place and Maier Schnaier's. And what do you suppose happened? Do you think they stopped sucking? They sucked as hard as ever!

From that time on they gave up trying to tell them apart. Let them be Maier-Schnaier and Schnaier-Maier. And they were given the name of the Maiers and the Schnaiers, as though each one was both a Maier and a Schnaier. More than once it happened in *cheder* that Maier was whipped when Schnaier should have got the whipping, or the other way around, Schnaier was punished for Maier's misdeeds. And in order to avoid hard feelings, the rabbi hit on this scheme (do they not say where there is learning there is wisdom?):

"You know what, children? Both of you stretch out. Then there will be no argument that I beat this one or that one. It will all remain in the family . . ."

But much, much later—after their *Bar Mitzvah,* when the Maiers and Schnaiers had reached manhood—something happened that made it possible to tell them apart a mile away even at night. What wonders God can devise! The brothers began to sprout beards (they must both have begun to smoke cigars too early) and on Maier's cheeks and upper lip there appeared black hairs (black as ink) and on Schnaier's face red hairs (red as fire). These beards grew as if the devil possessed them (they must both have continued to smoke cigars), so that by the time they were married they both had full beards. Did I say beards? Feather dusters was more like it. A black duster and a red one, that looked as if someone had glued them on.

Great are the works of the Lord, and His wonders are without end. For who knows what would have come to pass after their weddings if the beards, too, had been alike? In the confusion, even the wives might not have known which one of the brothers they had married . . . I do not know how it is with you in the big cities, but here in Kasrilevka it has never yet happened that husbands and wives should start exchanging each other. It is possible that there are husbands among us who would not object to this, but they know their wives and they know what they would get from them. However, all this is beside the point. The real story begins now.

Up till now we have concerned ourselves only with the Maiers and Schnaiers, that is with Maier and Schnaier, and we have become slightly acquainted with their mother and nurse, but we have not said a word about their father, as though they had never had a father. God forbid! Such a thing may have happened to others, but never to our kind of people. We have, thank God, no homes for foundlings where children are raised by strangers. It has never happened among us that a child should grow up and not know who his real father was. And if such a thing has happened, it has happened somewhere in Odessa or in Paris or in faraway America . . . As for Kasrilevka, I can swear that such a thing has never happened, and if it did, it happened to some servant girl or some other unfortunate maiden who was led astray by accident, through no fault of her own—an unhappy victim of another's lust . . .

In short, the Maiers and Schnaiers had a father, and a very fine father, too. He was a virtuous and an honest man named Reb Shimshen, and he had a magnificent beard, long and rich and luxurious. In fact, it could be said without exaggeration that Reb Shimshen had more beard than face. And for that reason he was known in Kasrilevka as Reb Shimshen Beard.

And this Reb Shimshen was—I don't even know what he was. But you can be sure that all his life he struggled and sweated for a meager living, waged constant warfare against poverty. Sometimes he overcame poverty; sometimes poverty overcame him, as is usual with Kasrilevkites, who are not afraid of want, but thumb their noses at it . . .

And Reb Shimshen lived out his life and finally he died. And when he died he was given a handsome burial. Almost the whole town followed his remains to the cemetery.

"Who is it that died?"

"Haven't you heard? Reb Shimshen."

"Which Reb Shimshen?"

"Reb Shimshen Beard."

"A great pity. So Reb Shimshen Beard is gone from us too."

That is what they said in Kasrilevka and mourned not so much for Reb Shimshen himself as for the fact that with his death there was one person less in Kasrilevka. Strange people, these Kasrilevkites! In spite of the fact that they are so poor that they almost never have enough for themselves, they would be pleased if no one among them ever died. Their only comfort is that people die everywhere, even in Paris, and that no one can buy his way out. Even Rothschild himself, who is greater than royalty, has to get up and go when the Angel of Death beckons.

Now let us turn back again to the Maiers and Schnaiers. As long as Reb Shimshen was alive the Maiers and Schnaiers lived as one, brothers in body and soul. But when their father died they became enemies at once, ready to tear each other's beards out. Perhaps you wonder why? Well, why do sons ever fight after a father's death? Naturally, over the inheritance. It is true that Reb Shimshen did not leave behind any farms or woodlands, houses or rental property, and certainly no cash. Nor did he leave any jewelry, silver or furniture to his children—not because he was mean or avaricious, but simply because he had nothing to leave. And yet don't think that Reb Shimshen left his children absolutely nothing. He left them a treasure that could be turned to money at any time, a treasure that could be pawned, rented or sold outright. This treasure we speak of was the seat he had had in the old Kasrilevka Synagogue, a seat along the east wall right next to Reb Yozifel, the Rabbi, who was next to the Holy Ark. It is true that Kasrilevka wits have a saying that it is better to have an acre outside than a seat inside, but that is only a saying, and when the Lord is kind and a person does have his own seat, and along the east wall at that, it's not so very bad—and certainly better than nothing . . .

In short, Reb Shimshen left behind a seat in the old Kasrilevka Synagogue. But he forgot one small detail. He didn't indicate who was to inherit the seat—Maier or Schnaier.

Obviously Reb Shimshen—may he forgive me—did not expect to die. He had forgotten that the Angel of Death lurks always behind our backs and watches every step we take, else he would surely have made a will or otherwise indicated in the presence of witnesses to which of his two sons he wanted to leave his fortune.

Well, what do you suppose? The very first Saturday after they arose from mourning, the quarrel began. Maier argued that according to law the seat belonged to him, since he was the older (by a good half-hour). And Schnaier had two arguments in his favor: first, they were not sure which of the two was older because according to their mother's story they had been exchanged as infants and he was really Maier and Maier was really Schnaier. In the second place, Maier had a rich father-in-law who also owned a seat along the east wall of the synagogue, and since the father-in-law had no sons the seat would eventually be Maier's. And when that happened Maier would have two seats by the east wall and Schnaier would have none whatever. And if that was the case, where was justice? Where was humanity?

When he heard of these goings-on, Maier's father-in-law, a man of means, but one who had made his money only recently, entered the battle. "You've got a lot of nerve!" he exclaimed. "I am not forty yet and I have every intention of living a long time, and here you are, dividing up my inheritance already. And besides, how do you know that I won't have a son yet? I may have more than one, see!" he stormed. "There is impudence for you!"

So their neighbors tried to make peace between them, suggested that they determine how much the seat was worth and then have one brother buy his share from the other. That sounds reasonable enough, doesn't it? The only trouble was that neither brother wanted to sell his share. They didn't care a thing about the money. What was money—compared to stubbornness and pride?

"How can one's own brother be so pigheaded as to keep a person away from his rightful seat?" "Why should you have our father's place, and not I?" It became a matter not so much of having things his own way as it was of preventing the other from having his. As the saying is: If I don't, you don't either. And the rivalry between the Maiers and the Schnaiers increased in fury. Stubbornness gave way to cunning as each tried to outwit the other!

The first Sabbath Maier came early and sat down in his father's seat; and Schnaier remained standing throughout the services. The second Sabbath Schnaier came first and occupied his father's place, while Maier remained standing. The third Sabbath Maier got there still earlier, spread himself out in the seat, pulled his *tallis* over his head, and there he was . . .

The next time it was Schnaier who hurried to get there first, sat down in the coveted seat, pulled his *tallis* over his face—and just try to budge him! The following week Maier was the first to get there . . . This went on week after week till one fine Sabbath both of them arrived at the same time—it was still dark outside—took their posts at the door of the synagogue (it was still shut) and glared at each other like roosters ready to tear each other's eyes out. It was like this that long ago the first two brothers stood face to face in an empty field, under God's blue sky, full of anger, ready to annihilate one another, devour each other, spill innocent blood . . .

But let us not forget that the Maiers and Schnaiers were young men of good family, respectable and well behaved—not rowdies who were in the habit of assaulting each other in public. They waited for Ezriel, the *shammes*, to come and open the door of the synagogue. Then they would show the whole world who would get to their father's seat first—Maier or Schnaier . . .

The minutes passed like years till Ezriel arrived with the keys. And when Ezriel, with his tangled beard, arrived he was not able to reach the door because the brothers stood against it—one with the left foot, the other with the right foot, and would not budge an inch.

"Well, what's going to happen?" said Ezriel casually, taking a pinch of snuff. "If the two of you insist on standing there like mean scarecrows I won't be able to open the door and the synagogue will have to remain closed all day. Go ahead and tell me: does that make sense?"

Apparently these words had some effect, because the Maiers and Schnaiers both moved back, one to the right, the other to the left, and made way for Ezriel and his key. And when the key turned in the lock and the door swung open, the Maiers and Schnaiers tumbled in headlong.

"Be careful, you're killing me!" yelled Ezriel the *shammes*, and before he could finish the words the poor man lay trampled under their feet, screaming in horror: "Watch out! You're trampling all over me—the father of a family!"

But the Maiers and Schnaiers cared nothing for Ezriel and his family. Their only thought was for the seat, their father's seat, and jumping over benches and praying stands they made for the east wall. There they planted themselves firmly against the wall with their shoulders and the floor with their feet and tried to shove each other aside. In the scuffle they caught each other's beards, grimaced horribly, gritted their teeth and growled: "May the plague take you before you get this seat!"

In the meantime Ezriel got up from the floor, felt to see if any of his bones were broken, and approached the brothers.

He found them both on the floor clutching each other's beards. At first he tried to reason with them.

"Shame on you! Two brothers—children of the same father and mother—tearing each other's beards out! And in a Holy Place at that! Be ashamed of yourselves!"

But Ezriel gathered that at the moment his lecture was in vain. Actually, his words added fuel to the flame so that the two children of one father became so enraged that one of them clutched in his fist a tuft of black hair (from Maier's beard) and the other a tuft of red (Schnaier's beard); blue marks showed on both faces and from the nose of one streamed blood.

As long as it was merely a matter of pulling beards, slapping and pummeling each other, the *shammes* could content himself with reading a lecture. But when he saw blood streaming, Ezriel could stand it no longer, for blood, even though only from a punched nose, was an ugly thing fit for rowdies and not God-fearing men.

He wasted no time, but ran to the tap, grabbed a dipper of water, and poured it over the two brothers. Cold water has always—since the world was created—been the best means of reviving a person. A man may be in the greatest rage, but as soon as he gets a cold bath he is strangely refreshed and cool; he comes to his senses. This happened to the Maiers and the Schnaiers. At the unexpected shower of cold water to which Ezriel had treated them, they woke up, looked each other in the eyes, and grew ashamed—like Adam and Eve when they had tasted of the forbidden fruit of the Tree of Knowledge and saw their nakedness . . .

And that very Saturday night the Maiers and Schnaiers went together with their friends and neighbors to the home of Reb Yozifel, the Rabbi, to have the dispute settled.

If Kasrilevka had not been such a tiny place, stuck away in a forgotten corner, far from the great world, and if newspapers and periodicals had been printed there, the world would surely have come to know the works of our Rabbi,

Reb Yozifel. The papers would have been full of tales about him and his wisdom. The great, the wise and the famous of the world would have traveled far to see him in person and to hear from his own lips the words of wisdom. Photographers and painters would have made portraits of him and spread them to the four corners of the earth. Interviewers would have plagued him, given him no rest. They would have asked him all his views—what his favorite dishes were, how many hours a day he slept, what he thought about this and that, about cigarette smoking and bicycle riding . . . But since Kasrilevka is a tiny place stuck away in a forgotten corner, far from the world, and papers and periodicals are not printed there, the world knows nothing of the existence of Reb Yozifel. The papers never mention his name. The great, the wise and the famous do not come to him, photographers and painters do not make pictures of him. Interviewers leave him alone. And Reb Yozifel lives his life quietly, modestly, without noise or fanfare. No one knows anything about him except the town of Kasrilevka, which marvels at him, glories in his wisdom, and pays him great honor (of riches there is little in Kasrilevka, but honor they will give one as much as he deserves). They say that he is a man who modestly conceals his wisdom and it is only when you come to him for judgment that you find out how deep he is, how profound, how sharp. Another Solomon!

With the Sabbath over and the benedictions completed, the Maiers and Schnaiers came to Reb Yozifel to have their dispute settled, and there they found the house already full of people. The whole town was anxious to hear how he would settle it, how he would divide one seat between two brothers.

First he gave both sides a chance to unburden themselves. Reb Yozifel works according to this theory: that before the verdict is handed down the litigants should have the right to say anything they want to—because after the verdict all the talking in the world won't help. After that he let Ezriel, the *shammes*, talk. After all, he was the chief witness. And

then other townspeople had their turn—everyone who had
the public welfare at heart. And they talked as long as they
wanted. Reb Yozifel is the kind of person who lets everyone
talk. He is something of a philosopher. He feels this way
about it: that no matter how long a person talks, he will
have to stop some time.

And that is just what happened. They talked and talked
and talked, and finally stopped talking. And when the last
person was through, Reb Yozifel turned to the Maiers and
Schnaiers and spoke to them quietly, calmly, as his custom
was.

"Hear ye, my friends—this is my opinion. According to
what I have heard from you and from all the other citizens
it is apparent that both of you are right. You both had one
father, and a very noble father, too—may he enjoy the blessings of Paradise. The only trouble is that he left you only
one seat in the synagogue. Naturally, this seat is very dear to
both of you. After all—it is something to own one's seat
along the east wall of the old, old Kasrilevka Synagogue.
You can't dismiss that with a wave of the hand. What then?
Just as it is impossible for one person to use two seats, so it
is impossible for two people to use a single one. On the contrary, it is much easier for one person to use two seats than
for two to use one."

And so with example and precept he went on to explain
the difficulty of the situation.

"But there is one way," he continued, "in which each of
you can sit along the eastern wall in adjoining seats. I have
come upon this solution after much reflection. And this is
what I have to say. My seat in the synagogue is right next to
the one your father left. One of you can have my seat and
then both of you brothers can sit next to each other in peace
and amity, and you will have no need to quarrel any more.
And if you will ask what will I do without a seat? then I
will answer you with another question: Where is it written
that a rabbi or any other man, for that matter, must have his
own seat and especially at the east wall, and at the old

Kasrilevka Synagogue at that? Let us stop to consider. What is a synagogue? A house of prayer. And why do we go to the synagogue? To pray. To whom? To the Almighty. And where is He found? Everywhere. All the world is filled with His glory. If that is the case, then what difference does it make whether it is east or north or south, whether it is near the Ark or by the door? The important thing is to come to the synagogue and to pray.

"Let me give you an example. Once there was a king . . ."

And there followed another of Reb Yozifel's parables of the two servants who began to tear each other's beards in the presence of the king. And they were sent away with this admonition: "If you want to tear each other's beards, go outside and do it as much as your heart desires, but do not defile my palace . . ."

Thus Reb Yozifel chided them gently, and then he said, "Go home now, my children, in peace and let your father be an advocate in heaven for you, for us, and for all Israel."

Thus the Rabbi handed down his verdict and all the people went home.

The following Sabbath, the Maiers and Schnaiers came to the synagogue and stationed themselves near the door. No matter how much they were entreated by the *shammes* on one side and the Rabbi on the other, they refused to occupy the seats by the east wall.

If there is anyone who would like to have his own seat by the east wall in the old, old Kasrilevka Synagogue, the seat next to Reb Yozifel, the Rabbi, at a reasonable price, let him go to Kasrilevka and see the children of Reb Shimshen Beard, either Maier or Schnaier, it does not matter which. They will sell it to you at any price you say, because neither of them uses that seat any more. It stands there—unoccupied.

What a waste!

TEVYE WINS A
FORTUNE

Who raiseth up the poor out of the dust,
And lifteth up the needy out of the dunghill.
        —PSALMS, 113:7.

If you are destined to draw the winning ticket in the lottery,
Mr. Sholom Aleichem, it will come right into your house
without your asking for it. As King David says, "It never
rains but it pours." You don't need wisdom or skill. And, on
the contrary, if you are not inscribed as a winner in the
Books of the Angels, you can talk yourself blue in the face
—it won't help you. The *Talmud* is right: "You can lead a
horse to water, but you cannot make him drink." A person
slaves, wears himself to the bone, and gets nowhere. He
might as well lie down and give up his ghost. Suddenly, no
one knows how or for what reason, money rolls in from all
sides. As the passage has it, "Relief and deliverance will
come to the Jews." I don't have to explain that to you. It
should be clear to both of us that so long as a Jew can still
draw breath and feel the blood beating in his veins, he must
never lose hope. I have seen it in my own experience, in the
way the Lord dealt with me in providing me with my present livelihood. For how else should I happen to be selling
cheese and butter all of a sudden? In my wildest dreams I
had never seen myself as a dairyman.

Take my word for it, the story is worth hearing. I'll sit
down for a little while here near you on the grass. Let the

horse do a little nibbling meanwhile. After all, even a horse is one of God's living creatures.

Well, it was in the late spring, around *Shevuos* time. But I don't want to mislead you; it may have been a week or two before *Shevuos,* or—let's see—maybe a couple of weeks after *Shevuos.* Don't forget, this didn't happen yesterday. Wait! To be exact, it was nine or ten years ago to the day. And maybe a trifle more.

In those days I was not the man I am today. That is, I *was* the same Tevye, and yet not exactly the same. The same old woman, as they say, but in a different bonnet. How so? I was as poor as a man could be, completely penniless. If you want to know the truth I'm not a rich man now either, but compared with what I was then I can now really call myself a man of wealth. I have a horse and wagon of my own, a couple of cows that give milk, and a third that is about to calve. We can't complain. We have cheese and butter and fresh cream all the time. We make it ourselves; that is, our family does. We all work. No one is idle. My wife milks the cows; the children carry pitchers and pails, churn the butter. And I myself, as you see, drive to market every morning, go from *datcha* to *datcha* in Boiberik, visit with people, see this one and that one, all the important businessmen from Yehupetz who come there for the summer. Talking to them makes me feel that I am somebody, too; I amount to something in the world.

And when Saturday comes—then I really live like a king! I look into the Holy Books, read the weekly portion of the Bible, dip into the commentaries, Psalms, *Perek,* this, that, something else . . . Ah, you're surprised, Mr. Sholom Aleichem! No doubt you're thinking to yourself, "Ah, that Tevye —there's a man for you!"

Anyway, what did I start to tell you? That's right. Those days. Oh, was Tevye a pauper then! With God's help I starved to death—I and my wife and children—three times a day, not counting supper. I worked like a horse, pulling wagonloads of logs from the woods to the railroad station for

—I am ashamed to admit it—half a *ruble* a day. And that not every day, either. And on such earnings just try to fill all those hungry mouths, not counting that boarder of mine, the poor horse, whom I can't put off with a quotation from the *Talmud*.

So what does the Lord do? He is a great, all-powerful God. He manages His little world wisely and well. Seeing how I was struggling for a hard crust of bread, He said to me: "Do you think, Tevye, that you have nothing more to live for, that the world has come to an end? If that's what you think, you're a big lummox. Soon you will see: if I will it, your luck can change in one turn of the wheel, and what was dark as the grave will be full of brightness." As we say on *Yom Kippur,* the Lord decides who will ride on horseback and who will crawl on foot. The main thing is—hope! A Jew must always hope, must never lose hope. And in the meantime, what if we waste away to a shadow? For that we are Jews—the Chosen People, the envy and admiration of the world.

Anyway, this is how it happened. As the Bible says, "And there came the day . . ." One evening in summer I was driving through the woods on my way home with an empty wagon. My head was bent, my heart was heavy. The little horse, poor thing, was barely dragging its feet. "Ah," I said to it, "crawl along, *shlimazl!* If you are Tevye's horse you too must know the pangs of hunger . . ." All around was silence, every crack of the whip echoed through the woods. As the sun set the shadows of the trees stretched out and lengthened—like our Jewish exile. Darkness was creeping in and a sadness filled my heart. Strange, faraway thoughts filled my mind, and before my eyes passed the images of people a long time dead. And in the midst of it all I thought of my home and my family. And I thought, "Woe unto us all." The wretched dark little hut that was my home, and the children barefoot and in tatters waiting for their father, the *shlimazl.* Maybe he would bring them a loaf of bread or a few stale rolls. And my wife, grumbling as a wife will:

"Children I had to bear him—seven of them. I might as well take them all and throw them into the river—may God not punish me for these words!"

You can imagine how I felt. We are only human. The stomach is empty and words won't fill it. If you swallow a piece of herring you want some tea, and for tea you need sugar. And sugar, I am told, is in the grocery store. "My stomach," says my wife, "can get along without a piece of bread, but if I don't take a glass of tea in the morning, I am a dead woman. All night long the baby sucks me dry."

But in spite of everything, we are still Jews. When evening comes we have to say our prayers. You can imagine what the prayers sounded like if I tell you that just as I was about to begin *Shmin-esra* my horse suddenly broke away as if possessed by the devil and ran wildly off through the woods. Have you ever tried standing on one spot facing the east while a horse was pulling you where *it* wanted to go? I had no choice but to run after him, holding on to the reins and chanting, *"God of Abraham, God of Isaac, and God of Jacob."* A fine way to say *Shmin-esra!* And just my luck, at a moment when I was in the mood to pray with feeling, out of the depths of my heart, hoping it would lift my spirits . . .

So there I was, running after the wagon and chanting at the top of my voice, as if I were a cantor in a synagogue: *"Thou sustainest the living with loving kindness* (and sometimes with a little food) *and keepest thy faith with them that sleep in the dust.* (The dead are not the only ones who lie in the dust; Oh, how low we the living are laid, what hells we go through, and I don't mean the rich people of Yehupetz who spend their summers at the *datchas* of Boiberik, eating and drinking and living off the fat of the land . . . Oh, Heavenly Father, why does this happen to me? Am I not as good as others? Help me, dear God!) *Look upon our afflictions.* (Look down, dear God! See how we struggle and come to the aid of the poor, because who will look out for us if you don't?) *Heal us, O Lord, and we shall be healed.* (Send us the cure, we have the ailment already.) *Bless this year for us, O Lord, our God, with every kind of produce* (corn and wheat and every other grain, and if you do, will I get anything out of it, *shlimazl* that I am? For instance, what difference does it make to my poor horse whether oats are dear or cheap?)."

But that's enough. Of God you don't ask questions. If you're one of the Chosen People you must see the good in everything and say, "This too is for the best." God must have willed it so . . .

"And for slanderers let there be no hope," I chant further. The slanderers and rich scoffers who say there is no God—a fine figure they'll cut when they get *there.* They'll pay for their disbelief, and with interest too, for He is one who "breaketh his enemies and humbleth the arrogant." He pays you according to your deserts. You don't trifle with Him; you approach Him humbly, pray to Him and beg His mercy. *"O Merciful Father, hear our voice, pay heed to our lamentations. Spare us and have mercy upon us* (my wife and children too—they are hungry). *Accept, O Lord, thy people Israel and their prayer, even as you did in the days of the Holy Temple, when the priests and the Levites . . ."*

Suddenly the horse stopped. In a hurry I finish *Shmin-esra,* lift up my eyes, and behold two mysterious creatures coming toward me out of the forest, disguised or at least dressed in the strangest fashion. "Thieves," I thought, but corrected myself at once. "What is the matter with you, Tevye? You've been driving through this forest for so many years by day and by night; why should you suddenly begin to worry about thieves?" And swinging my whip over my head, I yelled at the horse, "Giddap!"

"Mister!" one of the two creatures called out to me. "Stop! Please stop! Don't run away, mister, we won't do you any harm!"

"An evil spirit!" I said to myself, and a second later, "You ox, Tevye, you ass! Why should evil spirits come to you all of a sudden?" And I stop the horse. I look the creatures over

from head to foot: they are ordinary women. One elderly
with a silk shawl on her head and the other a younger one
with a *sheitel*. Both flushed and out of breath.

"Good evening," I cry out loud, trying to sound cheerful.
"Look who's here! What is it you want? If you want to buy
something, all I have is a gnawing stomach, a heart full of
pain, a head full of worries, and all the misery and wretchedness in the world."

"Listen to him going on," they say. "That's enough. You
say one word to a man and you get a lecture in return.
There is nothing we want to buy. We only want to ask: do
you know where the road to Boiberik is?"

"To Boiberik?" I say, and let out a laugh, still trying to
sound cheerful. "You might as well ask me if I know my
name is Tevye."

"Oh? So that's what they call you—Tevye? Good evening,
then, Mr. Tevye. What is there to laugh at? We are strangers here. We are from Yehupetz, and we are staying at a
datcha in Boiberik. This morning we went out for a short
walk in the woods, and we've been wandering ever since, going round and round in circles. A little while ago we heard
someone singing in the forest. At first we thought it was a
highwayman, but when we came closer and saw it was only
you, we felt relieved. Now do you understand?"

"Ha-ha!" I laughed. "A fine highwayman! Have you ever
heard the story about the Jewish highwayman who waylaid
a traveler in the forest and demanded—a pinch of snuff? If
you'd like, I could tell it to you . . ."

"Leave that for some other time," they said. "Right now,
show us how to get back to Boiberik."

"To Boiberik?" I said again. "Why, this is the way to
Boiberik. Even if you don't want to, you couldn't help getting there if you followed this path."

"Oh," said they. "Is it far?"

"No, not far. Only a few *versts*. That is, five or six. Maybe
seven. But certainly not more than eight."

"Eight *versts!*" they both cried out, wringing their hands

and all but bursting into tears. "Do you know what you're saying? Only eight *versts!*"

"What do you want me to do about it?" I asked. "If it were up to me, I'd have made it a little shorter. But people have to have all sorts of experiences. How would you like to be in a carriage crawling up a hill through mud in a heavy rain, late Friday afternoon and almost time to light the candles for the Sabbath? Your hands are numb, you're faint with hunger . . . And crash! The axle breaks!"

"You talk like a half-wit," they said. "You must be out of your head. Why do you tell us these old-wives' tales? We're too tired to take another step. We've had nothing to eat all day except for a glass of coffee and a butter roll in the morning, and you come bothering us with foolish tales."

"Well, that's different," I told them. "You can't expect a person to dance before he's eaten. The taste of hunger is something I understand very well. You don't have to explain it to me. It's quite possible that I haven't even seen a cup of coffee or butter roll for the past year . . ." And as I utter these words a glass of steaming coffee with milk in it appears before my eyes, with rich, fresh butter rolls and other good things besides. "Oh, *shlimazl,*" I say to myself, "is that what you've been raised on—coffee and butter rolls? And a plain piece of bread with herring isn't good enough for you?" But there, just to spite me, the image of hot coffee remained; just to tempt me the vision of rolls hovered before my eyes. I smelled the odor of the coffee, I savored the taste of the butter roll on my tongue—fresh and rich and sweet . . .

"Do you know what, Reb Tevye?" the women said to me. "Since we are standing right here, maybe it would be a good idea if we jumped into your wagon and you took us home to Boiberik. What do you say?"

"A fine idea," I said. "Here am I, coming *from* Boiberik, and you're going *to* Boiberik. How can I go both ways at the same time?"

"Well," they said, "don't you know what you can do? A

wise and learned man can figure it out for himself. He would turn the wagon around and go back again—that's all. Don't be afraid, Reb Tevye. You can be sure that when you and the Almighty get us back home again, we'll see to it that your kindness won't go unrewarded."

"They're talking Chaldaic," I told myself. "I don't understand them. What do they mean?" And the thought of witches and evil spirits and goblins returned to me. "Dummy, what are you standing there for?" I asked myself. "Jump into the wagon, show the horse your whip, and get away from here!" But again, as if I were under a spell, these words escaped me: "Well, get in."

The women did not wait to be asked again. Into the wagon they climb, with me after them. I turn the wagon around, crack the whip—one, two, three, let's go . . . Who? What? When? The horse doesn't know what I'm talking about. He won't move an inch. "Ah-ha," I think to myself. "Now I can see what these women are. That's all I had to do —stop in the middle of the woods to make conversation with women!" You get the picture: on all sides the woods, silent, melancholy, with night coming on, and here behind me these two creatures in the guise of women. My imagination runs away with me. I recall a story about a teamster who once was riding through the woods by himself when he saw lying on the road a bag of oats. He jumped down, heaved the heavy sack to his back and just managed to tip it into the wagon, and went on. He rode a *verst* or two, looked around at the sack—but there was neither sack nor oats. In the wagon was a goat, a goat with a beard. The teamster tried to touch it with his hand, but the goat stuck out his tongue—a yard long—and let out a wild, piercing laugh and vanished into air . . .

"Well, what's keeping you?" ask the women.

"What's keeping me? Can't you see what's keeping me? The horse doesn't want to play. He is not in the mood."

"Well, you've got a whip, haven't you? Then use it."

"Thanks for the advice," I say. "I'm glad you reminded me.

The only trouble with that is that my friend here is not afraid of such things. He is as used to the whip as I am to poverty," I add, trying to be flippant, though all the time I am shaking as if in a fever.

Well, what more can I tell you? I vented all my wrath on the poor animal. I whipped him till with God's help the horse stirred from his place, and we went on our way through the woods. And as we ride along a new thought comes to plague me. "Ah, Tevye, what a dull ox you are! You have always been good for nothing and you'll die good for nothing. Think! Here something happens to you that won't happen again in a hundred years. God Himself must have arranged it. So why didn't you make sure in advance how much it is going to be worth to you—how much you'll get for it? Even if you consider righteousness and virtue, decency and helpfulness, justice and equity and I don't know what else, there is still no harm in earning a little something for yourself out of it. Why not lick a bone for once in your life, since you have the chance? Stop your horse, you ox. Tell them what you want. Either you get so much and so much for the trip, or ask them to be so kind as to jump off the wagon at once! But then, what good would that do? What if they promised you the whole world on a platter? You have to catch a bear before you can skin it . . ."

"Why don't you drive a little faster?" the women ask again, prodding me from behind.

"What's your hurry?" I say. "Nothing good can come from rushing too much." And I look around at my passengers. I'll swear they look like women, just plain ordinary women, one with a silk shawl, the other with a *sheitel*. They are looking at each other and whispering. Then one of them asks: "Are we getting closer?"

"Closer, yes. But not any closer than we really are. Pretty soon we'll go uphill and then downhill, then uphill and downhill again, and then after that we go up the steep hill and from then on it's straight ahead, right to Boiberik."

"Sounds like a *shlimazl*," says one to the other.

"A seven-year itch," the other answers.

"As if we haven't had troubles enough already," says the first.

"A little crazy too, I'm afraid," answers the other.

"I must be crazy," I tell myself, "if I let them pull me around by the nose like that."

And to them I say, "Where do you want to be dropped off, ladies?"

"Dropped off? What do you mean—dropped off? What kind of language is that?"

"It's only an expression. You hear it among coarse and impolite drovers," I tell them. "Among genteel people like us we'd say it like this: 'Where would you wish to be transported, dear ladies, when with God's help and the blessings of Providence we arrive at Boiberik?' Excuse me if I sound inquisitive, but as the saying goes, 'It's better to ask twice than to go wrong once.'"

"Oh, so that's what you mean?" said the women. "Go straight ahead through the woods until you come to the green *datcha* by the river. Do you know where that is?"

"How could I help knowing?" I say. "I know Boiberik as well as I know my own home. I wish I had a thousand rubles for every log I've carried there. Last summer I brought a couple of loads of wood to that *datcha* you mention. Somebody from Yehupetz was living there then, a rich man, a millionaire. He must have been worth at least a hundred thousand *rubles*."

"He still lives there," they tell me, looking at each other, whispering together and laughing.

"In that case," I said, "if you have some connections with the man, maybe it would be possible, if you wanted to, that is, if you could say a word or two in my behalf . . . Maybe you could get some sort of job for me, work of some kind. I know a man, a young fellow called Yisroel, who lived not far from our village—a worthless good-for-nothing. Well, he went off to the city, no one knows how it happened, and today, believe it or not, he is an important man somewhere.

He makes at least twenty *rubles* a week, or maybe even forty. Who knows for sure? Some people are lucky, like our *shochet's* son-in-law. What would he ever have amounted to if he hadn't gone to Yehupetz? It is true, the first few years he starved to death. But now I wouldn't mind being in his boots. Regularly he sends money home, and he would like to bring his wife and children to Yehupetz to live with him, but he can't do it, because by law he isn't allowed to live there himself. Then how does he do it? Never mind. He has trouble aplenty, only if you live long enough . . . Oh, here we are at the river, and there is the green *datcha!*"

And I drive in smartly right up to the porch. You should have seen the excitement when they saw us. Such cheering and shouting! "Grandmother! Mother! Auntie! They've come home again! Congratulations! *Mazl-tov!* Heavens, where were you? We went crazy all day! Sent messengers in all directions. . . . We thought—who can tell? Maybe wolves, highwaymen—who knows? Tell us, what happened?"

"What happened? What should happen? We got lost in the woods, wandered far away, till a man happened along. What kind of a man? A *shlimazl* with a horse and wagon. It took a little coaxing, but here we are."

"Of all horrible things! It's a dream, a nightmare! Just the two of you—without a guide! Thank God you're safe!"

To make a long story short, they brought lamps out on the porch, spread the table, and began bringing things out. Hot samovars, tea glasses, sugar, preserves, and fresh pastry that I could smell even from where I was standing; after that all kinds of food: rich fat soup, roast beef, goose, the best of wines and salads. I stood at the edge of the porch looking at them from a distance and thinking, "What a wonderful life these people of Yehupetz must live, praise the Lord! I wouldn't mind being one of them myself. What these people drop on the floor would be enough to feed my starving children all week long. O God, All-powerful and All-merciful, great and good, kind and just, how does it happen that to some people you give everything and to others nothing?

To some people butter rolls and to others the plague?" But
then I tell myself, "You big fool, Tevye! Are you trying to
tell Him how to rule His world? Apparently if He wants it
that way, that's the way it ought to be. Can't you see? If it
should have been different it would have been? And yet,
what would have been wrong to have it different? True! We
were slaves in Pharaoh's day, too. That's why we are the
Chosen People. That's why we must have faith and hope.
Faith, first of all in a God, and hope that maybe in time,
with His help, things will become a little better . . ."

. But then I hear someone say, "Wait! Where is he, this
man you've mentioned? Did he drive away already—the
shlimazl?"

"God forbid!" I call out from the edge of the porch.
"What do you think? That I'd go away like this—without
saying anything? Good evening! Good evening to you all,
and may the Lord bless you. Eat well, and may your food
agree with you!"

"Come here!" they said to me. "What are you standing
there for in the dark? Let's take a look at you, see what you
are like! Maybe you'd like a little whiskey?"

"A little whiskey?" said I. "Who ever refused a drink of
whiskey? How does it say in the *Talmud?* 'God is God, but
whiskey is something you can drink!' To your health, ladies
and gentlemen."

And I turn up the first glass. "May God provide for you,"
I say. "May He keep you rich and happy. Jews," I say, "must
always be Jews. And may God give them the health and the
strength to live through all the troubles they're born to . . ."

The *nogid* himself, a fine-looking man with a skullcap,
interrupts me. "What's your name?" he asks. "Where do you
hail from? Where do you live now? What do you do for a
living? Do you have any children? How many?"

"Children?" I say. "Do I have children? Oh . . . if it is
true that each child were really worth a million, as my Golde
insists, then I should be richer than the richest man in
Yehupetz. The only thing wrong with this argument is that

we still go to bed hungry. What does the Bible say? 'The
world belongs to him who has money.' It's the millionaires
who have the money; all I have is daughters. And as my
grandmother used to say, 'If you have enough girls, the whole
world whirls.' But I'm not complaining. God is our Father.
He has His own way. He sits on high, and we struggle down
below. What do I struggle with? I haul logs, lumber. What
else should I do? The *Talmud* is right, 'If you can't have
chicken, herring will do.' That's the whole trouble. We still
have to eat. As my old grandmother—may she rest in peace
—used to say, 'If we didn't have to eat, we'd all be rich.' "

I realized that my tongue was going sideways. "Excuse me,
please," I said. "Beware of the wisdom of a fool and the
proverbs of a drunkard."

At this the *nogid* cries out, "Why doesn't somebody bring
something to eat?" And at once the table is filled with every
kind of food—fish and fowl and roasts, wings and giblets
and livers galore.

"Won't you take something?" they say. "Come on!"

"A sick person you ask; a healthy person you give," I say.
"Thanks, anyway. A little whiskey—granted. But don't expect me to sit down and eat a meal like this while there, at
home, my wife and children . . ."

Well, they caught on to what I was driving at, and you
should have seen them start packing things into my wagon.
This one brought rolls, that one fish, another one a roast
chicken, tea, a package of sugar, a pot of chicken fat, a jar
of preserves.

"This," they say, "take home for your wife and children.
And now tell us how much you'd want us to pay you for all
you did for us."

"How do I know what it was worth?" I answer. "Whatever you think is right. If it's a penny more or a penny less
I'll still be the same Tevye either way."

"No," they say. "We want you to tell us yourself, Reb
Tevye. Don't be afraid. We won't chop your head off."

I think to myself, "What shall I do? This is bad. What if

I say one *ruble* when they might be willing to give two? On
the other hand, if I said two they might think I was crazy.
What have I done to earn that much?" But my tongue
slipped and before I knew what I was saying, I cried out,
"Three *rubles!*"

At this the crowd began to laugh so hard that I wished I
was dead and buried.

"Excuse me if I said the wrong thing," I stammered. "A
horse, which has four feet, stumbles once in a while too, so
why shouldn't a man who has but one tongue?"

The merriment increased. They held their sides laughing.

"Stop laughing, all of you!" cried the man of the house,
and from his pocket he took a large purse and from the
purse pulled out—how much do you think? For instance,
guess! A ten-*ruble* note, red as fire! As I live and breathe
. . . And he says, "This is from me. And now, the rest of
you, dig into your pockets and give what you think you
should."

Well, what shall I tell you? Fives and threes and ones
began to fly across the table. My arms and legs trembled. I
was afraid I was going to faint.

"*Nu,* what are you standing there for?" said my host.
"Gather up the few *rubles* and go home to your wife and
children."

"May God give you everything you desire ten times over,"
I babble, sweeping up the money with both hands and
stuffing it into my pockets. "May you have all that is good,
may you have nothing but joy. And now," I said, "good
night, and good luck, and God be with you. With you and
your children and grandchildren and all your relatives."

But when I turn to go back to the wagon, the mistress of
the house, the woman with the silk shawl, calls to me, "Wait
a minute, Reb Tevye. I want to give you something, too.
Come back tomorrow morning, if all is well. I have a cow
—a milch cow. It was once a wonderful cow, used to give
twenty-four glasses of milk a day. But some jealous person

must have cast an evil eye on it: you can't milk it any more. That is, you can milk it all right, but nothing comes."

"Long may you live!" I answer. "Don't worry. If you give us the cow we'll not only milk it—we'll get milk too! My wife, Lord bless her, is so resourceful that she makes noodles out of almost nothing, adds water and we have noodle soup. Every week she performs a miracle: we have food for the Sabbath! She has brought up seven children, though often she has nothing to give them for supper but a box on the ear! . . . Excuse me, please, if I've talked too much. Good night and good luck and God be with you," I say, and turn around to leave. I come out in the yard, reach for my horse —and stop dead! I look everywhere. Not a trace of a horse!

"Well, Tevye," I say to myself. "This time they really got you!"

And I recall a story I must have read somewhere, about a gang of thieves that once kidnapped a pious and holy man, lured him into a palace behind the town, dined him and wined him, and then suddenly vanished, leaving him all alone with a beautiful woman. But while he looked the woman changed into a tigress, and the tigress into a cat, the cat into an adder.

"Watch out, Tevye," I say to myself. "No telling what they'll do next!"

"What are you mumbling and grumbling about now?" they ask.

"What am I grumbling about? Woe is me! I'm ruined! My poor little horse!"

"Your horse," they tell me, "is in the stable."

I come into the stable, look around. As true as I'm alive, there's my bony little old nag right next to their aristocratic horses, deeply absorbed in feeding. His jaws work feverishly, as if this is the last meal he'll ever have.

"Look here, my friend," I say to him. "It's time to move along. It isn't wise to make a hog of yourself. An extra mouthful, and you may be sorry."

I finally persuaded him, coaxed him back to his harness, and in good spirits we started for home, singing one hymn after another. As for the old horse—you would never have known him! I didn't even have to whip him. He raced like the wind. We came home late, but I woke up my wife with a shout of joy.

"Good evening!" said I. "Congratulations! *Mazl-tov*, Golde!"

"A black and endless *mazl-tov* to you!" she answers me. "What are you so happy about, my beloved bread-winner? Are you coming from a wedding or a *bris*—a circumcision feast—my goldspinner?"

"A wedding and a *bris* rolled into one," I say. "Just wait, my wife, and you'll see the treasure I've brought you! But first wake up the children. Let them have a taste of the Yehupetz delicacies, too!"

"Are you crazy?" she asks. "Are you insane, or out of your head, or just delirious? You sound unbalanced—violent!" And she lets me have it—all the curses she knows —as only a woman can.

"Once a wife always a wife," I tell her. "No wonder King Solomon said that among his thousand wives there wasn't one that amounted to anything. It's lucky that it isn't the custom to have a lot of wives any more!"

And I go out to the wagon and come back with my arms full of all the good things that they had given me. I put it all on the table, and when my crew saw the fresh white rolls and smelled the meat and fish they fell on it like hungry wolves. You should have seen them grab and stuff and chew—like the Children of Israel in the desert. The Bible says, "And they did eat," and I could say it, too. Tears came to my eyes.

"Well," says my helpmate, "tell me—who has decided to feed the countryside? What makes you so gay? Who gave you the drinks?"

"Wait, my love," I say to her. "I'll tell you everything. But first heat up the samovar. Then we'll all sit around the

table, as people should now and then, and have a little tea.
We live but once, my dear. Let's celebrate. We are inde-
pendent now. We have a cow that used to be good
for twenty-four glasses a day. Tomorrow morning, if the
Lord permits, I'll bring her home. And look at this, my
Golde! Look at this!" And I pull out the green and red and
yellow banknotes from my pockets. "Come, my Golde,
show us how smart you are! Tell me how much there is
here!"

I look across at my wife. She's dumbfounded. She can't say
a word.

"God protect you, my darling!" I say to her. "What are you
scared of? Do you think I stole it? I am ashamed of you,
Golde! You've been Tevye's wife so many years and you
think that of me! Silly, this is *kosher* money, earned honestly
with my own wit and my own labor. I rescued two women
from a great misfortune. If it were not for me, I don't know
what would have become of them."

So I told her everything, from *a* to *z*. The whole story of
my wanderings. And we counted the money over and over.
There were eighteen *rubles*—for good luck, you know—and
another eighteen for more good luck, and one besides. In
all—thirty-seven *rubles!*

My wife began to cry.

"What are you crying for, you foolish woman?" I ask.

"How can I help crying when my tears won't stop? When
your heart is full your eyes run over. May God help me,
Tevye, my heart told me that you would come with good
news. I can't remember when I last saw my Grandmother
Tzeitl—may she rest in peace—in a dream. But just before
you came home I was asleep and suddenly I dreamed I
saw a milkpail full to the brim. My Grandmother Tzeitl was
carrying it under her apron to shield it from an evil eye, and
the children were crying, 'Mama . . .' "

"Don't eat up all the noodles before the Sabbath!" I interrupt. "May your Grandmother Tzeitl be happy in Paradise—
I don't know how much she can help us right now. Let's

leave that to God. He saw to it that we should have a cow
of our own, so no doubt He can also make her give milk.
Better give me some advice, Golde. Tell me—what shall we
do with the money?"

"That's right, Tevye," says she. "What do you plan to do
with so much money?"

"Well, what do you think we can do with it?" I say.
"Where shall we invest it?"

And we began to think of this and that, one thing after
another. We racked our brains, thought of every kind of en-
terprise on earth. That night we were engaged in every type
of business you could imagine. We bought a pair of horses
and sold them at a profit; opened a grocery store in Boiberik,
sold the stock and went into the drygoods business. We
bought an option on some woodland and made something on
that, too, then obtained the tax concession at Anatevka, and
with our earnings began to loan out money on mortgages.

"Be careful! Don't be so reckless!" my wife warned me.
"You'll throw it all away. Before you know it, you'll have
nothing left but your whip!"

"What do you want me to do?" I ask. "Deal in grain and
lose it all? Look what's happening right now in the wheat
market. Go! See what's going on in Odessa!"

"What do I care about Odessa? My great-grandfather was
never there, and so long as I'm alive and have my senses,
my children will never be there, either!"

"Then what *do* you want?"

"What do I want? I want you to have some brains and
not act like a fool."

"So you're the brainy one! You get a few *rubles* in your
hand and suddenly you're wise. That's what always happens."

Well, we disagreed a few times, fell out, had some arguments, but in the end this is what we decided: to buy another cow—in addition to the one we were getting for nothing. A cow that would really give milk.

Maybe you'll say, "Why a cow?" And I'll answer, "Why
not a cow?" Here we are, so close to Boiberik, where all the

rich people of Yehupetz come to spend the summer at their *datchas*. They're so refined that they expect everything to be brought to them on a platter—meat and eggs, chickens, onions, pepper, parsnips—everything. Why shouldn't there be someone who would be willing to come right to their kitchen door every morning with cheese and butter and cream? Especially since the Yehupetzers believe in eating well and are ready to pay?

The main thing is that what you bring must be good—the cream must be thick, the butter golden. And where will you find cream and butter that's better than mine?

So we make a living . . . May the two of us be blessed by the Lord as often as I am stopped on the road by important people from Yehupetz—even Russians—who beg me to bring them what I can spare. "We have heard, Tevel, that you are an upright man, even if you are a Jewish dog . . ." Now, how often does a person get a compliment like that? Do our own people ever praise a man? No! All they do is envy him.

When they saw that Tevye had an extra cow, a new wagon, they began to rack their brains. "Where did he get it? How did he get it? Maybe he's a counterfeiter. Maybe he cooks alcohol in secret."

I let them worry. "Scratch your heads and rack your brains, my friends! Break your heads if you begrudge me my small living."

I don't know if you'll believe my story. You're almost the first person I've ever told it to.

But I'm afraid I've said too much already. If so, forgive me! I forgot that we all have work to do. As the Bible says, "Let the shoemaker stick to his last." You to your books, Mr. Sholom Aleichem, and I to my pots and jugs . . .

One thing I beg of you. Don't put me into one of your books, and if you do put me in, at least don't tell them my real name.

Be well and happy always.

A PAGE FROM THE
SONG OF SONGS

Buzie is a name. It is a diminutive of Esther-Libbe. First Esther-Libbe, then Libuzie, then Buzie. She is a year older than I, or maybe two years, and together we are not quite twenty years old. Now, I ask you, how old am I and how old is she? But that is not important. Instead let me give you a short sketch of her life.

My older brother Benny lived in a village, where he owned a mill. He was a wonder at shooting, riding and swimming. One summer day while bathing in the river, he drowned. Thus the old adage that the best swimmers drown was borne out. He left the mill, two horses, a young widow and a child. The mill was abandoned, the horses were sold, the widow remarried and moved to some distant place, and the child was brought to us.

That child was Buzie.

That my father should love Buzie as his own is easy to understand, and that my mother should watch over her like an only daughter is natural. In her they found a comfort for their great sorrow. But that has nothing to do with me. Then why is it that when I come from *cheder* and find Buzie not at home my food is flat and tasteless? And why is it that when Buzie comes in the darkest corners are suddenly lit up? And why is it that when Buzie speaks to me I drop my eyes? And when Buzie laughs at me I weep?

And when Buzie . . .

All through the winter I had been looking forward to the Passover holidays. Then I would be free from *cheder,* free to play with Buzie, free to run outdoors with her. We would run down the hill to the river's edge, where I could show her how the ducklings learn to swim. When I try to tell her about it she only laughs at me. Buzie doesn't believe a thing I tell her. She doesn't believe that I can climb to the top of the highest tree—if I only wanted to. She doesn't believe that I can shoot—if I only had a gun to shoot with. She never says she doesn't believe, she only laughs at me. And I hate nothing more than to be laughed at. But when Passover comes, the beautiful, free days of Passover, when we can run outdoors away from the watchful eyes of my parents, then I will show her such wonders that they will take her breath away.

The wonderful time, the most joyous time of the year, has come.

Buzie and I are dressed in our holiday clothes. Everything we have on twinkles and shines and crackles. I look at Buzie and I am reminded of the *Song of Songs* which I studied before Passover with my rabbi. Verse after verse, it comes back to me:

"Behold, thou art fair, my beloved, thou art fair; thy eyes are as doves, thy hair is a flock of goats that comes down from Mount Gilead.

"Thy teeth are like a flock of white lambs that come up from the river, all are alike; the same mother bore them.

"Thy lips are like a thread of scarlet; thy speech is full of sweetness."

Why is it that when you look at Buzie you are reminded of the *Song of Songs?* Why is it that when you study the *Song of Songs* Buzie comes into your thoughts?

We are ready to go. I can hardly stand still. My pockets are full of nuts. My mother gave us all we wanted. She filled our pockets and told us we could play with them to our hearts' content. But she made us promise not to crack any before Passover.

"Are you ready?" says Buzie.

I jump for the door. Away we go. The nuts make a drumming sound, they rattle as we run. At first we are dazzled by the brilliance outside. The sun is high up already; it is looking down on the other side of town. The air is free and fresh, soft and clear. Here and there on the hill beyond the synagogue there sprouts the first grass of spring, tender, quivering, green . . . With a scream and a flutter of wings a straight line of swallows flies over our heads and again I am reminded of the *Song of Songs:* "The flowers appear on the earth; the time of the song of birds has come and the voice of the turtle is heard in our land."

I feel strangely light. It seems to me that I have wings. Any minute now I will rise into the air and fly.

From the town strange sounds arise—a roaring, a boiling, a seething. It is the day before Passover, a rare and wonderful day. In one instant the world is transformed. Our yard is a king's court. Our house is a palace. I am a prince and Buzie is a princess. The logs of wood piled about our door are the cedars and cypresses that are mentioned in the *Song of Songs*. The cat that lies near the door warming herself in the sun is a roe or a young hart that is mentioned in the *Song of Songs*. The women and the girls who are working outdoors, washing and cleaning and getting ready for the Passover are the daughters of Jerusalem mentioned in the *Song of Songs*. Everything, everything is from the *Song of Songs*.

I walk about with my hands in my pockets and the nuts rattle. Buzie follows me step by step. I cannot walk slowly, I am treading on air. I want to fly, to swoop, to soar, like an eagle. I start running and Buzie runs after me. I leap onto the pile of logs and jump from one log to another. Buzie jumps after me. I jump up, she jumps up; I jump down, she jumps down. Who will get tired first? I guessed it.

"How-long-will-you-keep-it-up?" asks Buzie all out of breath.

And I answer her in the words of the *Song of Songs:* " 'Till the morning breeze come and the shadows flee away.' There! You are tired and I am not!"

I feel proud that Buzie cannot keep up with me. I gloat over her and at the same time I am sorry for her. My heart aches for her, because I imagine she is unhappy. That is Buzie—full of gaiety one moment, and the next she is hiding in a corner, quietly weeping. At times like these nothing helps. No matter how much my mother tries to comfort her, how much my father caresses her, she continues to cry. For whom does she cry? For her father who died when she was a baby? For her mother who married and went off without as much as a goodbye? Ah, that mother of hers. When you mention her mother her face turns fiery red, as though she were ashamed of her. She never says an unkind word about her, but she looks unhappy. I cannot bear to see Buzie looking so wretched. I sit near her on the logs and try to distract her thoughts.

Rolling a few nuts about, I start:

"Guess what I could do if I wanted to."

"What could you do?"

"If I wanted to, all your nuts would be mine."

"Would you win them away from me?"

"No. We wouldn't even start playing."

"Well then, would you take them away from me?"

"No. They would come to me by themselves."

She raises her eyes to me, her blue eyes, eyes straight out of the *Song of Songs.* I say, "You think I am joking. Well, I know a certain language, I know some magic words . . ."

She opens her eyes wider. I explain, feeling grown and important, all puffed up with pride. "We boys know a lot of things. There is a boy in *cheder,* Shaike, who is blind in one eye—he knows everything. He even knows *Kabala.* Do you know what *Kabala* is?"

"No. How should I know?"

I am suddenly lifted to the seventh heaven because I can give her a lesson in *Kabala*.

"*Kabala*, silly, is a useful thing. By means of *Kabala* I can make myself invisible. With *Kabala* I can draw wine from a stone and gold from a wall. With the help of *Kabala* you and I, just as we are sitting here, could rise to the clouds and above the clouds . . ."

To fly up to the clouds with Buzie and above the clouds, and fly away with her, far, far off over the ocean—that has been one of my fondest dreams. There, beyond the ocean, begins the land of the dwarfs who are descended from King David's time. These dwarfs are kindly little people who live on sweets and almond milk, play all day long on little flutes and dance in a ring, are afraid of nothing and are kind to strangers. When someone arrives from our world they give him food and drink and shower him with costly garments and gold and silver ornaments and before he leaves they fill his pockets with diamonds and jewels which lie about in their streets as trash does in ours.

"Really? Like trash in the streets?" asked Buzie, wonderingly, when I once told her about the dwarfs.

"Don't you believe it?"

"Do you?"

"Why shouldn't I?"

"Where did you hear about it?"

"In *cheder*, of course."

"Oh, in *cheder*!"

Lower and lower sinks the sun, painting the sky a fiery gold. . . . The gold is reflected in Buzie's eyes. They swim in molten gold.

I want very badly to impress Buzie with Shaike's ability and with the wonders I can perform by means of *Kabala*. But Buzie won't be impressed. Instead she laughs at me. She looks at me with her mouth half-open and all her pearly teeth showing, and laughs.

Annoyed, I ask, "Don't you believe me?"

Buzie laughs again.

"You think I am boasting. That I am making up lies."

Buzie laughs harder. I have to repay her for this. I know how, too.

"The trouble with you is that you don't know what *Kabala* is. If you knew, you wouldn't laugh. By means of *Kabala*, if I wanted to, I could bring your mother down here. Yes, I can. And if you begged me very hard I could bring her tonight, riding on a broomstick."

At once she stops laughing. A cloud crosses her lovely, bright face and it seems to me that the sun has suddenly disappeared and the day is done. I have gone too far. I have wounded her tenderest feelings. I am sorry I had ever started this. How can I make up to her now? I move closer to her. She turns away from me. I want to take her hand and speak to her with the words of the *Song of Songs:* "Return, return O Shulamite, turn back to me, Buzie . . ."

Suddenly a voice calls out, "Shimek, Shimek!"

Shimek—that's me. My mother is calling me, to go to the synagogue with my father.

To go with Father to the synagogue on the Eve of Passover is one of the pleasures of life. Just to be dressed in perfectly new clothes from head to foot and to show off before one's friends. And the services—the first evening prayer, the first benediction of the holiday season! What delights the Lord has provided for his Jewish children.

"Shimek! Shimek!"

My mother is in a hurry. "I am coming! I am coming right away, I just have to tell Buzie something, just one little thing!"

I tell her just one thing. That what I told her was not true. To make other people fly by means of *Kabala* is impossible. But I myself—I can fly, and I will show her right after the holidays. I will make my first attempt then. I will rise up here from these very logs where we are now sitting, and in one moment I will be above the clouds. From there I will turn to the right—there, see—there where everything ends and the Frozen Sea begins . . .

Buzie listens, absorbed in my story. The sun, about to sink, sends its last rays to kiss the earth.

"What," asks Buzie, "do you mean by the Frozen Sea?"

"Don't you know what the Frozen Sea is? That's far in the north. The water is as thick as jelly and as salty as brine. Ships cannot go there, and people who are caught in it never return."

Buzie looks at me wide-eyed. "Then why are you going there?"

"Am I going to touch the sea, you silly thing? I'll fly high up over it, like an eagle, and in a few minutes I shall be on dry land. That is where the twelve high mountains begin that belch fire and smoke. I shall stop on the tip of the twelfth mountain and walk from there for seven miles till I come to a thick forest. I will cross several forests till I come to a small lake. I shall swim across the lake and count seven times seven. Out of the ground will spring a dwarf with a long white beard. He will say to me, 'What is your wish?'

"And I will say to him: 'Lead me to the Queen's daughter!' "

"Which Queen's daughter?" asks Buzie, startled.

"The Queen's daughter," I explain, "is the beautiful princess who was snatched away from under the wedding canopy, bewitched, and carried far, far away and locked up in a crystal palace for seven years . . ."

"What is she to you?"

"What do you mean—what is she to me? I have to set her free, don't I?"

"You have to set her free?"

"Who, then?"

"You don't have to fly so far, believe me. You don't have to fly so far," says Buzie, and takes my hand. Her small, white hand is cold. I look into her eyes and see in them the last faint reflection of the gold that is draining from the sky.

Slowly the day is going, the first beautiful day of spring is passing away. Like a spent candle the sun goes down. The noises that we heard all day are dying too. There is hardly a person to be seen in the street. From the windows of the houses there wink the flames of candles lit for Passover Eve. A strange, a holy stillness surrounds us, and Buzie and I feel ourselves slowly merging with this stillness.

"Shimek! Shimek!"

This is the third time my mother has called me. As if I didn't know myself that I had to go to the synagogue! I'll stay only another minute, not more than a minute. But Buzie hears her too, pulls her hand out of mine, jumps to her feet and begins to push me.

"Shimek, your mother is calling you. You'd better go. It's late. Go."

I am getting ready to go. The day is done, the sun has been snuffed out. All the gold has turned to blood. A cool breeze has sprung up. Buzie keeps pushing me toward the house. I throw a last quick look at her. Her face has changed and it has a different, an unearthly beauty in the twilight. The thought of the bewitched princess flits through my head. But Buzie won't allow those thoughts. She keeps pushing me ahead. I start slowly to go and I look back just once at the bewitched princess who has now completely merged with the weird Passover twilight, and I stand rooted in one spot. But she waves her hand at me, bidding me to go, to go quickly. And it seems to me that I hear her speaking in the words of the *Song of Songs:*

"Make haste, my beloved, be thou like a gazelle or a young hart upon the mountain of spices."

TWO DEAD MEN

(A Tale for Purim)

You may think this is a strange title for a *Purim* tale; *Purim*
—when it is fitting and proper for a Jew to act the drunkard
and a storyteller to play the fool! Reader, I know that today is *Purim* and you are supposed to act the drunkard and
I the fool; and nevertheless I'll give you a story about two
dead men. That's final. All I can do for you is give you this
advice: if your nerves are weak, don't read this tale before
going to sleep.

1

Chlavne, a short, dark, heavy-set man, had always loved a
drink. Fortunately he was brought up in a decent and tem-
perate home, or he would surely have grown up a drunkard.
I do not guarantee that it was only his upbringing that saved
him from a drunkard's fate. It is possible that in spite of
that he might have been able to outdrink a squad of can-
noneers, if only he had the means. But his wife Gittel managed all his finances and did not let him have a *groschen*
to spend. Wherever money was involved Gittel took care of
it. The work itself, the labor that earned their bread,
was done by Chlavne (he was, alas, a shoemaker), but when

the work was finished it was Gittel who delivered it and collected the money. And naturally Chlavne was not pleased with this state of affairs.

"What do you think I am? A thief—or what?"

That is what Chlavne said to his wife Gittel, and he received a clear, unequivocal answer on the spot.

"Heaven forbid! Who said you were a thief? All you are is a soak. Do you dare tell me you aren't?"

To deny it outright was not easy. And yet to go ahead and confess that he loved to take the bitter drop was not so agreeable either. So he took refuge in a pun, as he frequently did, because Chlavne the shoemaker was fond not only of a glass of brandy, but also of a quip, a pun, a pithy saying, for he was a true Kasrilevkite. So he scratched his beard, looked up at the ceiling, and said:

"Listen to the woman! All she can say is soak. Soak! If I have a bottle in my hand, do I ever soak anybody with it? All I do is drink it."

"Oh, go to the devil!" his wife sputtered.

"Together with you, beloved, I'd go through the fires of hell."

"Here, go with this!" cried Gittel, and from the other side of the room she heaved a boot at him. This, too, Chlavne caught with a laugh, and he replied with a quip, as always.

And what did he do when Gittel came home with some money, and handed him a few *groschen* to go buy thread and wax and brushes? He became soft as butter and sweet as honey. And his respect for women in general and Gittel in particular rose immediately. He stroked his high, white forehead (all shoemakers have high, white foreheads) and mused thoughtfully, philosophically:

"I can't understand what a wise man like King Solomon had against you women. Do you know what King Solomon said about women? Or don't you?"

"Who cares what King Solomon said? You go to the market for thread and wax and brushes. And see that you don't lose your way in some tavern."

At this far-fetched idea, Chlavne burst out laughing.

"Next you'll be telling me not to wear my heavy mittens in July, or eat *matzo* on *Yom Kippur!* Which way is the market place and which way are the taverns? And besides, who would think, in the middle of the week, on a working day, of going off for a drink?"

But even while he was talking he was counting the money Gittel had given him by transferring it, coin by coin, from one hand to the other, and looking philosophically up at the ceiling with one eye closed, was figuring out exactly how much he would need for thread, how much for wax, and how much for brushes. And with a deep, deep sigh he quietly went out of the house, and straight to the tavern.

2

Who was that wise man, that sage, who after deep thought announced that on *Purim* all drunkards are sober? I doubt if he knew what he was talking about. Why should a drunkard miss his chance on a day when it is fitting and proper for everybody to get drunk as a lord? The first to protest against a notion like that would have been Chlvane the shoemaker. How eagerly he awaited that one day! What agony he suffered before it came! And when it finally arrived he went to the synagogue with everybody else, to settle his account with Haman and hang him up on a gallows fifty ells high together with his ten sons. And afterwards, instead of going home to taste the festive *hamantash* he stopped off for a while at the homes of one or two of his shoemaker friends, old comrades of the bottle, for a holiday toast. "May the good Lord spare Haman and his ten sons for another year so we can get together next *Purim* and hang them again on a fifty-ell gallows and take another drink in their honor. Amen."

And after this series of toasts our hero became so foggy that no matter how far he went, no matter how many corners he turned, he was unable to find his way home. It began to look as if the street in which he lived had decided to play hide-and-go-seek with him. There it was in front of him, winking to him with all the flickering candles in all the small windows, and when he took another step he found himself bumping his forehead into a wall. Where did the wall come from? As long as he could remember, there had never been a wall here in the middle of the street. Someone must have put up a woodshed here. Imagine the impudence —building woodsheds right in the middle of the street! Who would dare do a thing like that? It must have been Yossi the *nogid's* doings. But he'd never get away with it!

"As sure as my name is Ahasuerus, King of Persia!" cried Chlavne, and he reached up both hands to tear down the wall that Yossi the *nogid* had dared to build right in the middle of the street. But just then the wall moved away, Chlavne lost his balance, and stretched himself out like a baron, full length in the famous Kasrilevka mud.

And there let us leave him for a while, till we have introduced you to the second hero of our tale, a man who was known in our town by the glorious and opulent name of— Rothschild.

3

He was given the name of Rothschild in Kasrilevka obviously because he was the poorest man in town. Though poor people were as numerous in Kasrilevka as the stars in heaven, a pauper as completely wretched and miserable as he could not be duplicated even there. There is a proverb (it must have originated in Kasrilevka) that it takes a special kind of luck to be that unlucky. And as you know, every proverb is founded on truth.

Who this man Rothschild was and where he came from I cannot tell you. He was a pauper—that much you know already. And his occupation was—walking. And I don't mean walking from house to house, asking for alms. His walking was aimless. All day long he walked through the deep mud, with short, quick strides like a very busy man in a great hurry. He paused only when somebody stopped him.

"Greetings. And where are you going, Mr. Rothschild?"

Rothschild stopped, wiped the sweat off his forehead with his sleeve, looked with strangely frightened eyes at the person who spoke to him and his thin, yellow, hungry face wrinkled up into a sort of smile, as he answered so softly that he could barely be heard:

"Nowhere. I keep going . . . Maybe the good Lord will send something my way."

And having explained all this, he resumed his march with short, rapid strides. And the person who had stopped him remained standing a while looking after him, then shrugged his shoulders, spit into the mud, and laughed.

"There is a *shlimazl* for you!"

As long as this poor man had been known as Rothschild no one in Kasrilevka had ever seen him approach anyone with a plea for food, a request for drink or lodging, although every one knew very well that he was always hungry and had no place to lay his head. In Kasrilevka, there are experienced authorities on the subject of hunger, one might even say specialists. On the darkest night, simply by hearing your voice, they can tell if you are simply hungry and would like a bite to eat, or if you are really starving. No doubt they have their symptoms to judge by, like doctors who prod you here and there and can tell if you are slightly indisposed or if you are on the verge of giving up your ghost.

If we are to distinguish between the various degrees of hunger, between those who are simply hungry and those who are dead hungry, we must say without hesitation that our hero Rothschild was in the rank of the dead hungry. He was a man who frequently went along for days on end with nothing at all in his mouth. And more than once he would surely have passed out right on the broad highway if some

kind soul had not of his own accord noticed that here was
that unfortunate wretch, Rothschild. If you gave him something he did not refuse it, but if you asked him if he was
hungry he never answered. And if you asked if he was very
hungry he still did not answer, but his yellow, emaciated face
wrinkled up into something like a smile and his frightened
eyes looked down, apparently ashamed that a person could
ever be as hungry as he was, and a weak little sigh stole out
unwillingly. And who knows what that sigh meant?

The Kasrilevkites, who loved a jest, gave him something
to eat first, but afterwards could not refrain from teasing
him.

"Mr. Rothschild, tell us the truth. How many millions do
you have and where do you hide them all?"

Rothschild lowered his frightened eyes, wrinkled his
starved, waxen features, smiled weakly and said nothing.

And younger wags, who had no respect for anyone, came
close to him, pulled at his sleeve.

"Well, well! The great *M'sieu* Rothschild himself! And
how are things on the Paris Bourse?"

Again Rothschild lowered his eyes. What was there
to say?

Even the youngest of the lot, little school children, not
much more than toddlers, did not let him pass. They made
up a song about him:

> *Rothschild is a gentleman*
> *Rolling in riches.*
> *There's nothing he lacks*
> *But a pair of britches.*

He was especially afraid of these little children and he
ran away from them with his short quick strides. The children ran after him, they would not stop singing. And hearing them, their parents shouted:

"Go away, you scamps, you scoundrels! Go back to *cheder!*
Go back to school, you tramps!"

It is possible that there would have been plenty of people

in Kasrilevka to look after him and he would not have had to hunger at all. But who is to blame if this penniless wretch would rather die than hold out his hand for help? And besides, is Kasrilevka expected to support every pauper who comes her way? Do not the people have troubles and heartaches and anxieties enough of their own in their struggle for a livelihood? They thank the Lord that they are able to survive the day and live through the week with their wives and children.

And yet—let the truth be known—when the Holy Sabbath came around, Rothschild was provided for. All Kasrilevka was in the synagogue that day, and Rothschild was in front of their eyes. And seeing him there, would the people let him go hungry—on the Sabbath? After all, an extra person at the table means only that you lay another spoon. So one family or another would take him home. And if the feast was not so rich it was no tragedy. His stomach was tolerant. At least he sat at a table with other Jews. In front of them were a few slices of Sabbath bread, some fish bones and the brass candlesticks from the night before. All these things, taken together with the singing and chanting after the meal, had such an attraction for him that he was ready to forget all the fine dishes, the appetizers and the desserts that human fancy has invented in order to lure us and lead us more deeply into Gehenna.

Great is the power of the Holy Sabbath! On that day you would scarcely recognize the householder of Kasrilevka, or his guest, the derelict Rothschild.

4

Having fasted the whole day according to custom, the good householders of Kasrilevka finally saw the sun sinking and hastened to the synagogue to celebrate the *Purim* services, to chant the *Book of Esther* and take revenge on Haman. And having hurried through the final prayers standing on one foot, the hungry Kasrilevkites rushed out in a body the quicker to come home and the quicker to break the fast, each one under his own grapevine and his own fig tree, with a fresh, warm *hamantash* full of poppy seed. And in their great haste and desire to partake of food they completely forgot about Rothschild, as if there had never been a Rothschild in the whole world. And Rothschild, seeing that everyone was hurrying, hurried off too, with his short strides, over the muddy roads and alleys of the blessed Kasrilevka, without knowing where he was going.

Running past the half-fallen and dimly lighted shacks and cottages, from time to time our hungry hero stole a glance through a window and saw cheeks and jaws and necks, chewing and grinding and swallowing. What the bulging cheeks enclosed, what the jaws were grinding and the necks were swallowing, he could not see, but he felt fairly certain that it must be those sweet and fresh and wonderful triangular *hamantashen,* stuffed with honeyed poppy seed that melted in your mouth and tasted like something in Eden. And something woke inside of Rothschild and pulled at his heart and said to him, "Fool, why do you wander around in the darkness? Open one of those doors, go into the house and say, 'Good evening and a happy *Purim.* Do you have something that a person can break his fast with? It is the third day now since I have eaten anything.'" And Rothschild became frightened by his boldness. Such a thought had never come to him before—to force his way into a stranger's house like a thief! And lest his Evil Spirit take hold of him again he turned from the houses directly into the middle of the road where the mud was deepest, and in the darkness collided with something soft and broad and alive, and before he could regain his balance fell headlong over our hero number one—Chlavne the shoemaker.

Let us leave our Rothschild alone for a while and find out how Chlavne the shoemaker was doing.

5

Chlavne the shoemaker (we beg his pardon a hundred times for letting him lie in the mud so long) did not feel nearly as wretched in his new surroundings as the reader would imagine. It is an old-established trait of man to adapt himself to his surroundings, no matter how unfavorable they might be. As soon as he found that before resuming his journey he was destined to pause a while in this bed of mud, the famous Kasrilevka mud, he saw to it that he did it like a man, productively, and not idly and wastefully. Without rest and without pause he proceeded to pour his wrath out on the wealthy of the earth, and especially on Yossi the *nogid*. Did Yossi think that he, Chlavne, was drunk? He swore on his honor that he was not. Who could have started that rumor that he, Chlavne, was a drunkard? It must have been that wife of his, Vashti.

And having said the name Vashti, Chlavne the shoemaker became silent and thoughtful. This name—Vashti—came back to his mind again and again like nails being hammered into a shoe. He remembered quite clearly that his wife's name used to be Gittel—and now suddenly it was Vashti! How did that happen? Gittel—Vashti? And it was not only her name. Everything else about her was changed, too. She was dressed like a queen with a golden crown, and everything she wore from head to foot was gold. He decided that this was not the time to start a fight with her. With a beauty like that you made your peace. And he pulled himself through the mud, closer and closer to her; but she drew away. She spurned him. Apparently because of his other passion, drink. The devil take her! She was too proud to have people think that her husband was a drunkard!

"May I never live to get up from this spot if I ever let another drop of brandy touch my lips!" he swore. "Do you hear, Vashti? If you don't believe me, here is my hand. I promise . . ."

And Chlavne stretched out his thick, blackened hand with its stubby black fingers in the mud—and he was surprised to find that Vashti's hand was wet and cold and Vashti's fingers were damp and slippery. It was impossible to put one's arms around a woman like that. And once more he held out his arms, and embraced—the bony, shivering body of the unhappy Rothschild.

6

Philosophers tell you that many things can happen as a result of a shock. A woman can have a miscarriage because of a sudden fright. If the shock is great enough a person can go out of his mind, and in some cases—Heaven forbid!—it has even been suggested that it was possible for a drunkard to become suddenly sober. So say the philosophers. And therefore we should not be too much surprised to learn that as soon as our hero, Chlavne the shoemaker, had embraced the unfortunate Rothschild, he too became sober. That is, not entirely sober, not sober enough to pick himself out of the mud and stand like a man, but enough to make him regain his senses one by one. First of all, through his sense of touch, he became aware that Vashti was a man with a beard. Then, with the return of his sense of hearing, he made out these words distinctly: *"Shma Yisroel!* Help! Help! Save me!" Through his sense of sight he became aware that the two of them were lying in the mud, in the thick, suffocating Kasrilevka mud. But try as he might, he could not distinguish the person who was in his arms, for just then the moon had hidden behind a thick cloud and the dark night had spread its sable wings over all of Kasrilevka.

Rothschild too began slowly to collect his thoughts. His deathly fear gradually disappeared, and together our heroes recovered their speech. And what they said shall now be repeated, word for word:

Chlavne: Who are you?

Rothschild: It's me.

Chlavne: What are you doing here?

Rothschild: Not a thing.

Chlavne: How the devil did you get here?

Rothschild: I don't know.

Chlavne: Don't you know anything at all? What are you? One of us? A shoemaker?

Rothschild: No.

Chlavne: What then? A businessman?

Rothschild: Oh, no! No!

Chlavne: Then what on earth are you? Do you know? What *are* you?

Rothschild: I'm . . . I'm . . . dead . . . hungry . . .

Chlavne: So that's the story! You're dead hungry, and I'm dead drunk. But wait! If I'm not mistaken, aren't you Mr. Rothschild? Of course. I knew you at once. If that's the case, Brother Rothschild, maybe it would be a good idea if you helped me crawl out of this mud, and then if you are strong enough the two of us can go to my house and have a bite to eat. Something tells me that there is some sort of holiday being celebrated today. *Simchas-Torah? Purim?* I'm not sure which, but I know it's a holiday. If all the kings of the east and west insisted that it wasn't, I'd . . . I'd spit in their faces!

It took a little while before the two of them managed to drag themselves out of the mud, and with great effort they started on their way, each one holding on to the other. That is, Rothschild was doing his best to keep Chlavne upright, because so far only the shoemaker's head had sobered up. His feet still went this way and that. And when they came to . . .

But at this point let us leave both of our heroes, and let us glance for a moment into the home of Chlavne the shoemaker, to see how his wife Gittel was getting along.

7

No matter how much she may be criticized by cynics, no matter how much the humorists may joke about her, a wife is still a wife. As soon as it was dark, Gittel began to get things ready for her husband who ought to be coming home soon from the synagogue after his long day of fasting. In his behalf she spread a festive tablecloth and brought out those things that Chlavne loved so well—a bottle and a glass. It is possible that the bottle held no more than a single glassful, or perhaps in recognition of the holiday enough for two glasses. On the other hand, the *hamantash* which she placed on the table was a huge one. It was a giant of a *hamantash*, rich and golden, with honeyed poppy seed oozing out of its three corners. It cried aloud to be eaten. You could almost hear it plead: "Chlavne, where are you? Chlavne, come eat me!" But Chlavne did not hear. At that moment he was sitting with the other shoemakers pouring long drinks in honor of the holy *Purim*.

In vain did the shoemaker's wife look out of the window, in vain did she listen for a sound at the door. Every step she heard outside sounded like Chlavne's. But Chlavne was not walking just then. Chlavne was stretched out in the deep mud, whispering to Vashti. Gittel thought all the thoughts that a wife could ever think about her husband, but when it became really late she tore her jacket off its hook, threw it over her shoulders, and went out to search for Chlavne. She did not find him. The shoemakers with whom he had stopped to take a few drinks in honor of the holiday swore that they hoped they would not live till next *Purim* if Chlavne had not hurried straight home from the synagogue. And they swore that not one of them had so much as touched a single drop that evening. That is, unless—so said the shoemakers—he had met up somewhere with Shimen-Wolf . . .

At the mention of this name Gittel very noticeably trembled. This man, this Shimen-Wolf, was responsible for so many of her troubles . . .

Shimen-Wolf was also a shoemaker, and his greatest passion was the same as her husband's. But how could you compare Chlavne to him? He was notorious throughout that part of the country—he was known by only one name—Shimen-Wolf the Drunkard. The story is that he inherited this trait from his father, who had died of drink. One holiday long ago he drank so much that he caught fire inside and was burned to death. This had happened to Shimen-Wolf, too, on one occasion, but they had put out the fire in time and he was saved. Gittel could not believe that her husband had gone off with this drunkard. After all, he had given her his hand and sworn on his pair of *tfillin* that as long as he lived he would never have anything to do with Shimen-Wolf. Because she had insisted on this oath a feud had broken out at the time between Chlavne's Gittel and Shimen-Wolf's Hanna-Zissel. The feud had started with plain words which led to taunts and ended with something not at all pleasant to narrate: the two women became tangled up in each other's hair, and it was with the greatest difficulty that they were pulled apart alive. Since then they had not spoken to each other, and when they met somewhere by accident they stepped to the side of the road and spit three times, as one did when one encountered an evil spirit.

Gittel did not know what to do. Should she go to that shrew Hanna-Zissel to find out about her husband, or shouldn't she? She was afraid a new scandal might come of it. But the Lord himself came to her aid. Before she had time to move one way or the other she saw someone draped in black coming her way. She looked closer in the darkness and saw that it was Hanna-Zissel. Both women were ready to spring to the side of the road and spit three times, as always, but some strange power took hold of them and they began to talk. The conversation was short but to the point:

"What are you doing out here so late?"

"And what are you doing?"

"I'm looking for my husband."

"So am I."

"Where can they be?"

"I wish I knew."

"Mine was at the synagogue just a while ago."

"So was mine."

"Maybe they went somewhere together."

"It looks like it."

And both women let out a deep sigh, and continued on their way, one this way, the other that . . .

8

Sad and dejected, Gittel came home again, glanced at the *hamantash* on the table, and it seemed to her that the *hamantash* looked back at her and said: "What's the matter with Chlavne?" In her grief she threw herself on the bed and lay there so long that she fell asleep. She dreamt that someone knocked on the window and called her by name. Without moving she asked, "Who is that?" And she received the answer that it was Hanna-Zissel and the *shammes* of the burial society who had come to her for a shroud. Gittel felt so faint that she could not understand where she got the strength to ask as coldly as she might ask the butcher for a chickenwing: "Were they burned to death?" "Yes, they were burned to death." "Both together?" "Together."

In terror she sat up and heard something stirring on the other side of the door, as if several hands were passing over it. She was barely able to ask:

"Who is that?"

"Us."

"Who is us?"

"Unlock the door and you'll see."

"The door is unlocked."

"But we can't find the handle."

Gittel recognized her husband's voice. She sprang to the door, opened it, and saw two creatures covered with mud like some fiends from the depths of the earth. At this sight she leaped back.

"Happy *Purim,* my Gittel," said one of them, staggering into the room without letting go of his companion. "I'll swear that my name isn't Chlavne," he went on, "that you'll never guess who has come to see you. You have two guests for *Purim,* Gittel. Two dead men . . . God in heaven, Gittel, why do you look so scared? . . . Yes, we are dead, but we do not come from the Other World. One of us is dead drunk, the other dead hungry. And which is drunk and which is hungry you'll have to guess for yourself . . .

"What are you staring for, Gittel? Don't you know who this is? It's Rothschild. May Reb Yossi sink into the earth together with the Kasrilevka mud! Rothschild is so covered with the mud that you can't recognize him. You'd think he'd been rolling around in a pigsty."

Chlavne looked around the room, looked long at the table.

"Do you know, Gittel? You're a wise and thoughtful woman. Compared to you, Vashti is a silly little hen. You've put a bottle on the table, I see. Something must have told you what a holiday the whole world is celebrating today, and how we ought to celebrate it—with a prayer and a drink and a *hamantash.* To your health, Rothschild! May the Lord save Haman for another year, so we can hang him again with his ten sons on one gallows, fifty ells high!

"Gittel—why don't you say amen?"

THE CLOCK THAT
STRUCK THIRTEEN

The clock struck thirteen.

That's the truth. I wasn't joking. I am telling you a true story of what happened in Kasrilevka, in our own house. I was there.

We had a hanging clock. It was an ancient clock that my grandfather had inherited from his father and his father's father straight back to the days of Count Chmelnitski.

What a pity that a clock is a lifeless thing, mute and without speech. Otherwise what stories it could have told and told. It had a name throughout the town—Reb Nochem's clock—so unfaltering and true in its course that men came from all directions to set their own clocks and watches by it. Only Reb Leibesh Akoron, a man of learning and philosophy, who could tell time by the sun and knew the almanac by heart, said that our clock was—next to his little watch—just so much tin and hardware, not worth a pinch of snuff. But even he had to admit that it was still a clock. And you must remember that Reb Leibesh was the man who, every Wednesday night, climbed to the roof of the synagogue or to the hilltop nearby, before the evening prayers, to catch the exact moment when the sun went down—in one hand his watch, and in the other—his almanac. And just as the sun sank below the housetops he muttered to himself: "On the dot!"

He was always comparing the two timepieces. Walking in without so much as a Good Evening, he would glance up at our hanging clock, then down at his little watch, then over to his almanac, again at our clock, down to his watch, over to the almanac, several times, and away he went.

Only one day when he came in to compare the two time-pieces with his almanac, he let out a yell, "Nochem! Quick! Where are you?"

My father, more dead than alive, came running. "What— what's happened, Reb Leibesh?"

"You are asking me?" shouted Reb Leibesh, raising his lit-tle watch right up to my father's face, and pointing with his other hand up to our clock: "Nochem, why don't you say something? Can't you see? It's a minute and a half fast! A minute and a half! Cast out the thing!" He hurled the words like an angered prophet with a base image before him.

My father did not like this at all. What did he mean, tell-ing him to cast the clock out? "Where is it written, Reb Leibesh, that my clock is a minute and a half *fast?* Maybe we can read the same sentence backward—that your watch is a minute and a half *slow.* How do you like that?"

Reb Leibesh looked at my father as at a man who has just said that Sabbath comes twice a week or that the Day of Atonement falls on Passover. Reb Leibesh didn't say a word. He sighed deeply, turned around, slammed the door and away he went.

But we didn't care. The whole town knew that Reb Lei-besh was a man whom nothing could please. The best cantor you ever heard sounded like a crow; the wisest man was— an ass; the best marriage—a failure; the cleverest epigram— a dull commonplace.

But let us return to our clock. What a clock that was! Its chimes could be heard three doors away. Boom . . . Boom . . . boom . . . Almost half of the town ordered its life ac-cording to it. And what is Jewish life without a clock? How many things there are that must be timed to the minute—the lighting of the Sabbath candles, the end of the Sabbath, the daily prayers, the salting and the soaking of the meat, the intervals between meals . . .

In short, our clock was the town clock. It was always faithful to us and to itself. In all its existence it never knew a repair man. My father, himself, was its only master. He had "an intuitive understanding of how it worked." Every year before Passover he carefully removed it from the wall, cleaned the insides with a feather duster, took out from within a mass of spiderwebs, mutilated flies which the spiders had lured inside, along with dead cockroaches that had lost their way and had met their sad fate there. Then, cleaned and sparkling, he hung the clock on the wall again, and it glowed. That is, they both glowed, the clock because it had been polished and cleaned, and my father—because the clock did.

But there came a day when a strange thing happened. It was on a beautiful cloudless day when we were sitting at the noonday meal. Whenever the clock struck I liked to count the strokes, and I did it out loud.

"One, two, three . . . seven . . . eleven, twelve, thirteen . . ."

What . . . thirteen!

"Thirteen!" cried my father, and burst out laughing. "A fine mathematician you are—may the evil eye spare you. Whoever heard of a clock striking thirteen?"

"Thirteen," I said. "On my word of honor. Thirteen."

"I'll give you thirteen smacks," cried my father, aroused. "Don't ever repeat such nonsense. Fool! A clock can't strike thirteen."

"Do you know what," my mother broke in, "I'm afraid that the child is right. It seems to me that I counted thirteen, too."

"Wonderful," said my father. "Another village heard from."

But at the same time he too began to suspect something. After dinner he went to the clock, climbed on a stool, and prodded around inside until the clock began to strike. All three of us counted, nodding our heads at each stroke: "One, two, three . . . seven . . . nine . . . eleven, twelve, thirteen."

"Thirteen," repeated my father, with a look in his eye of a man who had just beheld the wall itself come to life and start talking. He prodded once more at the wheels. Once more the clock struck thirteen. My father climbed down from the stool pale as a sheet and remained standing in the middle of the room, looking down at the floor, chewing his beard and muttering to himself, "It struck thirteen . . . How is that? What does it mean? If it was out of order it would have stopped. What then?"

"What then?" said my mother. "Take down the clock and fix it. After all, you're the expert."

"Well," agreed my father, "maybe you're right." And taking down the clock he busied himself with it. He sweated over it, he worked all day over it, and at last hung it back in its place. Thank the Lord, the clock ran as it should, and when midnight came we all stood around it and counted each stroke till twelve. My father beamed at us.

"Well," he said, "no more thirteen."

"I've always said you were an expert," my mother said. "But there is one thing I don't understand. Why does it wheeze? It never used to wheeze like this before."

"You're imagining it," my father said. But listening carefully, we heard the clock wheeze when it got ready to ring, like an old man catching his breath before he coughs— "wh-wh-wh"—and then the boom . . . boom . . . boom. But even the boom itself was not the boom of olden days. The old boom had been a happy one, a joyous one, and now something sad had crept in, a sadness like that in the song of an old, worn-out cantor toward the end of the Day of Atonement . . .

As time went on the wheezing became louder and the ringing more subdued and mournful, and my father became melancholy. We could see him suffering as though he watched a live thing in agony and could do nothing to help it. It seemed as though at any moment the clock would stop altogether. The pendulum began to act strangely. Something shivered inside, something got caught and dragged, like an old man dragging a bad leg. We could see the clock getting ready to stop forever. But just in time, my father came to the decision that there was nothing wrong with the clock itself. What was wrong was the weight. Not enough weight. And so he fastened to the weight the pestle of my mother's mortar a matter of several pounds. The clock began to run like a charm, and my father was happy again, a new man.

But it didn't last long. Again the clock began to fail. Again the pendulum began to act strangely, swinging sometimes fast and sometimes slow. It was heartrending, it tore you apart, to see the clock languish before your eyes. And my father, watching it, drooped also, lost interest in life, suffered anguish.

Like a good doctor devoted to his patient, considering every known treatment or possible remedy, my father tried every way imaginable to save the clock.

"Not enough weight, not enough life," said my father, and attached to the weight more and more objects. First an iron frying pan, and then a copper pitcher, then a flatiron, a bag of sand, a couple of bricks . . . Each time the clock drew fresh life and began to run. Painfully, with convulsions, but it worked. Till one night when a catastrophe took place.

It was a Friday night in winter. We had just eaten the Sabbath meal of delicious spicy fish with horseradish, fat chicken soup with noodles, pot roast with prunes and potatoes, and had said the grace that such a meal deserved. The candles were still flickering. The servant girl had just brought in the freshly roasted sunflower seeds, when in came Muma Yenta, a toothless, dark-skinned little woman whose husband had abandoned her years ago and gone off to America.

"Good Sabbath," said Muma Yenta, breathless as usual. "I

just knew you'd have sunflower seeds—the only trouble is—
what can I crack them with? May my old man have as few
years to live as I have teeth in my mouth . . .

"M-m-m," she went on, faster and faster, "I can still smell
your fish, Malka . . . What a time *I* had getting fish this
morning, with that Sarah-Pearl—the millionairess—standing
next to me at the market. I was just saying to Menasha
the fishman, 'Why is everything so high today?' when Sarah-
Pearl jumps up with, 'Quick, I'm in a hurry. How much does
this pickerel weigh?' 'What's your rush?' I say to her. 'The
town isn't on fire. Menasha won't throw the fish back into the
river. Among the rich,' I let them know, 'there is plenty of
money but not much sense.' Then she goes and opens her
mouth at me. 'Paupers,' says she, 'shouldn't come around
here. If you have no money you shouldn't hanker after
things.' What do you think of her nerve? What was she before she married—a peddler herself—standing in her mother's stall at the market?"

She caught her breath and went on: "These people and
their marriages! Just like Abraham's Pessel-Peiseh who is so
delighted with her daughter just because she married a rich
man from Stristch, who took her just as she stood, without
dowry. Wonderful luck she has. They say she is getting to
look a sight. The life those children lead her . . . What
do you think—it's so easy to be a stepmother? God forbid!
Look at that Hava for instance. A good, well-meaning soul
like that. But you should see the trouble she has with her
stepchildren. The screaming you hear day and night, the way
they talk back to her. And what's worse—pitch-patch—three
smacks for a penny . . ."

The candles begin to gutter. The shadows tremble on the
walls, they mount higher and higher. The sunflower seeds
crackle. All of us are talking, telling stories to the company
at large, with no one really listening. But Muma Yenta talks
more than anybody.

"Listen to this," she lets out, "there is something even
worse than all the rest. Not far from Yampola, a couple of

miles, some robbers attacked a Jewish tavern the other night, killed everyone in the family, even an infant in a cradle. The only one left was a servant girl asleep on top of the oven in the kitchen. She heard the shrieks, jumped down from the oven, and looking through a crack in the door, saw the master and mistress lying murdered on the floor in a pool of blood. She took a chance—this servant girl—and jumped out of the window, running all the way to town yelling, 'Children of Israel, save us! Help! Help! Help!' "

Suddenly, in the midst of Muma Yenta's yelling, "Help! Help!"—we hear a crash—bang—smash—boom—bam! Immersed in the story, all we could think was that robbers were attacking our own home, and were shooting at us from all sides—or that the room had fallen in—or a hurricane had hit us. We couldn't move from our seats. We stared at each other speechless—waiting. Then all of us began to yell, "Help! Help! Help!"

In a frenzy my mother caught me in her arms, pressed me to her heart, and cried, "My child, if it's going to happen, let it happen to me! Oh . . ."

"What is it?" cries my father. "What's happened to him?"

"It's nothing. Nothing," yells Muma Yenta, waving her arms. "Be quiet." And the girl runs in from the kitchen, wild-eyed.

"What's the matter? What's happened? Is there a fire? Where is it?"

"Fire? What fire?" shouts Muma Yenta at the girl. "Go burn, if you want to. Get scorched, if you like." She keeps scolding the girl as if it's all her fault, then turns to us.

"What are you all making this racket for? What are you frightened of? What do you think it is? Can't you see? It's just the clock. The clock fell down. Now do you know? Everything you could imagine was hung on it—a half a ton at least. So it fell down. What's strange about that? You wouldn't have been any better yourself . . ."

At last we come to our senses. We get up from the table one by one, go up to the clock and inspect it from all sides.

There it lies, face down, broken, shattered, smashed, ruined forever.

"It is all over," says my father in a dull voice. his head bent as if standing before the dead. He wrings his hands and tears appear in his eyes. I look at him and I want to cry too.

"Hush, be quiet," says my mother, "why do you grieve? Perhaps it was destined. Maybe it was written in heaven that today, at this minute, the end should come. Let it be an atonement for our sins—though I should not mention it on the Sabbath—for you, for me, for our children, for our loved ones, for all of Israel. Amen. *Selah*."

All that night I dreamed of clocks. I imagined that I saw our old clock lying on the ground, clothed in a white shroud. I imagined that I saw the clock still alive, but instead of a pendulum there swung back and forth a long tongue, a human tongue, and the clock did not ring, but groaned. And each groan tore something out of me. And on its face, where I used to see the twelve, I saw suddenly number thirteen. Yes, thirteen. You may believe me—on my word of honor.

HOME FOR PASSOVER

Two times a year, as punctually as a clock, in April and again in September, Fishel the *melamed* goes home from Balta to Hashtchavata to his wife and children, for Passover and for the New Year. Almost all his life it has been his destiny to be a guest in his own home, a most welcome guest it is true, but for a very short time, only over the holidays. And as soon as the holidays are over he packs his things and goes back to Balta, back to his teaching, back to the rod, to the *Gamorah* that he studies with the unwilling small boys of Balta, back to his exile among strangers and to his secret yearning for home.

However, when Fishel does come home, he is a king! Bath-Sheba, his wife, comes out to meet him, adjusts her kerchief, becomes red as fire, asks him quickly without looking him in the eye, "How are you, Fishel?" And he answers, "How are *you?*" And Froike, his boy, now almost thirteen, holds out his hand, and the father asks him, "Where are you now, Ephraim, in your studies?" And Reizel, his daughter, a bright-faced little girl with her hair in braids, runs up and kisses him.

"Papa, what did you bring me for the holidays?"

"Material for a dress, and for your mother a silk shawl. Here, give Mother the shawl."

And Fishel takes a new silk (or maybe half-silk) shawl out of his *tallis*-sack, and Bath-Sheba becomes redder than ever, pulls her kerchief low over her eyes, pretends to get busy around the house, bustles here and there and gets nothing done.

"Come, Ephraim, show me how far you've got in the *Gamorah*. I want to see how you're getting along."

And Froike shows his father what a good boy he has been, how well he has applied himself, the understanding he has of his work and how good his memory is. And Fishel listens to him, corrects him once or twice, and his soul expands with pride. He glows with happiness. What a fine boy Froike is! What a jewel!

"If you want to go to the Baths, here is a shirt ready for you," says Bath-Sheba, without looking him in the eye, and Fishel feels strangely happy, like a man who has escaped from prison into the bright, free world among his own people, his loved and faithful ones. And he pictures himself in the room thick with steam, lying on the top ledge together with a few of his cronies, all of them sweating, rubbing each other and beating each other with birch rods and calling for more, more . . .

"Harder! Rub harder! Can't you make it harder!"

And coming home from the bath, refreshed, invigorated, almost a new man, he dresses for the holiday. He puts on his best gabardine with the new cord, steals a glance at Bath-Sheba in her new dress with the new silk shawl, and finds her still a presentable woman, a good, generous, pious woman . . . And then with Froike he goes to the synagogue. There greetings fly at him from all sides. "Well, well! Reb Fishel! How are you? How's the *melamed?*" "The *melamed* is still teaching." "What's happening in the world?" "What should happen? It's still the same old world." "What's doing in Balta?" "Balta is still Balta." Always, every six months, the same formula, exactly the same, word for word. And Nissel the cantor steps up to the lectern to start the evening serv-

ices. He lets go with his good, strong voice that grows louder
and stronger as he goes along. Fishel is pleased with the per-
formance. He is also pleased with Froike's. The lad stands
near him and prays, prays with feeling, and Fishel's soul expands with pride. He glows with happiness. A fine boy,
Froike! A good Jewish boy!

"Good *yom-tev!* Good *yom-tev!*"

"Good *yom-tev* to you!"

They are home already and the *seder* is waiting. The wine
in the glasses, the horseradish, the eggs, the *haroses,* and all
the other ritual foods. His "throne" is ready—two stools
with a large pillow spread over them. Any minute now Fishel
will become the king, any minute he will seat himself on his
royal throne in a white robe, and Bath-Sheba, his queen, with
her new silk shawl will sit at his side. Ephraim, the prince, in
his new cap and Princess Reizel with her braids will sit facing
them.

Make way, fellow Israelites! Show your respect! Fishel the
melamed has mounted his throne! Long live Fishel!

The wits of Hashtchavata, who are always up to some
prank and love to make fun of the whole world (and especially of a humble teacher) once made up a story about
Fishel. They said that one year, just before Passover, Fishel
sent a telegram to Bath-Sheba reading like this: *Rabiata so-
brani. Dengi vezu. Prigotov puli. Yedu tzarstvovat.* In ordinary language this is what it meant: "Classes dismissed.
Purse full. Prepare *kneidlach.* I come to rule." This telegram, the story goes on, was immediately turned over to
the authorities in Balta, Bath-Sheba was searched but nothing
was found, and Fishel himself was brought home under police escort. But I can tell you on my word of honor that this
is a falsehood and a lie. Fishel had never in his life sent a
telegram to anyone. Bath-Sheba was never searched. And
Fishel was never arrested. That is, he was arrested once, but
not for sending a telegram. He was arrested because of a

passport. And that not in Balta but in Yehupetz, and it was not before Passover but in the middle of summer. This is what happened.

Fishel had suddenly decided that he would like to teach in Yehupetz that year, and had gone there without a passport to look for work. He thought it was the same as Balta, where he needed no passport, but he was sadly mistaken. And before he was through with that experience he swore that not only he but even his children and grandchildren would never go to Yehupetz again to look for work . . .

And ever since that time he goes directly to Balta every season and in the spring he ends his classes a week or two before Passover and dashes off for home. What do you mean —dashes off? He goes as fast as he can—that is, assuming that the roads are clear and he can find a wagon to take him and he can cross the Bug either over the ice or by ferry. But what happens if the snows have melted and the mud is deep, there is no wagon to be gotten, the Bug has just opened and the ferry hasn't started yet because of the ice, and if you try to cross by boat you risk your very life—and Passover is right in front of your nose? What can you do? Take it the way a man does if he's on his way from Machnivka to Berdichev for the Sabbath, or from Sohatchov to Warsaw—it's late Friday afternoon, the wagon is going up a hill, it's getting dark fast, suddenly they're caught in a cloudburst, he's dead hungry—and just then the axle snaps! It's a real problem, I can assure you . . .

Well, Fishel the *melamed* knows what that problem is. As long as he has been a teacher and has taken the trip from Hashtchavata to Balta and from Balta to Hashtchavata, he has experienced every inconvenience that a journey can offer. He has known what it is to go more than halfway on foot, and to help push the wagon too. He has known what it is to lie together with a priest in a muddy ditch, with himself on bottom and the priest on top. He has known how it feels to run away from a pack of wolves that followed his wagon from Hashtchavata as far as Petschani—although later, it is true, he found out that it was not wolves but dogs. . . . But all these calamities were nothing compared with what he had to go through this year when he was on his way to spend the Passover with his family.

It was all the fault of the Bug. This one year it opened up a little later than usual, and became a torrent just at the time when Fishel was hurrying home—and he had reason to hurry! Because this year Passover started on Friday night—the beginning of Sabbath—and it was doubly important for him to be home on time.

Fishel reached the Bug—traveling in a rickety wagon with a peasant—Thursday night. According to his reckoning he should have come there Tuesday morning, because he had left Balta Sunday noon. If he had only gone with Yankel-Sheigetz, the Balta coachman, on his regular weekly trip—even if he had to sit at the rear with his back to the other passengers and his feet dangling—he would have been home a long time ago and would have forgotten all about the whole journey. But the devil possessed him to go into the marketplace to see if he could find a cheaper conveyance; and it is an old story that the less you pay for something, the more it costs. Jonah the Drunkard had warned him, "Take my advice, Uncle, let it cost you two *rubles* but you'll sit like a lord in Yankel's coach—right in the very back row! Remember, you're playing with fire. There is not much time to lose!" But it was just his luck that the devil had to drag an old peasant from Hashtchavata across his path.

"Hello, Rabbi! Going to Hashtchavata?"

"Good! Can you take me? How much will it cost?"

How much it would cost—that he found it necessary to ask; but whether or not he would get home in time for Passover—that didn't even occur to Fishel. After all, even if he went on foot and took only tiny steps like a shackled person, he should have been able to reach Hashtchavata in less than a week . . .

But they had hardly started out before Fishel was sorry

that he had hired this wagon, even though he had all the room in the world to stretch out in. It became apparent very soon that at the rate at which they were creeping they would never be able to get anywhere in time. All day long they rode and they rode, and at the end of the day they had barely got started. And no matter how much he kept bothering the old peasant, no matter how many times he asked how far they still had to go, the man did not answer. He only shrugged his shoulders and said, "Who can tell?"

It was much later, toward evening, that Yankel-Sheigetz overtook them, with a shout and whistle and a crack of the whip—overtook them and passed them with his four prancing horses bedecked with tiny bells, and with his coach packed with passengers inside, on the driver's seat, and some hanging onto the rear. Seeing the teacher sitting alone in the wagon with the peasant, Yankel-Sheigetz cracked his whip in the air again and cursed them both, the driver and the passenger, as only he could curse, laughed at them and at the horse, and after he had passed them he turned back and pointed at one of the wheels:

"Hey, *shlimazl!* Look! One of your wheels is turning!"

"Whoa!" the peasant yelled, and together the driver and passenger climbed down, looked at every wheel, at every spoke, crawled under the wagon, searched everywhere, and found nothing wrong.

Realizing that Yankel had played a trick on them, the peasant began to scratch the back of his neck, and at the same time he cursed Yankel and every other Jew on earth with fresh new curses that Fishel had never heard in all his life. He shouted louder and louder and with every word grew angrier and angrier.

"*Ah, shob tubi dobra ne bulo!*" he cried. "Bad luck to you, Jew! I hope you die! I hope you never arrive! Every one of you die! You and your horse and your wife and your daughter and your aunts and your uncles and your cousins and your second-cousins and—and—and all the rest of your cursed Jews!"

It was a long time before the peasant climbed into his wagon again and was ready to start. But even then he was still angry; he couldn't stop yelling. He continued to heap curses at the head of Yankel-Sheigetz and all the Jews until, with God's help, they came to a village where they could spend the night.

The next morning Fishel got up very early, before dawn, said his morning prayers, read through the greater part of the *Book of Psalms,* had a *beigel* for breakfast, and was ready to go on. But Feodor was not ready. Feodor had found an old crony of his in the village and had spent the night with him, drinking and carousing. Then he slept the greater part of the day and was not ready to start till evening.

"Now, look here, Feodor," Fishel complained to him when they were in the wagon again, "the devil take you and your mother! After all, Feodor, I hired you to get me home for the holidays! I depended on you. I trusted you." And that wasn't all he said. He went on in the same vein, half pleading, half cursing, in a mixture of Russian and Hebrew, and when words failed him he used his hands. Feodor understood well enough what Fishel meant, but he did not answer a word, not a sound, as though he knew that Fishel was right. He was as quiet and coy as a little kitten until, on the fourth day, near Petschani, they met Yankel-Sheigetz on his way back from Hashtchavata with a shout and a crack of the whip and this good piece of news:

"You might just as well turn back to Balta! The Bug has opened up!"

When Fishel heard this his heart sank, but Feodor thought that Yankel was making fun of him again and began to curse once more with even greater vigor and originality than before. He cursed Yankel from head to foot, he cursed every limb and every bone of his body. And his mouth did not shut until Thursday evening, when they came to the Bug. They drove right up to Prokop Baraniuk, the ferryman, to find out when he would start running the ferry again.

And while Feodor and Prokop took a drink and talked things over, Fishel went off into a corner to say his evening prayers.

The sun was beginning to set. It cast its fiery rays over the steep hills on both sides of the river, in spots still covered with snow and in spots already green, cut through with rivulets and torrents that bounded downhill and poured into the river itself with a roar where they met with the running waters from the melting ice. On the other side of the river, as if on a table, lay Hashtchavata, its church steeple gleaming in the sun like a lighted candle.

Standing there and saying his prayers with his face toward Hashtchavata, Fishel covered his eyes with his hand and tried to drive from his mind the tempting thoughts that tormented him: Bath-Sheba with her new silk shawl, Froike with his *Gamorah*, Reizel with her braids, and the steaming bath. And fresh *matzo* with strongly seasoned fish and fresh horseradish that tore your nostrils apart, and Passover borsht that tasted like something in Paradise, and other good things that man's evil spirit can summon . . . And no matter how much Fishel drove these thoughts from his mind they kept coming back like summer flies, like mosquitoes, and they did not let him pray as a man should.

And when he had finished his prayers Fishel went back to Prokop and got into a discussion with him about the ferry and the approaching holiday, explaining to him half in Russian, half in Hebrew, and the rest with his hands, how important a holiday Passover was to the Jews, and what it meant when Passover started on Friday evening! And he made it clear to him that if he did not cross the Bug by that time tomorrow—all was lost: in addition to the fact that at home everybody was waiting for him—his wife and children (and here Fishel gave a heart-rending sigh)—if he did not cross the river before sunset, then for eight whole days he would not be able to eat or drink a thing. He might as well throw himself into the river right now! (At this point

Fishel turned his face aside so that no one could see that there were tears in his eyes.)

Prokop Baraniuk understood the plight that poor Fishel was in, and he answered that he knew that the next day was a holiday; he even knew what the holiday was called, and he knew that it was a holiday when people drink wine and brandy. He knew of another Jewish holiday when people drank brandy too, and there was a third when they drank still more, in fact they were supposed to become drunk, but what they called that day he had forgotten . . .

"Good, that's very good!" Fishel interrupted with tears in his voice. "But what are we going to do now? What if tomorrow—God spare the thought . . ." Beyond that poor Fishel could not say another word.

For this Prokop had no answer. All he did was to point to the river with his hand, as though to say, "Well—see for yourself . . ."

And Fishel lifted his eyes and beheld what his eyes had never before seen in all his life, and he heard what his ears had never heard. For it can truthfully be said that never before had Fishel actually seen what the out-of-doors was like. Whatever he had seen before had been seen at a glance while he was on his way somewhere, a glimpse snatched while hurrying from *cheder* to the synagogue or from synagogue to *cheder*. And now the sight of the majestic blue Bug between its two steep banks, the rush of the spring freshets tumbling down the hills, the roar of the river itself, the dazzling splendor of the setting sun, the flaming church steeple, the fresh, exhilarating odor of the spring earth and the air, and above all the simple fact of being so close to home and not being able to get there—all these things together worked on Fishel strangely. They picked him up and lifted him as though on wings and carried him off into a new world, a world of fantasy, and he imagined that to cross the Bug was the simplest thing in the world—like taking a pinch of snuff—if only the Eternal One cared to perform a tiny miracle and rescue him from his plight.

These thoughts and others like them sped through
Fishel's head and carried him aloft and bore him so far from
the river bank that before he was aware of it, night had
fallen, the stars were out, a cool wind had sprung up and
had stolen in under his gabardine and ruffled his undershirt.
And Fishel went on thinking of things he had never thought
of before—of time and eternity, of the unlimited expanse of
space, of the vastness of the universe, of the creation of
heaven and earth itself . . .

It was a troubled night that Fishel the *melamed* spent in
the hut of Prokop the ferryman. But even that night finally
came to an end and the new day dawned with a smile of
warmth and friendliness. It was a rare and balmy morning.
The last patches of snow became soft, like *kasha,* and the
kasha turned to water, and the water poured into the Bug
from all directions . . . Only here and there could be seen
huge blocks of ice that looked like strange animals, like po-
lar bears that hurried and chased each other, as if they were
afraid that they would be too late in arriving where they
were going . . .

And once again Fishel the *melamed* finished his prayers,
ate the last crust of bread that was left in his sack, and
went out to take a look at the river and to see what could
be done about getting across it. But when he heard from
Prokop that they would be lucky if the ferry could start
Sunday afternoon, he became terrified. He clutched his head
with both hands and shook all over. He fumed at Prokop,
and scolded him in his own mixture of Russian and Hebrew.
Why had Prokop given him hope the night before, why
had he said that they might be able to get across today? To
this Prokop answered coldly that he had not said a word
about crossing by ferry, he had only said that they might be
able to get across, and this they could still do. He could take
him over any way he wanted to—in a rowboat or on a raft,
and it would cost him another half-*ruble*—not a *kopek* more.

"Have it your own way!" sobbed Fishel. "Let it be a rowboat. Let it be a raft. Only don't make me spend the holiday here on the bank!"

That was Fishel's answer. And at the moment he would have been willing to pay two *rubles,* or even dive in and swim across—if he could only swim. He was willing to risk his life for the holy Passover. And he went after Prokop heatedly, urged him to get out the boat at once and take him across the Bug to Hashtchavata, where Bath-Sheba, Froike and Reizel were waiting for him. They might even be standing on the other side now, there on the hilltop, calling to him, beckoning, waving to him . . . But he could not see them or hear their voices, for the river was wide, so fearfully wide, wider than it had ever been before.

The sun was more than halfway across the clear, deep-blue sky before Prokop called Fishel and told him to jump into the boat. And when Fishel heard these words his arms and legs went limp. He did not know what to do. In all his life he had never been in a boat like that. Since he was born he had never been in a boat of any kind. And looking at the boat he thought that any minute it would tip to one side—and Fishel would be a martyr!

"Jump in and let's go!" Prokop called to him again, and reaching up he snatched the pack from Fishel's hand.

Fishel the *melamed* carefully pulled the skirt of his gabardine high up around him and began to turn this way and that. Should he jump—or shouldn't he? On the one hand—Sabbath and Passover in one, Bath-Sheba, Froike, Reizel, the scalding bath, the *seder* and all its ceremonial, the royal throne. On the other hand—the terrible risk, almost certain death. You might call it suicide. Because after all, if the boat tipped only once, Fishel was no more. His children were orphans. And he stood with his coat pulled up so long that Prokop lost his patience and began to shout at him. He warned him that if Fishel did not jump in at once he would spit at him and go across by himself to Hashtchavata. Hearing the beloved word Hash-tcha-va-ta, Fischel remembered his dear and true ones again, summoned up all his courage—

and fell into the boat. I say "fell into" because with his first step the boat tipped ever so slightly, and Fishel, thinking he would fall, drew suddenly back, and this time he really did fall, right on his face . . . Several minutes passed before he came to. His face felt clammy, his arms and legs trembled, and his heart pounded like an alarm clock: tick-tock, tick-tock, tick-tock!

As though he were sitting on a stool in his own home, Prokop sat perched in the prow of the boat and coolly pulled at his oars. The boat slid through the sparkling waters, and Fishel's head whirled. He could barely sit upright. No, he didn't even try to sit. He was hanging on, clutching the boat with both hands. Any second, he felt, he would make the wrong move, any second now he would lose his grip, fall back or tumble forward into the deep—and that would be the end of Fishel! And at this thought the words of Moses' song in *Exodus* came back to him: "They sank as lead in the mighty waters." His hair stood straight up. He would not even be buried in consecrated ground! And he made a vow . . .

But what could Fishel promise? Charity? He had nothing to give. He was such a poor, poor man. So he vowed that if the Lord brought him back home in safety he would spend the rest of his nights studying the Holy Writ. By the end of the year he would go, page by page, through the entire Six Orders of the *Talmud*. If only he came through alive . . .

Fishel would have liked to know if it was still far to the other shore, but it was just his luck to have sat down with his face to Prokop and his back to Hashtchavata. And to ask Prokop he was afraid. He was afraid even to open his mouth. He was so sure that if he so much as moved his jaws the boat would tip again, and if it did, where would Fishel be then? And to make it worse, Prokop became suddenly talkative. He said that the worst possible time to cross the river was during the spring floods. You couldn't even go in a straight direction. You had to use your head, turn this way and that. Sometimes you even had to go back a little and then go forward again.

"There goes one as big as an iceberg!" Propkop warned. "It's coming straight at us!" And he swung the boat back just in time to let a huge mass of ice go past with a strange roar. And then Fishel began to understand what kind of trip this was going to be!

"Ho! Look at that!" Prokop shouted again, and pointed upstream.

Fishel lifted his eyes slowly, afraid to move too fast, and looked—looked and saw nothing. All he could see anywhere was water—water and more water.

"There comes another! We'll have to get past—it's too late to back up!"

And this time Prokop worked like mad. He hurled the boat forward through the foaming waves, and Fishel became cold with fear. He wanted to say something, but was afraid. And once more Prokop spoke up:

"If we don't make it in time, it's just too bad."

"What do you mean—too bad?"

"What do you think it means? We're lost—that's what."

"Lost?"

"Sure! Lost."

"What do you mean—lost?"

"You know what I mean. Rubbed out."

"Rubbed out?"

"Rubbed out."

Fishel did not understand exactly what these words meant. He did not even like the sound—lost—rubbed out. He had a feeling that it had to do with eternity, with that endless existence on a distant shore. And a cold sweat broke out all over his body, and once again the verse came to him, "They sank as lead in the mighty waters."

To calm him down Prokop started to tell a story that had happened a year before at this same time. The ice of the Bug had torn loose and the ferry could not be used. And just his luck one day an important-looking man drove up and wanted to go across. He turned out to be a tax officer from Ouman, and he was ready to pay no less than a *ruble* for the trip. Halfway across two huge chunks of ice bore down upon them. There was only one thing for Prokop to do and he did it: he slid in between the two chunks, cut right through between them. Only in the excitement he must have rocked the boat a trifle too much, because they both went overboard into the icy water. It was lucky that he could swim. The tax collector apparently couldn't, and they never found him again. Too bad . . . A *ruble* lost like that . . . He should have collected in advance . . .

Prokop finished the story and sighed deeply, and Fishel felt an icy chill go through him and his mouth went dry. He could not say a word. He could not make a sound, not even a squeak.

When they were halfway over, right in the middle of the current, Prokop paused and looked upstream. Satisfied with what he saw, he put the oars down, dug a hand deep into his pocket and pulled out a bottle from which he proceeded to take a long, long pull. Then he took out a few black cloves and while he was chewing them he apologized to Fishel for his drinking. He did not care for the whisky itself, he said, but he had to take it, at least a few drops, or he got sick every time he tried to cross the river. He wiped his mouth, picked up his oars, glanced again upstream, and exclaimed:

"Now we're in for it!"

In for what? Where? Fishel did not know and he was afraid to ask, but instinctively he felt that if Prokop had been more specific he would have added something about death or drowning. That it was serious was apparent from the way Prokop was acting. He was bent double and was thrashing like mad. Without even looking at Fishel he ordered:

"Quick, Uncle! Lie down!"

Fishel did not have to be told twice. He saw close by a towering block of ice bearing down upon them. Shutting his

eyes, he threw himself face down on the bottom of the boat
and trembling all over began, in a hoarse whisper, to recite
Shma Yisroel. He saw himself already sinking through the
waters. He saw the wide-open mouth of a gigantic fish; he
pictured himself being swallowed like the prophet Jonah
when he was escaping to Tarshish. And he remembered
Jonah's prayer, and quietly, in tears, he repeated the words:
"The waters compassed me about, even to the soul; the deep
was round about me. The weeds were wrapped about my
head."

Thus sang Fishel the *melamed* and he wept, wept bitterly, at the thought of Bath-Sheba, who was as good as a
widow already, and the children, who were as good as orphans. And all this time Prokop was working with all his
might, and as he worked he sang this song:

> *"Oh, you waterfowl!*
> *You black-winged waterfowl—*
> *You black-winged bird!"*

And Prokop was as cool and cheerful as if he were on dry
land, sitting in his own cottage. And Fishel's "encompassed
me about" and Prokop's "waterfowl," and Fishel's "the weeds
were wrapped" and Prokop's "black-winged bird" merged
into one, and on the surface of the Bug was heard a strange
singing, a duet such as had never been heard on its broad
surface before, not ever since the river had been known as
Bug . . .

"Why is he so afraid of death, that little man?" Prokop
Baraniuk sat wondering, after he had got away from the ice-
floe and pulled his bottle out of his pocket again for another
drink. "Look at him, a little fellow like that—poor, in tatters
. . . I wouldn't trade this old boat for him. And he's afraid
to die!"

And Prokop dug his boot into Fishel's side, and Fishel
trembled. Prokop began to laugh, but Fishel did not hear.
He was still praying, he was saying *Kaddish* for his own soul,
as if he were dead . . .

But if he were dead would he be hearing what Prokop was saying now?

"Get up, Uncle. We're there already. In Hashtchavata."

Fishel lifted his head up slowly, cautiously, looked around on all sides with his red, swollen eyes.

"Hash-tcha-va-ta?"

"Hashtchavata! And now you can give me that half-*ruble!*"

And Fishel crawled out of the boat and saw that he was really home at last. He didn't know what to do first. Run home to his wife and children? Dance and sing on the bank? Or should he praise and thank the Lord who had preserved him from such a tragic end? He paid the boatman his half-*ruble,* picked up his pack, and started to run as fast as he could. But after a few steps he stopped, turned back to the ferryman:

"Listen, Prokop, my good friend! Come over tomorrow for a glass of Passover brandy and some holiday fish. Remember the name—Fishel the *melamed!* You hear? Don't forget now!"

"Why should I forget? Do you think I'm a fool?"

And he licked his lips at the thought of the Passover brandy and the strongly seasoned Jewish fish.

"That's wonderful, Uncle! That's wonderful!"

When Fishel the *melamed* came into the house, Bath-Sheba, red as fire, with her kerchief low over her eyes, asked shyly, "How are you?" And he answered, "How are *you?*" And she asked, "Why are you so late?" And he answered, "We can thank God. It was a miracle." And not another word, because it was so late.

He did not even have time to ask Froike how he was getting along in the *Talmud,* or give Reizel the gift he had brought her, or Bath-Sheba the new silk shawl. Those things would have to wait. All he could think of now was the bath. And he just barely made it.

And when he came home from the bath he did not say anything either. Again he put it off till later. All he said was, "A miracle from heaven. We can thank the Lord. He takes care of us . . ."

And taking Froike by the hand, he hurried off to the synagogue.

agogue.

THE ENCHANTED
TAILOR

Once there was a man named Shimmen-Eli who lived in
Zolodievka, a little town in the district of Mazapevka, not
far from Haplapovitch and Kozodoievka (between Yampoli
and Strishtch on the road that runs from Pischi-Yaboda
through Petchi-Hvost to Tetrevitz and from there to Yehupetz). And he was known as Shimmen-Eli *Shma-Koleinu,*
(the Hebrew for "Hear our voice, O Lord") because in the
synagogue he shouted louder, swayed more vigorously,
chanted and warbled with greater emotion than anyone else.
By trade Shimmen-Eli was a tailor; not, you understand, a
master tailor who sewed according to the latest fashion books,
but a mender of great skill who excelled at darning holes
and making patches that could never be detected, in turning
a garment inside out and making the old look like new. He
could take a threadbare coat and turn it into a gabardine,
the gabardine into a pair of trousers, cut the trousers into a
jacket, and the jacket into something else again.

This was by no means such easy work, but Shimmen-Eli
Shma-Koleinu was an artist at it, and Zolodievka being a
poor town where a new garment was a rare thing, Shimmen-
Eli was held in high esteem. His only drawback was that he
could never get along with the rich men of the town. He
was always interfering in public affairs, defending the rights

of the poor, speaking out bluntly about the town philan-
thropists, calling the tax-collector a blood-sucker and canni-
bal, and the rabbis and *shochtim* who worked together with
the tax-collector a band of thieves, murderers, scoundrels and
highwaymen. Let the devil take them all, together with their
fathers and grandfathers and Uncle Ishmael . . .

Among his fellow workers Shimmen-Eli was considered
a man of great and esoteric learning, for he was always full
of quotations. He quoted passages from the Bible, which
some of them knew, from *Gamorah* and *Midrash* which they
had heard about, and from other commentaries whose existence they had never even suspected. No matter what the occasion, he had a Hebrew quotation at the tip of his tongue.
If the quotation was usually garbled, if the beginning did
not match the ending, and if none of it suited the occasion,
that is not for us to judge.

In addition to his learning he had a voice that was not
so bad, though possibly a little too shrill. He knew all the
tunes and traditional renderings of all the prayers by heart,
and he loved to lead the services in the Tailors' Chapel,
where he was president—an office that brought him more
grief than honor. A box in the ear, a slap in the face, was
not uncommon at the Tailors' Chapel, and the president was
usually at the receiving end.

Although Shimmen-Eli had been wretchedly poor all his
life, a pauper actually, nevertheless he did not let his poverty
get the best of him. On the contrary, he always said, "The
poorer I am, the better I feel. The hungrier I am, the louder
I sing. As the *Gamorah* says . . ." And here he let fly one
of his famous quotations, one part Hebrew, one part Chaldaic, and the rest as often as not a knock-kneed, staggering
Russian.

In appearance Shimmen-Eli was short and homely, with
pins and needles sticking out all over him and bits of cotton
batting clinging to his curly black hair. He had a short beard
like a goat's, a flattened nose, a split lower lip and large
black eyes that were always smiling. His walk was a little

dance all his own and he was always humming to himself.
His favorite saying was, "That's life—but don't worry."

And Shimmen-Eli was blessed with sons and daughters of
all ages—mainly daughters. And he had a wife named
Tsippa-Baila-Reiza who was his exact opposite; a tall, strong,
red-faced, broad-shouldered woman, a regular Cossack in appearance. Ever since the day of their wedding she had taken
him in hand and never loosened her hold. She was the head
of the house, and her husband had the greatest respect for
her. She had only to open her mouth and he trembled. In
the Tailors' Chapel it was said openly that Shimmen-Eli may
have patched the pants, but his wife wore them. At times,
when they were alone, she was not above giving him a good
slap in the face. This slap Shimmen-Eli would put into his
pocket, and comfort himself with his favorite quotation:
"That's life—but don't worry. The Bible says, 'And he shall
rule over thee,' but it means nothing. Let all the kings of
East and West do what they will, it won't help."

2

And it came to pass that one summer day Shimmen-Eli's
wife, Tsippa-Baila-Reiza, came home from the market with
her basket of purchases, flung down the bunch of garlic, the
few parsnips and potatoes that she had bought, and cried out
angrily, "The devil with it! I'm sick and tired of it all. Day
after day, day after day, I break my head trying to think what
to cook for dinner. You need the brains of a prime minister
to think of something new. Every day it's dumplings and
beans, beans and dumplings. May God forgive me for complaining, but look at Nechama-Brocha, will you—a pauper
like that, without a *kopek* to her name or a whole dish in
her cupboard—and *she* has to have a goat! Why is it? Because her husband, though only a tailor, is still a man! So
they have a goat, and if there is a goat in the house you
can have a glass of milk for the children, you can cook por-

ridge with milk, you can make a milk soup for dinner, noodles and milk for supper, and besides you can count on a
pitcher of sour cream, a piece of cheese, a bit of butter.
Think of it. If we only had a goat!"

"You're quite right, I'm afraid," said Shimmen-Eli mildly.
"There is an ancient law that every Jew must own a goat.
Let me quote you . . ."

"What good are your quotations?" cried Tsippa-Baila-
Reiza. "I tell you about a goat and you give me quotations.
I'll give *you* a quotation in a minute and you'll see stars!
He feeds me quotations, that breadwinner of mine, the *shli-
mazl*. I wouldn't trade all your quotations and all your learn-
ing for one good borsht with cream! Do you hear?"

With broad hints like this Tsippa-Baila-Reiza plagued her
husband constantly, until Shimmen-Eli promised her on his
word of honor that from then on she could rest easily. With
God's help she would get a goat.

"But how?" asked Tsippa-Baila-Reiza.

"Don't worry," answered Shimmen-Eli.

From that time on Shimmen-Eli began to save his
groschens. He denied himself many necessary things, pawned
his Sabbath gabardine, and by the greatest economy managed
to save up a few *rubles*. It was decided that he should take
the money and go over to Kozodoievka to buy a goat. Why
to Kozodoievka? For two reasons. First of all, because Kozodoievka was famous for its goats, as the name implies—*koza*
meaning *goat* in Russian. And secondly, because Tsippa-Baila-
Reiza had heard from a neighbor of hers with whom she had
not been on speaking terms for a number of years, and who in
turn had heard it from her sister who lived in Kozodoievka
and who had visited her not long before, that there was a
melamed, a teacher, in that town, named Chaim-Chana the
Wise (because he was such a fool) who had a wife named
Tema-Gittel the Silent (because she was so talkative), and
this Tema-Gittel owned two goats, both giving milk.

"Now, I ask you," said Tsippa-Baila-Reiza, "why should she
have two goats, both of them giving milk? What harm

would there be if she had only one? There are plenty
of people who don't have even half a goat. And yet they
live."

"You are quite right, my wife," said Shimmen-Eli. "That
is an old complaint. As the saying goes . . ."

"There he goes again! Another quotation!" interrupted his
wife. "You talk about a goat and he comes to you with a
quotation. Take my advice. You go to that *melamed* in Kozodoievka and tell him this: 'It has come to our attention that
you have two goats, both giving milk. What do you need
two goats for? For pets? And since you don't need the two,
why don't you sell one of them to me? Will it hurt you?'
That's the only way to talk to these people, you understand?"

"Of course I understand. Why shouldn t I?" said Shimmen-
Eli. "For my good money do I have to beg them? With money
you can get anything in the world. 'Silver and gold,' said
our wise men, 'make even pigs clean.' The only thing that's
bad is not to have any money at all. As Rashi says, 'A poor
man is like a dead man.' Or as it is written elsewhere, 'Without fingers you can't even thumb your nose.' Or, as another
passage so appropriately puts it, '*Abracadabra* . . .'"

"Another passage! Another quotation! My head rings with
his quotations! Oh, why don't you sink into the earth!" cried
Tsippa-Baila-Reiza. "May you be buried nine feet deep!"
And once more she instructed her husband how to approach
the *melamed*, how to feel him out, and how to close the
deal.

But suppose he didn't want to sell his goat? . . . Why
shouldn't he want to sell it? Why should he have two goats,
both of them giving milk? There are so many people who
don't have even half a goat. Well, do these people die? They
manage to live.

And so on and so on, in the same vein.

3

And when it was light, our tailor arose from bed, said his prayers, took his staff and a rope, and started off on foot.

It was Sunday, a bright, warm, summer day. Shimmen-Eli could not remember when he had seen a beautiful day like this before. He could not remember the last time that he had been out in the open country. It had been a long time since his eyes had beheld such a fresh green forest, such a rich green carpet sprinkled with many-colored flowers. It had been a long time since his ears had heard the twitter of birds and the fluttering of small wings, such a long time since he had smelled the odors of the fresh countryside.

Shimmen-Eli *Shma-Koleinu* had spent his life in a different world from that. His eyes had beheld entirely different scenes: A dark cellar with an oven near the door, with pokers and shovels leaning against it, and nearby a slop-basin full to the brim. Near the oven and the basin, a bed made of three boards, with a litter of small children on it, half-naked, barefoot, unwashed, always hungry.

His ears had heard entirely different sounds: "Mother, I want some bread! Mother, I'm hungry!" And above these sounds the voice of Tsippa-Baila-Reiza herself: "You want to eat? May you eat worms! Together with that father of yours, the *shlimazl!* Oh, dear God in heaven!"

And his nose was accustomed to entirely different odors: the odor of damp walls that dripped in winter and molded in summer; the odor of sour dough and bran, of onions and cabbage, of wet plaster, of fish and entrails; the odor of old clothes steaming under the hot iron . . .

And now, having for the moment escaped from that poor, dark, unhappy world into the fragrant, unaccustomed brightness, Shimmen-Eli felt like a man who on a hot summer day dives into the ocean. The water lifts him up, the waves lap around him, he floats blissfully, deeply inhaling the fresh, salty air. He had never known anything like this before.

Shimmen-Eli walked slowly along thinking to himself, "What harm would it do if every workingman could come out here at least once a week, here in the open country, and enjoy the freedom of God's great world? Ah, what a world, what a world!" And Shimmen-Eli began to hum and then to sing under his breath. "Oh, Lord, Thou hast created Thine own world out beyond the town. Thou has decreed that we, Thy people, should live in Zolodievka, huddled together in stifling quarters. And Thou didst give us woe and troubles, illness and poverty. These things Thou gavest us, O Lord, in Thy boundless mercy . . ."

Thus sang Shimmen-Eli under his breath, and he wanted to throw himself down on the grass, look up at the blue sky and taste just for a moment the sweetness of God's great world. But he remembered that he had work to do and he said to himself, "Enough, Shimmen-Eli, you have loitered enough. On your way, brother! It is time to go! You will rest, God willing, when you come to the Oak Tavern, where your kinsman, Dodi Rendar, will give you a drink. As the passage goes: 'A drop of whisky gladdens man's life' . . ."

And Shimmen-Eli *Shma-Koleinu* hurried on.

4

On the road from Zolodievka, halfway to Kozodoievka, there stands a guest house called the Oak Tavern. This tavern has a power, the power of a magnet, which draws to itself all travelers who pass by. Whether they are going from Zolodievka to Kozodoievka or from Kozodoievka to Zolodievka, they all stop at the Oak Tavern, if only for a few minutes. No one has ever discovered the secret of this. Some say it is because the host, Dodi Rendar, is such a likable fellow and so hospitable. That is, for money he will give you a good glass of whisky and the best of food. Others say that it is because Dodi, although not a thief himself, has dealings with all the thieves in the vicinity, and at the same time protects all his customers from thieves. But since this is only a rumor, perhaps we had better say no more about it.

This Dodi we speak of was a coarse fellow, fat and hairy, with a large belly, a bulbous nose, and the voice of a wild boar. He had nothing to worry about. He made a good living, owned several cows, was a widower without any ties. He had no learning whatsoever; he scarcely knew the difference between a Bible and a prayer book. And for this reason Shimmon Eli was ashamed of him. He considered it a disgrace that he, a learned man and president of his synagogue, should have such a coarse and ignorant lout for a relative. And Dodi, for his part, was ashamed to have a worthless tailor for a kinsman. Thus each one was ashamed of the other. And yet, when Dodi caught sight of Shimmen-Eli, he greeted him handsomely, not because he respected his kinsman, but because he feared his loud mouth.

"Oh," he said cheerfully, "look who's here! How are you, Shimmen-Eli? How is your Tsippa-Baila-Reiza? And how are the children?"

" 'What are we and what have we been?' " answered Shimmen-Eli, with a quotation. "How should we be? 'Who shall perish in an earthquake and who in a plague?' Sometimes better, sometimes worse . . . The important thing is, we're still alive. As it is written, '*Abracadabra* . . .'

"But how are *you,* my dear kinsman? What is new here in the country? How are your *vareniki* this year? I remember the ones you served a year ago with your drinks. *Vareniki,* that's what's important to you. The Holy Books mean nothing; you never look into them. Ah, Reb Dodi, Reb Dodi, if your father, my Uncle Gedalia-Wolf—may his soul rest in peace—were to arise now and see his son living in the country among peasants, he would die all over again. Ah, what a father you had, Reb Dodi! He was a good and pious man . . . Ah, yes, no matter what we begin with, we always arrive at death. Come, Reb Dodi, give me a drink. As Reb Pimpon says in his sixth book of commentaries, '*Kapota bimashken,*' 'Pawn your shirt, and buy yourself a drink.' "

"So!" said Dodi, bringing him a glass of whisky. "So you're throwing the Bible at me already! Leave that for later, kinsman. First tell me, Shimmen-Eli, where are you traveling to?"

"I am not traveling," said Shimmen-Eli with a shrug. "I am just taking a walk. As we say in our prayers, 'If you have legs you can walk.' "

"If that's the case," said Dodi, "then tell me, my dear friend, where are your walking to?"

"To Kozodoievka," said Shimmen-Eli, making a face. "To Kozodoievka to buy goats. As it is written, 'Thou shalt buy thyself goats.' "

"Goats?" asked Dodi in surprise. "How does a tailor come to be dealing in goats?"

"That's just a way of talking," said Shimmen-Eli. "What I meant actually was just one goat, that is, if the Lord has mercy and sends me the right kind of goat, one that won't cost too much. As far as I'm concerned, I don't want a goat, but my dear wife, Tsippa-Baila-Reiza—you know what she's like when she makes up her mind—has decided once for all that she must have a goat. And a wife, you have always maintained, must be obeyed. That's an old law. It's in the *Talmud*. You remember what the *Talmud* says . . ."

"About these things," said Dodi, "you are better informed than I am. You know well enough that I'm not even on speaking terms with the *Talmud*. But there is one thing I'd like to know, dear kinsman. How do you happen to be such an authority on goats?"

"The same way you're an authority on prayers!" said Shimmen-Eli angrily. "What does an innkeeper know about holiness? And yet when Passover comes, you recite the *Yom Kippur* prayers as well as you can, and get by with it!"

Dodi the innkeeper understood the jibe. He bit his lip and thought to himself, "Wait, wait, you worthless tailor, you. You're a little too smart for your own good today. You're showing off your knowledge too much. You'll get a goat from me yet, and you'll be sorry!"

And Shimmen-Eli brought the conversation to an end by asking for another drink of that strong brew that is a cure for all troubles.

The truth can no longer be held back. Shimmen-Eli loved an occasional drink. But a drunkard he was not. God forbid! When was he able to buy enough whisky to become a drunkard? And yet he had this weakness: when he took one drink he had to have a second. And with the second he became quite jolly. His cheeks grew red, his eyes shone, his tongue loosened and wagged without stopping.

"Speaking of guilds," said Shimmen-Eli, "the one I belong to is the Tailors' Guild. Our emblem: Shears and Iron! Our people," he said, "have this one trait: we all like honors. At our synagogue, for instance, the least little shoemaker would like to be a chairman of something. If nothing else, then at least of the water basin. Says I, 'My friends, have it your own way. I can live without being president. Elect any shoemaker you want. I don't care for the honor and I don't want the headaches.' But they say, 'Nonsense! Once you've been elected you can't get out of it!' So I say, 'It is written in our Holy *Torah:* "Thou shalt take thy beatings and be a leader amongst men . . ."'

"But there! I've talked too much already. It's getting late. I forgot all about my goat. So goodbye, Reb Dodi, be well. Say your prayers, and look after your *vareniki.*"

"Don't forget," replied Dodi. "On your way back, if God permits, you must come in again."

"If God permits and allows and wills it," said Shimmen-Eli. "After all, I am human, nothing but flesh and blood. Where else should I stop? And as for you, be sure there is whisky on hand, and a bite to eat. In the meantime, goodbye. And remember our motto: Shears and Iron!"

5

And Shimmen-Eli *Shma-Koleinu* departed from the Oak Tavern in an exalted mood, cheerful as he could be. And he arrived in Kozodoievka without mishap. And as soon as he came there he began to inquire where he could find the *melamed,* Chaim-Chana the Wise, who had a wife Tema-Gittel the Silent and two goats. He did not have to search very long, since Kozodoievka is not such a large town that a person can get lost in it. The whole town lies spread out before your view. Here are the butchers' stalls with the cleavers and the dogs. Here is the marketplace where women go from one poultry-stand to another, picking up the chickens, and pinching and feeling them.

"What do you want for this hen?"

"Which hen? Oh, this one! That isn t a hen, it's a rooster."

"So let it be a rooster. But what do you want for it?"

And two steps farther along is the yard of the synagogue where old women sit over small baskets of pears, sunflower-seeds and beans; where the teachers conduct their classes and children recite their lessons out loud; and where goats—big goats, little goats, goats of all descriptions—jump about, pull straw off the roofs, or else sit on the ground warming themselves in the sun and chewing the cud. And only a few steps beyond that is the bath house, with its dark, smoke-stained walls. And beyond that, the pond covered with a green scum full of leeches and croaking frogs. The pond shines in the sun, sparkles like diamonds—and smells to high heaven. And on the other side of the pond is nothing but earth and sky. That is all there is to Kozodoievka.

When the tailor arrived at Chaim's house, he found him sitting over the *Gamorah* in his *tallis-kot'n* and skullcap, leading his pupils in a loud recitation:

"And—when—the—goat—saw—the—food—that—had—been—left—on—the—barrel—she—went—after—it—greed-ily . . ."

" '*Abracadabra d' barbanta,*' " said Shimmen-Eli *Shma-Koleinu* in his own Chaldaic, and quickly translated it into plain Yiddish. "Good morning to you, Rabbi, and to all your pupils. You are in the midst of the very subject about which I have come here to see your wife, Tema-Gittel, namely, a goat. True, if it depended on me, I would not be buying one, but my dear wife Tsippa-Baila-Reiza has set her heart on one once for all: she must have a goat. And a wife, you will tell me, should be obeyed. The *Gamorah* says so . . . But why are you staring at me like that? Because I am a plain workingman? 'Happy are ye who toil with your hands!'

"No doubt you have heard of me. I am Shimmen-Eli of Zolodievka, member of the Tailors' Guild and president of our synagogue, though I never asked to be chosen. 'I can get along without the honor,' I told them, 'and you keep the beatings for yourselves.' But they shouted, 'It's too late! Once we've picked you, you can't get out of it! A king and a leader you shall be to us. You'll *be* our leader, and you'll *get* the beatings!'

"But here I've been talking, and I almost forgot to greet you properly. How do you do, my Rabbi! How do you do, my boys! A fine crew of imps and mischief-makers, I see. Anxious to get on with your studies. Am I right?"

Hearing these words, the children began to pinch each other under the table and to giggle surreptitiously. They were, indeed, pleased with the interruption. They would have liked such visitors every day. But Chaim-Chana the Wise was not so pleased. He disliked to be interrupted when he was teaching. So he called in his wife Tema-Gittel and he himself returned with his pupils to the goat which had gotten hold of the food on the barrel. And again they began to chant at the tops of their voices:

"And—the—Rabbi—decreed—that—the—goat—must—pay—for—the—food—and—for—the—damage—to—the—barrel."

Shimmen-Eli, seeing that there was no use talking to the *melamed,* turned to his wife, Tema-Gittel the Silent.

"Here I am," said Shimmen-Eli. "As you see, a plain working-man. You may have heard of me, Shimmen-Eli of Zolo-dievka, member of the Tailors' Guild and president of our synagogue (though I didn't ask for the honor). I have come to see you about one of your goats. For my part I wouldn't be buying a goat now, but since my dear wife Tsippa-Baila-Reiza has made up her mind that she has to have a goat . . ."

Tema-Gittel, a tiny woman with a nose like a bean that she was always wiping with her two fingers, listened as long as she could, and then interrupted:

"So you want one of my goats, do you? Well, let me tell you this, my dear man. I'm not interested in selling the goat. For let's not fool ourselves: why should I sell it? For the money you offer? Money is round. It rolls away. But a goat is always a goat. Especially a goat like mine. Did I call it a goat? A sweetheart, that's what it is! How easy it is to milk her! And the amount of milk she gives! And how cheap it is to feed her! What does she eat? A measure of bran once a day, and for the rest she nibbles the straw from the roof of the synagogue. Still, if you're ready to pay what it's worth, I might think it over. Money is—how do you say it?—a temptation. If I get enough money I can buy another goat. Although a goat like mine would be hard to find. Did I call it a goat? A sweetheart, I tell you! But wait, why waste words? I'll bring the goat in and you'll see for your-self."

And Tema-Gittel ran out and came back leading a goat and carrying a pitcher full of milk that the goat had given that same day.

At the sight of the milk the tailor could not keep from licking his lips.

"Tell me, my dear woman, how much do you ask for this goat of yours? Remember, if it's too much, I'm not inter-ested. You see, I don't even want the animal, but since my wife, Tsippa-Baila-Reiza, has set her heart . . ."

"What do you mean—how much?" burst out Tema-Gittel,

wiping her tiny nose. "Let's hear first what you're willing to pay. But let me tell you, no matter how much you pay, you'll be getting a bargain. Because if you buy my goat . . ."

"Listen to that!" interrupted the tailor. "Why do you suppose I'm buying it? Because it's a goat! Naturally! I'm not looking for a snake, am I? Though to tell you the truth, I'd never have thought of buying a goat if my wife hadn't . . ."

"That's what I'm telling you," Tema-Gittel interrupted in her turn and began to recount the virtues of her goat again. But the tailor did not let her finish. They kept interrupting each other until anyone listening to them would have heard something like this:

"A goat? A sweetheart, not a goat . . . I would never be buying a goat . . . A measure of bran . . . Set her heart on it . . . Money is round . . . So easy to milk . . . Tsippa-Baila-Reiza . . . What does she eat? . . . Once for all . . . Straw from the roof of the synagogue . . . A wife must be obeyed . . . A goat? A sweetheart, not a goat!"

At this point Chaim-Chana broke in. "Maybe you've said enough about goats already? Who ever heard of such a thing? Here I am, right in the midst of a point of law, and all I hear is goat, goat, goat, goat! Heavens above! Either sell the goat, or don't sell the goat, but stop talking about it. Goats, goats, goats, goats, goats. My head is ringing with goats!"

"The rabbi is right," said Shimmen-Eli. "Where there is learning there is wisdom. Why do we have to talk so much? I have the money and you have the goat. That should be enough. Three words can settle it. As it is written . . ."

"What do I care what's written?" said Tema-Gittel softly, arching herself like a cat and brushing her hand back and forth over her lips. "Just tell me what you want to pay."

"What should I say?" Shimmen-Eli answered as softly "Who am I to say? Ah, well, it looks as if I've wasted a trip. Apparently I'm not buying a goat today. Forgive me for bothering you . . ."

And Shimmen-Eli turned to go.

"Now, look here, my good man," said Tema-Gittel, catching him by the sleeve. "What's your hurry? Is there a fire somewhere? It seems to me we were talking about a goat . . ."

At last the *melamed's* wife named her price, the tailor named his; they haggled back and forth, and finally agreed. Shimmen-Eli counted out the money and tied the rope around the goat's neck. Tema-Gittel took the money, spit on it to ward off the Evil Eye, wished the tailor luck, and muttering softly looked from the money to the goat, from the goat to the money. And she led the tailor out with many blessings.

"Go in good health, arrive in good health, use the goat in good health, and may God grant that she continue to be as she has been up to now. No worse. May you have her a long time, may she give milk and more milk, and never stop giving milk."

"Amen," said the tailor and started to leave. But the goat would not budge. She twisted her head, reared up her hind legs, and bleated shrilly, like a young cantor trying to impress his congregation.

But Chaim-Chana came to the rescue with the rod he used on the boys, and helped to drive the goat out of the house. And the children helped along by shouting: *"Koza! Koza! Get out, koza!"*

And the tailor proceeded on his way.

6

But the goat had no desire to go to Zolodievka. She thrust herself against the wall. She twisted and turned and reared her hind legs. And Shimmen-Eli pulled at the rope and gave her to understand that all her kicking and bucking was useless. He said to her:

"It is written that out of necessity must thou bear thy

exile. Whether thou wilt or not; nobody asks thee. I, too, was once a free Soul, a fine young man with a starched shirt and shiny boots that creaked and clattered as I walked. What more did I need? A headache? But the Lord said unto me, 'Get thee out of thy country. Crawl, Shimmen-Eli, into thy sack. Marry Tsippa-Baila-Reiza. Beget children. Suffer all thy days and thy years. For what art thou but a tailor?' "

Thus Shimmen-Eli addressed the goat, and pulling her by the rope, he went on his way, quickly, almost at a run. A warm breeze ruffled the skirts of his patched gabardine, stole under his earlocks and stroked his little beard. It brought to his nostrils the fragrance of mint, of rosemary, and other herbs and flowers whose heavenly odors he had never smelled before. And in a spirit of ecstasy and wonder he began the afternoon prayers, very handsomely, with a noble chant like a cantor performing in the presence of an admiring congregation. Suddenly—who knows how?—an Evil Spirit came to tempt him, and whispered these words into his ear:

"Listen to me, Shimmen-Eli, you fool, you! Of all things, why burst into song? It is almost evening, you haven't had a thing in your mouth all day (except two small glasses of whisky), and you gave your kinsman your word of honor that on your way home with the goat, if all was well, you would stop to have a bite with him. It was a promise, so you'll have to keep it."

And Shimmen-Eli finished his prayers as fast as he could. Then he made his way to Dodi Rendar's tavern, entering with a joyful greeting on his lips.

"Good evening to you, dear kinsman, Reb Dodi. I have news for you. Congratulate me. 'I have dwelt with Laban . . .' I have a goat. And such a goat! Straight from goatland! A goat such as our fathers and forefathers had never known. Look her over, Reb Dodi, and give us your opinion. After all, you're a man of experience. Well, make a guess. How much should I have paid for it?"

Dodi put up his hand to shield his eyes from the setting

sun, and like a true expert appraised the goat—at exactly double the figure that Shimmen-Eli had paid. At which Shimmen-Eli was so flattered that he slapped the innkeeper soundly on the back.

"Reb Dodi, dear kinsman, long life to you! This one time you didn't guess right! You were all wrong!"

Reb Dodi pursed his lips and shook his head in speechless admiration, as if to say, "What a bargain! You certainly put one over that time!"

Shimmen-Eli in his turn bent his head sideways, and with a quick gesture as if he were pulling a needle out of his vest and threading it hastily, said, "Well, Reb Dodi, what do you say now? Do I know how to look after my own affairs, or don't I? Why, if you saw how much milk she gave, you would die on the spot!"

"I'd rather see you die," said Dodi in a friendly tone.

"Amen," said Shimmen-Eli. "The same to you. And now, if I'm such a welcome guest, take my goat, Reb Dodi, and put her in the barn where no one can steal her. In the meantime I'll say my evening prayers, and then the two of us will make a toast and take a bite to eat. As the *Megila* says, 'Before eating, one is not disposed to dance.' Is that in the *Megila*, Reb Dodi, or is it somewhere else?"

"Who knows? If you say so, it must be so. After all, you're the scholar around here."

When he had finished his prayers, the tailor said to Dodi, " 'Let me swallow, I pray thee, some of this red, red pottage; for I am faint . . .' Come, my kinsman, pour out something out of that green bottle, and let us drink of it, for our health's sake. Good health, that is our first concern. As we say in our prayers every day: 'Cause us to lie down in peace and health . . .' "

Having taken a couple of drinks and a little to eat, our tailor became very talkative. He talked about his home town of Zolodievka, the community in general and his synagogue and Tailors' Guild ("Shears and Iron our emblem!") in particular. And in the process of his discourse he denounced all

the leading citizens of the town, the well-to-do and influ-
ential men, and swore that as sure as his name was Shimmen-Eli, every one of them deserved to be sent to Siberia.

"You understand, Reb Dodi?" he rounded out his disser-
tation. "May the devil take them, these givers of charity! Is
it their own money they give? All they do is suck the blood
of us poor people. Out of my three *rubles* a week they make
me pay twenty-five *kopeks!* But their time will come, never
fear. God shall hold them to account! Although to tell you
the truth, my cherished wife, Tsippa-Baila-Reiza, has long
told me that I am worse than a *shlimazl,* a fool and a coward,
because if I only wanted to use it, I could hold a strong
whip over them! But who listens to one s wife? After all, I
have something to say, too. Does not our Holy *Torah* tell us:
'V'hu yimshol b' cho?' Shall I translate that for you, kinsman? *'V'hu*—and he, that is, the husband'—*'yimshol*—shall
rule!' But instead, what happens? What should happen?
Since you have started pouring, so pour a little more. Remember what the Bible says: *'Abracadabra d' barbanta!'* "

The more Shimmen-Eli talked, the more he wandered. His
eyelids drooped and soon he was leaning against the wall
and nodding. His head was bent sideways, his arms were
crossed over his chest, and in his fingers he held his thin
little beard like a man deep in thought. Had it not been for
the fact that he was snoring out loud, a snore that was at
once a whistling, a wheezing and a blowing, no one in the
world would have dreamt that he was asleep.

But though he dozed, his brain worked busily, and he
dreamed that he was home at his workbench with a strange
garment spread out in front of him. Was it a pair of trousers? Then where was the crotch? There was no crotch. Was
it an undershirt? Then why did it have such long sleeves?
Then what could it be? It had to be something. Shimmen-
Eli turned it inside out—it was a gabardine. And what a
gabardine! Brand new, soft and silky to the touch, too new
to be made into something else. But out of habit he took a
knife out of his vest pocket and began to look for a seam.

Just then Tsippa-Baila-Reiza rushed in and began to curse him:

"What are you ripping it for? May your entrails be ripped out! You green cucumber, you fine kidney bean! Can't you see it's your Sabbath gabardine that I got for you with the money I earned from the goat?"

And Shimmen-Eli remembered that he had a goat, and he rejoiced. Never in his life had he seen so many pitchers of milk, so many cheeses, and so much butter—crocks and crocks of butter! And the buttermilk, the cream, the clabber! And rolls and biscuits baked with butter, sprinkled with sugar and cinnamon! What appetizing odors! Never in his life had he smelled such odors. And then another odor crept in—a familiar one—pugh! He felt something crawl over his neck, under his collar, around his ears and over his face. It crawled right up to his nose. He reached out his fingers and caught a bedbug. He opened first one eye, then the other, stole a look toward the window . . . Good heavens, day was breaking!

"What do you think of that! I must have dozed off!" Shimmen-Eli said to himself and shrugged his shoulders. He woke up the innkeeper, ran out into the yard, opened the barn, took the goat by the rope, and started for home as quickly as he could, like a man who is afraid that he will miss—the Lord alone knows what.

7

When Tsippa-Baila-Reiza saw that it was late and that her husband was not yet home, she began to wonder if some evil had not befallen him. Perhaps robbers had attacked him on the way, murdered him, taken his few *rubles* away and thrown him into a ditch; and here she was, a widow for the rest of her days, a widow with so many children. She might as well drown herself. All that night she did not shut her eyes, and when the first cock crowed at dawn she pulled on her dress and went outside and sat down on the doorstep to wait for her husband. Maybe God would have mercy and send him home. But what could you expect from a *shlimazl* when he goes off by himself, she thought; and she planned the welcome that he so richly deserved.

But when finally he appeared with the goat following on the rope behind him—both of them tied to the rope, the goat around the neck and Shimmen-Eli around the waist— she was so relieved that she greeted him affectionately:

"Why so late, my little canary, my almond cake? I thought you had been robbed and killed on the way, my treasure."

Shimmen-Eli loosened the rope around his waist, took the goat into the house, and breathlessly began to tell Tsippa-Baila-Reiza all that had happened to him.

"Behold, my wife, the goat which I have brought to you. A goat straight from goatland. The kind of goat that our forefathers dreamt about but never saw. She eats only once a day, a measure of bran, and otherwise she nibbles the straw from the roof of the synagogue. Milk she gives like a cow, twice a day. I saw a full pail with my eyes, I swear. Did I call it a goat? A sweetheart, not a goat. At least that's what Tema-Gittel said. And such a bargain! I practically stole it from her. Six and a half *rubles* was all I paid. But how long do you think I had to bargain with the woman? Actually she didn't want to sell the goat. All night long I had to fight with her."

And while he spoke, Tsippa-Baila-Reiza thought to herself: "So Nechama-Brocha thinks she's the only person in town who amounts to something! She can have a goat and the rest of us can't? Now watch her eyes pop out when she sees Tsippa-Baila-Reiza with a goat too! And Bluma-Zlata? And Haya-Mata? Friends they call themselves, well-wishers. May they have only half the misfortune they wish me!"

And meanwhile she made a fire in the stove and began to

prepare some buckwheat noodles for breakfast. And Shimmen-Eli put on his *tallis* and *tfillin* and started the morning prayers.

It was a long time since he had prayed with such feeling. He sang like a cantor on a holiday and made so much noise that he woke the children. When they found out from their mother that their father had brought home a goat and that she was cooking noodles with milk, they screamed with joy, sprang out of their bed still in their nightgowns, and taking each other's hands, started to dance in a circle. And while they danced, they sang this song they had just made up:

> *"A goat, a goat, a little goat!*
> *Papa brought a little goat!*
> *The goat will give us mi-i-lk*
> *And Mama will make noodles!"*

Watching his children dancing and singing, Shimmen-Eli expanded with pleasure. "Poor children," he thought, "so eager for a little milk. That's all right, my children. Today you'll have as much milk as you want. And from now on you'll have a glass of milk every day, *kasha* with milk, and milk with your tea. A goat is really a blessing. Now let Fishel charge as much for his meat as he wants to. He always gave us bones instead of meat, so let him choke on his bones. What do I need his meat for if we have milk? For the Sabbath? For Sabbath we can buy fish. Where is it written that a Jew must eat meat? I have not seen a law on that anywhere. If all good Jews only listened to me, they would all buy themselves goats."

With these thoughts Shimmen-Eli *Shma-Koleinu* put away his *tallis* and *tfillin*, washed himself, made a benediction over a slice of bread, and sat down to wait for the noodles. Instead, the door flew open and in rushed Tsippa-Baila-Reiza with an empty pail, sputtering with anger, her face aflame. And a shower of curses began to descend on the head of poor Shimmen-Eli—not curses but burning stones. Fire and brimstone poured from Tsippa-Baila-Reiza's mouth.

"May your father, that drunkard, move over in his grave and make room for you!" she cried. "May you turn into a stone, a bone! May you end in hell! I could shoot you, hang you, drown you, roast you alive! I could cut you, slice you, chop you to pieces! Go, you robber, murderer, apostate! Take a look at the goat you brought me! May a scourge descend upon your head and arms and legs! God in heaven! Dear, true, loving Father!"

That was all that Shimmen-Eli heard. Pulling his cap down over his eyes, he went out of the house to see the misfortune that had befallen him.

Coming outside and seeing the goat tethered to the gate-post calmly chewing her cud, he stood fixed in his tracks, not knowing what to do or where to turn. He stood there thinking and thinking, and at last said to himself, " 'Let me die with the Philistines!' I'll get even with them yet, that *melamed* and his wife! They found the right person to play tricks on! I'll show them a few tricks they won't forget. He looked so innocent, too, that *melamed:* he didn't want anything to do with the whole transaction. And this is what he did to me . . . No wonder the children laughed when the rabbi led me out with the goat and his wife wished all that milk onto us . . . Milk I'll give them! I'll milk the blood out of those holy Kozodoievkites, those cheats, those swindlers!"

And once more he set out for Kozodoievka, with the intention of giving the teacher and his wife what they had coming . . .

A little later, passing by the Oak Tavern and seeing the innkeeper in the doorway, with his pipe between his teeth, our tailor burst out laughing.

"What are you so happy about?" asked the innkeeper. "What are you laughing for?"

"Listen to this," said the tailor, "and maybe you'll laugh, too." And he roared as though ten devils were tickling him. "Well, what do you think of my luck? Everything has to happen to me! You should have heard what I got from my

wife this morning—what Pharaoh's chariots and horsemen
got from the Lord. She served it up in every kind of dish,
and I had to take it on an empty stomach. If I could only
pass it on to the *melamed* and his wife! Believe me, I'll
never let them get away with it. It will be an eye for an eye
and a tooth for a tooth. I don't like to have people play
tricks like this on me. But come, Dodi, put this cursed goat
into the barn for a few minutes, and then pour me a drink.
I'm a troubled man. I need a little strength before I face
those people again.

"Ah, Reb Dodi, here's to your health. We're still men,
that's the main thing. And remember what we are enjoined
in the Bible: 'Do not worry . . .' You can be sure that I'll
give them something to think about before this morning is
over. I'll show them how to play tricks on a member of the
Tailors' Guild (Shears and Iron our emblem!)."

"Who told you it was a trick?" asked the innkeeper innocently, puffing away at his pipe. "Maybe you made a mistake in picking the goat?"

Shimmen-Eli nearly sprang at the innkeeper's throat. "Do
you know what you're saying? I came and asked for a goat
that would give milk, even as Jacob asked for Rachel. And
I was tricked just as he was!"

Dodi puffed at his pipe, shrugged his shoulders, and threw
up his hands as if to say, "Is it my fault? What can I do
about it?"

And once more Shimmen-Eli took his goat and went on
his way to Kozodoievka. And his anger burned within him.

8

And the teacher labored with his pupils, still on the same
section in the *Gamorah* dealing with damages and injuries.
Their voices resounded over the whole synagogue yard:

"The—cow—swung—her—tail—and—she—broke—the—
pitcher!"

"Good morning to you, my Rabbi, and to you boys, and to all Israel," said Shimmen-Eli. "Give me a minute of your time, I pray you. The cow won't run away, and the broken pitcher surely will not mend itself!

"That was a fine trick you played on me, Rabbi. No doubt it was a joke, but I don't like such jokes. It's too much like that story about the two men who were taking their bath one Friday afternoon, stretched out on the top ledge at the bath house. Said one of the men to the other, 'Here is my besom. Whip me with it.' And the other, taking the besom, beat him till he was bleeding. Said the first, 'Listen, my friend! If I have wronged you and you want to pay me back now while I am naked and helpless, that is very well. But if you are doing it as a joke, I want to tell you: I don't care for such jokes!' "

"What is the point of that?" asked the *melamed,* taking off his glasses and scratching his ear with them.

"This is the point. Why did you trick me that way—giving me a goat like this? For that kind of trick," he said, showing him an open hand, "you may get something in return! You needn't think you're dealing with just anybody! I'm Shimmen-Eli of Zolodievka, member of the Tailors' Guild and president of our synagogue (Shears and Iron our emblem!)."

The tailor was so excited that he shook all over, and the *melamed,* putting on his glasses, stared at him in amazement. The whole room rocked with laughter.

"Why do you look at me like a crazy fool?" demanded the tailor angrily. "I come here and buy a goat from you, and you send me home with—the devil alone knows what!"

"You don't like my goat?" the teacher asked, slowly.

"The goat? If that's a goat, then you're the governor of this province."

The boys burst into laughter anew. And at this point Tema-Gittel the Silent came in and the real battle started. Shimmen-Eli yelled at Tema-Gittel and Tema-Gittel yelled back. The *melamed* looked from one to the other, and the boys laughed louder and louder. Tema-Gittel shrieked, Shimmen-Eli roared, with neither yielding, till Tema-Gittel caught the tailor by the hand and pulled him out through the door.

"Come!" she cried. "Come to the rabbi. Let the whole world see how a Zolodievka tailor can persecute innocent people—slander them!"

"Yes, let's go," said Shimmen-Eli. "Certainly let the world see how people who are considered honest, even holy, can rob a stranger and ruin him. As we say in our prayers, 'We have become a mockery and a derision . . .' And you come too, *melamed*."

Whereupon the *melamed* put on his plush hat over his skullcap, and the four of them went to the rabbi together— the tailor, the *melamed,* his wife, and the goat.

When the delegation arrived, they found the rabbi saying his prayers. When he was through, he gathered up the skirts of his long coat and seated himself on his chair, an ancient relic that was little more than feet and armrests, shaky as the last teeth of an old man.

When he had finished hearing both parties, who had hardly let each other talk, the rabbi sent for the elders and the *shochet* and the other leading citizens of the town, and when they arrived he said to the tailor:

"Now be so kind as to repeat your story from beginning to end, and then we'll let her tell hers."

And Shimmen-Eli willingly told his story all over again. He told them who he was—Shimmen-Eli of Zolodievka, member of the Tailors' Guild and president of the synagogue (though he needed that honor like a headache). Harassed by his wife, Tsippa-Baila-Reiza, who was suddenly determined to have a goat, he had come to Kozodoievka, and there had bought from the *melamed* an animal that was supposed to be a goat. But it turned out that these people had taken away his money and passed off on him the devil alone knew what—possibly as a joke, but he, Shimmen-Eli, hated such jokes. "No doubt you have heard," he said, "the story of the two men who were taking their bath on a Friday afternoon . . ."

And the tailor, Shimmen-Eli, repeated the story of the bath, and the rabbi and the elders and the other leading citizens nodded their heads and smiled.

"Now that we have heard one side," said the rabbi, "let us hear the other."

At this Chaim-Chana the Wise arose from his seat, pulled his plush hat down over his skullcap, and began:

"Hear me, O Rabbi, this is my story, just like this. I was sitting with my pupils, sitting and studying, I was studying the Order of Injuries, that's what we were studying. *Buhi-Kama?* Yes, *Buhi-Kama.* And there walks in this man from Zolodievka, and he says he's from Zolodievka, from Zolodievka, you understand, and he greets me and tells me a long story. He tells me that he's from Zolodievka, a Zolodievkite, that is, and he has a wife whose name is Tsippa-Baila-Reiza. Yes, I'm sure it's Tsippa-Baila-Reiza. At least so it seems to me. Isn't that it?"

And he leaned over to the tailor questioningly, and the tailor, who had been standing all this time with his eyes shut, fingering his little beard, his head a little to one side, swaying back and forth, answered, "That is true. She has all three names, Tsippa and Baila and Reiza. She has been called by these names as long as I have known her, which is now—let's see—about thirty years. And now, my dear friend, let's hear what else you have to say. Don't go wandering. Get down to business. Tell them what I said and what you said. In the words of King Solomon, 'Beat not around the bush.' "

"But I don't know anything about it. I don't," said the *melamed,* frightened, and pointed to his wife. "She talked to him. She did the talking. She made the deal with him. I don't know anything."

"Then," said the rabbi, "let's hear what you have to say." And he pointed to the *melamed's* wife.

Tema-Gittel wiped her lips, leaned her chin on one hand and with the other began to tell her side of the story. She talked quickly, without stopping for breath, and her face grew redder and redder as she spoke.

"Listen to me," she said. "Here is the real story of what happened. This tailor from Zolodievka is either crazy or drunk or just doesn't know what he's talking about. Have you ever heard of such a thing? A man comes to me all the way from Zolodievka and fastens himself to us like a grease spot. He won't leave us alone. He insists: I must sell him a goat. (As you know, I had two of them.)

"The tailor makes a speech. He himself would not be buying a goat, but since his wife Tsippa-Baila-Reiza has set her heart on a goat, and a wife, he says, must be obeyed . . . Do you follow me, Rabbi? So I told him, 'What difference does that make to me? You want to buy a goat? I'll sell you a goat. That is, I wouldn't sell it for any amount, for what is money? Money is round. It rolls away, but a goat remains a goat, and especially a goat like this. It's a sweetheart, not a goat. So easy to milk! And the milk she gives! And what does she eat? Once a day a measure of oats, and for the rest some straw from the roof of the synagogue.'

"But thinking it over, I decided: after all, I have two goats, and money is a temptation. Anyway, at this point my husband told me to make up my mind, and we agreed on the price. How much do you think it was? May my enemies never have any more than we asked for that goat. And I gave him the goat, a treasure of a goat. And now he comes back, this tailor does, and tries to tell me that it's not a goat. It doesn't give milk. Do you know what? Here is the goat. Give me a milk pail, and I'll milk her right here in front of your eyes."

And she borrowed a pail from the rabbi's wife and milked the goat right there in front of their eyes, and she brought the milk to each one separately to see. First, naturally, to the rabbi, then to the elders, then to the other leading citi-

zens, and finally to the assembled populace. And such a
clamor arose! Such a tumult! This one said, "We must punish this Zolodievka tailor. Let him buy drinks for us all."
Another said, "Punishing him like this is not enough. We
ought to take away the goat." Still another said, "The goat is
a goat. Let him keep it. Let him enjoy it to a ripe old age.
What we ought to do is give him a few good kicks and
send him and the goat both to the devil!"

When he saw this turn of events, Shimmon-Eli quietly
slipped out of the rabbi's house, and disappeared.

9

The tailor hastened away from the angry multitude like a
man running from a fire. From time to time he looked back
to see if anyone was following him, and he thanked the
Lord for having escaped without a beating.

When he approached the Oak Tavern, Shimmen-Eli said to
himself: "He'll never get the truth out of me."

"Well, what happened?" asked Dodi with feigned interest.

"What should happen?" said Shimmen-Eli. "People have
respect for a man like me. They can't play tricks on me.
After all, I'm not a schoolboy. I showed them a few things. I
had a little discussion with the *melamed* too, about a few
points in the *Gamorah,* and we found out that I knew more
than he did. Anyway, to make a long story short, they begged
my pardon and gave me the goat I had bought. Here she is.
Take her for a little while, my kinsman, and then give me a
drink."

"He is not only a braggart," thought Dodi to himself,
"but a liar as well. I'll have to play the same game once
more and see what he'll say next time."

And to the tailor he said: "I have just the thing for you—
a glass of old cherry wine."

"Cherry wine!" said Shimmen-Eli and licked his lips in anticipation. "Bring it out and I'll tell you what I think of it. Not everyone knows what good wine is."

When he had drained the first glass, the tailor's tongue began wagging again. He said, "Tell me, dear kinsman, you're no fool and you have dealings with many people. Tell me, do you believe in magic, in illusions?"

"For instance?" asked Dodi, innocently.

"Why," said Shimmen-Eli, "*dybbuks*, elves, evil spirits of all sorts, wandering souls . . ."

"What makes you ask?" said Dodi, puffing at his pipe.

"Just like that," said Shimmen-Eli, and went on talking about sorcerers, witches, devils, gnomes, werewolves.

Dodi pretended to listen attentively, smoked his pipe, and then he spat and said to the tailor, "Do you know what, Shimmen-Eli? I'll be afraid to sleep tonight. I'll tell you the truth: I have always been afraid of ghosts, but from now on I'll believe in *dybbuks* and gnomes as well."

"Can you help yourself?" said the tailor. "Try not believing! Just let one good gnome come along and start playing tricks on you—upset your borsht, pour out your water, empty all your pitchers, break your pots, tie knots in the fringes of your *tallis kot'n,* throw a cat into your bed and let it lie on your chest like a ten-pound weight . . ."

"Enough! Enough!" begged the innkeeper, spitting to ward off spirits. "Don't ever tell me stories like that so late at night!"

"Goodbye, Reb Dodi. Forgive me for teasing you. You know I'm not to blame. As the saying is, 'The old woman had no troubles . . .' You know that saying, don't you? Well, good night . . ."

10

When the tailor returned to Zolodievka he walked into the house boldly, determined to give his wife a piece of his mind; but he controlled himself. After all, what can you expect from a woman? And for the sake of harmony he told her this story:

"Believe me, Tsippa-Baila-Reiza, in spite of what you think, people have to look up to me. I wish you could have seen what I gave that *melamed* and his wife! It was as much as they could take. And then I dragged them off to the rabbi and he ruled that they must pay a fine, because when a man like Shimmen-Eli comes to buy a goat from them, he deserves the greatest consideration, for this Shimmen-Eli, says the rabbi, is a man who . . ."

But Tsippa-Baila-Reiza did not want to hear any more about the praise that had been showered on her husband. What she wanted was to see the real goat he had now brought with him, so she took her pail again and ran out of the house. But it was not long before she came running back, speechless with anger. Catching Shimmen Eli by the collar, she gave him three good shoves, pushed him out of the house, and told him to go to the devil together with his goat.

Outside, a crowd of men, women and children quickly gathered around the tailor and his goat, and he told them the story of the goat which in Kozodoievka had given milk, but every time he brought her home was no longer a she-goat. With many oaths he swore that he himself had seen the full pail of milk that she had given in the rabbi's house. More and more people came by, examined the goat with deep interest, listened to the story, asked to have it repeated, and wondered greatly at it. Others laughed and teased him, still others shook their heads, spat on the ground, and said, "A fine goat that is. If that's a goat, then I'm the rabbi's wife!"

"What then is it?" asked the tailor.

"A demon, can't you see? It's possessed. It's a *gilgul*."

The crowd caught the word *gilgul*, and soon they all began to tell each other stories about spirits and ghosts, incidents that had occurred right here in Zolodievka, in Kozodoievka, in Yampoli, in Pischi-Yaboda, in Haplapovitch, in Petchi-Hvost, and other places. Who had not heard the story of Lazer-Wolf's horse that had to be taken out beyond the town, killed, and buried in a shroud? Or about the fowl which had been served up for a Sabbath dinner, and when it was placed on the table began to flap its wings? Or many other such true and well-known happenings?

After several more minutes of this, Shimmen-Eli pulled once more at his rope and proceeded again on his way to Kozodoievka, followed by a band of schoolboys shouting, "Hurrah for Shimmen-Eli! Hurrah for the milking tailor!"

And everybody roared with laughter.

At this the tailor was deeply hurt. As if it were not enough to have this misfortune happen to him, they made a laughing-stock of him too. So, taking the goat, he went through the town and sounded an alarm among the members of his Guild. How could they stand by and be silent at such an outrage? And he told them the whole story of what had happened to him in Kozodoievka, showed them the goat, and at once they sent for liquor, held a meeting, and decided to go to the rabbi, the elders, and the leading citizens of the community and ask them to come to their aid. Why, who had ever heard of such an outrage? To cheat a poor tailor, take away his last few *rubles,* supposedly sell him a goat and actually palm off the devil alone knew what! And then to play the same trick on him a second time! Such an outrage had never been heard of even in Sodom!

And the delegation came to the rabbi, the elders and the leading men of the town and raised a hue and cry. Why, who had ever heard of such an outrage? To cheat a poor tailor, rob him of his last few *rubles?* And they recounted the story of the tailor and his goat in all its details.

The rabbi, the elders, and the leading men of the town listened to the complaints, and that evening held a meeting at the rabbi's house, where it was decided to write a letter then and there to the rabbi, elders and leading men of Kozodoievka. And this they did, producing a letter in classical Hebrew, written in a style as lofty as the occasion demanded.

And here is the letter, word for word, as it was written:

"To the honorable Rabbi, Elders, Sages, renowned scholars, pillars who uphold and support the entire house of Israel! Joy unto you and joy unto everyone within the sacred community of Kozodoievka! May all that is good come unto you and remain with you. Amen.

"It has come to our attention, worthy Rabbi and Elders, that a great wrong has been committed unto one of our towns-people, the tailor Shimmen-Eli, son of Bendit-Leib, known also as Shimmen-Eli *Shma-Koleinu,* as follows:

"Two of your inhabitants, the *melamed* Chaim-Chana and his spouse Tema-Gittel, did with cunning extort the following sum, six and one-half *rubles* in silver, which they took unto themselves, and wiping their lips said, 'We have done no wrong.' Now, mark you, honorable sirs, such things are not done by Jews! All of us here undersigned are witnesses that this tailor is a poor workingman and has many children whom he supports by the honest toil of his hands. As King David says in the Book of Psalms: 'When thou eatest the labor of thy hands, happy shalt thou be, and it shall be well with thee.' And our sages have interpreted it thus: happy in this world, and well in the next world. Therefore do we beg you to search out and inquire as to what has been done, so that your judgment may shine forth like the sun and you may pass this proper decision: that either the tailor receive his money back entirely or that he be given the goat that he had bought, for that one which he brought home with him is not truly a goat! To this last fact our whole town can swear.

"Then let there be peace among us. As our sages have said, 'There is nothing so blessed as peace.' Peace unto you, peace unto the farthest and the nearest, peace unto all Israel. Amen.

"From us, your servants . . ."

And then they all signed their names. First the rabbi himself, then the elders, then the leading citizens, and then, one after the other, proudly if not always legibly, the entire membership of the Tailors' Guild.

11

And it came to pass that night that the moon shone down on Zolodievka and on all its bleak tumbledown little houses huddled together without yards, without trees, without fences, like gravestones in an old cemetery. And though the air was by no means fresh and the odors of the square and the marketplace were hardly pleasant and the dust was thick everywhere, nevertheless the people all came out, like roaches from their cracks, men and women, old people and little children, for "a breath of fresh air" after the stifling hot day. They sat on their stoops, talking, gossiping, or simply looking up at the sky, watching the face of the moon and the myriads of stars that, if you had eighteen heads, you could not count.

All that night Shimmen-Eli the tailor wandered by himself through the side streets and alleys of the little town with his goat, hiding from the small mischief-makers who had followed him all through the day. He thought that when it was light enough he would start back again toward Kozodoievka. And meanwhile he slipped into Hodel's tavern to take a drink for his sorrow's sake; unburden his heart, and seek the sympathetic tavern-keeper's advice in his grievous plight.

Hodel the tavern-keeper was a widow, a woman with brains, who knew all the public officials and was a good friend in need to all the workingmen in town. As a girl she had been known as a great beauty and had almost married a wealthy man, an excise collector. The story went that once when he was passing through Zolodievka the collector had seen her leading some geese to the *shochet,* and wanted to marry her at once. But the town gossiped so much that the match fell through. Later, against her will, she married some poor fellow, an epileptic, and again the tongues of the gossips began to wag. They said she was still in love with the exciseman, and they made up this song about her, a song which the women and maidens still sing to this day in Zolodievka.

It starts like this:

> *The moon was shining.*
> *It was the middle of the night.*
> *Hodel sat at her door.*

And it ends with these words:

> *I love you, my soul,*
> *Without end.*
> *I cannot live without you.*

And it was to this same Hodel that our tailor now poured out his heart. It was to her that he came for advice. "What shall I do?" he asked. "Tell me. After all, you are not only beautiful but wise. As King David—or who was it?—said in the *Song of Songs:* 'I am black but comely, O ye daughters of Jerusalem.' So tell me what to do."

"What can you do?" answered Hodel, and spat vigorously. "Can't you see it's an evil spirit? What are you keeping it for? Get rid of her. Throw her out. Or the same thing may happen to you that once happened to my Aunt Pearl, may she rest in peace."

"And what happened to her?" asked Shimmen-Eli, frightened.

"This," said Hodel, with a sigh. "My Aunt Pearl was a good honest woman (all of us have been good and honest in our family, though here in this forsaken town—may it burn to the ground—everybody always has the worst to say about everyone). Well, one day my Aunt Pearl was going to market and on the ground in front of her she saw a spool of thread. 'A spool of thread,' she thought, 'comes in handy,' so she bent down and picked it up. The spool jumped in her face and then fell to the ground. She bent down and picked it up again. Again it jumped in her face and again fell down. This happened again and again till at last she spit on it, said, 'Let the devil take it,' and started back home. Once or twice she looked back, and there was the spool of thread rolling after her. Well, she came home frightened to death, fell in a faint, and was sick for almost a whole year afterward. Now, what do you think that was? Tell me. Guess."

"Ah, they're all alike, these women!" said Shimmen-Eli. "Old wives' tales, nonsense, poppycock! If you wanted to listen to what women babbled about, you'd soon be afraid of your own shadow. It is truly written: 'And a voice was given unto them.' Geese, that's what they are! But never mind. That is life; don't worry. Good night. Good night to you."

And Shimmen-Eli went on his way.

The night was sprinkled with stars. The moon floated past clouds that were like tall dark mountains inlaid with silver. With half a face the moon looked down on the town of Zolodievka sunk in deep slumber. Some of the people of the town who were afraid of bedbugs had gone to sleep out-doors, had covered their faces with homespun sheets and were snoring lustily, dreaming sweet dreams, dreams of prof-itable transactions, of considerate landlords, of baskets of food brought home, dreams of wealth and honor, or of honor alone: all sorts of dreams. There was not a living creature on the streets. Not a sound was to be heard. Even the butchers' dogs who had barked and fought all day, now burrowed themselves between the logs in the back yard, hid their muzzles in their paws, and slept. From time to time a short bark escaped one of them when he dreamed of a bone that another dog was gnawing or of a fly that was buzzing in his ear. Now and then a beetle flew by, humming like the string of a bass violin, zh-zh-zh-zh, then fell to the ground and was silent. Even the town watchman who went around every night, keeping an eye on the stores and rattling his sticks over the windows, had this night become drunk, and leaning against a wall, fell fast asleep. In this silence Shimmen-Eli was the only one awake, not knowing whether to move or to stand still or to sit down.

He walked and muttered to himself, "The old woman had no troubles, so she bought herself a horse . . . Oh, this goat, this goat! May it break a leg and die! A goat? Yes, a goat. A little goat. *Chad gadyo, chad gadyo.* One little goat . . ."

He burst out laughing and was frightened by his own laughter. Passing by the old synagogue renowned for the spirits of dead men who prayed there every Saturday night in their shrouds and prayer shawls, he thought he heard a weird singing as of the wind blowing down a chimney on a winter night. And quickly turning away he found himself near the Russian church, from whose steeple a strange bird whistled shrilly. A terrible fear seized him. He tried to take heart, to steel himself with a prayer, but the words would not come.

Then looming before his eyes he saw the forms of friends long dead. And he remembered the terrifying stories he had heard in bygone days of devils, spirits, vampires, ghouls, goblins, of strange creatures that moved on tiny wheels, of some that walked on their hands, others that looked at you through a single eye, and spirits that wandered through eternity in long white shrouds. Shimmen-Eli began to think that the goat he was leading was really not a goat at all, but a sprite of some sort that at any moment would stick out its long, pointed tongue, or flap a pair of wings and utter a loud cock-a-doodle-doo. He felt his head whirling. He stopped, loosened the rope that had been tied around his waist, and urged the goat to leave him. But the goat would not budge. Shimmen-Eli took a few steps; the goat followed. He turned to the right; so did the goat. He turned left; the goat did too.

"Shma Yisroel!" screamed Shimmen-Eli, and started to run as fast as he could. And as he ran he imagined that someone was chasing him and mocking him in a thin, goatlike

voice, but the words were the words of a human: "Blessed
art thou . . . O Lord . . . who quickenest the dead . . ."

12

When the next day dawned and the men arose to go to the
synagogue, the women to market, and the young girls to
lead the animals to pasture, they found Shimmen-Eli sitting
on the ground and near him the goat, wagging his beard and
chewing the cud. When they spoke to the tailor he did not
answer. He sat like a graven image staring in front of him.
Quickly a crowd gathered; people came running from all
over town, and a hubbub arose: "Shimmen-Eli . . . goat
. . . *Shma-Koleinu* . . . *gilgul* . . . demons . . . spirits . . .
werewolves . . ." Rumors flew about, with everybody telling a different story. Someone said he had seen him riding
through the night.

"Who rode whom?" asked a man, sticking his head into
the circle. "Did Shimmen-Eli ride the goat or did the goat
ride Shimmen-Eli?"

The crowd burst out laughing.

"What are you laughing at?" a workingman burst out.
"You ought to be ashamed of yourselves! Grown men with
beards. Married men with families. Shame on you! Making
fun of a poor tailor. Can't you see the man is not himself?
He is a sick man. Instead of standing around sharpening
your teeth, it would be better if you took him home and
called the doctor!"

These words brought the people to their senses, and they
stopped laughing at once. Someone ran off for water, others
to get Yudel the healer. They took Shimmen-Eli under the
arms, led him home and put him to bed. Soon Yudel came
running with all his paraphernalia and began to work on
him. He rubbed him, blew into his face, applied leeches,
tapped his vein and drew a panful of blood.

"The more blood we draw," explained Yudel, "the better

it will be, for all illnesses come from within, from the blood itself." And after presenting this bit of medical theory Yudel promised to come again in the evening.

And when Tsippa-Baila-Reiza saw her husband stretched out on the broken old couch, covered with rags, his eyes rolled upward, his lips parched, raving in fever, she began to wring her hands, beat her head against the wall, wailed and wept as one weeps for the dead.

"Woe is me, wind is me! What will become of me now? What will become of me and all my children?"

And the children, naked and barefoot, gathered about their mother and joined her in her lamentations. The older ones wept silently, hiding their faces; the smaller ones who did not understand what had happened wailed out loud. And the youngest of all, a little boy of three, with a pinched yellow face, stood close to his mother with his tiny crooked legs and protruding belly and screamed loudest of all. "Mama! I'm hun-gry!"

All the neighbors came to find out how Shimmen-Eli was, but the sight of the poor tailor and his family was so heart-rending that nobody could stay long. Only a few women remained, and stood with tear-stained faces near Tsippa-Baila-Reiza, their noses red from blowing, their mouths working, shaking their heads as though to say, "Poor Tsippa-Baila-Reiza. Nothing can help her now."

Wonder of wonders! For fifty years Shimmen-Eli *Shma-Koleinu* had lived in Zolodievka in poverty and oppression. For fifty years he had lain in obscurity. No one spoke of him, no one knew what sort of man he was. But now that he was so close to death, the town suddenly became aware of all his virtues. It suddenly became known that he had been a good and kind man, generous and charitable; that is to say, he had forced money out of the rich and divided it among the poor. He had fought everybody for those poor people, fought staunchly, and had shared his last bite with others. These and many other things they told about the poor tailor, as people tell about a dead man at his funeral. And they all came to see him from all directions. They did everything they could to save him, to keep him from dying before his time.

13

And when the sun had set and night had fallen, the members of the Tailors' Guild came together at Hodel's tavern, ordered whisky, and called a meeting. They argued, shouted, ranted, pounded on the table.

"Why isn't something done? A fine town like Zolodievka —may it burn to the ground!—with so many rich people in it, and not one of them willing to lift a finger! They all live off the sweat of us, and none of them will help us. Who puts all the money into the community fund? We do. Who is skinned alive to support the *shochet,* the bath house, the synagogue? We are! Do we have to stand for everything? Come on, let's go to the rabbi and the elders. Now it's their turn to be useful. They'll have to keep his family alive! Come, let us deal with them!"

And they went to the rabbi with their complaint. In reply, the rabbi read to them the letter that had just been brought by a teamster from Kozodoievka. And this is what it said:

"To the honorable Rabbis, Elders, Sages and scholars of Zolodievka! May peace reign eternally in your holy community!

"No sooner had we received your letter, which, let us assure you, was as honey in our mouths, than we congregated and carefully studied the matter you referred to. In answer we can say only this, that you have wrongfully accused a townsman of ours. This tailor of yours is a wicked man who with base slander has created a scandal between our two communities and deserves to be punished accordingly. We, the undersigned, are ready under oath to bear witness that with our own eyes we saw the goat give milk. May the goats of all our friends be as bountiful.

"Pay no heed to the accusations of the tailor. Pay no heed to the words of ignorant people who speak falsely.

"Peace be unto you and peace unto all Jews everywhere, now and forever, Amen.

"From your younger brothers who bow in the dust at your feet . . ."

When the rabbi had finished reading this letter, the delegation cried out in anger, "Aha, those Kozodoievka hooligans! They're making fun of us! Let's show them who we are and what our emblem is! Shears and Iron! Let them remember that!"

And at once they called another meeting, sent for more whisky, and it was decided to take this imitation of a goat straight to Kozodoievka, take vengeance on the teacher, wreck his *cheder* and overturn the whole town.

No sooner said than done. They mustered about sixty men for the trip, tailors, shoemakers, carpenters, blacksmiths, butchers, strong young men who enjoyed a fight, each one armed with the tools of his trade: this one with a wooden yardstick, that one with a flatiron, one with a last, another with an axe, some with hammers and cleavers, and others with ordinary household utensils, rolling pins, graters, carving knives . . . And it was decided without further delay that they should march off to Kozodoievka and make war on the town, kill and destroy and lay waste.

"Once for all!" they cried. " 'Let us die with the Philistines!' Let's kill them off and be done with it!"

"But wait," one of them called out. "You are ready for the slaughter, fully armed. But where is the goat?"

"That's right! Where did the demon go?"

"He's been swallowed up."

"Then he's not such a fool. But where could he have gone to?"

"Home to the *melamed*. Can't you understand?"

"He'd be crazy to do that!"

"Where else could he go?"

"What difference does it make? Guess what you want to. The point is, the goat has disappeared!"

14

Now let us leave the possessed tailor struggling with the Angel of Death and the workingmen of the town preparing for battle, and let us pass on to the demon himself, that is— the goat.

When the goat became aware of the uproar that had arisen in the town, he thought to himself: what was he going to get out of all this? What was the use of being tied to the tailor's waist and following him wherever he went and starving to death? It was better to run off into the wide world and see what freedom meant. So he made his escape, running off madly across the marketplace, his feet scarcely touching the earth, knocking over men and women, jumping over everything that stood in his way—tables of bread and rolls, baskets of grapes and currants. He leaped over crockery and glassware, scattered and shattered everything in his path. The women screamed, "Who is it? What is it? What happened? A goat, a possessed creature, a demon! Woe is me! Where is he? There, there he is! Catch him! Catch him!"

The men picked themselves up and ran after the goat as fast as they could, and the women, naturally, ran after the men. But in vain. Our goat had tasted the joys of freedom and was gone, never to be seen again.

And the unfortunate tailor? What became of him? And how did the story end? Reader, don't compel me to tell you. The end was not a happy one. The story began cheerfully enough, but it ended like most cheerful stories, very tragically. And since you know that I am not a gloomy soul who prefers tears to laughter and likes to point a moral and teach a lesson, let us part as cheerfully as we can. And I wish that all of you readers and everybody else in the world may have more opportunities to laugh than to cry.

Laughter is healthful. The doctors bid us laugh.

A YOM KIPPUR
SCANDAL

"That's nothing!" called out the man with round eyes, like an ox, who had been sitting all this time in a corner by the window, smoking and listening to our stories of thefts, robberies and expropriations. "I'll tell you a story of a theft that took place in our town, in the synagogue itself, and on *Yom Kippur* at that! It is worth listening to.

"Our town, Kasrilevka—that's where I'm from, you know —is a small town, and a poor one. There is no thievery there. No one steals anything for the simple reason that there is nobody to steal from and nothing worth stealing. And besides, a Jew is not a thief by nature. That is, he may be a thief, but not the sort who will climb through a window or attack you with a knife. He will divert, pervert, subvert and contravert as a matter of course; but he won't pull anything out of your pocket. He won't be caught like a common thief and led through the streets with a yellow placard on his back. Imagine, then, a theft taking place in Kasrilevka, and such a theft at that. Eighteen hundred *rubles* at one crack.

"Here is how it happened. One *Yom Kippur* eve, just before the evening services, a stranger arrived in our town, a salesman of some sort from Lithuania. He left his bag at an inn, and went forth immediately to look for a place of wor-

ship, and he came upon the old synagogue. Coming in just
before the service began, he found the trustees around the
collection plates. 'Sholom aleichem,' said he. 'Aleichem
sholom,' they answered. 'Where does our guest hail from?'
'From Lithuania.' 'And your name?' 'Even your grandmother
wouldn't know if I told her.' 'But you have come to our
synagogue!' 'Where else should I go?' 'Then you want to
pray here?' 'Can I help myself? What else can I do?' 'Then
put something into the plate.' 'What did you think? That I
was not going to pay?'

"To make a long story short, our guest took out three silver *rubles* and put them in the plate. Then he put a *ruble*
into the cantor's plate, one into the rabbi's, gave one for the
cheder, threw a half into the charity box, and then began to
divide money among the poor who flocked to the door. And
in our town we have so many poor people that if you really
wanted to start giving, you could divide Rothschild's fortune
among them.

"Impressed by his generosity, the men quickly found a
place for him along the east wall. Where did they find room
for him when all the places along the wall are occupied?
Don't ask. Have you ever been at a celebration—a wedding or circumcision—when all the guests are already seated
at the table, and suddenly there is a commotion outside—the
rich uncle has arrived? What do you do? You push and
shove and squeeze until a place is made for the rich relative.
Squeezing is a Jewish custom. If no one squeezes us, we
squeeze each other."

The man with the eyes that bulged like an ox's paused,
looked at the crowd to see what effect his wit had on us,
and went on.

"So our guest went up to his place of honor and called
to the *shammes* to bring him a praying stand. He put on his
tallis and started to pray. He prayed and he prayed, standing
on his feet all the time. He never sat down or left his
place all evening long or all the next day. To fast all day

standing on one's feet, without ever sitting down—that only a Litvak can do!

"But when it was all over, when the final blast of the *shofar* had died down, the Day of Atonement had ended, and Chaim the *melamed,* who had led the evening prayers after *Yom Kippur* from time immemorial, had cleared his throat, and in his tremulous voice had already begun—'*Ma-a-riv a-ro-vim* . . .' suddenly screams were heard. 'Help! Help! Help!' We looked around: the stranger was stretched out on the floor in a dead faint. We poured water on him, revived him, but he fainted again. What was the trouble? Plenty! This Litvak tells us that he had brought with him to Kas-rilevka eighteen hundred *rubles*. To leave that much at the inn—think of it, eighteen hundred *rubles*—he had been afraid. Whom could he trust with such a sum of money in a strange town? And yet, to keep it in his pocket on *Yom Kippur* was not exactly proper either. So at last this plan had occurred to him: he had taken the money to the syna-gogue and slipped it into the praying stand. Only a Litvak could do a thing like that! . . . Now do you see why he had not stepped away from the praying stand for a single min-ute? And yet during one of the many prayers when we all turn our face to the wall, someone must have stolen the money . . .

"Well, the poor man wept, tore his hair, wrung his hands. What would he do with the money gone? It was not his own money, he said. He was only a clerk. The money was his employer's. He himself was a poor man, with a houseful of children. There was nothing for him to do now but go out and drown himself, or hang himself right here in front of everybody.

"Hearing these words, the crowd stood petrified, forgetting that they had all been fasting since the night before and it was time to go home and eat. It was a disgrace before a stranger, a shame and a scandal in our own eyes. A theft like that—eighteen hundred *rubles!* And where? In the Holy of Holies, in the old synagogue of Kasrilevka. And on what day? On the holiest day of the year, on *Yom Kippur!* Such a thing had never been heard of before.

"'*Shammes,* lock the door!' ordered our Rabbi. We have our own Rabbi in Kasrilevka, Reb Yozifel, a true man of God, a holy man. Not too sharp witted, perhaps, but a good man, a man with no bitterness in him. Sometimes he gets ideas that you would not hit upon if you had eighteen heads on your shoulders . . . When the door was locked, Reb Yozifel turned to the congregation, his face pale as death and his hands trembling, his eyes burning with a strange fire.

"He said, 'Listen to me, my friends, this is an ugly thing, a thing unheard of since the world was created—that here in Kasrilevka there should be a sinner, a renegade to his people, who would have the audacity to take from a stranger, a poor man with a family, a fortune like this. And on what day? On the holiest day of the year, on *Yom Kippur,* and perhaps at the last, most solemn moment—just before the *shofar* was blown! Such a thing has never happened anywhere. I cannot believe it is possible. It simply cannot be. But perhaps—who knows? Man is greedy, and the temptation—especially with a sum like this, eighteen hundred *rubles,* God forbid—is great enough. So if one of us was tempted, if he were fated to commit this evil on a day like this, we must probe the matter thoroughly, strike at the root of this whole affair. Heaven and earth have sworn that the truth must always rise as oil upon the waters. Therefore, my friends, let us search each other now, go through each other's garments, shake out our pockets—all of us from the oldest householder to the *shammes,* not leaving anyone out. Start with me. Search my pockets first.'

"Thus spoke Reb Yozifel, and he was the first to unbind his gabardine and turn his pockets inside out. And following his example all the men loosened their girdles and showed the linings of their pockets, too. They searched each other, they felt and shook one another, until they came to Lazer Yossel, who turned all colors and began to argue that,

in the first place, the stranger was a swindler; that his
story was the pure fabrication of a Litvak. No one had stolen
any money from him. Couldn't they see that it was all a
falsehood and a lie?

"The congregation began to clamor and shout. What did
he mean by this? All the important men had allowed themselves to be searched, so why should Lazer Yossel escape?
There are no privileged characters here. 'Search him! Search
him!' the crowd roared.

"Lazer Yossel saw that it was hopeless, and began to
plead for mercy with tears in his eyes. He begged them not
to search him. He swore by all that was holy that he was as
innocent in this as he would want to be of any wrongdoing
as long as he lived. Then why didn't he want to be searched?
It was a disgrace to him, he said. He begged them to have
pity on his youth, not to bring this disgrace down on him.
'Do anything you wish with me,' he said, 'but don't touch
my pockets.' How do you like that? Do you suppose we listened to him?

"But wait . . . I forgot to tell you who this Lazer Yossel
was. He was not a Kasrilevkite himself. He came from the
devil knows where, at the time of his marriage, to live with
his wife's parents. The rich man of our town had dug him
up somewhere for his daughter, boasted that he had found a
rare nugget, a fitting match for a daughter like his. He knew
a thousand pages of *Talmud* by heart, and all of the Bible. He was a master of Hebrew, arithmetic, bookkeeping, algebra, penmanship—in short, everything you could think of.
When he arrived in Kasrilevka—this jewel of a young man
—everyone came out to gaze at him. What sort of bargain
had the rich man picked out? Well, to look at him you could
tell nothing. He was a young man, something in trousers.
Not bad-looking, but with a nose a trifle too long, eyes that
burned like two coals, and a sharp tongue. Our leading citizens began to work on him: tried him out on a page of
Gamorah, a chapter from the Scriptures, a bit of *Rambam*,
this, that and the other. He was perfect in everything, the

dog! Whenever you went after him, he was at home. Reb Yozifel himself said that he could have been a rabbi in any Jewish congregation. As for world affairs, there is nothing to talk about. We have an authority on such things in our town, Zaidel Reb Shaye's, but he could not hold a candle to Lazer Yossel. And when it came to chess—there was no one like him in all the world! Talk about versatile people . . . Naturally the whole town envied the rich man his find, but some of them felt he was a little too good to be true. He was too clever (and too much of anything is bad!). For a man of his station he was too free and easy, a hail-fellow-well-met, too familiar with all the young folk—boys, girls, and maybe even loose women. There were rumors . . . At the same time he went around alone too much, deep in thought. At the synagogue he came in last, put on his *tallis,* and with his skullcap on askew, thumbed aimlessly through his prayerbook without ever following the services. No one ever saw him doing anything exactly wrong, and yet people murmured that he was not a God-fearing man. Apparently a man cannot be perfect . . .

"And so, when his turn came to be searched and he refused to let them do it, that was all the proof most of the men needed that he was the one who had taken the money. He begged them to let him swear any oath they wished, begged them to chop him, roast him, cut him up—do anything but shake his pockets out. At this point even our Rabbi, Reb Yozifel, although he was a man we had never seen angry, lost his temper and started to shout.

" 'You!' he cried. 'You thus and thus! Do you know what you deserve? You see what all these men have endured. They were able to forget the disgrace and allowed themselves to be searched; but you want to be the only exception! God in heaven! Either confess and hand over the money, or let us see for ourselves what is in your pockets. You are trifling now with the entire Jewish community. Do you know what they can do to you?'

"To make a long story short, the men took hold of this

young upstart, threw him down on the floor with force, and
began to search him all over, shake out every one of his
pockets. And finally they shook out . . . Well, guess what!
A couple of well-gnawed chicken bones and a few dozen
plum pits still moist from chewing. You can imagine what
an impression this made—to discover food in the pockets
of our prodigy on this holiest of fast days. Can you imagine
the look on the young man's face, and on his father-in-law's?
And on that of our poor Rabbi?

"Poor Reb Yozifel! He turned away in shame. He could
look no one in the face. On *Yom Kippur,* and in his synagogue . . . As for the rest of us, hungry as we were, we
could not stop talking about it all the way home. We rolled
with laughter in the streets. Only Reb Yozifel walked home
alone, his head bowed, full of grief, unable to look anyone
in the eyes, as though the bones had been shaken out of his
own pockets."

The story was apparently over. Unconcerned, the man
with the round eyes of an ox turned back to the window
and resumed smoking.

"Well," we all asked in one voice, "and what about the
money?"

"What money?" asked the man innocently, watching the
smoke he had exhaled.

"What do you mean—what money? The eighteen hundred
rubles!"

"Oh," he drawled. "The eighteen hundred. They were
gone."

"Gone?"

"Gone forever."

IN HASTE

For in haste didst thou come forth out of the Land of Egypt.
—DEUTERONOMY, 16:3.

To my honored, beloved and respected friend, Sholom Alei-chem:

I want to begin by informing you that I am still—Bless the Lord—among the living, and that I hope to hear the same from you, Amen. Next I want to tell you that, with God's help, I am now a king; that is, I have come home to Kasrilevka to spend the Passover with my wife and children, my father-in-law and mother-in-law, and with all my loved ones. And at Passover, as we all know, a Jew surrounded by his family is always a king. If only briefly, I hasten to inform you of all this, my dear, true friend. For a detailed account there is no time. It is Passover Eve, and on this day we must all do everything in great haste, standing on one foot. As it is written, "For *in haste* didst thou come forth out of the Land of Egypt."

But what to write of first, I hardly know myself. It seems to me that before anything else I ought to thank you and praise you for the good advice you gave me, to try my hand at matchmaking. Believe me, I shall never, never forget what you have done for me. You led me forth from the Land of Bondage, from the Gehenna of Yehupetz; you freed me from the desolate occupation of a commission salesman, and lifted m⌐ to a noble, respected profession. And for this I am obligated to praise and exalt you, to bless and adorn your name, as you well deserve.

It is true that thus far I have not succeeded in negotiating a single match, but I have made a beginning. Things are stirring, and once things begin to stir there is always the possibility and the hope that with God's help something may come of it. Especially in view of the fact that I do not work alone. I operate in partnership with other matchmakers, the best matchmakers in the world. As a result of these connections I now have a reputation of my own. Wherever I come and introduce myself, Menachem-Mendel from Yehupetz, I am invited to sit down, I am given tea with preserves, I am treated like an honored guest. They introduce me to the daughter of the house, and the daughter shows me what she can do. She turns to her governess and begins to speak French with her. Words come pouring like peas out of a sack, and the mother sits gazing at her daughter proudly, as though to say, "What do you think of her? She speaks well, doesn't she?"

And listening to these girls, I have picked up some French myself and I can understand quite a bit of the language. For instance, if someone says to me, *"Parlez-vous Français?"* ("How are you feeling these days?") I say, *"Merci, bonjour."* ("Not bad, praise the Lord.")

Then, after she has given a demonstration of her French, they have her sit down at the pianola to play something— overtures and adagios and finales—so beautiful that it penetrates to the very depth of one's soul! In the meantime the parents ask me to stay for supper and I let them talk me into it. Why not? . . . At the table they serve me the best portions of meat and feed me *tzimmes* even on weekdays. Afterwards, I strike up a conversation with the daughter. "What," I ask, "is your heart's desire—a lawyer, an engineer, a doctor?" "Naturally," she says, "a doctor." And once more she starts jabbering in French with the governess, and at this point the mother has an opportunity to display her daughter's handiwork. "Her embroidery and her knitting are a feast to the eye," she says, "and her kindness, her goodness, her consideration for others—there is no one like her! And quiet—like a dove. And bright—as the day . . ."

And the father, in his turn, traces his pedigree for me. He tells me what a fine family he comes from, and his wife as well. He tells me who his grandfather was, and his great-grandfather, and all his wife's connections. Every one of them of the finest. Rich people, millionaires, famous and celebrated all over the world. "There is not a single common person in our whole family," he assures me. "And not one pauper," his wife adds. "Not a single workingman," he says. "No tailors and no cobblers," she adds. "You'll find no fakes or frauds among us," he tells me. "Or apostates either, I can assure you," she puts in.

In the doorway, when I'm ready to leave and they wish me a good journey, I sigh and let them know how expensive it is to travel these days. Every step costs money. And if he is not obtuse he knows what I mean, and gives me at least enough for expenses . . .

I tell you, my dear friend, that matchmaking is not at all such a bad profession—especially if God ever intercedes and you actually conclude a match! So far, as I have told you, I have not succeeded in marrying anyone off. I have had no luck. At the start everything looks auspicious. It could hardly be better. It was a match predestined since the Six Days of Creation. But at the last moment everything goes wrong. In this case the youth does not care for the maiden; in the other, the girl thinks the groom is too old. This one has too fine a pedigree; that one does not have enough money. This one wants the moon on a platter; that one doesn't know what he wants. There is plenty of trouble connected with it, and heartaches, and indigestion, I can assure you.

Right now I am on the verge of arranging a couple of matches—naturally with a few partners—which, if the Lord has mercy and they go through, will be something for the whole world to talk about. Both parties come from the wealthiest and finest and oldest families—there is none like them. And the girls are both the greatest beauties. You can't find their equal anywhere. Both are well-educated, gifted, kind, bright, quiet, modest—all the virtues you can think of. And what do I have to offer them? Real merchandise! One—a doctor from Odessa. But he wants no less than thirty thousand *rubles* dowry, and he has a right to it, because according to the practice that he says he has, he should be worth much more. I have another from Byelotzerkiev—a rare find! A bargain at twenty thousand! And another in Yehupetz only he doesn't want to get married. And a whole flock of young little doctors who are only too anxious to get married.

Besides these I have a pack of lawyers and attorneys and justices at fifteen thousand and ten thousand, and smaller lawyers—young ones just hatched—that you can have for six thousand or five thousand, or even less. On top of that I have a couple of engineers who are already earning a living, and a few engineers still looking for work. And that is not all. I have an assortment of miscellaneous clients, elderly men, relics of past campaigns from Tetrevitz, from Makarevka, from Yampola and from Strishtch, without diplomas, but fine enough specimens, distinguished, skilled, intelligent. In short, there are plenty to pick from. The only trouble is that if the gentleman wants the lady, the lady does not want the gentleman. If the girl is willing, the man is not. Perhaps then you will ask why the man who does not want girl number one will not take number two, and vice versa? I thought of that myself, but it doesn't seem to work. Do you know why? Because strangers are always mixing in. They may be good people. They mean no harm. But they spoil everything. And meanwhile letters are flying back and forth. I send telegrams and receive telegrams every day. The whole world rocks and rolls!

And in the midst of it all, Passover gets in the way, like a bone in the throat, blocking everything. I think it over. My fortune won't run away from me. The merchandise I deal in is not so perishable. Why shouldn't I take a few days off and go to see my family in Kasrilevka? It's been so long since I've been there. It is not fair to my wife and children to be away from them so long. It does not look good to others, and it is even embarrassing to myself. So, to make it short, I have come home for Passover, and that is where I am writing you this letter from.

Maybe you will ask, why have I not written to you before this? Here is the answer. People like us are always worn out, we never have time. We are always rushing about. We never rest. I always keep thinking: if not today, then tomorrow. Soon, soon, with God's help, I'll arrange a worthwhile match, and then I'll write you all about it in celebration. But as it happened that all my prospects dragged on and remained hanging in the air, I kept putting off writing to you till God should bring me safely home . . .

And now I shall tell you what my homecoming was like. I'll describe everything just the way you like it. But if my account does not seem rounded out as yours always are, please excuse me. Each one of us has to tell his story the way he can.

I arrived—that is, the train came into the station—yesterday. But around here the mud is so deep that it took the wagon all night to pull through to town. For a time it even looked as if I might have to spend the Passover on the way somewhere, axle-deep in mud, together with the driver and the horses. You must be familiar with our Kasrilevka mud from the olden times. But ever since they began to talk about paving the roads around here, it seems as if the mud has become thicker and deeper than ever. In fact, people have begun going around without their galoshes, because they were always losing them in the mud. And some women have started a fashion even better than that. They go around without shoes, either. I wonder what they'll think of next!

Well, this morning, when we reached Kasrilevka itself, all the passengers had to get out of the wagon and go the rest of the way by foot. A fine homecoming! I felt my face burning. Acquaintance after acquaintance stopped me on the way, greeted me broadly, shook hands with me knee-deep in the mud—each with his own questions, his own comments. "How goes it with you, Menachem-Mendel?" "What is the latest news on the Yehupetz market?" "Look at the man, will you! In a derby hat and rubber overshoes!"

"Laugh, laugh," I answered, barely able to pull one foot after another out of the mud. "You have the right to laugh! Everywhere else in the world people really need galoshes, but here you can get along without them! Here it's as dry and sandy as in Palestine!"

I barely managed to drag myself home, and here I found a Gehenna. Like the fumes over Gehenna was the thick smoke that rose from the yard and the kitchen, where silverware for the holidays was being boiled, and everything else was being cleaned and scrubbed and scoured. And food, the rich and wonderful Passover food, was being cooked and baked and broiled. The shouting and clamoring of everyone, of mistresses and servants, the commands, the exhortations, the complaints and the threats, were enough to make a person deaf. A small thing—Passover Eve!

The first one to greet me was my mother-in-law, bless her. She is the same as ever, she has not changed in the least. She was in the front yard, standing over a wooden cot, her kerchief tied around her head with two pointed wings sticking out. In one hand she held a can of kerosene, in the other a brush. She was pickling bedbugs. When she saw me, she managed to control her joy. She kept right on with her work, muttering to herself:

"Well, well! You mention the Messiah—and look who comes! Here he is, my bird of Paradise . . . If he doesn't spoil, he'll find his way home. Goats run away, chickens get lost, but men always come back . . . The only place they don't return from is the Other World. Now I know why the cat was washing herself yesterday, and the dog was eating entrails . . . Oh, Sheine-Sheindel, daughter, come here! Welcome your ornament, your jewel, your crown of gold and diamonds! Your holy of holies . . . Quick, take the garbage away!"

At this point my wife runs out, frightened, and sees me. Her welcome is more direct.

"Tfui!" she spat out. "You picked just the right time to come. All year long you roam around that dirty city, lying around in all the attics, engage in every idolatry—and here you come fluttering in on Passover Eve, when we're busy cleaning up and there is no time to say a word to each other. I don't even have the time to put on a clean dress. I look like a fright. And you—fresh from the fine ladies of Yehupetz—may they roast in hell!—who held you in their clutches all year—may they not live through the Passover! Look at him! A plague on him! He doesn't even ask how a person is getting along, how the children are! Soreleh, Feigeleh, Yoseleh, Nechamenu, Moishe-Hersheleh! Your father has come back! Suddenly remembered you! May my worst enemies look as beautiful as you look in that derby hat!"

I must tell you the truth, dear friend. I barely recognized the children. And as for them—they didn't know me at all. But though my wife's welcome was not as ardent as I had hoped for, I could see that she was happy, for when I had finished greeting and kissing each of the children, I saw that she had withdrawn to one side and was crying.

But best and friendliest of all was the welcome I received from my father-in-law. He was as happy as if it were his own child he was seeing, or happy like a man who had been locked up in prison all these years and suddenly he sees another prisoner . . . My father-in-law, a distinguished-looking man with fine, dark eyes and a rich beard, had aged noticeably in these past few years, become white as a dove. Quietly he shook hands with me, asked how I was, and with a wink called me into his little alcove, and only when we were there alone did he embrace me.

"Do you know what, Mendel," he said to me with a deep sigh, "I'm growing old. Every year I'm a year older . . . But come, Mendel, sit down. Tell me what's new. You have been all over the world. How are things going on among our people? What is the true story about Dreyfus? What is it people are saying about a new war? What is happening in Palestine? Here we know nothing, we live like cattle . . ."

My father-in-law was getting wound up for a good long talk, but suddenly from outside we heard my mother-in-law's melodious voice:

"Boruch! Boruch!?" (The first Boruch was a shout, the second had a questioning overtone of astonishment in it, as if to say, "Aren't you here yet?")

"Just a minute! Here I come! I'm coming! I'm coming!" answered my father-in-law, and he bounded from the room.

A few times this happened. No sooner had he got started talking, when her voice rang out, "Boruch! Boruch!?" And each time he jumped. "I'm coming! I'm coming!" A little later, after breakfast, after the last few bread crusts found on the premises had been burned and the house itself had been purified for the holidays, and he was given a clean shirt and told that now he could go to the Baths, he became a different man, as though a new soul had been installed in his body. There at least, in the bath house, he thought he would have a chance for a few words. But again he was mistaken, woefully mistaken. As soon as we came in the crowd swarmed about us like bees, like the locusts in a year of famine. They almost ate me up alive. Every one of them wanted me to tell him what was going on in Yehupetz. Was it true, what they had heard about the bad times everywhere, the failures and bankruptcies? Did millionaire Brodsky still have some money? How was the Dreyfus case going to come out? Why didn't they hear about it any more? And how did it happen that England was still messing around with the Boers? These questions and many more they put to me from all sides. They almost pulled me apart. They didn't let me rest. And my father-in-law could not get a word in anywhere.

The same thing happened when we went to buy wine for

the *seder*. As soon as we walked down into Yudel Veinshenker's cellar, I was greeted from all sides and had to
shake hands with everybody. In the midst of it someone
asked for Palestinian wine, and Yudel Veinshenker (much
older now, with all his teeth gone) kept shouting that there
was no such thing. There never had been and never would
be. But one young man who pretended to be more worldly
than the others, kept arguing that he had seen it himself in
the papers.

"Papers! What papers?" shouted Yudel Veinshenker. "Lies
and falsehoods! Some troublemakers must have thought it
up! Those Zionists you hear about!"

The young man was stubborn. "As sure as I see you in
front of me," he said, "I saw the Palestinian wines mentioned. And what's more, I'll tell you the exact name. Mount
Carmel wine. And they sell it in all the shops in Yehupetz."

"In Yehupetz, you say?" several bystanders broke in. "Here
is a man straight from Yehupetz. Menachem-Mendel Boruch-
Hersh Leah-Dvoshe's! Let's ask Menachem-Mendel. He'll
know!"

I tried to speak, but they wouldn't let me. For every word
I say they ask me ten questions, and before I'm through
with one answer another of them asks me ten more questions. "Why do they call it Mount Carmel wine? Is it from
Mount Carmel itself or just from Palestine? How do they
bring it from Mount Carmel? How much does it cost? Who
makes it? Jewish colonists? Our own colonists? How many
colonies do we have now in Palestine? What are their
names, and what connection do they have with Baron Rothschild? Oh, Rothschild! How much is he really worth? Who is
worth more—Rothschild or the Yehupetzer Brodsky? Why is
Rothschild a Zionist and Brodsky not? Is it true, what they
say, that Doctor Herzl is buying up Palestine from the Turks
for the Zionists?"

"Come," my father-in-law says to me, "they don't let us get
in a word anywhere."

And it was only later in the day, while he was grating

horseradish outside, that my father-in-law was able to say a few words to me. But only a few words, because every little while we were interrupted by my mother-in-law.

"Boruch! *Boruch!?*"

"Right away! Here I come! Here I come!"

In the meantime the women had finished their work and had dressed themselves in their finest clothes and all their jewelry, like queens. My mother-in-law wore a dark green poplin dress with a flowered silk kerchief on her head. And Sheine-Sheindel had a flowered yellow silk dress with a dark green poplin kerchief on her head. And even I slipped into the alcove and put on my best clothes. Are we not all kings on Passover? And in the meanwhile I took a few sheets of paper and I'm writing you this letter. And once more, dear friend, I beg you to pardon me if I appear to be in a hurry. It's Passover Eve! If all is well and the Lord grants me strength, I shall write to you again in a few days. Then I shall have more time and I shall be able to write at greater length.

From your truest friend,
Menachem-Mendel

P.S. It is not my fate to enjoy anything in this world. There everything was ready, all was serene. The holiday spirit was in the air, and suddenly a misfortune overtook us. A dog stole into the kitchen, no one knows how, and ate up the greens and the chicken neck and the rest of the symbolic trimmings for tonight's *seder*. Suddenly there was an uproar and a tumult. Heavens were splitting open. I was sure murder was being done, or a fire had broken out, or at least someone had been scalded with boiling water. Everybody was yelling at everybody else, and all the cries melted into one uproar. Sheine-Sheindel was yelling at the servant girl; the servant girl was yelling at my father-in-law. "It's all his fault!" she cried. "The master has no brains! He's always leaving the door open! Always!"

But above them all could be heard my mother-in-law.

"Woe is me! Thunder and lightning! When the world calls a man crazy, you may believe it! A fool is worse than a sinner! How should a person be a prophet and know that he would leave the door open, and suddenly, on Passover Eve, a dog would steal into the kitchen? And of all things to find the chicken bones? It never rains but it pours. I have always said: the dog always gets the best bite of food, and the pudding comes out according to the company (that must mean me!) . . . What can we do now? Boruch! *Boruch?*"

"Here I am! Right away! Here I am!"

I look at my father-in-law and think: "What a woeful lot is yours, poor unfortunate king, and what a woeful thing is thy kingdom."

Once more, be well, And enjoy a *kosher Pesach.*

Yours

M. M.

ETERNAL LIFE

If you are willing to listen, I shall tell you the story of how I once took a burden upon myself, a burden which almost, almost ruined my life for me. And why do you think I did it? Simply because I was an inexperienced young man and none too shrewd. So far as that goes, I may be far from clever now, too, because if I were clever, I might have had a little money by now. How does the saying go? If you have money, you are not only clever, but handsome too, and can sing like a nightingale!

Well, there I was, a young man living with my father- and mother-in-law, as was the custom with young married couples in those days. And, as was also the custom in those days, I sat in the synagogue all day studying the *Torah*. Now and then I glanced into secular books too, but that had to be done on the sly so my father- and mother-in-law should not find out; not so much my father-in-law as my mother-in-law, a woman who was the real head of the family. You can really say she wore the pants. She managed all their affairs herself, picked out the husbands for her daughters herself, and herself arranged the entire match. It was she who had picked me out too, she who examined me in the *Torah,* she who brought me to Zvohil from Rademishli. I am from Rademishli, you know—that's where I was born. You must have heard of the town; it was recently in the papers.

So I lived in Zvohil with my mother-in-law, struggled over the Rambam's *Guide to the Perplexed,* never stepping out of the house, you might say, till the time came when I had to register for military service. Then, as the custom was, I had to bestir myself, go back to Rademishli, straighten out my papers, see what exemption I could claim, and arrange for a passport which I would need if I ever left the district. That, you could say, was my first venture into the outside world. All by myself, to prove that I was now a responsible person, I went forth into the marketplace and hired a sleigh. God sent me a bargain. I found a peasant who was going back to Rademishli with a freshly-painted, broad-backed sleigh with wings at the sides like an eagle. But I had failed to pay attention to the fact that the horse was a white one, and a white horse, my mother-in-law said, was bad luck. "I hope I'm lying," she said, "but this trip will be an unlucky one." "Bite your tongue," burst out my father-in-law, and at once was sorry, because he had to take his punishment right on the spot. But to me he whispered, "Women's nonsense," and I began to pack up for the trip: my *tallis* and *tfillin,* some freshly baked rolls, a few *rubles* for expenses, and three pillows—a pillow to sit on, a pillow to lean against, and a pillow to keep my feet warm. And I was ready to go.

So I said goodbye to everybody, and started on my way to Rademishli. It was late in winter; the hard-packed snow made a perfect road for the sleigh. The horse, though a white one, went as smoothly as a breeze, and my driver turned out to be one of those silent fellows who answers everything either "Uh-huh," meaning "yes," or "Uh-uh" for "no." That's all. You couldn't get another word out of him.

I had left home right after dinner and made myself as comfortable as I could, with a pillow under me, a pillow at my back, and one at my feet. The horse pranced, the driver cluck-clucked, the sleigh slid along, the wind blew, and snowflakes drifted through the air like feathers and covered

the wide expanse around us. My heart felt light, my spirits
free. After all, it was my first trip alone into God's world. I
was all alone, a free man, my own master! I leaned back and
spread myself out in the sleigh like a lord. But in winter, no
matter how warmly you are dressed, when the frost goes
through you, you feel like stopping somewhere to warm
yourself and catch your breath before going on again. And
I began to dream of a warm inn, a boiling *samovar,* and a
fresh pot roast with hot gravy. These dreams made me crave
for food I actually became hungry. I began to ask the driver
about an inn, asked if the next one was far away. He answered, "Uh-uh," meaning "no." I asked if it was close, and
he answered, "Uh-huh," meaning "yes." "How close?" I
asked. But that he would not answer, no matter how hard I
tried to make him.

I imagined what it would have been like if this were a
Jew driving the sleigh. He would have told me not only
where the inn was, but who ran it, what his name was, how
many children he had, how much rent he paid, what he got
out of it, how long he had been there, who had been there
before him—in short, everything. We are a strange people,
we Jews.

But there I was, dreaming of a warm inn, seeing a hot
samovar in front of me, and other good things like that; till
God took pity on me, the driver clucked to the horse, turned
the sleigh a little aside, and there appeared before us a small
gray hut covered with snow, a country inn standing alone in
the wide, snow-covered field, like a forsaken, forgotten tomb-
stone.

Driving up to the inn with a flourish, the driver took the
horse and sleigh into the barn and I went straight toward the
inn itself, opened the door, and stopped dead. Here is what
I saw. On the floor in the middle of the room lay a corpse
covered with black, with two copper candlesticks holding
small candles at its head. All around the body sat small children in ragged clothes beating their heads with their fists
and screaming and wailing, "Mo-ther! Mother!" And a tall,

thin man with long, thin legs, dressed in a torn summer coat
entirely out of season, marched up and down the room with
long strides, wringing his hands and saying to himself,
"What shall I do? What shall I do? I don't know what to
do!"

I understood right away what a happy scene I had come
upon. My first thought was to run away. I turned to leave,
but the door was slammed shut behind me and my feet felt
rooted to the ground. I could not move from the spot. Seeing a stranger, the tall man with the long legs ran up to me,
stretched out both arms like a man seeking help.

"What do you think of my misfortune?" he asked, pointing to the weeping children. "Poor little things . . . their
mother just died. What shall I do? What shall I do? I don't
know what to do!"

"Blessed is He who gives, and He who takes," I said, and
started to comfort him with the words one uses on such occasions. But he interrupted me.

"She was as good as dead for the past year, poor thing. It
was consumption. She begged for death to come. And now
she's dead and here we are, stuck in this forsaken spot. What
can I do? Go to the village to find a wagon to take her to
town? How can I leave the children here alone in the middle of this field, with night coming on? God in heaven, what
shall I do? What shall I do? I don't know what to begin to
do!"

With these words the man began to weep, strangely, without tears, as though he were laughing, and a queer sound
came from his lips, like a cough. All my strength left me.
Who could think of hunger now? Who remembered the
cold?

I forgot everything and said to him, "I am driving from
Zvohil to Rademishli with a very fine sleigh. If the town you
speak of is not very far from here I can let you take the
sleigh and I'll wait here. If it won't take too long, that is."

"Long may you live!" he cried. "For this good deed you'll
earn eternal life! As I am a Jew, eternal life!" he exclaimed,

and threw his arms around me. "The town is not far away, only four or five *versts*. It will take no more than an hour and I'll send the sleigh right back. You are earning eternal life, I tell you! Eternal life! Children, get up from the ground and thank this young man. Kiss his hands and his feet! He is letting me use his sleigh to take your mother to the burial ground. Eternal life! As sure as I'm a Jew, eternal life!"

This news did not exactly cheer them. When they heard their father talk about taking their mother away they threw themselves around her again and began to weep louder than ever. And yet it was good news that a man had been found to do them this kindness. God himself had sent him there. They looked at me as at a redeemer, something like Elijah, and I must tell you the plain truth: I began to see myself as an extraordinary being. Suddenly in my own eyes I grew in stature and became what the world calls a hero. I was ready to lift mountains, turn worlds upside down. There was nothing that seemed too difficult for me, and these words tore themselves out of my lips:

"I'll tell you what. I'll take her there myself, that is, my driver and I. I'll save you the trouble of going and leaving the children behind."

The more I talked the more the little children wept, wept and looked up at me as at an angel from heaven, and I grew in my own eyes taller and taller, till I almost reached the sky. For the moment I forgot I had always been afraid to touch a dead body, and with my own hands helped to carry the woman out and lift her into the sleigh. I had to promise the driver another half-*ruble,* and a drink of whisky on the spot. At first he scratched the back of his neck and mumbled something in his nose. But after the third drink he softened up and we started on our way, all three of us, the driver and I and the innkeeper's wife, Chava Nechama. That was her name, Chava Nechama, daughter of Raphael Michel. I remember it as if it had been this morning, because all along the way I kept repeating to myself the name that her hus-

band had repeated to me several times. For when the time
came to bury her with the proper ceremony, her full name
would have to be given. So all the way I repeated to myself,
"Chava Nechama, daughter of Raphael Michel. Chava Nechama, daughter of Raphael Michel. Chava Nechama, daughter of Raphael Michel." But while I kept repeating the
woman's name, the husband's name escaped me completely.
He had told me his name too and assured me that when I
came to the town and mentioned the name, the corpse would
be taken from me at once and I would be able to go on my
way. He was well known there, he said. Year after year he
came there for the holidays, contributed money for the synagogue, for the bath house, and everywhere he paid well. He
told me more, filled my head with instructions, where I
should go, what I should say and do, and every bit of it
flew out of my head. You'd think that at least a word of it
would have remained. But it didn't. Not a word.

All my thoughts revolved about one thing only, here I
was, carrying a dead woman. That alone was enough to make
me forget everything, even my own name; for from early
childhood I had been mortally afraid of dead bodies. You'd
have to pay me a fortune to make me stay alone with a
corpse. And now it seemed to me that the glazed, half-open
eyes stared at me and the dead, sealed lips would open any
minute and a strange voice would be heard as though from
a sepulchre, a voice so terrible that merely thinking of it almost threw me into a faint. It is not for nothing that such
stories are told of the dead, of people who have fainted out
of mere fright, and lost their minds or their powers of
speech.

So we rode along, the three of us. I had given the dead
woman one of my pillows and had placed her crossways in
the sleigh, right at my feet. In order to keep myself from
thinking melancholy thoughts I turned away from the body,
began to watch the sky and softly to repeat to myself, "Chava
Nechama, daughter of Raphael Michel. Chava Nechama,
daughter of Raphael Michel," until the name became jumbled

in my mind and I found myself saying, "Chava Raphael,
daughter of Nechama Michel," and, "Raphael Michel, daughter of Chava Nechama."

I had not been aware that it was getting darker and
darker. The wind was blowing stronger all the time and the
snow continued to fall until it was so deep that we could
not find the road. The sleigh went hither and yon, without
direction, and the driver began to grumble at first softly, then
louder and more insistently, and I could swear that he was
blessing me with a threefold blessing. I asked him, "What
is the matter with you?" He spat into the snow and turned
upon me with such murderous anger that I shrank back.
"Look what you've done!" he cried. "You've been the ruina-
tion of me and my horse!" Because of this, because we had
taken a dead woman into the sleigh, the horse had strayed
from the road, and here we were wandering, and God alone
knew how long we would keep on wandering. For night was
almost here, and then we would really be lost.

At this good news I was ready to go back to the inn, un-
load our baggage, forget eternal life. But it was too late, said
the driver. We could neither go ahead nor turn back. We
were wandering in the middle of the field, the devil alone
knew where. The road was snowed under, the sky was black.
It was late. The horse was dead tired. May a bad end come
to that innkeeper and all the innkeepers of the world! Why
hadn't he broken a leg before he had stopped at the inn?
Why hadn't he choked on the first glass of whisky before he
had let himself be talked into this folly, and for a miserable
half-*ruble* perish here in the wilderness, together with his
poor little horse. As for himself, it didn't matter so much.
Maybe it was fated that he should come to a bad end, and at
this spot. But the poor little horse, what had he done? An
innocent animal, to be sacrificed like that?

I could swear that there were tears in his voice. And to
make him feel better I told him that I would give him another half-*ruble* and two more glasses of whisky. At this he
became furious and told me plainly that if I didn't keep my

mouth shut he would throw our cargo out of the sleigh altogether. And I thought to myself: what would I do if he
threw the corpse and me out into the snow? Who knew
what a man like that could do when he lost his temper? I
had better be quiet, sit in the sleigh buried in pillows and try
to keep from falling asleep, because in the first place, how
could a person fall asleep with a dead body in front of him?
And in the second place, I had heard that in wintertime you
mustn't fall asleep outside, because if you did you might fall
asleep forever.

But in spite of myself my eyes kept shutting. I would have
given anything at that moment for a short nap. And I kept
rubbing at my eyes but my eyes would not obey. They kept
shutting slowly and opening and shutting again. And the
sleigh slid over the soft deep white snow and a strange sweet
numbness poured through my limbs and I felt an extraordinary calm descend on me. And I wished that this sweet
numbness and calm would last and last. I wished it would
last forever. But an unknown force, I don't know where it
came from, stood by and prodded me. "Do not sleep. Do not
fall asleep." With a great effort I tore my eyes open and the
numbness resolved itself into a chill that went through my
bones and the calm turned to fear and shrinking and melancholy—may the Lord have mercy on me. I imagined that my
corpse was stirring, that it uncovered itself and looked at me
with half-shut eyes as though to say, "What did you have
against me, young man? Why did you drag me off, a dead
woman, the mother of young children, and then fail to bring
me to consecrated ground?"

The wind blew. It shrieked with a human voice, whistled
right into my ears, confided a horrible secret to me. Terrible
thoughts, frightful images followed one another in my mind
and it seemed to me that we were all buried under the snow,
all of us, the driver, the horse, the dead woman and I. We
were all dead, all of us. Only the corpse—isn't it remarkable?
—only the dead woman, the innkeeper's wife, was alive!

Suddenly I heard my driver clucking to his horse cheerfully, thanking God, and sighing and crossing himself in the dark. I sat up and looked around. In the distance I saw a gleam of light. The light glimmered, went out, and glimmered again. A house, I thought, and thanked God with all my heart. I turned to the driver. "We must have found the road," I said. "Are we close to town?"

"Uh-huh," said the driver in his usual brief manner, without anger, and I could have thrown my arms around his wide shoulders and kissed him, I was so happy to hear that pleasant brief "Uh-huh" which was more wonderful to me at that moment than the wisest discourse.

"What's your name?" I asked, surprised at myself for not having asked it before.

"Mikita," he answered, in one short word, as was his custom.

"Mikita," I repeated, and the name Mikita took on a strange charm.

He answered, "Uh-huh."

I wished that he would tell me more. I wanted to hear him say something more, at least a few words. Mikita had suddenly become something dear to me, and his horse too, a charming animal! I began a conversation with him about his horse, told him what a fine horse he had. A very fine horse!

To which Mikita answered, "Uh-huh."

"And your sleigh, Mikita, is a fine sleigh too!"

Again he answered, "Uh-huh."

Beyond that he would not say a word.

"Don't you like to talk, Mikita, old fellow?" I asked.

"Uh-huh," he said. And I burst out laughing. I was as happy as though I had found a treasure, or made a wonderful discovery. In a word, I was lucky. I was more than lucky. Do you know what I wanted to do? I wanted to raise my voice and sing. That's a fact. I have always had that habit. When I am feeling good I burst out singing. My wife, bless her, knows this trait of mine, and asks, "What happened now, Noah? How much have you earned today to make you so happy?" To a woman, with her woman's brains, it is possible for a man to be happy only when he has made some money. Why does it happen that women are so much more greedy than men? Who earns the money, we or they? But there! I'm afraid I've gone off on the road to Boiberik again.

Well, with God's help we came to the town. It was still very early, long before daybreak. The town was sound asleep. Not a glimmer of light showed anywhere. We barely distinguished a house with a large gate and a besom over the gate, the sign of a guest house or inn. We stopped, climbed down, Mikita and I, and began to pound at the gate with our fists. We pounded and pounded till at last we saw a light in the window. Then we heard someone shuffle up to the gate, and a voice called out, "Who's there?"

"Open, Uncle," I cried, "and you'll earn eternal life."

"Eternal life? Who are you?" came the voice from behind the gate, and the lock began to turn.

"Open the door," I said. "We've brought a corpse with us."

"A what?"

"A corpse."

"What do you mean, a corpse?"

"By a corpse I mean a dead person. A dead woman that we've brought from out in the country."

Inside the gate a silence fell. We heard only the lock being turned again and then the feet shuffling off. The lights went out and we were left standing in the snow. I was so angry that I told the driver to help me, and together we pounded at the window with our fists. And we pounded so heartily that the light went on again and the voice was heard once more, "What do you want? Will you stop bothering me!"

"In God's name," I begged as if pleading with a highwayman for my life, "have pity on me. We have a corpse with us, I tell you."

"What corpse?"

"The innkeeper's wife."

"What innkeeper are you talking about?"

"I've forgotten his name, but hers is Chava Michel, daughter of Chana Raphael, I mean Chana Raphael, daughter of Chava Michel, Chana Chava Chana, I mean . . ."

"Go way, you *shlimazl,* or I'll pour a bucket of water over you!"

And with this, the innkeeper shuffled off again and once more the light went out. There was nothing we could do. It was only an hour or so later, when day was beginning to break that the gate opened a crack and a dark head streaked with white popped out and said to me, "Was it you that banged at the window?"

"Of course! Who do you think?"

"What did you want?"

"I've brought a corpse."

"A corpse? Then take it to the *shammes* of the Burial Society."

"Where does your *shammes* live? What's his name?"

"Yechiel's his name, and he lives at the foot of the hill right near the Baths."

"And where are your Baths?"

"You don't know where the Baths are? You must be a stranger here! Where are you from, young man?"

"Where am I from? From Rademishli. That's where I was born. But right now I'm coming from Zvohil. And I'm bringing a corpse from a village close by. The innkeeper's wife. She died of consumption."

"That's too bad. But what's that got to do with you?"

"Nothing at all. I was driving by and he begged me, the innkeeper, that is. He lives all alone out there in the country with all those small children. There was nowhere to bury her, so when he asked me to earn eternal life, I thought to myself: why not?"

"That doesn't make sense," he said to me. "You'd better see the officers of the Burial Society first."

"And who are your officers? Where do they live?"

"You don't know the officers of our Burial Society? Well, first there's Reb Shepsel, who lives over there beyond the marketplace. Then there is Reb Eleazer-Moishe, who lives right in the middle of the marketplace. And then there is Reb Yossi, he's an officer too, who lives near the old synagogue. But the one you'd better see first is Reb Shepsel. He's the one who runs everything. A hard man, I'm warning you. You won't persuade him so easily."

"Thank you very much," I said. "May you live to tell people better news than you've told me. And when can I see these men?"

"When do you suppose? In the morning after services."

"Thanks again. But what shall I do until then? At least let me in so I can warm myself. What is this town anyway, another Sodom?"

At this the innkeeper locked the doors again, and once more it was as silent as a tomb. What could we do now? Here we were in the middle of the road with our sleigh, and Mikita fuming, grumbling, scratching his neck, spitting and roaring out his three-dimensional curses. "May that foul innkeeper roast in hell through all eternity, and every other innkeeper with him!" For himself he didn't care. Let the evil spirits take him. But his horse, what did they have against his poor little horse, to torture it, let it starve and freeze like that? An innocent animal being sacrificed. What had it ever done?

I felt disgraced before my driver. What could he be thinking of us? A Jew treating another Jew like this. We who were supposed to be the wise and merciful ones and they, the common, unlearned peasants. Thus I blamed the whole tribe for the discourtesy of one man, as is always our custom.

Well, we waited for daylight to come and the town to begin to show signs of life. And finally it did. Somewhere we heard the grating of a door, the sigh of a bucket. From a few chimneys smoke curled up, and in the distance roosters crowed louder and stronger. Soon the doors all opened and God's creatures appeared, in the image of cows, calves, goats, and also men, women and young girls, wrapped up in shawls, bundled from head to foot like mummies. In short the whole town had come to life as if it were a human being. It awoke,

washed, pulled on its clothes, and set out to work: the men
to the synagogue to pray and study and say *T-hilim;* the
women to the ovens, the calves and the goats; and I to inquire about the officers of the Burial Society, Reb Shepsel,
Reb Eleazer-Moishe, Reb Yossi.

Wherever I asked they put me through a cross-examination.
Which Shepsel? Which Eleazer-Moishe, which Yossi? There
were, they said, several Shepsels, Eleazers and Yossis in town.
And when I told them that I wanted the officers of the Burial Society, they looked frightened and tried to find out why
a young man should want the officers of the Burial Society so
early in the morning. I didn't let them feel me out long,
but opened my heart to them and told them the whole secret of the burden I had taken upon myself. You should have
seen what happened then. Do you suppose they rushed to
relieve me of my misfortune? God forbid! They ran out, all
right, every one of them, but it was only to see if there really
was a corpse or if I had invented the whole story. They
formed a ring about us, a ring that kept shifting because of
the cold, some people leaving and others taking their place,
looking into the sleigh, shaking their heads, shrugging their
shoulders, and asking over and over who the corpse was, and
where it came from, who I was, where I had got it, and
gave me no help whatever.

With the greatest of difficulty I managed to find out where
Reb Shepsel lived. I found him with his face turned to the
wall, wrapped in his *tallis* and *tfillin,* praying so ardently,
with such a melodious voice and so much feeling that the
walls actually sang. He cracked his knuckles, rocked back
and forth, made strange movements with his body. I enjoyed
it tremendously, because in the first place I love to listen to
such spirited praying, and besides, it gave me a chance to
warm my frozen bones. When Reb Shepsel finally turned his
face to me his eyes were still full of tears and he looked like
a man of God, his soul as far removed from earth as his big
fat body was from heaven. But since he was still in the midst
of his prayers and did not want to interrupt them with secu-

lar discourse, he spoke to me in the holy tongue, that is, in a language that consisted of gestures of the hands, winks of the eye, shrugs and motions of the head and even the nose, with a few Hebrew words thrown in. If you wish, I can relate the conversation to you word by word, and no doubt you will understand which words were his and which were mine.

"Sholom aleichem, Reb Shepsel."

"Aleichem sholom. I-yo. Nu-o."

"Thank you. I have been sitting all night."

"Nu-o? Ma?"

"I have a request to make of you, Reb Shepsel. You will earn eternal life."

"Eternal life? Good! In what way?"

"I have brought you a corpse."

"Corpse! What corpse?"

"Not far from here there is a country inn. The owner is a poor man whose wife just died of consumption, and she left him with several small children, may God have compassion on them. If I had not taken pity on them, I don't know what the poor innkeeper would have done, alone out there in the middle of the field with the corpse."

"God have mercy on them. Well . . . and did he give you anything for the Burial Society?"

"Where is he going to get the money for that? He's a poor man. Poor as can be, and with a houseful of children. You will earn eternal life, Reb Shepsel."

"Eternal life. Good. Very good! Jews. Poor people . . . ah, yes."

And here he broke in with a series of strange sounds accompanied by so many gestures, winks, blinks, shrugs and motions of the head that I could not begin to understand what he was driving at.

And seeing that I could not follow him, he turned his face to the wall in disgust and once more began to pray, but not with the same ardor as before. His voice was lower, but he rocked back and forth faster than ever, till he came to the end, threw off his *tallis* and *tfillin* and fell on me with such fury that you would have thought I had outwitted him in some transaction and ruined him completely.

"Look," he said to me, "our town is such a poor one, with so many paupers of our own for whom shrouds must be provided when they die, and here you come from some strange place with a corpse. They come here from everywhere. Everybody comes here!"

I defended myself as well as I could. I said I was an innocent man trying to do only what was proper with respect to the dead. Suppose a dead body had been found in the street and had to be buried, laid to his eternal rest. "You are," I said, "an honest man, a pious one. You can earn eternal life with this deed."

At this he became even angrier and began to lash out at me, not with blows, but with words.

"Is that so?" he cried. "You are a man who craves eternal life? Then take a walk around our town and see to it that our own people stop dying of hunger and freezing of cold. Then you will earn eternal life. Ah-hah! A young man who deals in eternal life! Go take your merchandise to the ne'er-do-wells. Maybe they will be interested. We have our own duties to perform, our own poor to bury. And if we suddenly began to yearn for this eternal life you talk about we could find our own way to earn it!"

With these words Reb Shepsel showed me out and slammed the door behind me. And I swear to you on my word of honor that from that morning on I have despised all those overly pious people who pray out loud and beat their breasts and bow low and make crazy motions. I have hated those holy ones who talk with God all the time, who pretend to serve Him, and do whatever they want, all in His name! True, you might say that these modern irreligious people nowadays are no better and may even be worse than the old-timers with their false piety. But they're not so revolting. At least they don't pretend to be on speaking terms with God. But there! I'm on the way to Boiberik again.

Well, the president, Reb Shepsel, had driven me off. So

what should I do next? Go to the other trustees, of course.
But at this point a miracle occurred. I saved myself the trouble of going to them, because they came to me instead. They
met me face to face at the door and said:

"Are you the young man we're looking for?"

"And what young man are you looking for?"

"The one who brought a body here. Is that you?"

"Yes, I'm the one. What do you want me for?"

"Come back with us to Reb Shepsel and we'll talk it over."

"Talk it over?" I asked. "What is there to talk over? You
take the body from me, let me go on my way—and you'll
earn eternal life."

"You don't like the way we do things? Is anyone keeping
you here?" they asked. "Go take your body anywhere you
want, even to Rademishli, and we'll be grateful to you."

"Thanks for the advice," I told them.

"You're welcome," said they.

So we went back into Reb Shepsel's house and the three
trustees began to talk. They argued and quarrelled, called
each other names. The other two said Reb Shepsel was stubborn, a hard man to deal with; and Reb Shepsel yelled back
at them, shouted, ranted, quoted the law: the town's own
poor came first. At this the other two fell on him.

"Is that so? Then you want the young man to take the
body back with him?"

"God forbid," I said. "What do you want, I should take the
body back? I barely came here alive, almost got lost on the
way. My driver wanted to throw me out of the sleigh in the
open field somewhere. I beg you. Have pity on me. Take the
corpse off my hands. You'll earn eternal life."

"Eternal life is a fine enough thing," answered one of
them, a tall thin man with bony fingers, the one called
Eleazer-Moishe. "We'll take the body away from you and
bury it, but it will cost you something."

"What do you mean?" I asked. "Here I undertook a respon-
sibility like this, at the risk of my life, almost got lost on
the way, and you want money!"

"But you're getting eternal life, aren't you?" said Reb Shepsel with such an ugly leer that I wanted to go after him as he deserved. But I managed to control myself. After all, I was still at their mercy.

"Let's get to work," said the one called Reb Yossi, a small man with a short scraggly beard. "I suppose you know, young man, that you have another problem on your hands. You have no papers, no papers at all."

"What papers?" I asked.

"How do we know whose body it is? Maybe it's not what you said it was," said the tall man with the bony fingers, the one called Eleazer-Moishe.

I stood looking from one to the other, and the tall one with the bony fingers, the one called Eleazer-Moishe, shook his head and pointed at me with his long fingers and said:

"Yes, yes. Maybe you murdered some woman yourself. Maybe it's your own wife that you brought here and made up this story about a country inn, the innkeeper's wife, consumption, small children, eternal life."

I must have looked frightened to death at these words, for the one they called Reb Yossi began to comfort me, telling me that they themselves had nothing against me. They understood very well that I was not a robber or a murderer, but still I was a stranger, and a dead body was not a sack of potatoes. We were dealing with a dead person, a corpse. They had, he explained, a rabbi and a police inspector in their town. A report had to be made out.

"Yes, of course. A report. A report," added the tall one, the one called Eleazer-Moishe, pointing with his finger and looking down at me accusingly as though I had committed some crime. I couldn't say another word. I felt a sweat break out on my forehead and I was ready to faint. I was well aware of the miserable plight I had fallen into. It was a disgrace, a sorrow and a heartache in one. But, I thought to myself, what was the use of starting the whole discussion over again with them? So I took out my purse and said to the three trustees of the Burial Society:

"Listen, my friends, here is the whole story. I see what I have fallen into. It was an evil spirit that made me stop at that country inn to warm myself just when the innkeeper's wife had to go ahead and die, and I had to listen to the poor wretch left with all the children begging me, promising eternal life. And now I have to pay for it. Here is my purse. You'll find about seventy-odd *rubles* in it. Take it and do what you think best. Just leave me enough to get me to Rademishli, and take the body away from me and let me go on my way."

I must have spoken with great feeling for the three trustees looked at each other and would not touch my purse. They told me that their town was not Sodom; they were not robbers. True, the town was a poor one, with more paupers than rich people, but to fall on a strange man and order him to hand over his money, that they would not think of. Whatever I wanted to give of my own free will was all right. To do it without charging at all was impossible. It was a poor town, and there were all the expenses, pallbearers, a shroud, drinks, the cost of the burial lot. But it was not necessary for me to throw my money away. If I started to do that, there would be no end to it.

Well, what more can I tell you? If the innkeeper had had two hundred thousand *rubles,* his wife could not have had a finer funeral. The whole town came to look at the young man who had brought the corpse. They told each other that it was the body of his mother-in-law, a rich woman. (I don't know where they got the mother-in-law story.) At any rate they came to welcome the young man who had brought the rich mother-in-law and was throwing out money right and left. They actually pointed their fingers at me. And as for beggars, they were like the sands of the ocean. In all my life I have never seen so many beggars in one place, not even in front of the synagogue on *Yom Kippur* eve. They pulled at the skirts of my coat, they almost tore me to pieces. How often do they see a young man who throws away money like that? I was lucky that the trustees came to my rescue and

kept me from giving away all I had. Especially the tall one
with the bony fingers, Eleazer-Moishe, did not step away
from me for a moment. He kept pointing at me with his
finger and saying, "Young man, do not hand out all your
money." But the more he spoke the closer the beggars gathered around me, tearing at my flesh. "It's nothing," yelled the
beggars. "It's nothing. When you bury such a rich mother-in-
law you can afford to spend a few extra *groschen*. She must
have left him enough money May we have as much!"

"Young man!" yelled one beggar, pulling at my coat,
"young man, give the two of us half a *ruble!* At least forty
kopeks. We were born like this, one lame, the other blind.
Give us at least a *gulden,* a *gulden* for two maimed ones.
Surely we deserve a *gulden!*"

"Don't pay attention to him!" shouted another, pushing the
first one aside. "Do you call them cripples? My wife is a real
cripple. She can't use her arms or legs, she can't move a
limb, and our children are sick too! Give me anything at all
and I'll say *kaddish* for your mother-in-law all year—may
she rest in Paradise!"

Now I can laugh about it. Then it was far from a laughing
matter, for the crowd of beggars grew and multiplied about
me. In half an hour they flooded the marketplace and it was
impossible to proceed with the coffin. The attendants had to
use sticks to disperse the mob, and a fight broke out. By that
time some peasants began to gather about us too, with their
wives and countless children, and at last the news reached the
town authorities. The police inspector appeared on horseback
with a whip in his hand and with one harsh look about him
and a few sharp lashes of the whip sent the mob flying in
all directions. He himself dismounted and came up to the
coffin to investigate. He started by questioning me, asked
who I was, where I had come from, and where I was going.
I was paralyzed with fear. I don't know why, but whenever
I see an officer of the law I go numb with fear, though I
have no real reason to worry. In all my life I have never as
much as touched a fly on the wall and I know quite well

that a policeman is an ordinary human being, flesh and blood like the rest of us. In fact, I know a Jew who is so friendly with the police officer that they visit each other frequently and when there is a holiday the officer eats fish at my friend's house, and when my friend visits the officer he's treated to hard-boiled eggs. He can't praise the officer highly enough. And yet every time I see a policeman I want to run. It must be something I inherited, because, as you know, I come from a region where pogroms came one after another in the days of Vassilchikov, and I'm descended from the victims of those pogroms. If I wanted to, I could tell you stories enough about those days—but there, I must be well past Boiberik this time.

As I said, the officer began to cross-examine me. He wanted to know who I was, and what I was, and where I was going. How could I tell him the whole story—that I live with my father-in-law in Zvohil and I'm going to Rademishli to get a passport? But the trustees, long may they live, saved me the trouble. Before I could even begin, one of them, the one with the thin beard, called the officer aside and began to talk with him, while the tall one with the bony fingers quickly and in guarded language taught me how to answer the officer.

"Be careful what you say," he whispered. "Tell him the whole truth. You live not far from town and this is your mother-in-law and you brought her here to be buried. Tell him your name and your mother-in-law's too. Your real names, you understand, straight out of the *Hagadah*. And give him the burial fee—don't forget."

And saying this he winked at me and continued, "In the meantime, your driver looks tired and thirsty. We'll take him across the street and give him a chance to rest."

Then the inspector took me into a large building and began to make out some papers. I have no idea at all what nonsense I told him. I said anything and everything that came to my mind and he wrote it all down.

"Your name?"

"Moishe."

"Your father's."

"Itzko."

"Your age?"

"Nineteen."

"Married?"

"Married."

"Children?"

"Of course."

"Your trade?"

"Merchant."

"Who is the dead person?"

"My mother-in-law."

"Her name?"

"Yenta."

"Her father's?"

"Gershon."

"Her age?"

"Forty."

"Cause of death?"

"Fright."

"Fright?"

"Yes, fright."

"What do you mean—fright?" he asked, laying down his pen and lighting a cigarette, looking me over from head to foot. Suddenly my tongue stuck to the roof of my mouth. I thought to myself, if I am inventing a story, I might as well do a good job. So I told him how my mother-in-law had been sitting all alone knitting some socks. She had forgotten that her young son, a boy named Ephraim, was in the room with her. A thirteen-year-old boy, very stupid, something of a clown. He was making shadow figures on the wall and he put his hands up high behind his mother's back, and making a goat's shadow on the wall, opened his mouth and bleated, "Ba-a-a-a." Struck with fright, she fell from her chair and died on the spot.

While I was telling him this story he kept looking at me strangely, not taking his eyes off me. He heard me out till the end, spat on the floor, wiped his red mustaches, and led me out again to the coffin. He removed the black cover, looked at the dead woman's face and shook his head. He looked from the corpse to me, and from me to the corpse, and then said to the trustees, "Well, you can go ahead and bury the woman. As for this young man, I'll have to keep him here until I satisfy myself that she was really his mother-in-law and that she died of fright."

You can imagine how I felt when I heard this. I turned aside—I couldn't help it—and burst out crying like a small child.

"Look here, what are you crying for?" asked the little man they called Reb Yossi, and comforted me, cheered me up as best he could. I was innocent, wasn't I? Then what did I have to be afraid of?

"If you don't eat garlic, they'll never smell it on your breath," put in Reb Shepsel with such a smirk that I wanted to give his fat cheeks a couple of good hard slaps.

God in heaven, what good did it ever do me to make up this big lie and drag my mother-in-law into it? All I needed now was to have her find out that I had buried her alive and spread the news that she had died of fright.

"Don't be afraid," Reb Eleazer broke in, prodding me with his bony fingers. "God will take care of you. The officer is not such a bad fellow. Just give him the burial fee I told you about. He'll understand. He knows that everything you told him is true."

I cannot tell you any more. I don't even want to remember what happened to me after that. You understand, of course, that they took the few *gulden* I had left, put me in jail and I had to stand trial. But that was child's play compared to what happened when the news reached my father- and mother-in-law that their son-in-law was in prison for having brought a dead woman from somewhere.

Naturally they came at once, identified themselves as my

parents-in-law, and then the excitement really began! On one side the police went after me. "A fine fellow you are! Now, if your mother-in-law Yenta, daughter of Gershon, is alive, then who was the dead woman you brought?" On the other side, my mother-in-law, may she live long! "There is only one thing I want to ask you," she kept saying to me. "What did you have against me, to take me and bury me alive?"

Naturally at the trial it turned out that I was innocent, free from all guilt. Of course that cost some money too. Witnesses had to be brought in, the innkeeper and his children, and finally I was set free. But what I went through afterwards, especially from my mother-in-law, that I don't wish my worst enemy to have to go through!

And from that time on, when anybody mentions eternal life, I run away as fast as I can.

HANNUKAH MONEY

Can you guess, children, which is the best of all holidays? *Hannukah*, of course.

You don't go to *cheder* for eight days in a row, you eat pancakes every day, spin your *dreidel* to your heart's content, and from all sides *Hannukah* money comes pouring in. What holiday could be better than that?

Winter. Outside it's cold, a bitter frost. The windows are frozen over, decorated with beautiful designs, the sills piled high wih snow. Inside the house it's warm and cheerful. The silver *Hannukah* lamp stands ready on the table and my father is walking back and forth, his hands behind his back, saying the evening prayers. When he is almost through, but while still praying, he takes out of the chest a waxen candle (the *shammes,* to light the others with) and starting *Oleinu,* the last prayer in the regular services, signals to us:

." 'Shehu noteh shomayim . . .' Nu! Nu-o!"

My brother and I don't know what he means. We ask, "What do you want? A match?"

My father points with his hand toward the kitchen door, " 'Al-kein n'kaveh l'cho . . .' E-o-nu!"

"What then? A bread knife? Scissors? The mortar and pestle?"

My father shakes his head. He makes a face at us, comes

to the end of the prayer, and then, able to speak again,
says, "Your mother! Call your mother! I'm ready to light the
candle!"

The two of us, my brother and I, leap for the kitchen,
almost falling over each other in our haste.

"Mother! Quick! The *Hannukah* candles!"

"Oh, my goodness! Here I am! *Hannukah* lights!" cries
my mother, leaving her work in the kitchen (rendering
goose fat, mixing batter for pancakes) and hurries into the
parlor with us. And after her comes Braina the cook, a
swarthy woman with a round plump face and mustache,
her hands always smeared with grease. My mother stands at
one side of the room with a pious look on her face, and
Braina the cook remains at the door, wipes her hand on
her dirty apron, draws her greasy hand over her nose, and
leaves a black smear across her face.

My father goes up to the lamp with his lighted candle,
bends down and sings in the familiar tune, "Blessed art thou,
O Lord . . ." and ends ". . . to kindle the lights of *Hannukah*."

My mother, in her most pious voice, chimes in, "Blessed
be He and blessed be His name." And later, "Amen." Braina
nods her approval and makes such queer faces that Motel
and I are afraid to look at each other.

"These lights we kindle," my father continues, marching
up and down the room with an eye on the *Hannukah* lamp.
He keeps up this chant till we grow impatient and wish that
he would reach his hand into his pocket and take out his
purse. We wink at each other, nudge and push each other.

"Motel," I say, "go ask him for *Hannukah* money."

"Why should I ask?"

"Because you're younger. That's why."

"That's why I shouldn't. You go. You're older."

My father is well aware of what we are talking about, but
he pretends not to hear. Quietly, without haste, he walks
over to the cupboard and begins to count out some money.
A cold shiver runs down our backs, our hands shake, our

hearts pound. We look up at the ceiling, scratch our earlocks, try to act as if this meant nothing at all to us.

My father coughs.

"H'm . . . Children, come here."

"Huh? What is it?"

"Here is *Hannukah* money for you."

The money in our pockets, we move off, Motel and I, at
first slowly, stiffly, like toy soldiers, then faster and faster
with a skip and a hop. And before we have reached our room
we lose all restraint and turn three somersaults one after the
other. Then hopping on one foot we sing:

> *"Einga beinga*
> *Stupa tzeinga*
> *Artze bartze*
> *Gola shwartze*
> *Eimelu reimelu*
> *Beigeli feigeli*
> *Hop!"*

And in our great joy and exuberance we slap our own
cheeks twice, so hard that they tingle.

The door opens and in walks Uncle Benny.

"Come here, you rascals. I owe you some *Hannukah*
money."

Uncle Benny puts his hand into his vest pocket, takes
out two silver *gulden,* and gives us each one.

2

Nobody in the world would ever guess that our father and
Uncle Benny are brothers. My father is tall and thin; my
uncle is short and fat. My father is dark, my uncle is fair.
My father is gloomy and silent, my uncle jolly and talkative.
As different as day and night, summer and winter. And yet
they are blood brothers.

My father takes a large sheet of paper ruled off into

squares, black and white, and asks us to bring him a handful
of dry beans from the kitchen, dark ones and white ones.
They are going to play checkers.

(Once a miracle happened, and this is our celebration.)

Mother is in the kitchen rendering goose fat and frying
pancakes. My brother and I are spinning our *dreidel*. My
father and Uncle Benny sit down and play checkers.

"One thing I'll have to ask you," my father says. "Once
you've made a move it's a move. You can't keep changing
your mind."

"A move is a move," my uncle agrees, and makes a move.

"A move is a move," repeats my father and jumps my
uncle's bean.

"That's right," says Uncle Benny, "a move is a move," and
jumps twice.

The longer they play the more absorbed they become.
They chew their beards, beat time under the table with their
feet, and together they hum one song:

"Oh, what shall I do? What shall I do? What shall I do?"
sings my father, chewing an end of his beard. "If I move
here," he chants, as one does over the *Gamorah,* "then he'll
move there. Maybe I'd better move . . . over here."

"Over here . . . over here," echoes Uncle Benny in the
same tone.

"Why should I worry?" my father hums again. "If he
should take this *one* then I'll take those *two*. On the other
hand, maybe he thinks he can take three . . ."

"Take three . . . take three . . . take three . . ." Uncle
Benny helps him out.

"Ah, you're no good, Benny. You're no good at all," sings
my father and makes a move.

"You're worse than no good, my brother," sings Uncle
Benny and pushes a bean forward, then snatches it back.

"You can't do that, Benny," my father cries. "You said a
move was a move!" And he catches Uncle Benny's hand.

"No!" Uncle Benny insists. "If I haven't finished I can still
move."

"No!" my father declares just as emphatically. "We decided on that before we started. Remember. You can't change your mind."

"I can't?" asks Uncle Benny. "How many times did you change yours?"

"I?" says my father indignantly. "See! That's why I hate to play with you, Benny!"

"Who is forcing you to play with me?"

At this point my mother comes in from the kitchen, her face flaming from the heat.

"Already? Fighting already?" she asks. "Over a few beans?"

Behind her comes Braina with a large platter of steaming pancakes. We all move toward the table. My brother Motel and I, who only a moment ago had been fighting like cat and dog, make up quickly, become friends again, and go after the pancakes with the greatest gusto.

3

In bed that night I lie awake and think: how much would I be worth if all my uncles and aunts and other relatives gave me *Hannukah* money? First of all there is Uncle Moishe-Aaron, my mother's brother, stingy but rich. Then Uncle Itzy and Aunt Dveira, with whom my father and mother have not been on speaking terms for years and years. Then Uncle Beinish and Aunt Yenta. And how about our sister Ida and her husband Sholom-Zeidel? And all the other relatives?

"Motel, are you asleep?"

"Yes. What do you want?"

"How much *Hannukah* money do you think Uncle Moishe-Aaron will give us?"

"How should I know? I'm not a prophet."

A minute later: "Motel, are you sleeping?"

"Yes. What now?"

"Do you think anyone else in the whole world has as many uncles and aunts as we have?"

"Maybe yes . . . and maybe no."

Two minutes later: "Motel, are you asleep?"

"Of course."

"If you're asleep, how can you talk to me?"

"You keep bothering me so I have to answer."

Three minutes later: "Motel, are you awake?"

This time he answers with a snore. I sit up in bed, take out my father's present, smooth it out, examine it. A whole *ruble*.

"Think of it," I say to myself. "A piece of paper, and what can't you buy with it! Toys, knives, canes, purses, nuts and candy, raisins, figs. Everything."

I hide the *ruble* under my pillow and say my prayers. A little later Braina comes in from the kitchen with a platter full of *rubles* . . . She isn't walking, she's floating in the air, chanting, "These lights we kindle . . ." And Motel begins to swallow *rubles* as if they were pancakes.

"Motel!" I scream with all my might. "God help you, Motel! What are you doing? Eating money?"

I sit up with a start . . . spit three times. It was a dream. And I fall asleep again.

4

The next morning after we have said our prayers and eaten breakfast, our mother puts on our fur-lined jackets and bundles us up in warm shawls and we start off for our *Hannukah* money. First of all, naturally, we stop off at Uncle Moishe-Aaron's.

Our Uncle Moishe-Aaron is a sickly man. He has trouble with his bowels. Whenever we come we find him at the wash bowl after having come in from the back yard, washing and drying his hands with the appropriate prayer.

"Good morning, Uncle Moishe-Aaron!" we cry out together, my brother and I. Our Aunt Pessil, a tiny woman with one black eyebrow and one white one, comes forward to meet us. She takes off our coats, unwinds our shawls, and proceeds to blow our noses into her apron.

"Blow!" says Aunt Pessil. "Blow hard. Don't be afraid. Again! Again! That's the way!"

And Uncle Moishe-Aaron, a little man with a moth-eaten mustache and ears stuffed with cotton, dressed in his old ragged fur-lined jacket and with his quilted skullcap on his head, stands at the wash bowl, wiping his hands, wrinkling his face, blinking at us with his eyes, while he groans out his prayer.

My brother and I sit down uneasily. We are always miserable and frightened in this house. Aunt Pessil sits opposite us, her arms folded across her chest, and puts us through her usual examination.

"How is your father?"

"All right."

"And your mother?"

"All right."

"Have they killed any geese yet?"

"Oh, yes."

"Did they have much fat?"

"Quite a lot."

"Did your mother make pancakes yet?"

"Yes."

"Has Uncle Benny come yet?"

"Yes."

"Did they play checkers?"

"Yes."

And so on and so on . . .

Aunt Pessil blows our noses again and turns to Uncle Moishe-Aaron.

"Moishe-Aaron, we ought to give the children some *Hannukah* money."

Uncle Moishe-Aaron doesn't hear. He keeps on drying his
hands, and comes to the end of his prayer with a drawn-out
groan.

Aunt Pessil repeats: "Moishe-Aaron! The children! *Hannukah* money."

"Huh? What?" says Uncle Moishe-Aaron, and shifts the
cotton from one ear to the other.

"The children. *Hannukah* money!" Aunt Pessil shouts right
into his ear.

"Oh, my bowels, my bowels," groans Uncle Moishe-
Aaron (that's the way he always talks), holding his belly
with both hands. "Did you say *Hannukah* money? What do
children need money for? What will you do with it, huh?
Spend it? Squander it? How much did your father give you?
Huh?"

"He gave me a *ruble*," I say, "and him a half."

"A *ruble!* Hm . . . Some people spoil their children, ruin
them. What will you do with the *ruble,* huh? Change it?
Huh? No! Don't change it. Do you hear what I say? Don't
change it. Or do you want to change it? Huh?"

"What does it matter to you whether they change it or
don't change it?" breaks in Aunt Pessil. "Give them what
they have coming and let them go on their way."

Uncle Moishe-Aaron shuffles off to his room and begins
to search through all the chests and drawers, finds a coin
here, a coin there, and mutters to himself:

"Hm . . . How they spoil their children. Ruin them.
Simply ruin them."

And coming back, he pushes a few hard coins into our
hands. Once more (for the last time) Aunt Pessil blows our
noses, puts on our coats, wraps the shawls around us, and we
go on our way. We run over the white frozen crunchy snow,
counting the money that Uncle Moishe-Aaron has given us.
Our hands are frozen, red and stiff. The coins are copper,
large and heavy, very old six-*kopek* pieces, strange, old-
fashioned three-*kopek* pieces rubbed smooth and thin, *gros-*

chens that we've never seen before, thick and green with age. It's hard for us, in fact impossible, to figure out how much *Hannukah* money Uncle Moishe-Aaron has given us.

5

Our second stop for *Hannukah* money is at Uncle Itzy's and Aunt Dveira's, with whom my parents have not been on speaking terms for many years. Why they don't speak to each other I don't know, but I do know that they never speak, although they go to the same synagogue and sit next to each other on the same bench. And at the holidays when it comes to auctioning off the various honors, they always try to outbid each other. A fierce battle takes place each time. The whole congregation takes sides, helps them to bid, eggs them on.

The *shammes*, who acts as auctioneer, stands on the platform, working hard. His skullcap is off to one side, his prayer-shawl keeps slipping off his shoulders.

"Eighteen *gulden* for *Shi-shi!*

"Twenty *gulden* for *Shi-shi!*"

The bidding gets hotter and hotter. My father and Uncle Itzy are bent over their Bibles, from all appearances unaware of what is going on. But every time one of them bids the other one raises it.

The congregation enjoys the spectacle and helps along. "Thirty . . . thirty-five . . . thirty-seven and a half . . ." But the battle is between my father and Uncle Itzy, and they continue the bidding until one or the other has to give up.

And yet whenever there is a celebration in the family, a birth, a circumcision, a *Bar Mitzvah,* an engagement party, a wedding or a divorce, the feud is forgotten. We all attend, exchange gifts, make merry, drink together and dance together like the best of friends.

"Good morning, Uncle Itzy! Good morning, Aunt

Dveira!" we cry out together, my brother Motel and I, and they receive us like honored guests.

"Did you come all this way just to see us, or was there something else on your mind?" Uncle Itzy asks and pinches our cheeks. He opens his purse and gives us our *Hannukah* money, a new silver twenty-*kopek* piece to me and another one to my brother. And from there we go straight to Uncle Beinish's.

6

If you want a picture of complete chaos, go to our Uncle Beinish's house. No matter when you come you find a perfect bedlam. They have a house full of children, half-naked, dirty, unkempt, unwashed, always bruised, usually scratched, often bloodied and with black eyes. One of the children may be laughing, another crying; one singing, another shrieking; one humming, another whistling; this one has put on his father's coat with the sleeves rolled up, and that one is riding a broomstick; this one is drinking milk from a pitcher, that one is cracking nuts, another is walking about with a herring's head in his hand, and still another is sucking on a stick of candy while from his nose two runnels flow down toward his mouth. Aunt Yenta must be strong as an ox to put up with this crew. She curses them, pinches them, shakes them all day long. She isn't particular. Whichever one comes within reach gets a slap or a shove or a prod in the side.

An ordinary slap by itself is not worth mentioning. "I hope you choke; I hope you die; why doesn't someone kidnap you!" These are the lesser curses. And words like "the plague" and "cholera" and "violent death" are uttered casually, without anger, as one might say "Good evening" or "Good Sabbath." The house becomes quiet only when Uncle Beinish comes home. But since Uncle Beinish is a busy man who spends all his time at the store, coming home only for meals, their house is a perpetual Gehenna.

When we come in we find little Ezriel riding on his older brother Getzi's back, with Froike and Mendel whipping Getzi on, one with the sleeve of an old jacket, the other with the cover of a prayer book. Chaim'l, who has found the windpipe of a slaughtered goose somewhere, is blowing at it until he is blue in the face, and succeeds in producing an eerie sound like the squeal of a stuck pig. Zeinvilleh is playing a tune on a comb and David, a small boy of about four, has put his shoes on his hands and beats time with them. Sender'l rushes by carrying a kitten by the scruff of the neck. The kitten's tongue hangs out, its eyes are shut, its feet hang limply. You can almost hear it say, "See how I suffer here; they torture me, they make life unbearable." In another corner Esther, the oldest girl, is trying to comb and braid her little sister Haska's hair, but since the hair is curly and has not been combed for a long time, the child stands shrieking at the top of her voice and Esther keeps slapping her to make her stop. The only quiet one is Pinny, a tiny boy with crooked legs, his shirt tail pinned up behind him. The only trouble with him is that wherever he goes he leaves a trail behind him.

But none of this disturbs Aunt Yenta in the least. It does not prevent her from sitting calmly at the table drinking chicory, with an infant at her breast and an older child on her knee. Between sips of chicory she cuddles the baby at her breast and digs her elbow into the child on her knee. "Look at you eat, you pig! May the worms eat you! Esther, Rochel, Haska, where the devil are you? Quick, wipe his nose! Bring me a saucer, quick! Here I am, drinking without a saucer! Mendel, don't make so much noise! I'll give you such a crack that you'll turn over three times! Oh, my heart, my soul, my comfort. What, murderers, you want more food? All you do all day is eat, eat, eat! Why don't you choke!"

When they catch sight of the two of us the children fall on us like locusts, grabbing us by our hands, our feet, some leaping at our heads. Chaim'l blows the windpipe right into

my ear. David, still wearing his shoes on his hands, throws
his arms around us. Pinny, with the shirt tail pinned behind
him, gets hold of one of my legs and wraps himself about it
like a little snake. A confusion of sounds and voices surrounds us, deafens our ears.

"May you scream with a toothache!" shouts Aunt Yenta
from the other room. "A person can get deaf here! They're
devils, not children! May your souls burn forever and ever!"

And in the midst of all this noise and confusion Uncle
Beinish comes in with his *tallis* and *tfillin,* apparently on his
way from the synagogue, and at once everything becomes
quiet. The children vanish.

"Good morning, Uncle Beinish!" we cry out together, my
brother Motel and I.

"What are you doing here, you *shkotzim?*" asks Uncle
Beinish. "Ah, *Hannukah* money!" And he gives us each a
ten-*kopek* piece.

The children peek at us from their corners with bright
little eyes like mice, wink and signal with their hands,
make strange faces at us, try hard to make us laugh. But
with great effort we control ourselves, take the money, and
run off as fast as we can from this living Gehenna.

7

The next place we go to for *Hannukah* money is our sister
Ida's. Since she was a child Ida has always been a lugubrious
creature. No matter what silly little thing happened, she
could always be counted on to burst out crying. She was always shedding tears over her own or other people's troubles.
But when she became engaged to Sholom-Zeidel, that was
when she really cried! Perhaps you think it was because the
young man didn't please her? God forbid! She had never
even seen the man! No, she wept because a bride is supposed to weep before her wedding. When the tailors brought
her trousseau she wept all night long. Later, when her girl

friends came for their last party together she ran off to her room every few minutes to weep into her pillows. But she was really at her best on her wedding day! That day she didn't stop crying for a minute.

But the climax came at the veiling, when Menashe Fiddele, the fiddler, led her to the dais and Reb Boruch B'dachun climbed up on the table, folded his arms over his ample stomach, lowered his head as though he were bemoaning the dead, and began, in a mournful tone that could move a stone to tears, the following song:

> Dearest Bride, dearest bride!
> Weep all you please;
> Your tears are becoming,
> They need not cease.

> Weeping is ordained
> For brides to be.
> And soon you will stand
> Under the canopy.

> For you must learn
> That now your life
> Is full of sadness,
> Woe and strife;

> That man is not made
> Of iron or stone.
> He is only a being
> Of flesh and bone;

> That sinners are lashed
> In the depths of hell,
> And they scream and howl
> And lament as well.

Then learn to practice virtue
And humility.
Weep, maiden, weep,
Let your tears run free."

And so on and so on without end.

The women who stood around her, helping to undo her beautiful long braids, could not control themselves. They gave themselves up to their lamentations wholeheartedly, made the oddest faces, wiped their eyes and blew their noses. And poor Ida wept loudest of all. She wailed and moaned and blubbered so hard that she fainted three times and they barely revived her in time for the ceremony.

But our brother-in-law, on the other hand, was as merry as our sister Ida was sad. If anything, Sholom-Zeidel was too merry, a practical joker, a clown, a zany, who fastened himself to you like a leech and got under your skin. He was always teasing us, my brother and me, pinching our ears and filliping our noses. That gave him his greatest pleasure. The first year they were married there were times when for days Motel and I went around with swollen noses, stinging ears. So when we heard that the young couple was leaving our home to set up their own establishment we were really overjoyed. But for the rest of the family the day they moved was a day of mourning. Ida wept, poured buckets of tears, and my mother, watching her, wept also. Sholom-Zeidel, who was supposed to be doing the packing, skipped back and forth, stole up behind us cunningly, and pinched our ears or filliped our noses. And when he bade us farewell he had the impudence to tell us not to wait to be invited but to come as often as we liked. We swore to each other on our honor, my brother and I, never to set foot in his house as long as we lived.

But a person forgets all things, even a pinched ear. How can you keep from going to your own married sister for *Hannukah* money?

When we come into the house, Sholom-Zeidel greets us heartily.

"Well, well! Look who's here! I'm glad you came. I've been waiting. I have some *Hannukah* money for you!"

And Sholom-Zeidel takes out his purse and hands each one of us several shiny silver coins. And before we can even count how many he has given us, his hand flies out, pinch, fillip go his fingers, and once more our ears and noses feel the sharp sting.

"Leave them alone! Haven't you tortured them enough?" our sister Ida begs him with tears in her eyes, and calling us aside, fills our pockets with cake, nuts and figs, and gives us *Hannukah* money besides.

We make our escape as quickly as we can and hurry home.

8

"Well, Motel," I say, "let's get down to business. Let's figure out how much money we've collected. But I'll tell you what. You wait. First let me count mine and then you'll count yours."

And I begin to count. A *ruble* and three twenty-*kopek* pieces, four *gulden,* five *grivnye,* six *piatekas* . . . how much is that altogether? It must be a *ruble* and three twenties and four *gulden* and five *grivnye* and six *piatekas* . . .

My brother Motel won't wait until I am through, and he gets busy with his own finances. He moves each coin from one hand to the other and counts.

"A twenty and a twenty are two twenties, and one more is three. And two *gulden* is three twenties and two *gulden* and a *grivnye* and another *grivnye* and one more—that makes two twenties and three *gulden,* I mean three *gulden* and two twenties . . . What am I talking about? I'll have to start all over again from the beginning."

And he starts all over from the beginning. We count and

we count and we can't get the total. We figure and we figure and we can't get it straight. When we get to Uncle Moishe-Aaron's old *piatekas,* huge sixes, smoothly rubbed threes and swollen *groschens* we get so mixed up that we don't know where in the world we are. We try to exchange these coins with our mother, our father, with Braina the cook, but it doesn't work. Nobody wants to have anything to do with them.

"What sort of *piatekas* are those? Who palmed them off on you?"

We are ashamed to tell, and we keep quiet.

"Do you know what," says my brother Motel, "let's throw them into the oven, or outside in the snow, when no one is looking."

"What a smart boy you are!" I tell him. "It would be better to give them to a beggar."

But just to spite us no one comes to our door. We wait and we wait and not a single one appears. We can't get rid of Uncle Moishe-Aaron's present.

TIT FOR TAT

Once I was a rabbiner. A rabbiner, not a rabbi. That is, I was called rabbi—but a rabbi of the crown.

To old-country Jews I don't have to explain what a rabbi of the crown is. They know the breed. What are his great responsibilities? He fills out birth certificates, officiates at circumcisions, performs marriages, grants divorces. He gets his share from the living and the dead. In the synagogue he has a place of honor, and when the congregation rises, he is the first to stand. On legal holidays he appears in a stovepipe hat and holds forth in his best Russian: *"Gospoda Prihozhane!"* To take it for granted that among our people a rabbiner is well loved—let's not say any more. Say rather that we put up with him, as we do a government inspector or a deputy sheriff. And yet he is chosen from among the people, that is, every three years a proclamation is sent us: *"Na Osnavania Predpisania . . ."* Or, as we would say: "Your Lord, the Governor, orders you to come together in the synagogue, poor little Jews, and pick out a rabbiner for yourselves . . ."

Then the campaign begins. Candidates, hot discussions, brandy, and maybe even a bribe or two. After which come charges and countercharges, the elections are annulled, and we are ordered to hold new elections. Again the proclamations: *"Na Osnavania Predpisania . . ."* Again candidates,

discussions, party organizations, brandy, a bribe or two . . .
That was the life!

Well, there I was—a rabbiner in a small town in
the province of Poltava. But I was anxious to be a modern
one. I wanted to serve the public. So I dropped the formali-
ties of my position and began to mingle with the people—
as we say: to stick my head into the community pot. I got
busy with the *Talmud Torah*, the charity fund, interpreted
a law, settled disputes or just gave plain advice.

The love of settling disputes, helping people out, or ad-
vising them, I inherited from my father and my uncles. They
—may they rest in peace—also enjoyed being bothered all the
time with other people's business. There are two kinds of
people in the world: those that you can't bother at all, and
others whom you can bother all the time. You can climb
right on their heads—naturally not in one jump, but gradually. First you climb into their laps, then onto their shoulders, then their heads—and after that you can jump up
and down on their heads and stamp on their hearts with
your heavy boots—as long as you want to.

I was that kind, and without boasting I can tell you that
I had plenty of ardent followers and plain hangers-on who
weren't ashamed to come every day and fill my head with
their clamoring and sit around till late at night. They never
refused a glass of tea, or cigarettes. Newspapers and books
they took without asking. In short, I was a regular fellow.

Well, there came a day . . . The door opened, and in
walked the very foremost men of the town, the sparkling
best, the very cream of the city. Four householders—men
of affairs—you could almost say: real men of substance.
And who were these men? Three of them were the *Troika*
—that was what we called them in our town because they
were together all the time—partners in whatever business
any one of them was in. They always fought, they were always suspicious of each other, and watched everything the
others did, and still they never separated—working always
on this principle: if the business is a good one and there

is profit to be made, why shouldn't I have a lick at the bone too? And on the other hand, if it should end in disaster— you'll be buried along with me, and lie with me deep in the earth. And what does God do? He brings together the three partners with a fourth one. They operate together a little less than a year and end up in a brawl. That is why they're here.

What had happened? "Since God created thieves, swindlers and crooks, you never saw a thief, swindler or crook like this one." That is the way the three old partners described the fourth one to me. And he, the fourth, said the same about them. Exactly the same, word for word. And who was this fourth one? He was a quiet little man, a little innocent-looking fellow, with thick, dark eyebrows under which a pair of shrewd, ironic, little eyes watched everything you did. Everyone called him Nachman Lekach.

His real name was Nachman Noss'n, but everybody called him Nachman Lekach, because as you know, *Noss'n* is the Hebrew for "he gave," and *Lekach* means "he took," and in all the time we knew him, no one had ever seen him give anything to anyone—while at taking no one was better.

Where were we? Oh, yes . . . So they came to the rabbiner with the complaints, to see if he could find a way of straightening out their tangled accounts. "Whatever you decide, Rabbi, and whatever you decree, and whatever you say, will be final."

That is how the three old partners said it, and the fourth, Reb Nachman, nodded with that innocent look on his face to indicate that he too left it all up to me: "For the reason," his eyes said, "that I know that I have done no wrong." And he sat down in a corner, folded his arms across his chest like an old woman, fixed his shrewd, ironic, little eyes on me, and waited to see what his partners would have to say. And when they had all laid out their complaints and charges, presented all their evidence, said all they had to say, he got up, patted down his thick eyebrows, and not looking at the others at all, only at me, with those deep, deep, shrewd little eyes of his, he proceeded to demolish their claims and charges—so completely, that it looked as if they were the thieves, swindlers and crooks—the three partners of his— and he, Nachman Lekach, was a man of virtue and piety, the little chicken that is slaughtered before *Yom Kippur* to atone for our sins—a sacrificial lamb. "And every word that you heard them say is a complete lie, it never was and never could be. It's simply out of the question." And he proved with evidence, arguments and supporting data that everything he said was true and holy, as if Moses himself had said it.

All the time he was talking, the others, the *Troika,* could hardly sit in their chairs. Every moment one or another of them jumped up, clutched his head—or his heart: "Of all things! How can a man talk like that! Such lies and falsehoods!" It was almost impossible to calm them down, to keep them from tearing at the fourth one's beard. As for me —the rabbiner—it was hard, very hard to crawl out from this horrible tangle, because by now it was clear that I had a fine band to deal with, all four of them swindlers, thieves and crooks, and informers to boot, and all four of them deserving a severe punishment. But what? At last this idea occurred to me, and I said to them:

"Are you ready, my friends? I am prepared to hand down my decision. My mind is made up. But I won't disclose what I have to say until each of you has deposited twenty-five *rubles*—to prove that you will act upon the decision I am about to hand down."

"With the greatest of pleasure," the three spoke out at once, and Nachman Lekach nodded his head, and all four reached into their pockets, and each one counted out his twenty-five on the table. I gathered up the money, locked it up in a drawer, and then I gave them my decision in these words:

"Having heard the complaints and the arguments of both parties, and having examined your accounts and studied your evidence, I find according to my understanding and deep conviction, that all four of you are in the wrong, and not only in the wrong, but that it is a shame and a scandal for Jewish people to conduct themselves in such a manner—to falsify accounts, perjure yourselves and even act as informers. Therefore I have decided that since we have a *Talmud Torah* in our town with many children who have neither clothes nor shoes, and whose parents have nothing with which to pay their tuition, and since there has been no help at all from you gentlemen (to get a few pennies from you one has to reach down into your very gizzards) therefore it is my decision that this hundred *rubles* of yours shall go to the *Talmud Torah,* and as for you, gentlemen, you can go home, in good health, and thanks for your contribution. The poor children will now have some shoes and socks and shirts and pants, and I'm sure they'll pray to God for you and your children. Amen."

Having heard the sentence, the three old partners—the *Troika*—looked from one to the other—flushed, unable to speak. A decision like this they had not anticipated. The only one who could say a word was Reb Nachman Lekach. He got up, patted down his thick eyebrows, held out a hand, and looking at me with his ironic little eyes, said this:

"I thank you, Rabbi Rabbiner, in behalf of all four of us, for the wise decision which you have just made known. Such a judgment could have been made by no one since King Solomon himself. There is only one thing that you forgot to say, Rabbi Rabbiner, and that is: what is your fee for this wise and just decision?"

"I beg your pardon," I tell him. "You've come to the wrong address. I am not one of those rabbiners who tax the living and the dead." That is the way I answered him, like a real gentleman. And this was his reply:

"If that's the case, then you are not only a sage and a rabbi among men, you're an honest man besides. So, if you would care to listen, I'd like to tell you a story. Say that we will pay you for your pains at least with a story."

"Good enough. Even with two stories."

"In that case, sit down, Rabbi Rabbiner, and let us have your cigarette case. I'll tell you an interesting story, a true one, too, something that happened to me. What happened to others I don't like to talk about."

And we lit our cigarettes, sat down around the table, and Reb Nachman spread out his thick eyebrows, and looking at me with his shrewd, smiling, little eyes, he slowly began to tell his true story of what had once happened to him himself.

All this happened to me a long time ago. I was still a young man and I was living not far from here, in a village near the railroad. I traded in this and that, I had a small tavern, made a living. A Rothschild I didn't become, but bread we had, and in time there were about ten Jewish families living close by—because, as you know, if one of us makes a living, others come around. They think you're shoveling up gold . . . But that isn't the point. What I was getting at was that right in the midst of the busy season one year, when things were moving and traffic was heavy, my wife had to go and have a baby—our boy—our first son. What do you say to that? "Congratulations! Congratulations everybody!" But that isn't all. You have to have a *bris,* the circumcision. I dropped everything, went into town, bought all the good things I could find, and came back with the *Mohel* with all his instruments, and for good measure I also brought the *shammes* of the synagogue. I thought that with these two holy men and myself and the neighbors we'd have the ten men that we needed, with one to spare. But what does God do? He has one of my neighbors get sick—he is sick in bed and can't come to the *bris,* you can't carry him. And another has to pack up and go off to the city. He can't wait another day! And here I am without the ten men. Go do something. Here it is—Friday! Of all days, my wife has to pick Friday to have the *bris*—the day before the Sabbath. The *Mohel* is frantic—he has to go back right away. The *shammes* is actually in tears. "What did you ever drag

us off here for?" they both want to know. And what can I
do?

All I can think of is to run off to the railroad station. Who
knows—so many people come through every day—maybe
God will send some one. And that's just what happened. I
come running up to the station—the agent has just called
out that a train is about to leave. I look around—a little
roly-poly man carrying a huge traveling bag comes flying by,
all sweating and out of breath, straight toward the lunch
counter. He looks over the dishes—what is there a good
Jew can take in a country railroad station? A piece of herring—an egg. Poor fellow—you could see his mouth was
watering. I grab him by the sleeve. "Uncle, are you looking
for something to eat?" I ask him, and the look he gives me
says: "How did you know that?" I keep on talking: "May
you live to be a hundred—God himself must have sent you."
He still doesn't understand, so I proceed: "Do you want to
earn the blessings of eternity—and at the same time eat a
beef roast that will melt in your mouth, with a fresh, white
loaf right out of the oven?" He still looks at me as if I'm
crazy. "Who are you? What do you want?"

So I tell him the whole story—what a misfortune had
overtaken us: here we are, all ready for the *bris,* the *Mohel*
is waiting, the food is ready—and such food!—and we need a
tenth man! "What's that got to do with me?" he asks, and I
tell him: "What's that got to do with you? Why—everything depends on you—you're the tenth man! I beg you—
come with me. You will earn all the rewards of heaven—
and have a delicious dinner in the bargain!" "Are you crazy,"
he asks me, "or are you just out of your head? My train is
leaving in a few minutes, and it's Friday afternoon—almost
sundown. Do you know what that means? In a few more
hours the Sabbath will catch up with me, and I'll be
stranded." "So what!" I tell him. "So you'll take the next
train. And in the meantime you'll earn eternal life—
and taste a soup, with fresh dumplings, that only my wife
can make . . ."

Well, why make the story long? I had my way. The roast
and the hot soup with fresh dumplings did their work. You
could see my customer licking his lips. So I grab the traveling bag and I lead him home, and we go through with the
bris. It was a real pleasure! You could smell the roast all
over the house, it had so much garlic in it. A roast like that,
with fresh warm twist, is a delicacy from heaven. And when
you consider that we had some fresh dill pickles, and a bottle
of beer, and some cognac before the meal and cherry cider
after the meal—you can imagine the state our guest was in!
His cheeks shone and his forehead glistened. But what then?
Before we knew it the afternoon was gone. My guest jumps
up, he looks around, sees what time it is, and almost has a
stroke! He reaches for his traveling bag: "Where is it?" I
say to him, "What's your hurry? In the first place, do you
think we'll let you run off like that—before the Sabbath?
And in the second place—who are you to leave on a journey
an hour or two before the Sabbath? And if you're going to
get caught out in the country somewhere, you might just as
well stay here with us."

He groans and he sighs. How could I do a thing like that
to him—keep him so late? What did I have against him?
Why hadn't I reminded him earlier? He doesn't stop bothering me. So I say to him: "In the first place, did I have to
tell you that it was Friday afternoon? Didn't you know it
yourself? And in the second place, how do you know—
maybe it's the way God wanted it? Maybe He wanted you
to stay here for the Sabbath so you could taste some of my
wife's fish? I can guarantee you, that as long as you've eaten
fish, you haven't eaten fish like my wife's fish—not even in a
dream!" Well, that ended the argument. We said our evening prayers, had a glass of wine, and my wife brings the
fish to the table. My guest's nostrils swell out, a new light
shines in his eyes and he goes after that fish as if he hadn't
eaten a thing all day. He can't get over it. He praises it to
the skies. He fills a glass with brandy and drinks a toast to
the fish. And then comes the soup, a specially rich Sabbath

soup with noodles. And he likes that, too, and the *tzimmes* also, and the meat that goes with the *tzimmes,* a nice, fat piece of brisket. I'm telling you, he just sat there licking his fingers! When we're finishing the last course he turns to me: "Do you know what I'll tell you? Now that it's all over, I'm really glad that I stayed over for *Shabbes.* It's been a long time since I've enjoyed a Sabbath as I've enjoyed this one." "If that's how you feel, I'm happy," I tell him. "But wait. This is only a sample. Wait till tomorrow. Then you'll see what my wife can do."

And so it was. The next day, after services, we sit down at the table. Well, you should have seen the spread. First the appetizers: crisp wafers and chopped herring, and onions and chicken fat, with radishes and chopped liver and eggs and *gribbenes.* And after that the cold fish and the meat from yesterday's *tzimmes,* and then the jellied neat's foot, or *fisnoga* as you call it, with thin slices of garlic, and after that the potato *cholent* with the *kugel* that had been in the oven all night—and you know what that smells like when you take it out of the oven and take the cover off the pot. And what it tastes like. Our visitor could not find words to praise it. So I tell him: "This is still nothing. Wait until you have tasted our borsht tonight, then you'll know what good food is." At that he laughs out loud—a friendly laugh, it is true— and says to me: "Yes, but how far do you think I'll be from here by the time your borsht is ready?" So I laugh even louder than he does, and say: "You can forget that right now! Do you think you'll be going off tonight?"

And so it was. As soon as the lights were lit and we had a glass of wine to start off the new week, my friend begins to pack his things again. So I call out to him: "Are you crazy? Do you think we'll let you go off, the Lord knows where, at night? And besides, where's your train?" "What?" he yells at me. "No train? Why, you're murdering me! You know I have to leave!" But I say, "May this be the greatest misfortune in your life. Your train will come, if all is well, around dawn tomorrow. In the meantime I hope your appetite and digestion are good, because I can smell the borsht already! All I ask," I say, "is just tell me the truth. Tell me if you've ever touched a borsht like this before. But I want the absolute truth!" What's the use of talking—he had to admit it: never before in all his life had he tasted a borsht like this. Never. He even started to ask how you made the borsht, what you put into it, and how long you cooked it. Everything. And I say: "Don't worry about that! Here, taste this wine and tell me what you think of it After all, you're an expert. But the truth! Remember—nothing but the truth! Because if there is anything I hate, it's flattery . . ."

So we took a glass, and then another glass, and we went to bed. And what do you think happened? My traveler overslept, and missed the early morning train. When he wakes up he boils over! He jumps on me like a murderer. Wasn't it up to me, out of fairness and decency, to wake him up in time? Because of me he's going to have to take a loss, a heavy loss—he doesn't even know himself how heavy. It was all my fault. I ruined him. I! . . . So I let him talk. I listen, quietly, and when he's all through, I say: "Tell me yourself, aren't you a queer sort of person? In the first place, what's your hurry? What are you rushing for? How long is a person's life altogether? Does he have to spoil that little with rushing and hurrying? And in the second place, have you forgotten that today is the third day since the *bris?* Doesn't that mean a thing to you? Where we come from, on the third day we're in the habit of putting on a feast better than the one at the *bris* itself. The third day—it's something to celebrate! You're not going to spoil the celebration, are you?"

What can he do? He can't control himself any more, and he starts laughing—a hysterical laugh. "What good does it do to talk?" he says. "You're a real leech!" "Just as you say," I tell him, "but after all, you're a visitor, aren't you?"

At the dinner table, after we've had a drink or two, I call out to him: "Look," I say, "it may not be proper—after all, we're Jews—to talk about milk and such things while we're eating meat, but I'd like to know your honest opinion: what do you think of *kreplach* with cheese?" He looks at me with distrust. "How did we get around to that?" he asks. "Just like this," I explain to him. "I'd like to have you try the cheese *kreplach* that my wife makes—because tonight, you see, we're going to have a dairy supper . . ." This is too much for him, and he comes right back at me with, "Not this time! You're trying to keep me here another day, I can see that. But you can't do it. It isn't right! It isn't right!" And from the way he fusses and fumes it's easy to see that I won't have to coax him too long, or fight with him either, because what is he but a man with an appetite, who has only one philosophy, which he practices at the table? So I say this to him: "I give you my word of honor, and if that isn't enough, I'll give you my hand as well—here, shake—that tomorrow I'll wake you up in time for the earliest train. I promise it, even if the world turns upside down. If I don't, may I—you know what!" At this he softens and says to me: "Remember, we're shaking hands on that!" And I: "A promise is a promise." And my wife makes a dairy supper—how can I describe it to you? With such *kreplach* that my traveler has to admit that it was all true: he has a wife too, and she makes *kreplach* too, but how can you compare hers with these? It's like night to day!

And I kept my word, because a promise is a promise. I woke him when it was still dark, and started the samovar. He finished packing and began to say goodbye to me and the rest of the household in a very handsome, friendly style. You could see he was a gentleman. But I interrupt him: "We'll say goodbye a little later. First, we have to settle up." "What do you mean—settle up?" "Settle up," I say, "means to add up the figures. That's what I'm going to do now. I'll add them up, let you know what it comes to, and you will be so kind as to pay me."

His face flames red. "Pay you?" he shouts. "Pay you for what?" "For what?" I repeat. "You want to know for what? For everything. The food, the drink, the lodging." This time he becomes white—not red—and he says to me: "I don't understand you at all. You came and invited me to the *bris*. You stopped me at the train. You took my bag away from me. You promised me eternal life." "That's right," I interrupt him. "That's right. But what's one thing got to do with the other? When you came to the *bris* you earned your reward in heaven. But food and drink and lodging—do I have to give you these things for nothing? After all, you're a businessman, aren't you? You should understand that fish costs money, and that the wine you drank was the very best, and the beer, too, and the cherry cider. And you remember how you praised the *tzimmes* and the puddings and the borsht. You remember how you licked your fingers. And the cheese *kreplach* smelled pretty good to you, too. Now, I'm glad you enjoyed these things; I don't begrudge you that in the least. But certainly you wouldn't expect that just because you earned a reward in heaven, and enjoyed yourself in the bargain, that *I* should pay for it?" My traveling friend was really sweating; he looked as if he'd have a stroke. He began to throw himself around, yell, scream, call for help. "This is Sodom!" he cried. "Worse than Sodom! It's the worst outrage the world has ever heard of! How much do you want?" Calmly I took a piece of paper and a pencil and began to add it up. I itemized everything, I gave him an inventory of everything he ate, of every hour he spent in my place. All in all it added up to something like thirty-odd *rubles* and some *kopeks*—I don't remember it exactly.

When he saw the total, my good man went green and yellow, his hands shook, and his eyes almost popped out, and again he let out a yell, louder than before. "What did I fall into—a nest of thieves? Isn't there a single human being here? Is there a God anywhere?" So I say to him, "Look, sir, do you know what? Do you know what you're yelling about? Do you have to eat your heart out? Here is my suggestion: let's ride into town together—it's not far from here —and we'll find some people—there's a rabbiner there— let's ask the rabbi. And we'll abide by what he says." When

he heard me talk like that, he quieted down a little. And—
don't worry—we hired a horse and wagon, climbed in, and
rode off to town, the two of us, and went straight to the
rabbi.

When we got to the rabbi's house, we found him just
finishing his morning prayers. He folded up his prayer shawl
and put his philacteries away. "Good morning," we said to
him, and he: "What's the news today?" The news? My
friend tears loose and lets him have the whole story—everything from A to Z. He doesn't leave a word out. He tells
how he stopped at the station, and so on and so on, and
when he's through he whips out the bill I had given him
and hands it to the rabbi. And when the rabbi had heard
everything, he says: "Having heard one side I should now
like to hear the other." And turning to me, he asks, "What
do you have to say to all that?" I answer: "Everything he
says is true. There's not a word I can add. Only one thing
I'd like to have him tell you—on his word of honor: did he
eat the fish, and did he drink the beer and cognac and the
cider, and did he smack his lips over the borsht that my wife
made?" At this the man becomes almost frantic, he jumps
and he thrashes about like an apoplectic. The rabbi begs
him not to boil like that, not to be so angry, because anger
is a grave sin. And he asks him again about the fish and the
borsht and the *kreplach,* and if it was true that he had drunk
not only the wine, but beer and cognac and cider as well.
Then the rabbi puts on his spectacles, looks the bill over
from top to bottom, checks every line, and finds it correct!
Thirty-odd *rubles* and some *kopeks,* and he makes his judgment brief: he tells the man to pay the whole thing, and for
the wagon back and forth, and a judgment fee for the rabbi
himself . . .

The man stumbles out of the rabbi's house looking as if
he'd been in a steam bath too long, takes out his purse, pulls
out two twenty-fives and snaps at me: "Give me the change."
"What change?" I ask, and he says: "For the thirty you
charged me—for that bill you gave me." "Bill? What bill?

What thirty are you talking about? What do you think I am,
a highwayman? Do you expect me to take money from you?
I see a man at the railroad station, a total stranger; I take his
bag away from him, and drag him off almost by force to our
own *bris,* and spend a wonderful *Shabbes* with him. So am
I going to charge him for the favor he did me, and for the
pleasure I had?" Now he looks at me as if I really am crazy,
and says: "Then why did you carry on like this? Why did
you drag me to the rabbi?" "Why this? Why that?" I say to
him. "You're a queer sort of person, you are! I wanted to
show you what kind of man our rabbi was, that's all . . ."

When he finished the story, my litigant, Reb Nachman
Lekach, got up with a flourish, and the other three partners
followed him. They buttoned their coats and prepared to
leave. But I held them off. I passed the cigarettes around
again, and said to the storyteller:

"So you told me a story about a rabbi. Now maybe you'll
be so kind as to let me tell you a story—also about a rabbi,
but a much shorter story than the one you told."

And without waiting for a yes or no, I started right in,
and made it brief:

This happened, I began, not so long ago, and in a large
city, on *Yom Kippur* eve. A stranger falls into the town—a
businessman, a traveler, who goes here and there, everywhere, sells merchandise, collects money . . . On this day
he comes into the city, walks up and down in front of the
synagogue, holding his sides with both hands, asks everybody
he sees where he can find the rabbi. "What do you want the
rabbi for?" people ask. "What business is that of yours?" he
wants to know. So they don't tell him. And he asks one
man, he asks another: "Can you tell where the rabbi lives?"
"What do you want the rabbi for?" "What do you care?"
This one and that one, till finally he gets the answer, finds
the rabbi's house, goes in, still holding his sides with both
hands. He calls the rabbi aside, shuts the door, and says,

"Rabbi, this is my story. I am a traveling man, and I have money with me, quite a pile. It's not my money. It belongs to my clients—first to God and then to my clients. It's *Yom Kippur* eve. I can't carry money with me on *Yom Kippur,* and I'm afraid to leave it at my lodgings. A sum like that! So do me a favor—take it, put it away in your strong box till tomorrow night, after *Yom Kippur.*"

And without waiting, the man unbuttons his vest and draws out one pack after another, crisp and clean, the real red, crackling, hundred *ruble* notes!

Seeing how much there was, the rabbi said to him: "I beg your pardon. You don't know me, you don't know who I am." "What do you mean, I don't know who you are? You're a rabbi, aren't you?" "Yes, I'm a rabbi. But I don't know *you* —who you are or what you are." They bargain back and forth. The traveler: "You're a rabbi." The rabbi: "I don't know who you are." And time does not stand still. It's almost *Yom Kippur!* Finally the rabbi agrees to take the money. The only thing is, who should be the witnesses? You can't trust just anyone in a matter like that.

So the rabbi sends for the leading townspeople, the very cream, rich and respectable citizens, and says to them: "This is what I called you for. This man has money with him, a tidy sum, not his own, but first God's and then his clients'. He wants me to keep it for him till after *Yom Kippur.* Therefore I want you to be witnesses, to see how much he leaves with me, so that later—you understand?" And the rabbi took the trouble to count it all over three times before the eyes of the townspeople, wrapped the notes in a kerchief, sealed the kerchief with wax, and stamped his initials on the seal. He passed this from one man to the other, saying, "Now look. Here is my signature, and remember, you're the witnesses." The kerchief with the money in it he handed over to his wife, had her lock it in a chest, and hide the keys where no one could find them. And he himself, the rabbi, went to *shul,* and prayed and fasted as it was ordained, lived through *Yom Kippur,* came home, had a bite to eat, looked

up, and there was the traveler. "Good evening, Rabbi."
"Good evening. Sit down. What can I do for you?" "Nothing. I came for my package." "What package?" "The
money." "What money?" "The money I left with you to
keep for me." "You gave *me* money to keep for you?
When was that?"

The traveler laughs out loud. He thinks the rabbi is joking with him. The rabbi asks: "What are you laughing at?"
And the man says: "It's the first time I met a rabbi who
liked to play tricks." At this the rabbi is insulted. No one,
he pointed out, had ever called him a trickster before. "Tell
me, my good man, what do you want here?"

When he heard these words, the stranger felt his heart
stop. "Why, Rabbi, in the name of all that's holy, do you
want to kill me? Didn't I give you all my money? That is,
not mine, but first God's and then my clients'? I'll remind
you, you wrapped it in a kerchief, sealed it with wax, locked
it in your wife's chest, hid the key where no one could find
it. And here is better proof: there were witnesses, the leading citizens of the city!" And he goes ahead and calls them
all off by name. In the midst of it a cold sweat breaks out on
his forehead, he feels faint, and asks for a glass of water.

The rabbi sends the *shammes* off to the men the traveler
had named—the leading citizens, the flower of the community. They come running from all directions. "What's the
matter? What's happened?" "A misfortune. A plot! A millstone around our necks! He insists that he brought a pile
of money to me yesterday, to keep over *Yom Kippur,* and
that you were witnesses to the act."

The householders look at each other, as if to say: "Here
is where we get a nice bone to lick!" And they fall on the
traveler: how could he do a thing like that? He ought to be
ashamed of himself! Thinking up an ugly plot like that
against their rabbi!

When he saw what was happening, his arms and legs went
limp, he just about fainted. But the rabbi got up, went to
the chest, took out the kerchief and handed it to him.

"What's the matter with you! Here! Here is your money! Take it and count it, see if it's right, here in front of your witnesses. The seal, as you see, is untouched. The wax is whole, just as it ought to be."

The traveler felt as if a new soul had been installed in his body. His hands trembled and tears stood in his eyes.

"Why did you have to do it, Rabbi? Why did you have to play this trick on me? A trick like this."

"I just wanted to show you—the kind—of—leading citizens—we have in our town."

MODERN CHILDREN

Modern children, did you say? Ah, you bring them into the world, sacrifice yourself for them, you slave for them day and night—and what do you get out of it? You think that one way or another it would work out according to your ideas or station. After all, I don't expect to marry them off to millionaires, but then I don't have to be satisfied with just anyone, either. So I figured I'd have at least a little luck with my daughters. Why not? In the first place, didn't the Lord bless me with handsome girls; and a pretty face, as you yourself have said, is half a dowry. And besides, with God's help, I'm not the same Tevye I used to be. Now the best match, even in Yehupetz, is not beyond my reach. Don't you agree with me?

But there is a God in heaven who looks after everything, "a Lord merciful and compassionate" who has His way with me summer and winter, in season and out. And He says to me, "Tevye, don't talk like a fool. Leave the management of the world to Me."

So listen to what can happen in this great world of ours. And to whom does it have to happen? To Tevye, *shlimazl*.

To make a long story short, I had just lost everything I had in a stock market investment I had gotten involved in through that relative of mine, Menachem-Mendel (may his

name and memory be forever blotted out), and I was very
low. It looked as if it was all over with me. No more Tevye,
no more dairy business.

"Fool," my wife says to me. "You have worried enough.
You'll get nowhere worrying. You'll just eat your heart out.
Pretend that robbers had broken in and taken everything
away . . . I'll tell you what," she says to me. "Go out for
a while. Go see Lazer-Wolf, the butcher, at Anatevka. He
wants to see you about something very important."

"What's the matter?" I asked. "What is he so anxious to
see me about? If he is thinking of that milch cow of ours,
let him take a stick and knock that idea out of his head."

"What are you so anxious about her for?" she says to me.
"The milk that we get out of her, or the cheese or butter?"

"I'm not thinking about that," I answer. "It's just the idea.
It would be a sin to give the poor thing away to be slaughtered. You can't do that to a living creature. It is written in
the Bible . . ."

"Oh, enough of that!" she comes back at me. "The whole
world knows already that you're a man of learning! You do
what I tell you. You go over and see Lazer-Wolf. Every
Thursday when our Tzeitl goes there for meat, he won't
leave her alone. 'You tell your father,' he keeps saying, 'to
come and see me. It's important.' "

Well, once in a while you have to obey your wife. So I
let her talk me into it, and I go over to Anatevka, about
three miles away. He wasn't home. "Where can he be?" I
ask a snubnosed woman who is bustling around the place.

"They're slaughtering today," says the woman, "and he
went down to bring an ox. He'll be coming back pretty
soon."

So I wait. And while I'm waiting I look around the house
a little. And from what I see, it looks as if Lazer-Wolf has
been a good provider. There is a cupboard filled with cop-
perware—at least a hundred and fifty *rubles'* worth; a couple
of samovars, some brass trays, silver candlesticks and gilded

goblets. And a fancy *Hannukah* lamp and some trinkets made of porcelain and silver and everything.

"Lord Almighty!" I think to myself. "If I can only live to see things like that at my children's homes . . . What a lucky fellow he is—such wealth, and nobody to support! Both his children are married, and he himself is a widower . . ."

Well, at last the door opens and in stamps Lazer-Wolf.

"Well, Reb Tevye," he says. "What's the matter? Why is it so hard to get hold of you? How goes it?"

"How should it go?" I say to him. "I go and I go, and I get nowhere. 'Neither gold nor health nor life itself,' as the *Torah* says."

"Don't complain, Reb Tevye," he answers me. "Compared with what you were when I first knew you, you're a rich man today."

"May we both have what I still need to make me a rich man," I say. "But I am satisfied, thank God. '*Abracadabra askakudra*,' as the *Talmud* says."

"You're always there with a line of *Talmud*," he comes back. "What a lucky man you are, Reb Tevye, to know all these things. But what does all that wisdom and knowledge have to do with us? We have other things to talk about. Sit down, Tevye." He lets out a yell, "Let's have some tea!" And as if by magic the snubnosed woman appears, snatches the samovar, and is off to the kitchen.

"Now that we are alone," he says to me, "we can talk business. Here is the story. I've been wanting to talk to you for a long time. I tried to reach you through your daughter. How many times have I begged you to come? You understand, I've been casting an eye . . ."

"I know," I say, "that you have been casting an eye on her, but it's no use. Your pains are wasted, Reb Lazer-Wolf. There's no use talking about it."

"Why not?" he asks, with a frightened look.

"Why yes?" says I. "I can wait. I'm in no hurry. My house isn't on fire."

"But why should you wait, if you can arrange it now?"

"Oh, that's not important," I say. "Besides, I feel sorry for the poor thing."

"Look at him," says Lazer-Wolf with a laugh. "He feels sorry for her . . . If somebody heard you, Reb Tevye, he'd have sworn that she was the only one you had. It seems to me that you have a few more without her."

"Does it bother you if I keep them?" I say. "If anyone is jealous . . ."

"Jealous? Who is talking of jealousy?" he cries. "On the contrary, I know they're superior, and that is exactly why —you understand? And don't forget, Reb Tevye, that you can get something out of it too!"

"Of course . . . I know all a person can get from you . . . A piece of ice—in winter. We've known that from way back."

"Forget it," he says to me, sweet as sugar. "That was a long time ago. But now—after all—you and I—we're practically in one family, aren't we?"

"Family? What kind of family? What are you talking about, Reb Lazer-Wolf?"

"You tell me, Reb Tevye. I'm beginning to wonder . . ."

"What are you wondering about? We're talking about my milch cow. The one you want to buy from me."

Lazer-Wolf throws back his head and lets out a roar. "That's a good one!" he howls at me. "A cow! And a milch cow at that!"

"If not the cow," I say, "then what *were* we talking about? You tell me so I can laugh too."

"Why, about your daughter. We were talking about your daughter Tzeitl the whole time. You know, Reb Tevye, that I have been a widower for quite a while now. So I thought, why do I have to go looking all over the world—get mixed up with matchmakers, those sons of Satan? Here we both are. I know you, you know me. It's not like running after a stranger. I see her in my shop every Thursday. She's made a good impression on me. I've talked with her a few times.

She looks like a nice, quiet girl. And as for me—as you see
for yourself—I'm pretty well off. I have my own house. A
couple of stores, some hides in the attic, a little money in
the chest. I live pretty well . . . Look, Tevye, why do we
have to do a lot of bargaining, try to impress each other,
bluff each other? Listen to me. Let's shake hands on it and
call it a match."

Well, when I heard that I just sat and stared. I couldn't
say a word. All I could think was: Lazer-Wolf . . . Tzeitl
. . . He had children as old as she was. But then I reminded
myself: what a lucky thing for her. She'll have everything
she wants. And if he is not so good-looking? There were
other things besides looks. There was only one thing I really
had against him: he could barely read his prayers. But then,
can everybody be a scholar? There are plenty of wealthy
men in Anatevka, in Mazapevka, and even in Yehupetz who
don't know one letter from another. Just the same, if it's
their luck to have a little money they get all the respect and
honor a man could want. As the saying goes, "There's learning in a strongbox, and wisdom in a purse . . ."

"Well, Reb Tevye," he says. "Why don't you say something?"

"What do you want me to do? Yell out loud?" I ask
mildly, as if not wanting to look anxious. "You understand,
don't you, that this is something a person has to think over.
It's no trifle. She's my eldest child."

"All the better," he says. "Just because she is your eldest
. . . That will give you a chance to marry off your second
daughter, too, and then, in time with God's help, the third.
Don't you see?"

"Amen. The same to you," I tell him. "Marrying them off
is no trick at all. Just let the Almighty send each one her
predestined husband."

"No," he says. "That isn't what I mean. I mean something
altogether different. I mean the dowry. That you won't need
for her. And her clothes I'll take care of too. And maybe
you'll find something in your own purse besides . . ."

"Shame on you!" I shout at him. "You're talking just as if you were in the butcher shop. What do you mean—my purse? Shame! My Tzeitl is not the sort that I'd have to sell for money!"

"Just as you say," he answers. "I meant it all for the best. If you don't like it, let's forget it. If you're happy without that, I'm happy too. The main thing is, let's get it done with. And I mean right away. A house must have a mistress. You know what I mean . . ."

"Just as you say," I agree. "I won't stand in your way. But I have to talk it over with my wife. In affairs like this she has her say. It's no trifle. As Rashi says, 'A mother is not a dust rag.' Besides, there's Tzeitl herself to be asked. How does the saying go? 'All the kinsmen were brought to the wedding—and the bride was left home . . .' "

"What foolishness!" says Lazer-Wolf. "Is this something to *ask* her about? *Tell* her, Reb Tevye! Go home. Tell her what is what, and get the wedding canopy ready."

"No, Reb Lazer-Wolf," I say. "That's not the way you treat a young girl."

"All right," he says. "Go home and talk it over. But first, Reb Tevye, let's have a little drink. How about it?"

"Just as you say," I agree. "Why not? How does the saying go? 'Man is human—and a drink is a drink.' There is," I tell him, "a passage in the *Talmud* . . ." And I give him a passage. I don't know myself what I said. Something from the *Song of Songs* or the *Hagadah* . . .

Well, we took a drop or two—as it was ordained. In the meantime the woman had brought in the samovar and we made ourselves a glass or two of punch, had a very good time together, exchanged a few toasts—talked—made plans for the wedding—discussed this and that—and then back to the wedding.

"Do you realize, Reb Lazer-Wolf, what a treasure she is?"

"I know . . . Believe me, I know . . . If I didn't I would never have suggested anything . . ."

And we both go on shouting. I: "A jewel! A diamond! I

hope you'll know how to treat her! Not like a butcher . . ."

And he: "Don't worry, Reb Tevye. What she'll eat in my house on weekdays she never had in your house on holidays."

"Tut, tut," I said. "Feeding a woman isn't everything. The richest man in the world doesn't eat five-*ruble* gold pieces, and a pauper doesn't eat stones. You're a coarse fellow, Lazer-Wolf. You don't even know how to value her talents —her baking—her cooking! Ah, Lazer-Wolf! The fish she makes! You'll have to learn to appreciate her!"

And he: "Tevye, pardon me for saying it, but you're somewhat befuddled. You don't know your man. You don't know me at all . . ."

And I: "Put gold on one scale and Tzeitl on the other . . . Do you hear, Reb Lazer-Wolf, if you had a million *rubles,* you wouldn't be worth her little finger."

And he again: "Believe me, Tevye, you're a big fool, even if you are older than I am."

We yelled away at each other that way for a long time, stopping only for a drink or two, and when I came home it was late at night and my feet felt as if they had been shackled. And my wife, seeing right away that I was tipsy, gave me a proper welcome.

"Sh . . . Golde, control yourself," I say to her cheerfully, almost ready to start dancing. "Don't screech like that, my soul. We have congratulations coming."

"Congratulations? For what? For having sold that poor cow to Lazer-Wolf?"

"Worse than that," I say.

"Traded her for another one? And outsmarted Lazer-Wolf —poor fellow?"

"Still worse."

"Talk sense," she pleads. "Look, I have to haggle with him for every word."

"Congratulations, Golde," I say once more. "Congratulations to both of us. Our Tzeitl is engaged to be married."

"If you talk like that then I know you're drunk," she says.

"And not slightly, either. You're out of your head. You must have found a real glassful somewhere."

"Yes. I had a glass of whisky with Lazer-Wolf, and I had some punch with Lazer-Wolf, but I'm still in my right senses. Lo and behold, Golde darling, our Tzeitl has really and truly and officially become betrothed to Lazer-Wolf himself."

And I tell her the whole story from start to finish, how and what and when and why. Everything we discussed, word for word.

"Do you hear, Tevye," my wife finally says, "my heart told me all along that when Lazer-Wolf wanted to see you it was for something. Only I was afraid to think about it. Maybe nothing would come of it. Oh, dear God, I thank Thee, I thank Thee, Heavenly Father . . . May it all be for the best. May she grow old with him in riches and honor—not like that first wife of his, Fruma-Sarah, whose life with him was none too happy. She was, may she forgive me for saying it, an embittered woman. She couldn't get along with anybody. Not at all like our Tzeitl . . . Oh, dear God, I thank Thee, dear God . . . Well, Tevye, didn't I tell you, you simpleton . . . Did you have to worry? If a thing has to happen it will happen . . ."

"I agree with you," said I. "There is a passage in the *Talmud* that covers that very point . . ."

"Don't bother me with your passages," she said. "We've got to get ready for the wedding. First of all, make out a list for Lazer-Wolf of all the things Tzeitl will need. She doesn't have a stitch of underwear, not even a pair of stockings. And as for clothes, she'll need a silk dress for the wedding, and a cotton one for summer, a woolen one for winter, and petticoats, and cloaks—she should have at least two— one, a fur-lined cloak for weekdays and a good one with a ruffle for Saturdays. And how about a pair of button-shoes and a corset, gloves, handkerchiefs, a parasol, and all the other things that a girl nowadays has to have?"

"Where, Golde, darling, did you get acquainted with all these riggings?" I ask her.

"Why not?" says she. "Haven't I ever lived among civilized people? And didn't I see, back in Kasrilevka, how ladies dressed themselves? You let me do all the talking with him myself. Lazer-Wolf, is, after all, a man of substance. He won't want everybody in the family to come bothering him. Let's do it properly. If a person has to eat pork, let him eat a bellyful . . ."

So we talked and we talked till it was beginning to get light. "My wife," I said, "it's time to get the cheese and butter together so I can start for Boiberik. It is all very wonderful indeed, but you still have to work for a living."

And so, when it was still barely light I harnessed my little old horse and went off to Boiberik. When I got to the Boiberik marketplace—Oho! Can a person ever keep a secret? Everybody knew about it already, and I was congratulated from all sides. "Congratulations, congratulations! Reb Tevye, when does the wedding come off?"

"The same to you, the same to you," I tell them. "It looks as if the saying is right: 'The father isn't born yet and the son is dancing on the rooftops . . .'"

"Forget about that!" they cry out. "You can't get away with that! What we want is treats. Why, how lucky you are, Reb Tevye! An oil well! A gold mine!"

"The well runs dry," I tell them, "and all that's left is a hole in the ground."

Still, you can't be a hog and leave your friends in the lurch. "As soon as I'm through delivering I'll be back," I tell them. "There'll be drinks and a bite to eat. Let's enjoy ourselves. As the Good Book says, 'Even a beggar can celebrate.'"

So I got through with my work as fast as I could and joined the crowd in a drink or two. We wished each other good luck as people do, and then I got back into my cart and started for home again, happy as could be. It was a beautiful summer day, the sun was hot, but on both sides of the road there was shade, and the odor of the pines was wonderful. Like a prince I stretched myself out in the wagon and eased up on the reins. "Go along," I said to the little old horse, "go your own way. You ought to know it by now." And myself, I clear my throat and start off on some of the old tunes. I am in a holiday mood, and the songs I sing are those of *Rosh Hashono* and *Yom Kippur*. As I sing I look up at the sky but my thoughts are concerned with things below. The heavens are the Lord's, but the earth He gave to the Children of Adam, for them to brawl around in, to live in such luxury that they have time to tear each other apart for this little honor or that . . . They don't even understand how one ought to praise the Lord for the good things that He gives them . . . But we, the poor people, who do not live in idleness and luxury, give us but one good day and we thank the Lord and praise Him; we say, *"Ohavti, I love Him"* —the Highest One—*"for He hears my voice and my prayer, He inclines His ear to me . . . For the waves of death compassed me, the floods of Belial assailed me . . ."* Here a cow falls down and is injured, there an ill wind brings a kinsman of mine, a good-for-nothing, a Menachem-Mendel from Yehupetz who takes away my last penny; and I am sure that the world has come to an end—there is no truth or justice left anywhere on earth . . . But what does the Lord do? He moves Lazer-Wolf with the idea of taking my daughter Tzeitl without even a dowry . . . And therefore I give thanks to Thee, dear God, again and again, for having looked upon Tevye and come to his aid . . . I shall yet have joy. I shall know what it is to visit my child and find her a mistress of a well-stocked home, with chests full of linens, pantries full of chicken fat and preserves, coops full of chickens, geese and ducks . . .

Suddenly my horse dashes off downhill, and before I can lift my head to look around I find myself on the ground with all my empty pots and crocks and my cart on top of me! With the greatest difficulty I drag myself out from under and pull myself up, bruised and half-dead, and I vent my wrath on the poor little horse. "Sink into the earth!" I shout. "Who asked you to show that you know how to run? You almost ruined me altogether, you devil!" And I gave him as much as he could take. You could see that he realized he had gone a little too far. He stood there with his head down, humble, ready to be milked . . . Still cursing him, I turn the cart upright, gather up my pots, and off I go. A bad omen, I tell myself, and I wonder what new misfortunes might be awaiting me . . .

That's just how it was. About a mile farther on, when I'm getting close to home, I see someone coming toward me. I drive up closer, look, and see that it's Tzeitl. At the sight of her my heart sinks, I don't know why. I jump down from the wagon.

"Tzeitl, is that you? What are you doing here?"

She falls on my neck with a sob. "My daughter, what are you crying about?" I ask her.

"Oh," she cries, "Father, Father!" And she is choked with tears.

"What is it, daughter? What's happened to you?" I say, putting my arm around her, patting and kissing her.

"Father, Father, have pity on me. Help me . . ."

"What are you crying for?" I ask, stroking her head. "Little fool, what do you have to cry for? For heaven's sake," I say, "if you say *no* it's *no*. Nobody is going to force you. We meant it for the best, we did it for your own sake. But if it doesn't appeal to you, what are we going to do? Apparently it was not ordained . . ."

"Oh, thank you, Father, thank you," she cries, and falls on my neck again and dissolves in tears.

"Look," I say, "you've cried enough for one day . . . Even eating pastry becomes tiresome . . . Climb into the wagon and let's go home. Lord knows what your mother will be thinking."

So we both get into the cart and I try to calm her down. I tell her that we had not meant any harm to her.

God knows the truth: all we wanted was to shield our daughter from poverty. "So it was not meant," I said, "that you should have riches, all the comforts of life; or that we should have a little joy in our old age after all our hard work, harnessed, you might say, day and night to a wheel-barrow—no happiness, only poverty and misery and bad luck over and over . . ."

"Oh, Father," she cries, bursting into tears again. "I'll hire myself out as a servant. I'll carry rocks. I'll dig ditches . . ."

"What are you crying for, silly child?" I say. "Am I forcing you? Am I complaining? It's just that I feel so wretched that I have to get it off my chest; so I talk it over with Him, with the Almighty, about the way He deals with me. He is, I say, a merciful Father, He has pity on me, but He shows me what He can do, too; and what can I say? Maybe it has to be that way. He is high in heaven, high up, and we are here below, sunk in the earth, deep in the earth. So we must say that He is right and His judgment is right; because if we want to look at it the other way round, who am I? A worm that crawls on the face of the earth, whom the slightest breeze—if God only willed it—could annihilate in the blink of an eye. So who am I to stand up against Him with my little brain and give Him advice on how to run this little world of His? Apparently if He ordains it this way, it has to be this way. What good are complaints? Forty days before you were conceived, the Holy Book tells us, an angel appeared and decreed: 'Let Tevye's daughter Tzeitl take Getzel, the son of Zorach, as her husband; and let Lazer-Wolf the butcher go elsewhere to seek his mate.' And to you, my child, I say this: May God send you your predestined one, one worthy of you, and may he come soon, Amen. And I hope your mother doesn't yell too much. I'll get enough from her as it is."

Well, we came home at last. I unharnessed the little horse and sat down on the grass near the house to think things over, think up some fantastic tale to tell my wife. It was late, the sun was setting; in the distance frogs were croaking; the old horse, tied to a tree, was nibbling at the grass; the cows, just come from pasture, waited in the stalls to be milked. All around me was the heavenly smell of the fresh grass—like the Garden of Eden. I sat there thinking it all over . . . How cleverly the Eternal One has created this little world of His, so that every living thing, from man to a simple cow, must earn its food. Nothing is free. If you, little cow, wish to eat—then go, let yourself be milked, be the means of livelihood for a man and his wife and children. If you, little horse, wish to chew—then run back and forth every day with the milk to Boiberik. And you, Man, if you want a piece of bread—go labor, milk the cows, carry the pitchers, churn the butter, make the cheese, harness your horse, drag yourself every dawn to the *datchas* of Boiberik, scrape and bow to the rich ones of Yehupetz, smile at them, cater to them, ingratiate yourself with them, see to it that they are satisfied, don't do anything to hurt their pride . . . Ah, but there still remains the question: *Mah nishtano?* Where is it written that Tevye must labor in their behalf, must get up before daybreak when God Himself is still asleep, just so that they can have a fresh piece of cheese, and butter for their breakfasts? Where is it written that I must rupture myself for a pot of thin gruel, a loaf of barley bread, while they—the rich ones of Yehupetz—loll around in their summer homes without so much as lifting a hand, and are served roast ducks and the best of *knishes, blintzes* and *vertutin?* Am I not a man as they are? Would it be a sin, for instance, if Tevye could spend one summer himself in a *datcha* somewhere? But then—where would people get cheese and butter? Who would milk the cows? The Yehupetz aristocrats, maybe? And at the very thought of it I burst out laughing. It's like the old saying: "If God listened to every fool what a different world it would be!"

And then I heard someone call out, "Good evening, Reb Tevye." I looked up and saw a familiar face—Motel Kamzoil, a young tailor from Anatevka.

"Well, well," I say, "you speak of the Messiah and look

who's here! Sit down, Motel, on God's green earth. And what brings you here all of a sudden?"

"What brings me here?" he answers. "My two feet."

And he sits down on the grass near me and looks off toward the barn where the girls are moving about with their pots and pitchers. "I have been wanting to come here for a long time, Reb Tevye," he says at last, "only I never seem to have the time. You finish one piece of work and you start the next. I work for myself now, you know, and there is plenty to do, praise the Lord. All of us tailors have as much as we can do right now. It's been a summer of weddings. Everybody is marrying off his children—everybody, even the widow Trihubecha."

"Everybody," I say. "Everybody except Tevye. Maybe I am not worthy in the eyes of the Lord."

"No," he answers quickly, still looking off where the girls are. "You're mistaken, Reb Tevye. If you only wanted to you could marry off one of your children, too. It all depends on you . . ."

"So?" I ask. "Maybe you have a match for Tzeitl?"

"A perfect fit!" the tailor answers.

"And," I ask, "is it a good match at least?"

"Like a glove!" he cries in his tailor's language, still looking off at the girls.

I ask, "In whose behalf is it then that you come? If he smells of a butcher shop I don't want to hear another word!"

"God forbid!" he says. "He doesn't begin to smell of a butcher shop!"

"And you really think he's a good match?"

"There never was such a match!" he answers promptly. "There are matches and matches, but this one, I want you to know, was made exactly to measure!"

"And who, may I ask, is the man? Tell me!"

"Who is it?" he says, still looking over yonder. "Who is it? Why, me—myself!"

When he said that I jumped up from the ground as if I'd

been scalded, and he jumped too, and there we stood facing each other like bristling roosters. "Either you're crazy," I say to him, "or you're simply out of your mind! What are you— everything? The matchmaker, the bridegroom, the ushers all rolled into one? I suppose you'll play the wedding march too! I've never heard of such a thing—arranging a match for oneself!"

But he doesn't seem to listen. He goes right on talking.

"Anyone who thinks I'm crazy is crazy himself! No, Reb Tevye, I have all my wits about me. A person doesn't have to be crazy in order to want to marry your Tzeitl. For example, the richest man in our town—Lazer-Wolf, the butcher—wanted her too. Do you think it's a secret? The whole town knows it. And as for being my own match- maker, I'm surprised at you! After all, Reb Tevye, you're a man of the world. If a person sticks his finger in your mouth you know what to do! So what are we arguing about? Here is the whole story: your daughter Tzeitl and I gave each other our pledge more than a year ago now that we would marry . . ."

If someone had stuck a knife into my heart it would have been easier to endure than these words. In the first place, how does a stitcher like Motel fit into the picture as my son- in-law? And in the second place, what kind of words are these, "We gave each other our pledge that we would marry?" And where do I come in? . . . I ask him bluntly, "Do I still have the right to say something about my daugh- ter, or doesn't anyone have to ask a father any more?"

"On the contrary," says Motel, "that's exactly why I came to talk with you. I heard that Lazer-Wolf has been discussing a match, and I have loved her now for over a year. More than once I have wanted to come and talk it over with you, but every time I put it off a little. First, till I had saved up a few *rubles* for a sewing machine, and then till I got some decent clothes. Nowadays almost everybody has to have two suits and a few good shirts . . ."

"You and your shirts!" I yell at him. "What childish nonsense is this? And what do you intend to do after you're
married? Support your wife with shirts?"

"Why," he says, "why, I'm surprised at you, Reb Tevye!
From what I hear, when you got married you didn't have
your own brick mansion either, and nevertheless here you
are . . . In any case, if the whole world gets along, I'll get
along, too. Besides, I have a trade, haven't I?"

To make a long story short, he talked me into it. For after
all—why should we fool ourselves?—how do all Jewish children get married? If we began to be too particular, then no
one in our class would ever get married at all . . . There
was only one thing still bothering me, and that I still
couldn't understand. What did they mean—pledging their
troth? What kind of world has this become? A boy meets a
girl and says to her, "Let us pledge our troth." Why, it's
just too free-and-easy, that's all!

But when I looked at this Motel standing there with his
head bent like a sinner, I saw that he was not trying to get
the best of anybody, and I thought: "Now, what am I becoming so alarmed about? What am I putting on such airs
for? What is my own pedigree? Reb Tzotzel's grandchild!
And what huge dowry can I give my daughter—and what
fine clothes? So maybe Motel Kamzoil is only a tailor, but
at the same time he is a good man, a worker; he'll be able to
make a living. And besides, he's honest too. So what have I
got against him?"

"Tevye," I say to myself, "don't think up any childish arguments. Let them have their way." Yes . . . but what am I
going to do about my Golde? I'll have plenty on my hands
there. She'll be hard to handle. How can I make her think
it's all right? . . .

"You know what, Motel," I said to the young suitor. "You
go home. I'll straighten everything out here. I'll talk it over
with this one and that one. Everything has to be done right.
And tomorrow morning, if you haven't changed your mind
by that time, maybe we'll see each other."

"Change my mind!" he yells at me. "You expect me to change my mind? If I do, I hope I never live to go away from here! May I become a stone, a bone, right here in front of you!"

"What's the use of swearing?" I ask him. "I believe you without the oath. Go along, Motel. Good night. And may you have pleasant dreams."

And I myself go to bed, too. But I can't sleep. My head is splitting. I think of one plan and then another, till at last I come upon the right one. And what is that? Listen, I'll tell you . . .

It's past midnight. All over the house we're sound asleep. This one is snoring, that one is whistling. And suddenly I sit up and let out a horrible yell, as loud as I can: "Help! Help! Help!" It stands to reason that when I let out this yell everybody wakes up, and first of all—Golde.

"May God be with you, Tevye," she gasps, and shakes me. "Wake up! What's the matter with you? What are you howling like this for?"

I open my eyes, look around to see where I am, and call out in terror, "Where is she? Where is she?"

"Where is who?" asks Golde. "What are you talking about?"

I can hardly answer. "Fruma-Sarah. Fruma-Sarah, Lazer-Wolf's first wife . . . She was standing here a minute ago."

"You're out of your head," my wife says to me. "May God save you, Tevye. Do you know how long Fruma-Sarah has been dead?"

"I know that she's dead," I say, "but just the same she was here just a minute ago, right here by the bed, talking to me. Then she grabbed me by the windpipe and started to choke me . . ."

"What on earth is the matter with you, Tevye?" says my wife. "What are you babbling about? You must have been dreaming. Spit three times and tell me what you dreamt, and I'll tell you what it meant."

"Long may you live, Golde," I tell her. "It's lucky you

woke me up or I'd have died of fright right on the spot.
Get me a drink of water and I'll tell you my dream. Only I
beg you, Golde, don't become frightened: the Holy Books
tell us that sometimes only three parts of a dream come true,
and the rest means nothing. Absolutely nothing. Well, here
is my dream . . .

"In the beginning I dreamt that we were having a celebration of some kind, I don't know what. Either an engagement or a wedding. The house was crowded. All the men
and women we knew were there—the *rov* and the *shochet*
and everybody. And musicians, too . . . In the midst of the
celebration the door opens, and in comes your grandmother
Tzeitl, may her soul rest in peace . . ."

"Grandmother Tzeitl!" my wife shouts, turning pale as a
sheet. "How did she look? How was she dressed?"

"How did she look?" I say . . . "May our enemies look
the way she looked. Yellow. A waxen yellow. And she was
dressed—how do you expect?—in white. A shroud. She came
up to me. 'Congratulations,' she said, 'I am so happy that you
picked such a fine young man for your Tzeitl who bears my
name. He's a fine, upstanding lad—this Motel Kamzoil . . .
He was named after my uncle Mordecai, and even if he is a
tailor he's still an honest boy . . .'"

"A tailor!" gasps Golde. "Where does a tailor come into
our family? In our family we have had teachers, cantors,
shamosim, undertakers' assistants, and other kinds of poor
people. But a tailor—never!"

"Don't interrupt me, Golde," I tell her. "Maybe your
grandmother Tzeitl knows better . . . When I heard her
congratulate me like that, I said to her, 'What is that you
said, Grandmother? About Tzeitl's betrothed being a tailor?
Did you say Motel? . . . You mean a butcher, don't you? A
butcher named Lazer-Wolf?'

" 'No,' says your grandmother again. 'No, Tevye. Your
daughter is engaged to Motel, and he's a tailor, and she'll
grow old with him—if the Lord wills—in comfort and
honor.'

" 'But, Grandmother,' I say again, 'what can we do about Lazer-Wolf? Just yesterday I gave him my word . . .'

"I had barely finished saying this when I looked up, and your grandmother Tzeitl is gone. In her place is Fruma-Sarah—Lazer-Wolf's first wife—and this is what she says: 'Reb Tevye, I have always considered you an honest man, a man of learning and virtue. But how does it happen that you should do a thing like this—let your daughter take my place, live in my house, carry my keys, wear my clothes, my jewelry, my pearls?'

" 'Is it my fault,' I ask her, 'if Lazer-Wolf wanted it that way?'

" 'Lazer-Wolf!' she cries. 'Lazer-Wolf will have a terrible fate, and your Tzeitl too, if she marries him. It's a pity, Reb Tevye. I feel sorry for your daughter. She'll live with him no more than three weeks, and when the three weeks are up I'll come to her by night and I'll take her by the throat like this . . .' And with these words Fruma-Sarah grabs me by the windpipe and begins choking me—so hard that if you hadn't waked me up, by now I'd have been—far, far away . . ."

"Ptu, ptu, ptu," spits my wife three times. "It's an evil spirit! May it fall into the river; may it sink into the earth; may it climb into attics; may it lie in the forest—but may it never harm us or our children! May that butcher have a dream like that! A dark and horrible dream! Motel Kamzoil's smallest finger is worth more than all of him, even if Motel is only a tailor; for if he was named after my uncle Mordecai he couldn't possibly have been a tailor by birth. And if my grandmother—may she rest in peace—took the trouble to come all the way from the other world to congratulate us, why, all we can do is say that this is all for the best, and it couldn't possibly be any better. Amen. Selah . . ."

Well, why should I go on and on?

The next day they were engaged, and not long after were

married. And the two of them, praise the Lord, are happy.
He does his own tailoring, goes around in Boiberik from one
datcha to another picking up work; and she is busy day and
night, cooking and baking and washing and tidying and
bringing water from the well . . . They barely make enough
for food. If I didn't bring her some of our cheese and butter
once in a while—or a few *groschen* sometimes—they would
never be able to get by. But if you ask her—my Tzeitl, I
mean—she says everything is as good as it could be. Just let
Motel stay in good health.

So go complain about modern children. You slave for
them, do everything for them! And they tell you that they
know better.

And . . . maybe they do . . .

YOU MUSTN'T WEEP—
IT'S YOM-TEV

I am willing to bet any amount you want that no one in
the world was as happy at the coming of spring as were the
two of us—I, the cantor Peisi's son, Motel, and the neighbor's calf, Meni. (It was I who had given him that name.)
Both of us together had crept out of our narrow winter quarters to greet the first day of spring, both of us together had
felt the warm rays of the sun and together we had smelled
the fresh odors of the newly sprouted grass. I, Motel, the
cantor's son, came out of a cold, damp cellar that smelled of
sour dough and medicine and Meni, the neighbor's calf, was
let out of even the worse stench of a smell, filthy shed with
flimsy walls through whose chinks the snow sifted in winter and the rain beat in summer.

Having escaped into God's free world, the two of us, Meni
and I, began to show our unbounded joy, each in his own
way. I, Motel, the cantor's son, lifted up both my arms above
my head, opened my mouth, and drew in as much of the
fresh warm air as my lungs could contain. And I felt as
though I were growing in height, as though I were drawn up
there into the blue sky where the fleecy clouds drifted, up
there where the birds dipped and rose and were lost to view.
And from my overfilled breast there escaped a song that was

even lovelier than the songs my father used to lead in the synagogue during holidays, a song without words, without notes, without motif—more like the song of a waterfall or the waves of the ocean—a sort of *Song of Songs,* a hymn of praise: "O Father," I sang, "O Heavenly Father . . ."

Meni, the neighbor's calf, showed his joy quite differently. First of all, he buried his black, wet muzzle in the dirt, poked at the earth three or four times with his forepaws, lifted up his tail, reared himself up and let out a loud ma-a-a-a. This sounded so funny to me that I had to burst out laughing and to mimic the ma-a-a-a. The calf apparently was pleased by this, for it was not long before he repeated it all once more with the same intonation and the same leap. Naturally I did it over again, in every detail. This was repeated, several times—I leaped, the calf leaped; the calf let out his ma-a-a-a. I let out a ma-a-a-a. Who knows how long this might have gone on if it hadn't been for my brother Elihu who came up from behind and slapped me sharply across the neck.

"What's the matter with you! A boy like you, almost nine years old, dancing with a calf! Into the house, you good-for-nothing. You'll get it from Father."

Nonsense! My father won't do anything to me. My father is sick. He hasn't led the prayers in the synagogue since the Autumn Festivals. All night long I hear him coughing, and every day the doctor comes to the house. The doctor is a large, heavy-set man with a black mustache and laughing eyes—a cheerful man. He has only one name for me—*Pupik.* Whenever he sees me he pokes me in the belly. He keeps telling my mother not to stuff me with potatoes, and for the patient he prescribes bouillon and milk, milk and bouillon. My mother listens to him quietly and when he is gone she hides her face in her apron and her shoulders shake. Then she wipes her eyes, calls my brother Elihu aside and they whisper in low voices. What they are talking about I do not know, but they seem to be quarreling. My mother wants to send Elihu somewhere and he won't go. He says to

her, "Rather than go to them for help I'd kill myself. I'd
sooner die."

"Bite your tongue," says my mother in a low voice, gritting
her teeth and looking as if she wanted to slap him. But soon
she calms down and pleads with him: "What can I do, my
son? You see how ill he is. We must do something for him."

"Then sell something," says my brother, looking out of the
corners of his eyes at the glass cabinet. My mother follows
his glance, wipes her eyes again and sighs, "What can I sell?
My soul? There is nothing left. Or shall I sell the empty
cabinet?"

"Well, why not?" says my brother.

"Murderer!" cries out my mother. "How did I ever get
such murderers for children?"

My mother fumes and rages, cries her heart out, then
wipes her eyes and forgives him. The same thing also happened with the books, with the silver collar on my father's
tallis, with the two gilded goblets, with my mother's silk dress,
and all the other things which were sold one by one, each
to a different buyer . . .

The books were sold to Michal, the baggage-man, a man
with a thin beard which he was constantly scratching. My
poor brother had to go to him three times before he brought
him to the house. My mother, relieved and happy to see him
at last, put her finger across her lips to show him that he
must speak softly so my father shouldn't hear. Michal understood, raised his eyes to the shelf, scratched his beard and
said to her, "Well, show us, what have you got up there."

My mother beckoned to me to climb up on the table and
take down the books. I didn't have to be told twice. I
jumped up so eagerly that I sprawled over the table and my
brother, snapping at me to stop jumping like a crazy fool,
pushed me aside. He climbed up on the table himself and
handed the books down to Michal who scratched his beard
with one hand, while with the other he leafed through the
books and found fault with each one. This one had a poor

b.nding, that one had a worn back, another was simply worthless. And after he had looked through half of them, examined all the bindings, felt all the backs, he scratched his beard again:

"If it was a complete set of *Mishnayos,* I might consider buying it . . ."

My mother turned pale, and my brother on the contrary became red as fire. He leaped angrily at the baggage-man, "Why didn't you tell us in the beginning that all you wanted to buy were *Mishnayos?* What did you have to come here and take up our time for?"

"Be quiet!" my mother begged him, and a hoarse voice was heard from the next room where my father lay.

"Who is there?"

"Nobody," my mother said and pushing my brother Elihu into my father's room, began to bargain with Michal herself and finally sold him the books, apparently for very little, because when my brother came back again and asked her how much, she pushed him aside, saying, "It's none of your business." And Michal snatched up the books quickly, shoved them into his bag and disappeared.

Of all the things in the house that we sold none gave me as much pleasure as the glass cabinet.

It is true that when they ripped the silver collar off my father's *tallis,* it was a treat, too. First of all there was the bargaining with Yosel the goldsmith, a pale man with a red birthmark on his face. Three times he went away, but in the end he won out, and he sat down crosslegged near the window with my father's *tallis,* took out a small knife with a yellow, bone handle, bent his middle finger and began to rip the collar with such skill that I envied him! And yet you should have seen how my mother carried on. She cried and cried and cried. Even my brother Elihu, who has been confirmed already and is practically a man, ready to be married, turned toward the door and pretended to be blowing his nose.

"What's going on there?" called my father from the sick-room.

"Nothing," my mother answered, wiping her eyes, and her lower lip and the whole lower part of her face trembled so that it was all I could do to keep from laughing.

But how does that compare with the taking away of the glass cabinet?

First of all, how could anybody take it away? I had always taken it for granted that the cabinet was built into the wall, so how could it be moved? And if it was, where would my mother keep the bread and the dishes and the pewter spoons and forks (our two silver spoons and one silver fork, had been sold long ago). And where would we keep the *matzos* at Passover? These thoughts went through my head while Nachman the carpenter was measuring the cabinet with the big red thumbnail of his dirty right hand. He kept insisting that the cabinet wouldn't go through the door. "Here," he said, "is the width of the cabinet, and here is the width of the door—it will never go through here."

"Then how did it ever get in?" asked my brother Elihu.

"Don't ask me," answered Nachman angrily. "Go ask the cabinet. How should I know how it got in?"

For one moment I was really afraid for the cabinet. That is, I was afraid it would remain at our house. But it wasn't long before Nachman returned with his two tall sons, both of them also carpenters, and they took hold of the cabinet as easily as the devil took hold of the *melamed*. First came Nachman, then the two sons, and behind them came I. The father directed them; "Kopel, this way. Mendel, to the right. Kopel, don't rush. Mendel, wait . . ." I imitated the gestures of all three, but my mother and brother refused to have anything to do with it. They stood looking at the empty wall, now covered with cobwebs and wept . . . A regular circus. Always crying. Suddenly we heard a loud crash. Right in the doorway the glass had shattered. The carpenter and his sons began to roar at each other, and curse, each blaming the other for the broken glass. "Graceful as a lead bird!" "Bears' feet." "The devil take you." "Go break your head in hell."

"What's going on there?" a weak voice called from the sick-room.

"Nothing," my mother answered, wiping her eyes.

But these experiences were as nothing compared with the selling of my brother's couch and my cot. My brother's couch was once the sofa we all sat on, but after Elihu became engaged he began to sleep on it, and I inherited his old cot. Long ago when times were good and my father was still well and conducted services in the butchers' synagogue with his choir of four, the sofa still had springs. Now the springs belonged to me. I did all sorts of tricks with them; cut my hands and almost poked my eyes out. One day I put them around my neck and nearly choked to death. Finally, my brother spanked me and threw the springs up into the attic.

It was old Hannah who bought the couch and the cot from us. Before she paid her deposit my mother wouldn't let her look under the covers.

"You can buy what you see in front of you. There is nothing more to look at." But after she had finished bargaining and had given my mother a deposit she went up to the couch and the cot, lifted up the bedclothes, looked slowly into every corner, and spat violently. My mother resented her spitting and was ready to return the money, but my brother Elihu interfered:

"Once you've bought it, it's final."

That night we put the bedclothes on the floor and my brother and I spread ourselves out like lords, covered ourselves with one blanket (his blanket had already been sold) and I was pleased to hear my brother say that sleeping on the floor wasn't so bad. I waited till he had said his prayers and gone to sleep and then I began to roll around on the floor, over and over again. There was plenty of room, praise the Lord. It was like a field, a field in paradise . . .

"What can we do now?" said my mother one morning, as she looked around with a deep frown at the four empty walls. My brother and I followed her glance. Then looking at me with pity in his eyes my brother said sternly:

"Go outside, Motel. We have something to talk about."

I ran out, skipping on one foot. Naturally I went straight to the neighbor's calf. In the last few months Meni had grown into a handsome calf, with a lovely black muzzle, and brown eyes full of understanding. It was always looking for something to eat and liked to have its throat scratched.

"Again. So you're playing with that calf again? You can't stay away from your dear friend?"

It was my brother Elihu speaking, this time without anger, without curses. And taking my hand he led me to Hirsch-Ber the cantor. There, at Hirsch-Ber's, he told me I would be well off. First of all I would have enough to eat. At home things were bad, he said. Our father was very ill: we had to do everything we could for him. And we were doing everything we could. And he unbuttoned his coat and showed me his vest underneath.

"This is where I used to wear my watch," he said. "A gift from my father-in-law and I sold it. If he ever found out—I don't know what he'd do. The world would turn upside down.

"Well, here we are," my brother said, in a friendly tone. Hirsch-Ber the cantor was a good musician. That is, he couldn't sing himself, he had no voice at all, poor fellow (so said my father) but he understood music. He had fifteen boys in his choir and he was a terribly mean master. That much I knew. He listened to me sing one or two pieces with all the frills and flourishes, then patted my head and told my brother that my soprano wasn't bad. Not only wasn't it bad, my brother insisted, but it was excellent. Elihu bargained with him, took a payment, and told me I was going to stay here for a while. He told me to obey Hirsch-Ber and not to get homesick.

It was easy for him to say, "Don't get homesick." But how could I keep from being homesick in the summer time when the sun shone, the sky was clear as crystal, and even the mud had already dried up? In front of our house there was a pile of logs, not ours, but Yossi, the *nogid's*. He was planning to build a dwelling and since he had nowhere to keep the logs he kept them in front of our house. God bless Yossi, the *nogid,* for that. Out of his logs I made myself a fortress. In this fortress I was happy, Meni the calf was happy, we ruled alone here. So how could I keep from being homesick?

I have been at Hirsch-Ber's for three weeks already and I have hardly done any singing at all. I have another job—I take care of his Dobtzie. Dobtzie is a deformed child, a hunchback. She is not quite two, but I have to hold her all the time and she is heavy. It's all I can do to lift her. Dobtzie is fond of me. She puts her thin arms about me and clutches me with her thin fingers. She calls me Kiko—I do not know why. But she loves me. She won't let me sleep at night. "Kiko ki." That means that she wants me to rock her. Dobtzie adores me. When I am eating she tears the food out of my hands. "Kiko pi." That means, "Give it to me." How I long for home. The food is not so wonderful here, either. It's a holiday—*Shevuos* eve. I wish I could go outside and see the heavens split open, as they do on *Shevuos,* but Dobtzie won't let me. Dobtzie loves me too much to let me out of her sight. "Kiko ki." She wants me to stay and rock her. I rock and I rock until I fall asleep. In my sleep a visitor comes to me—Meni, the neighbor's calf. He looks at me with his big eyes, like a human being's and says, "Come." And we both run, downhill to the river. I roll up my pants. Hop! I am in the river. I swim and Meni swims after me. It's lovely on the other side. There is no cantor, no Dobtzie, no sick father. I wake. It was all a dream. Oh, if I could only run away, run away. But how can I run away? Where could I run? Home, of course.

Hirsch-Ber is up already. He tells me to dress quickly and go with him to the synagogue. There is a big morning ahead of us. There are some special pieces to sing today. When we get there I see my brother Elihu. What is he doing here? He usually goes to the butchers' synagogue, where our father is cantor. What does this mean? My brother goes up and talks something over with Hirsch-Ber, who does not seem to be well-pleased. Finally he says, "But remember, bring him back right after dinner."

"Come along," my brother says to me, "you're going home to see Father." And we start to go off together, Elihu walking sedately, and I skipping along.

"What's your hurry?" says my brother, holding me back. He apparently wants to talk to me.

"You know Father is sick. He's very, very sick. God knows what will become of him. We have to save him, but have nothing left and no one wants to help. Mother absolutely won't let him go to the hospital. She will sooner die than let him go there. Here she comes. Be quiet."

With outstretched arms my mother comes to meet me. She falls on my neck and I feel a tear not my own fall on my cheek. My brother Elihu goes inside to my father, and my mother and I remain standing outside. A group of women gather about us—our neighbor's wife, Fat Pessie, and her daughter Mindel and her daughter-in-law Pearl and several others.

"Oh! A guest for *Shevuos*," they say. "May you enjoy his company!"

My mother lowers her tear-swollen eyes. "A guest?" she says. "The child has only come to see his sick father." And then turning to Pessie she adds in a whisper, "A town full of people, but does anyone care? Twenty-three years in one synagogue; he ruined his health. I might still be able to save him, but I have nothing to do it with. We've sold everything, even the pillows. Sent the child out to a cantor. Everything for him. Everything to help him . . ."

While my mother talks I keep turning my head this way and that.

"What are you looking for?" my mother asks.

"What do you suppose?" says Pessie. "He must be looking for the calf." And she turns to me with a strangely pleasant tone in her voice.

"Ah, little one, the calf is gone. We had to sell it to the butcher. What else could we do? It's enough to feed one animal without having two to worry about."

So the calf had become just a mouth to feed!

A strange woman, Pessie. She sticks her nose into everything. She wants to know what we're going to have for dinner.

"Why do you ask?" my mother wants to know.

"Just like that," says Pessie, carelessly, and lifting up her shawl pushes into my mother's hands a bowl of thick cream. My mother shoves it back with both hands.

"For heaven's sake, Pessie, what are you doing? What do you think we are? Beggars? Don't you know us better than that?"

"It's because I do know you," Pessie defends herself. "I'm not giving you anything, just lending it to you. Our cow has been good to us lately. We've had more than we can use. You'll return it some day."

The women talk and I keep thinking of the pile of logs, and my playmate the calf whom I won't see any more. If I weren't ashamed I'd burst out crying.

"If your father asks how you're getting along," my mother tells me, "say, 'God be thanked.'"

My brother explains this further:

"Don't complain about anything to him. Don't tell him any of your childish stories. Just say, 'God be thanked.' Understand?" And with these words my brother Elihu took me into the sick-room to see my father. The table was crowded with jars and bottles and boxes of pills. The air smelled like a druggist's shop. The window was tightly closed. In honor of *Shevuos* the room had been decorated with greens. The floor was covered with sweet-smelling grass. My brother had done it all.

When my father saw me come in he beckoned to me with a long, thin finger. My brother pushed me forward. I could hardly recognize my father. His face was like chalk. His gray hairs shone on his head, each hair singly as if pasted on. His dark eyes were sunken deep into his head. His teeth looked artificial. His neck was so thin that it could barely support his head. He made strange movements with his lips, like a tired swimmer trying to breathe. As I approached the bed he placed his hot, bony fingers on my face, and twisted his mouth into a wan smile that was like the smile of death.

Just then my mother came into the room, followed by the jolly doctor with the big, black mustache. He greeted me like an old friend, poked me in the belly and said cheerfully to my father:

"So you have a guest for *Shevuos!* May you enjoy his company!"

"Thank you," said my mother and beckoned to the doctor to examine the patient and prescribe something for him. The doctor threw the window open and began to scold my brother for keeping it shut. "I've told you a thousand times that a window likes to be kept open."

My brother Elihu pointed at my mother. It was her fault. She wouldn't let him open the window because she was afraid my father would catch cold. My mother motioned to the doctor to hurry and examine the patient, give him something. The doctor calmly took out his big gold watch. I could see my brother staring at it. The doctor saw it, too.

"Do you want to know what time it is? I have four minutes to half past eleven. What do you have?"

"My watch has stopped," said my brother, turning red from the tip of his nose to the backs of his ears.

My mother was becoming restless. She wanted the doctor to hurry up and give something for the patient. But the doctor was in no hurry. He asked my mother all sorts of trivial questions. When was my brother getting married? What did Hirsch-Ber think of my singing? I ought to have a good voice, because a voice is inherited. My mother answered him patiently. Suddenly the doctor turned his chair around and faced my father and took the dry, feverish hand in his.

"Well, Cantor," he said, "how were the Services this *Shevuos?*"

"God be praised," answered my father, with the smile of a ghost.

"That's good. And the coughing? Are you coughing less? Are you sleeping better?" asked the doctor, bending closer.

"No," said my father, barely catching his breath. "On the contrary, I cough as much as ever. I sleep very little. But God be praised. It's *Shevuos*—a holy day. We received the Commandments this day. And we have a guest—a guest for *Shevuos* . . ."

Everyone's eyes were turned on the "guest," and the guest looked down on the floor. His thoughts were elsewhere. They were outdoors with the logs where reeds and stickers grew, with the neighbor's calf that had been like a dear human friend, and now had been sold to the butcher. They were down by the river that tumbled downhill—far from the sick room that smelled like a drugstore.

The bowl of cream that our neighbor Pessie had lent to us was very useful. My brother and I made a feast out of it, both of us dipping chunks of fresh white bread into the chilled sour cream, and finding it very good.

"The only trouble with it is that there isn't enough . . ." said my brother. He was being unusually friendly that day. He didn't even make me go back to Hirsch-Ber right away. He let me play at home a while instead.

"After all, you're a guest here today," he said, and told me I could go outside and play on the logs for a while. But he warned me not to climb too much and tear my best pair of pants. My best pair of pants! That was a good joke. You should have seen those pants. But let's not talk about them . . . Let's talk about Yossi the *nogid's* logs instead. Yossi the *nogid* thought the logs belonged to him. That's what he

thought! Really they were my logs. I made a palace out of
them and a vineyard. I was a prince. The prince walked
proudly in his vineyard, tore up a reed and marched back and
forth with it. Everyone envied me. Even the *nogid's* son, Hennich with the squinting eye, begrudged me my good fortune.
He went by in his shiny new clothes, pointed at my pants and
laughed and squinted his eye and shouted:

"Watch out, you'll be losing something."

"Better run along," I said, "before I call my brother Elihu."

All the little boys were afraid of my brother Elihu. Hennich with his squinting eyes moved off and I was again
alone, once more a prince in his vineyard. What a pity that
Meni couldn't be here with me. He had been sold to the
butcher, said Pessie. Why? To be slaughtered? Was he born
for this—to be slaughtered? For what end is a calf ever born,
and for what end a human being?

Suddenly I hear a terrible screaming and wailing from our
house. I recognize my mother's voice. I look up. People are
running in and out of the house. I continue to lie stretched
out on a log. I feel good. But what's this? Here comes Yossi
the *nogid*. Yossi is the president of the butchers' synagogue
where my father has been cantor for twenty-three years.
Yossi was once a butcher himself, but he now deals in cattle
and furs, and is a rich man, a very, very rich man.

Yossi is waving his arms, shouting angrily at my mother:

"Why wasn't I told that Peisi the cantor was so sick? Why
was everybody so quiet about it?"

"Did you want me to shout?" says my mother, weeping.
"The whole town saw how I struggled, how I tried to save
him. And he wanted to be saved, too . . ."

My mother was unable to say any more. She wrung her
hands and threw her head back. My brother caught her in his
arms.

"Mother, why do you have to explain to him? Mother,
don't forget this is *yom-tev*—it's *Shevuos!* You mustn't
weep! Mother!"

But Yossi continues to shout. "The whole town? Who is

the town? You should have come to me! I'll take care of everything. The funeral, the attendants, the shroud, everything! I'll pay for it all. And if something has to be done for the children, come to me, too, don't be ashamed to come."

But that comforted my mother not at all. She kept on weeping and wailing and fainting in my brother's arms. And my brother, who was almost in tears himself, kept reminding her, "Today is *yom-tev,* Mother! It's *Shevuos,* you mustn't cry, Mother."

And then at once it all became clear to me. My heart shrank. I felt lost. I wanted to burst out crying, and I didn't know for whom. I was so sorry for my mother, I couldn't bear to see her cry like that.

And I left my palace and my vineyard and I came up to her from behind and cried in the same tone as my brother.

"Mother! Today is *yom-tev.* It's *Shevuos,* Mother! You mustn't weep!"

I'M LUCKY—I'M AN ORPHAN

Never before in my life have I been the privileged character I am now. What is the reason for this?

As you know, my father, Peisi the cantor, died the first day of *Shevuos,* and I was left an orphan.

The first day after *Shevuos* my brother and I began to say *kaddish,* the prayer for the dead. It was my brother Elihu who taught me how to say it. My brother Elihu is a devoted brother, but a poor teacher. He is quick tempered and he beats me. Taking the prayer book in his hand, that first day after *Shevuos,* he sat down with me and began to teach me the words: *"Yisgadal v'yiskadash shmei rabo."* He expected me to know it by heart right away. He repeated it with me one time after another from beginning to end and then told me to say it by myself. I tried, but it didn't work.

The first few lines weren't bad, but after that I always got stuck. Every time this happened he prodded me with his elbow, and said my mind must be elsewhere (how did he guess?), that I must be thinking about the calf (how could he know?). But he didn't give up. He repeated it with me once more. I started out like a flash, but again, after a few lines, I got stuck. The words wouldn't come. So he grabbed me by the ear and shouted, "If Father could only get up from his grave now and see what a stupid child he had . . . !"

"Then I wouldn't have to be saying *kaddish* for him!" I said, promptly.

For this I caught a juicy slap on the cheek. Hearing the noise my mother cried out, "God be with you! What are you doing? Whom are you slapping? Have you forgotten that the child is an orphan?"

I sleep with my mother now in the bed my father had slept in—the only piece of furniture left in the house. She lets me have most of the blanket.

"Cover yourself," she says to me, "and go to sleep, my poor little child. You might as well try to sleep; I have no food to give you."

I cover myself with the blanket, but I can't fall asleep. I keep repeating the words of *kaddish* to myself.

I don't go to *cheder* these days. I am not learning anything these days. I don't even pray, I don't sing in the choir.

I'm lucky. I'm an orphan.

Congratulate me. I know the whole *kaddish* by heart now —every bit of it. In the synagogue I stand on a bench and rattle it off without a pause. I have a good singing voice— inherited from my father—a real soprano. All the boys stand around me and envy me. The women weep. Some of the men even give me a *kopek*. Yossi the *nogid's* son, Hennich with the squinting eye (who is by nature very jealous), stands in front of me and sticks out his tongue. He is eager —he is anxious—he is dying—to make me laugh. But just to spite him I won't laugh. One time Aaron the *shammes* caught him at it, and grabbing him by the ear, led him to the door. Served him right!

Since I have to say *kaddish* in the morning and at night, I don't stay with Hirsch-Ber any more, and I don't have to carry Dobtzie around all the time. I am a free man. I spend all day at the river, either fishing or bathing. I have figured out for myself a good way to catch fish. If you like, I'll teach it to you. You take off your shirt, tie your sleeves into knots, and walk slowly through the water up to your neck. You have to keep going a long, long time. When you feel the shirt growing heavy it's a sign that it is full. Then you come out as quickly as you can, and shake out the weeds and mud, and look carefully inside. Tangled in the weeds you will sometimes find a few little tadpoles. These you can throw back; it's a pity to let them die. In the thick mud you may find a leech. These are worth money: for ten you can get three *groschen,* a *kopek* and a half. But it isn't easy work . . . For fish there is no use even looking. At one time there may have been fish in the river, but now there are none. I don't care. I'd be glad enough just to find leeches, but you don't even always find those. This summer I didn't catch a single one.

How my brother Elihu found out that I have been going fishing I don't know. When he did find out he almost pulled my ear off. It was lucky that Fat Pessie, our neighbor, saw him do it. One's own mother couldn't take up for her child any better.

"Is that the way to treat an orphan?" she cried.

My brother Elihu is ashamed and lets go my ear. Everybody takes up for me these days.

I'm lucky. I'm an orphan.

Our neighbor, Fat Pessie, must have fallen in love with me. She goes after my mother and won't stop bothering her. She wants me to go and live at her house.

"Why should it bother you?" she asks. "I have twelve at the table already, so he'll be one more." She almost got my mother to consent that time, but my brother Elihu spoke up.

"Who will keep an eye on him and see that he goes to say *kaddish?*"

"I'll see that he goes," said Pessie. "There, does that satisfy you?"

Pessie is not a rich woman. Her husband is a bookbinder;

his name is Moishe. He is known as a very skilled workman, but being skilled is not enough. You need luck besides. That is what Pessie tells my mother. My mother goes her one better. She says that even to be unlucky, to be a *shlimazl,* you have to have luck. As an example she points at me. Here I am, an orphan—and everybody wants me! There are some people who are willing to keep me for good, but my mother says that as long as she is alive she won't give me up. And she bursts out crying. Later she asks my brother's advice.

"What do you think? Should we let him stay at Pessie's?"

My brother is almost a grown man now. If he weren't, would my mother be asking his advice? With his hand he strokes his chin, as though he had a beard already. He likes to talk like a grown man.

"Let him go. So long as he doesn't become a *sheigetz.*"

And it is agreed that I should live at Pessie's for the time being, provided that I don't become a *sheigetz.* What do they call being a *sheigetz*? To tie a piece of paper to the cat's tail so she'll chase it around and around—that is being a *sheigetz.* Rattling a stick along the fence around the priest's house and making a lot of noise—that is being a *sheigetz.* Pulling the cork out of the water carrier's tank so that half the water runs out—that is being a *sheigetz.*

"It's your luck that you're an orphan!" cries Leibke the water carrier. "If you weren't, I'd break every bone in your body! You can believe me, too!"

I believe him all right, but I also know that he won't touch me. For I am an orphan.

I'm lucky. I'm an orphan.

Our neighbor Pessie told a big lie. She said she feeds twelve at her table, but according to my reckoning I am the fourteenth. She must have forgotten their blind Uncle Boruch. Maybe she didn't count him because he is so old and has no teeth to chew with. I won't argue about that. It is true that he can't chew, but he still knows how to swallow. He swallows like a goose, and grabs all the food he can reach. Everybody grabs there. I grab too, and for that they jump on me. Under the table each one kicks me. The one who kicks the hardest is Vashti. Vashti is a terror. His name is really Hershel, but they call him Vashti. Everyone in this house has a nickname.

You can be sure that there is a reason for each name. Pinny is called "Barrel" because he is round and fat. Haym is rough and shaggy so they call him "Buffalo." Mendel has a pointed nose so they call him "Sharpnose." Feitel is called "Petelili" because he stammers. Berel is never satisfied with one slice of bread smeared with chickenfat; he always says, "Give me more!" In short, everyone in this house has a nickname. Even the cat—poor innocent creature. What harm did she ever do anyone? And yet she has a nickname too. They call her "Feiga-Leah the *shammeste*." Do you want to know why? Because she is fat and Feiga-Leah, the wife of the *shammes,* is also fat. You can't imagine how many times every one of them has been beaten for calling the cat by a human name. But beatings have no effect. Once they have given someone a nickname, the name sticks.

I have a nickname too. Guess what it is . . . "Motel with the Lips." They don't like my lips. They say that when I eat I always smack my lips. I would like to see a person who can eat without smacking his lips! I am not one of those proud people whose feelings are easily hurt, but this nickname I simply can't stand. And just because I can't stand it they keep on teasing me and calling me by it all the time. Nothing can make them stop. First I was "Motel with the Lips," then "The Lips," and finally just "Lippy."

"Lippy, where have you been?"

"Lippy, wipe your nose."

It annoys me and then it hurts me so that I start crying. Seeing me, their father, Pessie's husband, Moishe the book-binder, asks, "Why are you crying?"

I answer, "Why shouldn't I cry? My name is Motel and they call me Lippy."

He asks who called me that, and I say Vashti.

He was going to beat Vashti and Vashti said it wasn't he, it was Barrel. And Barrel said it was Buffalo.

And so it went. One blamed another and the other blamed a third. It was like a circle without an end. At last their father made up his mind. He laid them down one by one and gave each one a good whipping with the cover of a prayerbook.

"You rascals!" he cried. "I'll show you how to make fun of an orphan! The devil take every one of you!"

And so it goes. Everybody comes to my defense. Everybody takes up for me.

I'm lucky. I'm an orphan.

DREYFUS IN KASRILEVKA

I doubt if the Dreyfus case made such a stir anywhere as it did in Kasrilevka.

Paris, they say, seethed like a boiling vat. The papers carried streamers, generals shot themselves, and small boys ran like mad in the streets, threw their caps in the air, and shouted wildly, "Long live Dreyfus!" or "Long live Esterhazy!" Meanwhile the Jews were insulted and beaten, as always. But the anguish and pain that Kasrilevka underwent, Paris will not experience till Judgment Day.

How did Kasrilevka get wind of the Dreyfus case? Well, how did it find out about the war between the English and the Boers, or what went on in China? What do they have to do with China? Tea they got from Wisotzky in Moscow. In Kasrilevka they do not wear the light summer material that comes from China and is called pongee. That is not for their purses. They are lucky if they have a pair of trousers and an undershirt, and they sweat just as well, especially if the summer is a hot one.

So how did Kasrilevka learn about the Dreyfus case? From Zeidel.

Zeidel, Reb Shaye's son, was the only person in town who subscribed to a newspaper, and all the news of the world they learned from him, or rather through him. He read and they interpreted. He spoke and they supplied the commentary. He told what he read in the paper, but they turned it around to suit themselves, because they understood better than he did.

One day Zeidel came to the synagogue and told how in Paris a certain Jewish captain named Dreyfus had been imprisoned for turning over certain government papers to the enemy. This went into one ear and out of the other. Someone remarked in passing, "What won't a Jew do to make a living?"

And another added spitefully, "A Jew has no business climbing so high, interfering with kings and their affairs."

Later when Zeidel came to them and told them a fresh tale, that the whole thing was a plot, that the Jewish Captain Dreyfus was innocent and that it was an intrigue of certain officers who were themselves involved, then the town became interested in the case. At once Dreyfus became a Kasrilevkite. When two people came together, he was the third.

"Have you heard?"

"I've heard."

"Sent away for good."

"A life sentence."

"For nothing at all."

"A false accusation."

Later when Zeidel came to them and told them that there was a possibility that the case might be tried again, that there were some good people who undertook to show the world that the whole thing had been a plot, Kasrilevka began to rock indeed. First of all, Dreyfus was one of *ours*. Secondly, how could such an ugly thing happen in Paris? It didn't do any credit to the French. Arguments broke out everywhere; bets were made. Some said the case would be tried again, others said it would not. Once the decision had been made, it was final. All was lost.

As the case went on, they got tired of waiting for Zeidel

to appear in the synagogue with the news; they began to go
to his house. Then they could not wait that long, and they
began to go along with him to the postoffice for his paper.
There they read, digested the news, discussed, shouted, ges-
ticulated, all together and in their loudest voices. More than
once the postmaster had to let them know in gentle terms
that the postoffice was not the synagogue. "This is not your
synagogue, you Jews. This is not *kahal shermaki*."

They heard him the way Haman hears the *grager* on
Purim. He shouted, and they continued to read the paper
and discuss Dreyfus.

They talked not only of Dreyfus. New people were always coming into the case. First Esterhazy, then Picquart,
then General Mercies, Pellieux Gonse . . .

There were two people whom Kasrilevka came to love
and revere. These were Emile Zola and Labori. For Zola
each one would gladly have died. If Zola had come to
Kasrilevka the whole town would have come out to greet
him, they would have borne him aloft on their shoulders.

"What do you think of his letters?"

"Pearls. Diamonds. Rubies."

They also thought highly of Labori. The crowd delighted
in him, praised him to the skies, and, as we say, licked their
fingers over his speeches. Although no one in Kasrilevka had
ever head him, they were sure he must know how to make a
fine speech.

I doubt if Dreyfus' relatives in Paris awaited his return
from the Island as anxiously as the Jews of Kasrilevka. They
traveled with him over the sea, felt themselves rocking on
the waves. A gale arose and tossed the ship up and down,
up and down, like a stick of wood. "Lord of Eternity,"
they prayed in their hearts, "be merciful and bring him
safely to the place of the trial. Open the eyes of the judges,
clear their brains, so they may find the guilty one and the
while world may know of our innocence. Amen. *Selah*."

The day when the good news came that Dreyfus had arrived was celebrated like a holiday in Kasrilevka. If they had not been ashamed to do so, they would have closed their shops.

"Have you heard?"

"Thank the Lord."

"Ah, I would have liked to have been there when he met his wife."

"And I would have liked to see the children when they were told, 'Your father has arrived.' "

And the women, when they heard the news, hid their faces in their aprons and pretended to blow their noses so no one could see they were crying. Poor as Kasrilevka was, there was not a person there who would not have given his very last penny to take one look at the arrival.

As the trial began, a great excitement took hold of the town. They tore not only the paper to pieces, but Zeidel himself. They choked on their food, they did not sleep nights. They waited for the next day, the next and the next.

Suddenly there arose a hubbub, a tumult. That was when the lawyer, Labori, was shot. All Kasrilevka was beside itself.

"Why? For what? Such an outrage! Without cause! Worse than in Sodom!"

That shot was fired at their heads. The bullet was lodged in their breasts, just as if the assassin had shot at Kasrilevka itself.

"God in Heaven," they prayed, "reveal thy wonders. Thou knowest how if thou wishest. Perform a miracle, that Labori might live."

And God performed the miracle. Labori lived.

When the last day of the trial came, the Kasrilevkites shook as with a fever. They wished they could fall asleep for twenty-four hours and not wake up till Dreyfus was declared a free man.

But as if in spite, not a single one of them slept a wink that night. They rolled all night from side to side, waged war with the bedbugs, and waited for day to come.

At the first sign of dawn they rushed to the postoffice. The outer gates were still closed. Little by little a crowd gathered outside and the street was filled with people. Men walked up and down, yawning, stretching, pulling their earlocks and praying under their breath.

When Yadama the janitor opened the gates they poured in after him. Yadama grew furious. He would show them who was master here, and pushed and shoved till they were all out in the street again. There they waited for Zeidel to come. And at last he came.

When Zeidel opened the paper and read the news aloud, there arose such an outcry, such a clamor, such a roar that the heavens could have split open. Their outcry was not against the judges who gave the wrong verdict, not at the generals who swore falsely, not at the French who showed themselves up so badly. The outcry was against Zeidel.

"It cannot be!" Kasrilevka shouted with one voice. "Such a verdict is impossible! Heaven and earth swore that the truth must prevail. What kind of lies are you telling us?"

"Fools!" shouted Zeidel, and thrust the paper into their faces. "Look! See what the paper says!"

"Paper! Paper!" shouted Kasrilevka. "And if you stood with one foot in heaven and the other on earth, would we believe you?"

"Such a thing must not be. It must never be! Never! Never!"

And—who was right?

THE CONVOY

1 HAMAN IVANOVITCH PLISETSKY

That was what they called the new Government Inspector who had recently come to Teplik. To be accurate, his real name was Agamemnon Afonagenovitch, but the Jews of Teplik, who love to tamper with names, changed his for two reasons: first, because Haman Ivanovitch was shorter and easier to say. Just try, for instance, to roll your tongue around in your mouth and say, A-ga-mem-non A-fo-na-ge-no-vitch! That is the first reason. And the second is that since Teplik was founded, no one remembers ever having heard of an Inspector so much like the Haman of Scriptures as this Haman Ivanovitch Plisetsky of whom we speak.

In Teplik they have had all kinds of Inspectors—good ones, bad ones, those who take bribes eagerly and those who would not touch a *kopek*—except possibly as a New Year gift, which doesn't count, or a birthday present, which you could hardly refuse. All of us have birthdays, and everywhere a birthday is celebrated as a holiday. It has been that way since the dawn of history, since Pharaoh was king of Egypt, as we read in *Genesis*. Pharaoh, when his birthday came, ordered a feast for all his slaves, set his cupbearer free from prison, and hanged his baker on a tree, as Joseph had foretold in interpreting the dreams three days before.

But let us go back to this other tyrant, this Haman we

have been talking about. When he arrived in Teplik, the first
thing he did was to start cleaning up the town. And when
I say cleaning, I mean just that. The horse thieves of Teplik, renowned throughout the world, were smoked out in a
month or two. Even if you needed one for an exhibit you
couldn't find one. If there was any person he had any reason to
suspect, he did not wait or hesitate, but packed him off by
convoy to the prison at Heissin. Let them reckon with him
there.

After the thieves and petty pilferers, he turned his attention to the streets of the town and to the Jews. He issued
the order that from that day on, the streets must all be kept
clean. No one must empty rubbish into the streets, pour slops
out of the front door, or do anything else unseemly. And the
Jews, he declared, must not open their shops before noon on
Sunday, teachers must not hold classes without a special
permit, and to make it complete, he forbade the *eirev,* the
zone of exemption. As you recall, on the Sabbath we must
not carry anything on our persons, not even a handkerchief.
In our own house we could, and in our yard also, but in the
city at large not a thing. So every Friday afternoon we used
to make a fence around the entire Jewish settlement. A
fence? You could call it that, though it consisted of no
more than a strong piece of cord that ran from tree to tree
around the entire village. This we called an *eirev,* and it
made all the village one's own yard, and people could carry
whatever they needed without fear of committing a sin.

But now Haman said that the *eirev* had to go. The Jews
could get along without their telegraph, without these wires
strung all around the town. Even in the synagogue itself,
when some of the men had a fight over this or that honor and
slapped each other in the face, he liked to interfere. That's
the kind of tyrant he was!

Well, he had his way. The stores were closed Sunday till
noon. And if not right on the dot—if some of them opened
a minute or two earlier—he pretended not to notice. For
what choice did he have? He did as much as he could. But

to be a watchman at every Jewish shop, to catch anyone who opened the door just an inch—that was not humanly possible.

But the *eirev,* the zone of exemption, gave him trouble at first. Every Friday afternoon the cord was strung up all around the town, and Saturday morning he had it torn down. But the next week a new *eirev* appeared, and the week after that another one. This happened several weeks in succession. No matter how much his spies watched, they could not find the culprit, until he condescended to go himself, hide behind a hedge and spend the whole night watching. Finally toward daybreak he caught Peisi, the *shammes'* son, in the very act of stretching the cord. Without ceremony he grabbed Peisi by the left ear and dragged him off to jail and locked him up for the whole day. From that day on Teplik had to get along without an *eirev.* And still people carried their handkerchiefs and watches around on the Sabbath— with no apparent consequences.

Not so simple was the war he waged against the teachers. They made life wretched for him. Here he arrested a teacher with twenty pupils and closed his *cheder,* and there he discovered him with the same pupils in another street. He closed up this *cheder* too, swore out a warrant; looked around—and there was the same man, high up in the women's balcony of the synagogue with the same twenty pupils shouting at the tops of their voices. A curse on these Jewish children, you couldn't drive them away from their studies! "For heaven's sake, if you have to go up there with those pupils of yours, stay there and be damned! But don't make so much noise! Don't force me to listen to you!"

That is how Plisetsky appealed to the teacher, and he swore that if he ever caught him again he would banish him from Teplik within twenty-four hours. The teacher heard him out with the greatest respect and discontinued his classes in the women's balcony. But the next day he started again in a cellar not far away, and went on teaching with the very same ear-splitting chant as before—that familiar, deafening chant without which the study of Hebrew apparently has no more flavor than the cold puddings that wealthy people in the big cities eat these days.

Haman Ivanovitch battled with these teachers so long, till with a final curse he shut his eyes and pretended not to know that they were there.

2 THE NOGID OF TEPLIK, SHOLOM-BER TEPLIKER OF TEPLIK

Since most of the inhabitants of Teplik were Jews, the new Inspector had to spend the greater part of his time dealing with Jews, and in a short time he became acquainted with most of them, knew them by name, learned all their secrets, spoke to them in a half-Yiddish, half-Russian language of his own, and became quite intimate with many of them—almost like one of the family.

The richer townspeople, the leading citizens—the soup ladles, as we call them, because they are always stirring the community pot—in their turn, when they saw how friendly he was, began to win their way into his good favor—first, with a piece of Sabbath fish ("Jew fish," he called it), a glass of Passover brandy ("Jew brandy"), and a few pieces of *matzo* ("Jew *matzo*"). And afterward, with a fawning smile, they moved on to the next stage—of slipping something into his hand. But his response to this gesture was so unexpected and sharp that they learned something that they remembered forever after, and they passed it on to their children and grandchildren: "Never bribe a man—until you know who he is and what he is."

"If you're trying to bribe me," cried Haman, "it must mean that you've committed some crime. Here, take him and put him away!"

The words, "Take him and put him away!" were always at the tip of his tongue. They meant several different things: to throw a person in jail for a day or two; to put him away for several weeks; or even to send him off to Heissin, where the prison was, by convoy. And once he had given this order, nothing more could be done about it. Not all the kings of east or west could help. That's the kind of a man he was! And yet so inconsistent was he that if some penniless wretch fell into his hands, this tyrant reached into his own pocket and gave the fellow a *ruble* or two, and said to him in his mixture of Russian and Yiddish:

"Here is a loan to help you on your way."

But considerate as he was of poor people, so intolerant was he of the rich. And especially if the rich man was from Teplik. And most especially the *nogid* of Teplik, Sholom-Ber Tepliker of Teplik. Him he could not tolerate at all, and for a long, long time he tried to catch the man at some misdemeanor, without success, till God came to his aid and he had him in his hands. This is how it happened.

This Sholom-Ber Tepliker of Teplik, in addition to being a man of wealth, was as stubborn and proud a creature as you would ever find. If he ever decided to do something, nothing could stop him. It would be easier to pick up all of Teplik and move it somewhere else than to make him change his mind. Thus when Haman Ivanovitch decreed that no one was to throw rubbish or slops out into the street, Sholom-Ber Tepliker of Teplik asked this question, "Whose business is that? It's my rubbish and my slops, and I can do with it as I wish!"

"But, Reb Sholom-Ber," people tried to tell him, "if this Haman ever catches you, there'll be trouble!"

"Don't worry," said Sholom-Ber. He was a man who did not like to waste his words.

"But, Reb Sholom-Ber, he'll serve a warrant."

"Let him serve seventy-seven warrants!"

"But, Reb Sholom-Ber, what if someone should slip in front of your house and break a leg?"

"Let that Haman break a leg!" cried Sholom-Ber, and ordered his servant girl to throw as much rubbish in front of the house as she wanted to.

So Plisetsky came to him with the police and served papers on him, and Sholom-Ber protested vociferously, and told them all what he thought of them, as only a *nogid* can. Plisetsky told him to shut his mouth, and in the course of giving this advice threw in a few words like, "the nerve of the Jew," and "dirty Jewish mouth," and a few other pleasant remarks of the same general type. At this Sholom-Ber became angry and let it be known before all those present that the Inspector was a second Haman, in fact he was Haman himself, the very same one they told about in the Bible. All this was added as an extra clause to the complaint, and between one thing and another, the leading citizen of Teplik, Sholom-Ber himself, was sentenced to two weeks in the district jail. And all the prayers and all the vows and all the pledges to the Almighty could not help him!

It is to be understood that all of Teplik rocked at the news. Imagine it! Two weeks behind bars for Teplik's Sholom-Ber! And the whole town came to see him being led off to jail. They say that not even a babe was left in its cradle. Everybody who could see was there to watch him. And as they led him through the marketplace to the town jail, Sholom-Ber Tepliker of Teplik lowered his eyes for the first time in his life. And his wife, Stissi-Pearl, for very shame, hid herself in her house. And everybody else in town stood along the road watching the spectacle and saying nothing, although deep in their hearts many of them were glad.

In the first place, he had it coming. Just because he was rich was no reason for a man to be so insolent. And in the second place he was disliked by everyone because in spite of his haughty manner he was a low and petty creature and his wife, Stissi-Pearl, begrudged a person a dry crust of bread, though, as everybody in Teplik knew well enough, their very gizzards were stuffed with gold and they had no one to spend it on—not even a child.

"If I had their money," every Tepliker was in the habit of saying, "if I only had half as much, or a third as much, the town would get more pleasure out of it than it does now . . ." And that might very well have been so, but since in all of Tepik there was no one else who had any money at all, there was no one who got any pleasure out of it— neither the town itself, nor Sholom-Ber, nor his wife Stissi-Pearl. Though it may be that the latter two did get some joy out of it. It all depends what you call joy. If you measured it by the position one held in the community, then Sholom-Ber had it. Wherever he was, whether in the synagogue or at a public gathering or a celebration, he had the place of honor. It was always the others who came up to him to wish him a good Sabbath, a good morning, or greet him at the holidays. When Sholom-Ber spoke, the others listened in silence, and whatever he said was a thing of wisdom. And more than that—every year, at *Simchas-Torah,* it was at his home that the whole town gathered. Sholom-Ber sat like a king and asked everyone who came to take some brandy, and Stissi-Pearl his wife watched every glass. There were other occasions also during the year, which, if you were a Tepliker, would have some meaning, but if you were not, would have none at all. And besides all this, there was the simple fact that Sholom-Ber was convinced that he was the only one who was anything at all. Only he, and no one else.

In Teplik there was only one Sholom-Ber Tepliker. In Teplik there was only one like that. There was no other . . .

3 A CHEERFUL PAUPER

In Teplik, if there had been no meddlers and informers, that is, if there had been no people who paid attention to what everybody else was doing, ninety-nine out of every hundred transgressions would have gone unpunished, and Teplik would have had as many sinners as Sodom itself. But since the people of Teplik have a way of keeping very well informed of the activities of their neighbors, every time they see anything that looks wrong, or hear anything, or smell anything, or even imagine anything that might not be just right, they make a note of it and see to it that the information reaches the proper authorities in the proper manner. And Plisetsky could boast that he did not ever have to hire any spies. The householders of Teplik were competent enough spies themselves.

After an introduction like this, you will not be surprised to hear that one bright morning the police surrounded the hut of·Berel the Redhead with the crooked leg, just as he was sitting on the ground, the skirts of his gabardine rolled up around his waist, pouring from a large jug into small bottles the raisin wine that he sold to his neighbors for sacramental purposes. With great absorption he pressed each cork in and pounded it down. Plisetsky opened the door quietly, observed the red-haired Berel at his work, remaining standing a few minutes on the threshold, and beckoned to his assistants. When Berel raised his eyes and saw Haman Ivanovitch standing over him, he got up from the ground, came up to the Inspector with his strange limp, and looked him right in the eye as though to say, "Are you going to punish me for this? Go ahead, punish me! What can you take away from me? The hole in my pocket?"

How did it happen that Berel was so bold? Because he had nothing to be afraid of. True, he had made wine out of raisins, poured it into small bottles and sold it to his acquaintances for the Sabbath, and in that way earned his livelihood. But what a wine it was, and what a livelihood! The wine was no wine; the livelihood no livelihood. And yet both served their purpose. Every Friday night a benediction had to be made over wine, so this was wine. And it kept him occupied, gave him something to live on—not much, but enough, as he said, for a thin gruel to dip his hard crust into. And that was better than nothing. Think of how many people there are in Teplik who have no work at all and earn nothing at all and have nothing at all! Really nothing! Absolutely nothing at all!

And it was these very men, who did nothing and earned

nothing and had nothing, who were most envious of Berel
the Redhead, who had the reputation among them of living
like a mogul. Was there not a rumor current that he had
fish and meat every Sabbath, and certainly white bread? And
did he not send his children to *cheder?* And didn't he clothe
them, and have a goat of his own? And all from these raisins
that he shook up and made into wine! So they sat down
and wrote a letter to Plisetsky with all the necessary information. And this is how it read:

"Whereas we have always been concerned with the public
welfare, and whereas the public welfare is threatened by all
illegal transactions, and whereas Berel the Redhead, here-
after referred to by his legal name of Berko Krivak, has for
so many years dealt in wine without a permit, and whereas
the aforementioned Berko Krivak manufactures this wine
with his own hands, also without a permit, therefore . . ."
And so on and so on and so on . . .

The pride of a pauper is nothing to sneer at. The poorer
a man is, the prouder he is—prouder than some of the richest people in the world. I once knew a pauper who met
another on the street.

"How can you compare yourself to me, you idiot!" said the
first. "You still have a pair of boots and a torn old overcoat, and I don't have these things even in my dreams!"

This was said in such a tone of boastfulness that if Rothschild himself had been standing there, he would have lost
confidence in himself.

In the meantime, returning to our story, Haman Ivanovitch
stood contemplating Berel's apartments, which consisted of
three rooms, or to be more accurate, of two small alcoves
and a kitchen, and each of these rooms was filled with beds
and the beds were full of children. The children were half-
dressed and half-naked, that is, they were dressed from the
neck to the navel, and from there down they were naked.
To this half-naked audience the Inspector was a rare sight,
the like of which they had never seen. Without hesitation
the children jumped out of bed, quietly stole up to the

dazzling figure and stared up at him, examined his gold buttons and felt the scabbard at his side. And while they drank in all the details of his attire, this conversation took place above their heads:

Plisetsky: According to what they wrote about you, you must be making a lot of money.

Berel: It could have been a little worse. It could have been a lot better.

Plisetsky: Then why are your children naked and barefoot?

Berel: They grow better that way.

Plisetsky: And what do you do with your money?

Berel: I do as the *Talmud* advises us.

Plisetsky: The *Talmud?* And what does that say?

Berel: It tells us to divide our money three ways. One third is to be put away; one third is to be kept in cash, and the rest in merchandise.

Plisetsky: I see you're in good spirits.

Berel: What do I have to worry about? What do I need and what do I have? But tell me, my Lord and Master, what is it that my good neighbors said about me, and what is it that I can expect as a result of this visit of yours?

Plisetsky: If you want to know so much you'll be old and gray in a hurry. But first show me all your chests and drawers. I have to search your home. Maybe in addition to the wine I'll find other good things too.

Berel: With the greatest pleasure. Only this: if you discover any gold or silver or government bonds, let's divide it, half for me and half for you.

Plisetsky: You're a little too cheerful—like some people before their death.

Berel: It may be so. No one knows what tomorrow will bring. As the *Talmud* says, "Repent for your sins a day before you die." And as we never know when the Angel of Death might grab us by the neck, so . . .

At this point Plisetsky interrupted him, called in the police and told them to take him to jail. When he heard the word "jail," Berel felt a chill pass through him, and a wailing arose among the children as if a corpse were being carried out.

Naturally in Teplik it did not take long for the news to get around, and from all sides people came crowding to see another Jew being led off to prison—no one knew why. That is, why he was being led was no secret. How could a thing like that be kept a secret in Teplik? Especially when they saw Haman Ivanovitch carrying a small bottle of wine, the kind they knew Berel made without a license. The only thing they did not know was what would come of it. A fine —or prison? They tried to figure out which. And yet they had much more sympathy for this pauper than for Sholom-Ber the *nogid*. But they could do nothing to help him, except sigh as he walked past.

4 ANOTHER TRANSGRESSOR

That same day Haman Ivanovitch went after the Jews of Teplik in one more way. He arrested another Jew, one who, quite obviously, had not committed any crime. This is how it happened:

There was a young man in town, a boy you might call him, named Hennich. This Hennich had an older brother, David-Leib, who was to be called up for military service that year, and David-Leib claimed exemption because Hennich was not yet eighteen years old and thus was technically dependent on him. That was as the law provided. The papers were all made out and filed with the authorities in Heissin. But filing papers was not enough. They also had to produce the brother in person so that the authorities could see for themselves how old he was. The order came to Plisetsky, and when Plisetsky was ordered to produce, he produced. He sent the constable and had Hennich brought to him at the station.

Hennich, you could see at a glance, was not a very gifted

youth. His complexion was pasty, almost lifeless; he had a
cataract in one eye, and his head shook with some nervous
disorder. In addition to this, his fright at being picked up by
the constable was such that it gave a touch of madness to
his appearance, and the impression he made on the Inspector
was not a very good one.

"Are you Hennich Tellerlecker?" Plisetsky asked, grabbing
hold of him and looking him over from head to foot.

"I am Hennich Tellerlecker," answered the boy, and then
realizing that he was there on account of his brother, he
blurted out, "And I'm not eighteen yet! I swear I'm not!"

"So I see," said Plisetsky. "Only seventeen and a half—not
counting Sundays and Holidays." And he looked at Hennich
so fiercely that the poor lad went hot and cold all over, his
heart sank, and he said to himself, "It's all up. David-Leib is
gone from us . . ." But he still wanted to do something for
his brother, and suddenly he became bold and cried out, "I
swear that I am not more than seventeen and a month. Not
a day more. If I am lying I hope I may never come home
again. Maybe I look older, but I am not! We are all like
that in our family. By fifteen our beards start growing . . ."

Plisetsky looked at him, shook his head and smiled, as
though to say, "That's all you need besides the cataract and
that complexion of yours—a handsome beard." And then he
told his deputy to put him away until he could examine the
papers more carefully. And Hennich was put away.

So a third citizen of Teplik took up his residence that day
in the town jail.

He was greeted at once by Berel. "Look who's here! And
what was it you did now, my little bird, and who was it that
told them you had done it?"

Sholom-Ber was more reserved. From his corner he looked
the lad over coldly, as if he were a thief who had just been
caught stealing. And Hennich looked back like a half-wit,
with his mouth open, at the sight of the town's *nogid* in the
same cell with him, and he began to babble, without knowing what he was saying.

"I don't know what I did. I don't know anything. It's on account of David-Leib. If I'm more than eighteen . . ."

Berel interrupted him. "What are you flapping your mouth for? Say something! Make sense!"

"I am telling you about my brother . . ." And suddenly he turned upon Berel with these words: "Tell me! How do I look to you?"

"How do you look? You look like a wild man!" Berel answered with a laugh and looked at Sholom-Ber to see if he was laughing too. But the *nogid* was not laughing at all. He was looking at the wretched Hennich shaking in his rags and tatters, wondering why things like that had to go on living in this world.

"No," said Hennich, looking at the rich man with his good eye and at Berel with the other. "That isn't what I meant. What I mean is, how old do I look?"

"Oh, how old? Well, I'd say about twenty-two or so—or a trifle more . . ."

In his great sorrow and anger Hennich let out a shriek and turned on Berel:

"Are you crazy? What are you talking about? David-Leib was just twenty and he is almost three years older than me. So what are you talking about?"

And he looked so mournful and woebegone that Sholom-Ber himself became interested and asked him:

"There are two of you then—two brothers—is that it?"

"Two brothers and our old mother. And a sister of thirteen who is out doing housework. And a younger brother apprenticed to a shopkeeper. And two smaller girls and a little boy in *Talmud Torah*. And all of us depend on him, on David-Leib—all of us. If they send him away we'll have to get sacks and go begging. House to house. What else can we do?"

And he told the whole story as well as he could—not too clearly, not too consecutively, but always insisting that he was not yet eighteen in spite of the beard and in spite of what everybody said. And he turned aside with a cough, wiping his nose and his eyes.

"It's a pity, the poor fellow," said the *nogid* in spite of himself.

"A *shlimazl*," added Berel with a half-smile. "And his brother, in some ways, is not much better. He'd make as good a soldier as I would." And he stuck out his lame leg and looked at it from all sides.

5 THE CONVOY STARTS

Until the day that we now come to, and until the last minute, Sholom-Ber Tepliker of Teplik did not believe that he would be compelled to go with the convoy to Heissin. All the time that he waited he busied himself, writing letters to the proper people, using what influence he had to free himself. But Plisetsky was busy too and his influence was greater, and he saw to it that our fine citizen of Teplik took that trip to Heissin with the convoy—and on foot!

"I'll see to it that you go," Haman Ivanovitch said to him in half-Russian, half-Yiddish, "with your own feet." And to make it worse, the day was bright and hot, a midsummer day. No one could escape the heat, it was like a furnace, a limekiln. Shopkeepers closed their shops, workers left their tools, teachers their schools, and they all went to see the *nogid* being led away. And the people of Teplik, seeing him standing with lowered head, said to each other, "Let that be a lesson to us." But in their hearts they rejoiced. They were having their revenge. Pity they had only for Berel the Redhead and for Hennich.

For Sholom-Ber's journey his wife had sent a large basket with fresh white loaves, roast duck and other good things. Berel's wife and all their children came to bid Berel farewell, bringing a small loaf of bread, boiled fish and potatoes and a bunch of fresh garlic. Only Hennich had no food at all to take along, but some strangers in the crowd collected enough to buy him a dark loaf, a couple of small salted fish, and onions. And all these delicacies were handed over to the guard, who took them willingly, promising that every bit of it would be safe in his hands. And then Haman Ivanovitch appeared on his porch and told the guard to start moving. The guard moved, and the prisoners with him, and after them all of Teplik.

The convoy consisted of one Lavre, the guard, a hairy creature with a fur jacket that he wore winter and summer, a tall fur hat, and a long knotty staff with a large wooden knob at one end and a sharp iron point at the other. The roast duck and the salt fish under one arm, the bread and garlic under the other, his report for the district officials stuck in his bosom, he started off quickly with his wards, much more quickly than you would have imagined. That was because our prisoners wanted to get rid of their followers, and when the older people had dropped away, they begged the guard to chase the little children back. They had kept them company out beyond the town, beyond the mill, and showed no signs of weariness. Lavre raised his staff with the iron point and the youngsters disappeared like frightened birds, and the prisoners remained alone in the open fields. They did not have to hurry any more, they began to take shorter steps and slower ones, and one of them suggested to the guard that it might be well to sit down for a while on the fresh green grass and take a little rest.

The guard was not such an evil man, and it did not take long to convince him. In fact, it is hard to say who was more eager to stop. He too was willing to rest and to sample the baskets he had been carrying, and to see what those odors were that had been tickling his nostrils all the way. He had already broken off a few twists of one of the large white loaves and found them to his liking. He had tasted one of the fishes too and found that with garlic it was not at all bad. Walking behind the prisoners, he was able to taste this and that without their knowledge, until Sholom-Ber hap-

pened to look around and caught him pinching his large
white loaf and nibbling at what he had pinched off.

"Our protector," he said to the others guardedly, "has good
active jaws."

"Pray that he doesn't choke," said Berel, cheerfully. "Now
that you mention it, my own appetite is not so bad either.
What do you say, Hennich, are you beginning to feel a little
weak inside too?"

Hennich moistened his lips and said in his own strange
manner:

"Very hungry, no. But a little something to chew, maybe.
If I had something."

"I have everything," said Sholom-Ber with a quick glance
back at their guard.

"Everything?" wondered Berel. "Without a glass of brandy
you can never say everything." And to make sure that the
guard caught the full meaning, he said it over, in Russian:
"Isn't it true, Lavre, that a meal without brandy is like eating
without teeth?"

"True . . . very true . . ." the guard answered earnestly.

And they juggled their words so long, till they all understood and agreed that as it was not very far from where they
were to Granov, at most a couple of *versts,* one of the prisoners—naturally Hennich, the youngest—should dash off for
a bottle of brandy; and the other two prisoners, Sholom-Ber
Tepliker of Teplik and Berel the Redhead, guaranteed that
he would not try to escape. And when they had sent him
off, the others sat down on the grass in the middle of the
field, under a tree on a hillock, the prisoners talking with
each other in low tones, and the guard sitting near them but
looking with both eyes up the road to Granov.

6 HE REMINDS HIM OF OLD WRONGS

If I were a painter or a photographer I would have taken
a picture of this group, the three figures sitting there in the

middle of the field on the hillock under a wild pear tree with small green leaves and those small, hard pears that no one can eat and that no one ever knows what to do with.

Between Lavre, the guard, with the tall fur cap, on one side, and Berel the Redhead with the crooked leg and the red, freckled face on the other, our Sholom-Ber Teplike of Teplik, with the small eyes and the thin beard, with his black, satin gabardine and with his black, silk hat, looked like a man of state among two common fellows. A man like that usually knows how to conduct himself. He may act like anybody else, like a plain and modest man, and yet he is not just like anybody else. Other people talk about the things' that *he* wants to talk about, and when *he* talks, others listen. and when others talk, he has the right to interrupt.

"What do you think of this heat?" he said to Berel with a sigh and a glance in all directions. And he rolled his sleeves up to the elbows and fanned himself with his silk hat.

"It's not at all cold," answered Berel, following the rich man's glance.

"I hope it doesn't rain," the other went on, with a look up at the sky.

Berel looked up too. "It would be a pity," he agreed, "with all of us dressed up like this."

"Not a bad fellow, this guard of ours," continued Sholom-Ber, with his eyes on a long, empty wagon that a pair of large oxen were pulling up the road, with a little boy on the driver's seat dangling a whip above their ears.

"Our guard?" echoed Berel. "He's a gentleman compared with those good neighbors of mine who ran to the police with the news that a poor hardworking man was selling a few bottles of raisin wine. It wasn't even anything new. It's been going on for years . . ."

"What do you think," interrupted the *nogid* again, with his eyes on the road that led to Granov. "What do you think? He couldn't have lost his way, could he? I mean, made tracks? That boy—what's his name?"

"Him?" said Berel. "Why should he do a thing like that?

What did he ever do that was wrong? He's no more a criminal than I am."

"Speaking of that," said Sholom-Ber, "what do you think they'll do to you?" He was sitting now with his eyes closed, meditatively chewing at a blade of grass.

"For what? For that raisin wine? They won't hang me, that much I know. But beyond that—" he shrugged his shoulders, "let them do what they want. What can they take away from me? The holes in my pockets? And if they want me to sit a while, I'll sit. But what I want to know is what will they do with *you?* You're somebody! You have money, position, property . . .

"I'll tell you the truth, Reb Sholom-Ber. Don't be offended. But if I were you I'd never have given them a chance to throw me into jail like this; for a little thing like that, a bit of rubbish, a pan of dirty water! In the first place, I would not have been so stubborn, especially with the police. In the second, if I were you, I wouldn't have let them march me off this way. Teplik itself should never have allowed it, letting its *nogid* be sent to jail by convoy, like a common nobody, a penniless lout."

At another time Berel would have paid dearly for talking like this to Sholom-Ber. He would certainly have been sent flying head first. But now on his way by convoy to Heissin, Sholom-Ber was not a privileged character. Now a person could say anything he wanted to him. And Berel the Redhead got even with him as well as he could, smoothly, without ever losing his temper. He edged up close to Sholom-Ber with his crooked leg, so close that the rich man had to move away a little, and he spoke to him like this:

"Do you know, Reb Sholom-Ber, how long we have known each other? It's been a long, long time. I remember when you were a brat no taller than that" (Berel held his hand down close to the ground). "You must be about my age, at the most a year older, or two, and you ought to remember me from those days because my grandfather and your father were—don't be afraid, I was not going to say relatives, although they were that too, forty-second cousins once removed on my mother's side. What I was going to say was that we sat close to each other in the synogogue, your father along the east wall and my grandfather in the opposite row so that when we all stood facing east I had your back right in my face. I still remember your father's shiny silk coat and his broad shoulders and the silver stripes on his *tallis;* and my grandfather, Reb Naftali the vintner—you must remember him—used to pull his own yellow *tallis* over his head and pinch me every time I looked up from my prayerbook. Because apparently I was just as anxious to be praying as you were . . . When we were supposed to be standing motionless you were always looking down at your new boots that squeaked. And how I used to envy you, always with new boots while mine were always old, always patched. I could never get good boots on account of my foot. And that was not the only trouble I had on account of that foot. It was hard for me to walk, but that too was nothing. What was worse was being called Limpy and being mimicked. And worst of all was the way you did it, Reb Sholom-Ber—don't be offended! You and others like you, from the richer families, spoiled little brats . . ."

"I?" cried the *nogid* with a start, and then he remembered that it was true, they used to mimic Berel, make fun of the way he jumped on one foot.

"And making fun of me would not have been so bad either, but what was even worse than that was that you never let me play with the rest of you. You chased me away with sticks and stepped with your heels on my ailing foot, right on my toes, and pretended it had been an accident. Stepped on them to make me scream, so I screamed, and you laughed and held your sides . . ."

"Now, *that* you simply made up!" the *nogid* called out, his face red with shame, and he remembered how spoiled he had been as a child. He had been able to do anything that he wanted to.

"No, I'm not making it up. It was true and I'll prove it

to you. I told my grandfather and he went and told your
father, and your father would not believe it. He scolded my
grandfather, swore that his child was a well-behaved boy
who wouldn't have a thing to do with paupers' children.
How do you like that? Paupers' children! From that time on
I knew what I was—a pauper's child. But I did not know
what it meant and I asked my grandfather, and he told me.
He taught me what it meant to be a poor man's child, and
what it was to be a rich man's. But I still could not understand why a rich man's child could step on the toes of a poor
man's child, and the poor man's child could do nothing about
it. So I asked my grandfather that too, and he explained it
to me this way: that a rich man is not a poor man and a
poor man is not a rich man. In short, the rich were rich and
the poor were poor. And still that did not make sense, so I
looked into his eyes, maybe there I could find an explanation
that his words could not give me. But all I saw was something like a dark cloud pass over his face, and the wrinkles
on his forehead. And that was all . . . And I must admit
there is nothing I can do about it. Ever since that time I
have had nothing but scorn for the rich and the children of
the rich, and most of all I have scorned and hated you . . ."

"Me?"

"You. Yes, you! You were just a child then, no larger than
a grasshopper. We were both children. But even later, when
we were older, when we were *Bar-Mitzvah,* young men already, you always turned away from me, as if you didn't
know me. You were afraid that I might greet you, and you
might have to answer me. You begrudged me even that, apparently. It was not worth your time . . ."

The *nogid* of Teplik, Sholom-Ber Tepliker, squirmed and
made a weak gesture with his hands. "That couldn't have
been," he said without conviction, and at the same time he
admitted to himself that it was possible. He remembered
that his father was always reminding him that he was not
like other children, that the others were not his equal.

"Don't be offended, Reb Sholom-Ber. Foolish little things

are never forgotten. When I was married the first time (you were married a short time earlier) I sent you an invitation, but you did not even acknowledge it."

"I swear I don't remember that."

"How should you remember? I bet you don't remember this either, that when my wife died, I sent my Uncle Yossi (my grandfather was dead already by that time) to tell you that I was alone with two small children, forlorn and helpless. Your answer was that you were a man who did not meddle in public affairs."

"Did *I* say that? Oh, no! Your uncle must have told you a lie."

"That may be so. Maybe *you're* right. All I know is that you did nothing to help me that time, or later either, when my house burned down and I was left as naked as when I was born. Or later yet, that time we met at Heissin at the inn, if you remember, during the Fair. You had come, if I remember correctly, to buy some horses or a cow, or maybe to sell some grain."

The rich man rubbed his forehead, like a man trying to remember something, something that eluded him. And he wondered why he should have forgotten and the other had not. And he did not like it that Berel the Redhead, who in Teplik would not have dared say two superfluous words to him, should point out all his shortcomings and remind him of all his past misdeeds. He did not like it at all, and he was on the point of saying so when Hennich arrived from Granov with the bottle of brandy, all out of breath from running, afraid that someone might catch him with the bottle and have him arrested . . .

And the three transgressors sat down to their feast, beginning with a drop of brandy. They offered the guard a glass too, and he did not refuse. But they could see that the drink did not appeal to him. He made a face, wiped his thick mustache with his sleeve, and cursed forsaken Granov and its fiery brandy.

"May seven devils take it! It's too bitter!" he swore, and

he lifted up his hand as if he were taking an oath that as
long as he lived he would never take another drop. And yet,
when they had finished the fish and were about to attack the
roast duck, they prevailed upon him to try another sip. It
was hard work, but they succeeded, and he agreed to try it
again, and when they urged him to finish the glass because
they wanted him to take another, he agreed to that too.

When they had finished eating, the four of them lay
down under the pear tree for a little while, not to take a
nap—that they did not even have in mind—but simply to
look up at the deep blue heavens and watch the tiny white
clouds that passed by overhead and disintegrated and then
disappeared like smoke, and the ravens that swept and
turned and at the same time appeared motionless.

Lying on the ground after eating, and looking up at the
sky, is an excellent way of overcoming sleeplessness. The
first to prove this was the guard himself, who almost at once
let out a snore like a frightened horse. And shortly afterward
was heard the only slightly more modest accompaniment that
issued from the capable though less consistent nostrils of the
boy Hennich. He did well while he tried, but he awoke too
often, sat up too frequently to babble something that was on
his mind:

"So tired . . . ran four versts . . . afraid, afraid he'd
catch me . . . the Inspector . . ."

The only ones who did not sleep were the rich man,
Sholom-Ber Tepliker of Teplik, and Berel the winemaker.
Sholom-Ber was worrying. He wanted to know what it was
that had happened that time in Heissin at the Fair, what it
was he had refused to do. And Berel did him a favor and
told him the whole story in these words.

7 A TRIVIAL INCIDENT IS NOT FORGOTTEN

"Don't be offended," Berel began. "A trivial incident is never forgotten. I came to Heissin not for the Fair. My oxen were still in pasture and my ships were still at sea. Then why did I have to come to Heissin at that very time? I came to look over a boy whom the *shadchan* had found for my older daughter, by my first wife. I had finally decided to marry her off. She was still young, poor child, but her stepmother kept nagging me. She wanted her out of the house. And what could I do? I asked what good it would do her. Who would help her cook and bake and scrub the smaller children's heads, and whom would she be able to curse and pull around by the hair? But try to convince a woman! So we decided to marry her off.

"That's easy to say. But how? What with? With your five fingers? There isn't much that people in our class can do, but clothes at least we have to get. Do I mean fine clothes? No. But even a cotton dress and some shoes and stockings cost money. And you have to get a few nightgowns, a couple of pillows, a bedspread, maybe a blanket. That's not counting the dowry, and how can a person give less than a hundred *rubles*? And here I was, with less than a hundred *kopeks*.

"And as if to tease me, Moishe-Aaron, the matchmaker, keeps swamping me with letters, one letter after another, saying that he had found a young man in Heissin, just the right boy for my daughter, one boy in a hundred, one in a million. I'd never find another one like him. And whose boy is it? Yankel the carpenter's, a poor man's child, but a very gifted one, advanced in his studies, a good penman—everything! And he played the fiddle like the devil himself!

"So I wrote to Moishe-Aaron and told him that first of all I was in no hurry to consider a match, and in the second place I had to know how much dowry he expected, because maybe it was not for my purse at all. And in the third place,

why didn't Yankel come here first, at least to take a look at
the girl. So he answers me at once—Moishe-Aaron, that is
—and tells me that my first point, that I was not interested
in a match, was nonsense, because he knew and everybody
else knew that a daughter is not a son, and it's never too
soon to marry her off. And as for what I had said about a
dowry, that was foolish of me. Were we talking about an ox
or a cow that we should start bargaining? These were his
very words. And as for coming to look at my daughter, that
was not necessary, either. Yankel knew all about her already.
A neighbor of his from Heissin had been in my house and
had seen the girl and he could not begin to praise her
highly enough.

"At any rate—a letter here, a letter there—I took my feet
in my hands, as the saying is, and went off to Heissin. And
when I saw the boy I felt as if I had never seen anyone
like him in my life before. His face was like that of a prince,
his brain a prime minister's. When he spoke, every word
was a jewel. And when he played the fiddle you could forget
every musician who ever lived! I was in love with him myself and I swore that no matter what happened I would have
him for my daughter. But go do something when your pocket's empty! If I only had a hundred *rubles!* Or even part of
it to give as a deposit! The boy himself did not care about
a dowry. Give it to him or don't give it to him, it was all
the same. But the carpenter, the devil take him, was stubborn and you couldn't budge him. If a grand duchess herself
wanted to marry his son she'd have to pay a dowry before
she could lead him to the canopy.

"I turned to the *shadchan.* 'Reb Moishe-Aaron,' I said, 'do
something. Say something.' 'What can I say?' he asked. 'Do
something quick. It looks bad. You'll never get anywhere
with this stubborn ox. Only yesterday I almost hit him over the
head with his plane.' Did you ever hear anything like that?
Yet there was the boy before my eyes. I couldn't drive him
out. I simply had to have him for my daughter. I'd die if I
didn't have him!

"In the meantime, I looked around at the inn, and whom did I see? Reb Sholom-Ber Tepliker! God alone, I told myself, could have brought him there. And I wasn't shy. I went right up and greeted you, like an old friend. I was so happy to see you! Why? Because, I thought to myself, you would surely ask me what I was doing here in Heissin, and I would tell you that I was here for a match. And you would say, 'With whom?' And I would say, 'With Yankel the carpenter.' And you would say, 'How much dowry are you giving?' And I would say, 'Ah, that's the whole problem! The carpenter says that I'll have to lay down a hundred, and all I have is a fig.' And then you would say . . .

"But what happened really? You didn't ask me a thing. So without your asking, I told you that I had come not for the Fair, but to arrange a match for my daughter. Why did I do that? Because I thought that then you would have to ask with whom, and then I could say, 'With Yankel the carpenter.' And then you would say, 'What dowry are you giving?' And I'd say . . . But you know already what I was going to say, and yet what happened? Not the trace of a question!

"So I decided to tell you without being asked. I told you whom the match was with, and I praised the boy to the skies, as I could do in all truthfulness. Well . . . I did all the talking. You didn't say a word. My story made no impression, as if it went through one ear and out through the other. So I said to myself, why should I be a diplomat? The time had come to say it directly—tear the tooth out by the root! And what did you do then? You refused me outright. And scolded me besides."

"I scolded you? What did I say?"

"Do you want me to tell you? Ah, trivial things are never forgotten. And so I remember. You asked me what right did I have to bother you, what right did I have to expect you to go throwing out a hundred *rubles* at a time . . ."

"But did you tell me what you needed the money for?"

"Did I tell you? Don't you remember? And this was your

answer: 'What makes you so anxious to marry off your daughter to a millionaire?' And when I told you how well the boy played the fiddle, you said to me, 'It's lucky he plays the fiddle. What if it was a trumpet?' Here I was, suffering anguish, desperate for help, and you made fun of me, practiced your jokes on me . . . Apparently you were feeling good that day."

Reb Sholom-Ber Tepliker of Teplik listened to the whole story, sweated, said nothing. What had really happened that day he did not remember, but there had been something to do with a hundred *rubles*. That much he remembered. And he was ashamed of himself, ashamed to think that he had once refused a small thing like that which would have meant so much to this man and his family. The story itself now interested him too, and he asked: "Well, how did the match turn out?"

"There wasn't any."

"What do you mean—there wasn't any?"

"The carpenter wouldn't have anything more to do with me. The devil take him!"

"And your daughter? The girl?"

"My daughter? I buried her long ago. I killed her and buried her myself. You don't believe me? Well, what could I do? Could I make a dowry with my own hands? . . . A year went by, two years went by. There is no such thing, you know, as a Jewish convent. And the stepmother continued to nag. So I married the child off to a bookbinder as penniless as myself. A good man, an honest one, but sickly, tubercular. He struggled along a few years and then he died, leaving me this inheritance—three little children. Yes, I was the one to inherit them, because my daughter had caught his disease and she died too, a year later. Do you see? So now I have not only children from my own two marriages, but three little orphans besides. But such children! You won't find their equal in the richest families. 'Grandpa, where are you going?' they asked when Haman had me taken away. 'To Heissin,' I told them. 'When I come back I'll bring you all some chocolate.' And do you think they didn't know that I was telling them a lie? You should have seen them stand around me, like little lambs, without a sound, but with tears in their eyes. You can imagine what they looked like—if I tell you that Haman Ivanovitch himself reached into his pocket and gave them a *gulden* to buy sweets with."

8 WHICH PERTAINS TO HENNICH AND HIS FAMILY

Berel the Redhead had nothing more to say. After a pause he stood up, straightened his ailing leg, and limping over to Hennich snapped his finger across the lad's nose.

"Look here!" he said. "Haven't you slept long enough already?"

Hennich awoke with a start, wiped his eyes, and seeing the *nogid* looking at him, picked himself up quickly and began to babble:

"I didn't begin to sleep! I was thinking about poor David-Leib. They say more than eighteen. And what will happen to the poor children?"

"Listen to him talk!" said Berel to Sholom-Ber. "A real *shlimazl!* I was telling you just now about my bad luck, but compared to him I'm a rich man, a millionaire! And a man of influence, too . . . I'm the man who got David-Leib the job that he supports the family with. Eight mouths!"

"Nine you can say," Hennich corrected him. "Two brothers and an old mother. A sister of thirteen who does house work. And a younger brother in a shop. And two smaller girls. And a boy in *cheder,* a younger one. And where am I?"

"You? You are as good as buried!" Berel told him. "What are you now, and what will you ever be?" And turning to Sholom-Ber he said, "Now his brother David-Leib compared to him is a prime minister. A genius he's not; but he's not a fool, either. He's honest. The whole family is honest; they wouldn't steal a *beigel* from anyone. But David-Leib is both honest *and* capable.

"Well, one day he came to me with this story. In Heissin a sugar refinery had just been built that was owned by Reb Zalmen Rademishler, and Reb Zalmen Rademishler belonged to the Sadagora *chassidim.* Now I belong to the Sadagora *chassidim* too, and David-Leib's father—may he rest in peace —was also one of them. So he wanted me to go to see Reb Zalmen and ask him if he would find work somewhere in his refinery for him. 'What kind of work would you want?' I asked, and he told me, 'Anything at all, so long as it's work.' 'Idiot,' I said, 'tell me what you can do.' And he said, 'I can do anything. I know arithmetic and bookkeeping. I can write and I can copy.' 'Where did you learn all that?' I asked him. 'By myself,' he said, and took a piece of paper out of his pocket for me to show Reb Zalmen what his handwriting was like.

"Well, he bothered me so much that in order to get rid of him I put on my shoes and again went to Heissin, on foot. And when I came to Reb Zalmen's refinery they wouldn't let me in. What's the matter? And they tell me this. If I came just to visit Reb Zalmen, he did not have time to see me. And if I had some business to do, I should go into the office. I said to myself, 'Bah! I don't like this at all!' What kind of talk was this—no time—business—office? We Sadagora *chassidim* don't believe in such tricks. 'Go,' I said, 'tell Reb Zalmen that I, Berel the Redhead from Teplik, am here to see him about something important, and *not* on business, and I *can't* wait, because I have no time either!' So they tell me that Reb Zalmen is at his prayers, he just started a little while ago. 'If so,' I said, 'that's different.' But at the same time, was that an excuse? Couldn't he see me anyway? But the answer to that is that he was a rich man and people had to show respect for him. If I were rich, the whole world would respect me too.

"So I sat down and waited. I waited an hour and two and

three, right by the door. All around me was rush and bustle. People came and went, this one in, that one out. It was getting late. Someone came past me with a tray and a *samovar* and food that I'd never even seen before. So I said to myself, 'This I don't like either!' And I decided: why be formal? So I opened the door and in I went. 'How do you do, Reb Zalmen,' I said. 'How do you do,' said he, 'and where are you from?' 'From Teplik,' I answer him. 'Didn't you recognize me? I'm Berel. I was in Sadagora together with you once, to see our Rabbi.' 'Maybe so,' he said, 'but I didn't remember you and I still don't know you. My eyesight is not so good any more, not good at all. I went to all the doctors around here and then I went to Mendelstam, and he gave me black glasses to wear and told me not to read or write and keep away from sunlight.' 'Oh-ho,' I said to myself, 'you're telling me a story I heard from my grandmother!' And then to him, 'Listen to me, Reb Zalmen. This is what I came for. You remember Benny from Teplik, don't you?' And he said, 'Which Benny?' 'Benny Tellerlecker,' I tell him. 'No,' he says, 'this is the first time I've heard the name —Tellerlecker.' 'That,' I said, 'won't help you. You knew him well enough. We all drank wine together in Sadagora and danced together on the Rabbi's table, and more than once embraced each other, you and he and I, and now he's in Eternity—may he intercede for us there.'

"When he heard this, Reb Zalmen became another man altogether. These rich men must be very much afraid of death. 'What do you want?' he asks, 'what do you want of me?' 'What should I want?' I say, 'I want to fulfill my promise to the dead. A few hours before he died, this same Benny Tellerlecker called me and a few other friends together and told us that he had gone to see you a couple of times here in Heissin, wanted to talk with you about something, but had not been allowed to come in. He was a quiet little man, you remember, and he never liked intrigue or politics; so when he saw that he was not wanted he turned around and went back home again. But now, that he was about to begin an-

other journey, and a longer one, from which no one ever
returns, he wanted to bid farewell to each of us separately,
and through each of us he sent his regards first to the Rabbi
of our order, and then to you. And he asked me to give
this message to you: he leaves everything he has to you—
that is, he leaves his whole family to you, and he knows
that you will never abandon them.'

" 'What can I do for them?' said he, reaching into his
pocket. 'Ah-ha,' thought I, 'a donation. Never!' And I said,
'What I want you to do is to take his eldest son, David-Leib,
and give him work, a job.' When a rich man hears the
word *job* he has a stroke. 'Where can I get him a job?
Where can I find work for him? Every job is taken.' 'That
story,' I said, 'you can tell someone else, not me! I don't want
to hear any excuses from you. You have to find a job for
Benny's son. He knows arithmetic and bookkeeping, he can
copy and write. So please be so kind now and call for a
glass of brandy and a bite to eat, because I'm starved. I've had
nothing in my mouth all day.'

"Well, why should I drag out the story? We Sadagora
chassidim are simple people. Reb Zalmen promised me that
he would take the boy, so when I came home I sent David-
Leib back to Heissin. For a while he lay around, waiting.
Reb Zalmen told him that he would have to talk it over
with his son first, his son Reb Yossil, and Reb Yossil was
not in town. Later, when Reb Yossil returned, Reb Zalmen
was out of town. But at last they had to take him in, and
today he is their chief executioner."

"Cashier," corrected Hennich, and explained to them what
a cashier was. "He has to do with money. He takes it and he
gives it out."

"Thanks for making it clear," said Berel. "Otherwise we
would never have known."

And he went over to the guard, pulled him by the sleeve,
and woke him up.

"Hey, Lavre, what's the matter with you? It's time to sober
up."

And Lavre obeyed him. Slowly he got up from the ground, slowly he looked up at the sky to see where the sun was, then he picked up his staff, lined up and counted his three wards, and together they continued their journey.

9 THE *NOGID* REPENTS

The sun was close to setting, the heat had begun to abate, and the convoy was near the outskirts of Granov, the first scheduled stop on their journey, when the three prisoners stopped near a windmill, turned their faces toward the east, and began their evening prayers. Lavre stood a little to one side leaning against his staff, his cap pushed back, and looked with curiosity at the Jews nodding and swaying and once or twice beating their breasts.

Of the three, it was Reb Sholom-Ber Tepliker of Teplik who prayed with the greatest feeling. That evening he was not satisfied with merely touching his breast twice, he really beat it. "Forgive us, Our Father, for we have sinned; pardon us, Our King, for we have transgressed." With all his heart he regretted his past behavior, the things he had done and the things he had neglected to do. And he compared himself to this tattered creature, Berel the Redhead, and he was ashamed of himself. Berel, who had hardly enough to keep himself alive, had not hesitated to go a long distance on foot in someone else's behalf, to force his way into a rich man's presence, humble himself in order to do someone else a favor. And he, Sholom-Ber Tepliker of Teplik, had been unwilling even to hear about someone else's troubles; he had been cold, cold as ice. And he was sorry that he had acted that way, and most of all he was sorry for the way he had treated Berel in connection with the match he had tried to arrange for his young daughter, in Heissin, at the time of the Fair.

He felt now that he owed something to Berel the Redhead for the share he might have had in the killing of his

daughter. For if he had listened to Berel's request, if he had
shown a trace of pity, a trace of love for a poor man, his
daughter might still be alive and happy. And Sholom-Ber felt
that if he could still right at least a small part of the wrong,
he would feel much better. But he did not know how to
do it. And as he went on with his prayers his whole life
passed in review before his eyes, almost for the first time.
And he could not understand how he had ever been so
satisfied with himself, and had thought that he had done his
duty if only he said his prayers every day and dropped an
occasional three-*kopek* piece in the charity box.

The Tepliker *nogid*, Sholom-Ber Tepliker of Teplik, remembered how he had bargained for every *groschen* that
had to be torn from him by force. He had given the Holy
Scrolls to the synagogue for his own glory, but he had refused a small loan to the scribe who had made the scrolls.
And he burned with shame. He felt that until that day his
soul had been asleep, that his heart had lain under a weight
somewhere, with ice around it. And he wanted to do something for Berel, and he did not know how.

He had lived fifty-six years, more than three-quarters of
the seventy he hoped to live, and all his life had been one
long war to add one *groschen* to another. To whom would
he leave it all? He had no children, and his kinsmen all
hated him. And he remembered things he had long forgotten,
and a cold chill gripped his heart. He promised that from
now on, at least, in his old age, he would be more considerate
of his fellow men.

Having finished their prayers, our convoy resumed its journey. Berel limped along, joking with Hennich, and the *nogid*
walked alone, deep in thought. He walked faster and faster,
without looking to left or right, without knowing that he
was getting ahead of the others.

"What's your hurry, Reb Sholom-Ber?" the redhead called
to him. "I can't keep up with you."

"Is it hard for you to walk, Reb Berel?" the *nogid* asked.
"Here, give me your hand and we'll go together. And when

we come home again, with the Lord's help, I want you to come to me, both of you. There is something I have to tell you."

Berel could not understand. What did he have to tell them? And why at his home? Why not now, where they were? And why had he suddenly become so humble?

Hennich did not even try to understand. All he said was, "If only the Lord has mercy. If only David-Leib is saved."

"Don't worry," said Sholom-Ber. "Even if he goes, I'll take care of all of you. I'll take care of everybody."

When the convoy entered Granov the sun had already set, all but a bright golden strip along the horizon. They were greeted with music, a chorus of the croaking of frogs mingled with the bleating of sheep and goats being led home for the night in a cloud of dust. And that was their good fortune.

In the cloud of dust the people did not see *who* was being led through their town! Otherwise the good people of Granov might have welcomed them with the same respect and escorted them beyond the town with the same parade with which they were greeted and escorted at Michaelovka and Mitchulka and Krasnopilka and Zdakovitz and all the other points along the way between Teplik and Heissin.

THE FIDDLE

Today I'll play you something on the fiddle.

I don't know how you feel, but as for me, there is nothing more wonderful than to be able to play a fiddle. As far back as I can remember my heart has gone out to the fiddle. In fact, I loved everything about music. Whenever there was a wedding in our town I was the first one on hand to greet the musicians. I would steal up behind the bass violin, pluck a string—boom!—and run off. Boom—and run off again. For doing this I once caught the devil from Berel Bass. Berel Bass, a fierce-looking man with a flat nose and a sharp eye, pretended not to see me as I stole up behind his bass violin. But just as I was stretching my hand out to pull at the string he caught me by the ear and led me to the door with a great show of courtesy.

"Don't forget to kiss the *mazuza* on your way out," he said.

But that experience taught me nothing. I couldn't stay away from musicians. I was in love with every one of them, from Shaike Fiddele, with his fine black beard and slim white fingers to round-shouldered Getzie Peikler with the big bald spot that reached down to his ears. Many a time when they chased me away, I hid myself under a bench and listened to them playing. From under the bench I watched

Shaike's nimble fingers dancing over the strings and listened to the sweet tones that he so skillfully drew out of his little fiddle.

After that I would go around for days in a trance with Shaike and his fiddle constantly before my eyes and moving through my dreams at night. Pretending that I was Shaike, I would crook my left arm, move my fingers, and draw the right arm across as though I held a bow. All this while I threw my head to one side and dreamily shut my eyes. Just like Shaike. Exactly like him.

When the rabbi caught me—this was in *cheder*—drumming my finger in the air, throwing my head back and rolling my eyes, he gave me a loud smack. "You rascal, you are supposed to be learning something, and here you are—fooling around—catching flies!"

I vowed to myself, "Let the world come to an end, I must have a fiddle. No matter what it cost, I must have one." But how do you make a fiddle? Naturally, of cedarwood. It is easy to say—cedarwood. But where do you get this wood that is supposed to grow only in the Holy Land? So what does God do? He gives me this idea: we had an old sofa at our house, an inheritance from my grandfather, Reb Anshel, over which my two uncles and my father had quarreled for a long time. My uncle Ben argued that he was the oldest son, therefore the sofa was his. Uncle Sender argued that he was the youngest, therefore the sofa belonged to him. My father admitted that he, being only a son-in-law, had no claim to the sofa, but since his wife, my mother, was my grandfather's only daughter, the sofa rightfully belonged to her. All this time the sofa remained at our house. But my two aunts, Aunt Itke and Aunt Zlatke, entered the feud. They carried their bickerings back and forth between them. The sofa this, the sofa that. Your sofa, my sofa. The whole town rocked with it. Meanwhile, the sofa remained our sofa.

This sofa of which I speak had a wooden frame with a thin veneer which was loose and puffed out in several places.

Now this veneer, which was loose in spots, was the real cedarwood that fiddles are made of. That was what I had heard in *cheder*. The sofa had one drawback which was really a virtue. When you sat down on it you couldn't get up, because it sloped—there was a bulge on one end and a depression in the middle. This meant that no one wanted to sit on it. So it was put away in a corner and was pensioned off.

But now I began to cast an eye at this sofa. I had already arranged for a bow a long time ago. I had a friend, Yudel the teamster's Shimeleh, and he promised me as many hairs as I would need from the tail of his father's horse. And a piece of resin, to rub the bow with, I had all my own. I hated to rely on miracles. I got it in a trade with another friend of mine—Maier, Lippe-Sarah's boy—for a small piece of steel from my mother's old crinoline that had been lying up in the attic. Later, out of this piece of steel, Maier made himself a knife sharpened at both ends, and I was even ready to trade back with him, but he wouldn't think of it. He shouted at me:

"You think you're smart! You and your father, too! Here I go and work for three nights, sharpening and sharpening, and cut all my fingers, and you come around and want it back again!"

Well, I had everything. There was only one thing to do—to pick off enough of the cedar veneer from the sofa. And for that I chose a very good time—when my mother was out shopping and my father lay down for his afternoon nap. I crept into the corner with a big nail and began clawing away with real energy. In his sleep my father heard someone burrowing, and apparently thought it was a mouse. He began to hiss: "Shhh, shhhhh." I didn't move, I didn't breathe.

My father turned over on his other side and when I heard that he was snoring again I went back to my work. Suddenly I looked up—there stood my father, watching me with a puzzled look. At first he didn't seem to know what was going on, but when he saw the gouged-out sofa he dragged

me out by the ear and shook me till I rattled. I thought I
was going to faint.

"God help you—what are you doing to the child?" my
mother screamed from the threshold.

"Your pride and joy! He's driving me into my grave!"
gasped my father, pale as the white-washed wall, as he
clasped at his heart and went into a coughing spell.

"Why do you eat yourself up like that?" asked my mother.
"You're sick enough without that. Just take a look at yourself, just look!"

The desire to play the fiddle grew as I grew. The older I
grew, the more anxious I was to be able to play, and as if
in spite I had to listen to music every day. Just about halfway between home and *cheder* there was a small sod-covered
shack, and whenever you passed that shack you heard all
sorts of sounds, the strains of all kinds of instruments, and
especially the sound of a fiddle. It was the home of a musician, Naftaltzi Bezborodka, a Jew with a shortened coat, with
clipped earlocks and with a starched collar. His nose was
large and looked almost as if it were pasted on, his lips were
thick, his teeth black, his face was pockmarked and without
the trace of a beard. And that was why they called him
Bezborodka, the beardless one. His wife was a crone who
was known as Mother Eve, and they had at least a dozen
and a half children—tattered, half-naked, barefoot, and every
one of them, from the oldest to the youngest, played on
some instrument—this one the fiddle, that one the cello, the
other the bass, one the trumpet, another the flute, the bas-
soon, the harp, the cymbal, the balalaika, the drum. Some of
them could whistle the most complicated melody with their
lips, or through their teeth, on glass tumblers or pots, or on
pieces of wood. They were magicians—or devils of some
sort!

With this family I became acquainted in a most unexpected way. I was standing under their window one day,
drinking in the music, when one of the boys caught sight of

me and came out. He was Pinny, the flutist, a boy about
fifteen, but barefoot like the rest.

"What do you think of the music?" he asked.

"I wish I could play that well in ten years," I told him.

"You can," he said, and explained that for two *rubles* a
month his father would teach me to play. Or, if I wanted, he
himself would teach me.

"What instrument would you like to play?" he asked. "The
fiddle?"

"The fiddle," I said.

"The fiddle," he repeated. "Could you pay a *ruble* and a
half a month—or are you as penniless as I am?"

"I can pay," I told him. "But there is one thing. Neither
my father nor my mother nor my rabbi must know a thing
about it."

"God forbid!" he exclaimed. "Why should anyone find
out?" He moved up closer to me and whispered, "Have you
got a cigar butt—or a cigarette?" I shook my head. "No?
You don't smoke? Well, then, lend me a few *groschen* so I
can buy some cigarettes. But don't tell anybody. My father
doesn't know that I smoke, and if my mother found out she'd
take the money away and buy some bread."

He took the money and said in a friendly voice, "Come on
in. You'll get nothing done standing out here."

With great fear, my heart pounding and my legs trembling, I crossed the threshold of this small paradise.

My new friend Pinny introduced me to his father. "This
is Sholom—Nochem-Vevik's. A rich man's son . . . He
wants to learn to play the fiddle."

Naftaltzi Bezborodka pulled at his earlock, straightened his
collar, and buttoned up his coat. Then he began a long and
detailed lecture on the subject of music in general and fiddle-
playing in particular. He gave me to understand that the
fiddle was the best and finest of all instruments—there was
no instrument that ranked higher. Else why is the fiddle the
chief instrument in an orchestra, and not the trombone or

the flute? Because the fiddle is the mother of all instruments . . .

Thus Naftaltzi spoke, accompanying his words with motions of his hands and large nose. I stood gaping at him, swallowing every word that came out.

"The fiddle," Naftaltzi continued, apparently pleased with his lecture, "the fiddle, you understand, is an instrument that is older than all other instruments. The first fiddler in the world was Tubal Cain or Methuselah, I am not sure which. You may know, you study such things in *cheder*. The second fiddler was King David. The third, a man named Paganini, also a Jew. The best fiddlers have always been Jews. I can name you a dozen. Not to mention myself . . . They say I don't play badly, but how can I compare myself to Paganini? Paganini, we are told, sold his soul to the devil for a fiddle. He never would play for the great of the world—the kings and the princes—no matter how much they gave him. He preferred to play for the common people in the taverns and the villages, or even in the woods for the beasts and birds. Ah, what a fiddler Paganini was!"

Suddenly he turned around: "Fellow artists—to your instruments!"

Thus Naftaltzi called out to his band of children, who gathered about him immediately, each with his own instrument. Naftaltzi himself struck the table with his bow, threw a sharp look at each child separately and at all of them at once, and the concert began. They went at it with such fury that I was almost knocked off my feet. Each one tried to outdo the other, but loudest of all played a little boy named Chemeleh, a thin child with a running nose and bare spindly legs. Chemeleh played a strange instrument—some sort of a sack—and when he blew, it gave out an unearthly shriek, like a cat when its tail is stepped on. With his bare foot Chemeleh marked time and all the while watched me out of his small impish eyes and winked at me as if to say, "I am doing well, ain't I?" . . . But hardest of all worked Naftaltzi himself. He both played and conducted, working with his

hands, his feet, his nose, his eyes, his whole body; and if
anyone made a mistake, he gritted his teeth and yelled out:
"*Forte*, you fool! *Forte, fortissimo!* Count, stupid—count!
One, two, three! One, two, three!"

I arranged with Naftaltzi Bezborodka to take three lessons
a week, an hour and a half each time, for two *rubles* a
month I begged him over and over to keep this a secret, or
I would get into trouble. He gave me his word of honor that
he would breathe it to no one.

"We are people," he said gravely, adjusting his collar, "of
small means, but when it comes to honor and integrity, we
have more than the richest of the rich. By the way—can you
spare me a few *groschen?*"

I pulled a *ruble* out of my pocket. Naftaltzi took it from
me like a professor—very refined—with the tips of his fingers. Then he called Mother Eve, and hardly looking at her,
said, "Here, get something for dinner."

Mother Eve took the money from him with both hands
and every one of her fingers, inspected it carefully, and said,
"What shall I buy?"

"Anything you want," he said with a show of indifference.
"Get a few rolls—two or three herring—a sausage. And
don't forget—an onion, some vinegar and oil—and, maybe,
a bottle of brandy . . ."

When the food was laid out on the table the crowd fell
on it with such gusto as after a fast. Watching them made
me so ravenous that when they asked me to join them I
couldn't refuse. And I don't know when I enjoyed any food
as much as I did that meal.

When we were through, Bezborodka winked at the crowd,
signaled for them to reach for their instruments, and I was
treated to another concert, this time an "original composition." This they played with such verve and spirit that my
ears rang and my head swam and I left the house drunk with
Naftaltzi Bezborodka's "composition."

All that day in *cheder* the rabbi, the boys and the books

all danced before my eyes and the music rang incessantly in my ears. At night I dreamed of Paganini riding the devil. He hit me over the head with his fiddle. I woke screaming, my head splitting, and I began to babble—I don't know what. Later my older sister Pessel told me that I was out of my head. What I said made no sense—crazy words like "composition," "Paganini," "the devil" . . . Another thing my sister told me was that while I was sick someone came to ask about me—somebody from Naftaltzi the musician—a barefoot boy. He was chased away and told never to come back.

"What did that fiddler's boy want from you?" my sister nagged, but I held my tongue.

"I don't know. I don't know a thing. What are you talking about?"

"How does it look?" my mother said. "You are a grown boy already—we are trying to arrange a match for you—and you pick yourself friends like these. Barefoot fiddlers! What have you got to do with musicians anyway? What did Naftaltzi's boy want of you?"

"Which Naftaltzi?" I asked innocently. "What musicians?"

"Look at him!" my father broke in. "He doesn't know a thing. Poor little fellow! At your age I was engaged a long time already, and you are still playing games with children. Get dressed and go to *cheder*. And if you meet Hershel Beltax on the way and he asks what was the matter with you, tell him you had a fever. Do you hear what I said? A fever."

I didn't begin to understand. What did I have to do with Hershel Beltax? And why did I have to tell him about a fever? In a few weeks my question was answered.

Hershel Beltax (he was called that because he and his father and his grandfather had all worked for the tax collector) was a man with a round little belly, a short red beard, small moist eyes and a broad white forehead—the mark of a wise man. He had the reputation in town of being an intelligent man, accomplished and learned—up to a cer-

tain point—in the *Torah*. He was a fine writer—that is, he
had a clear handwriting. It was said that at one time his
writings were known all over the countryside. And besides
that he had money and a daughter, an only daughter, with
red hair and moist eyes—the exact image of him. Her name
was Esther, she was called by a nickname—Flesterl. She was
timid and delicate, and terribly afraid of us schoolboys because we teased her all the time. When we met her we sang
this song:

> *Esther, Flester,*
> *Where is your sister?*

What was so terrible about that? Nothing, it seemed to
me, and yet when Esther heard it she covered her ears and
ran off crying. She would hide in her room and not go out
on the street for days.

But that was a long time ago when she was a child. Now
she was a grown girl with long red braids and went about
dressed in the latest fashion. My mother was very fond of
her. "Gentle as a dove," she used to say. Sometimes on Saturday Esther used to come to visit my sister and when she saw
me she would turn even redder than she was and drop her
eyes. And my sister would call me over and start asking me
questions—and watch us both to see how we acted.

One day—into the *cheder* walked my father with Hershel
Beltax, and behind them trailed Reb Sholom-Shachne, the
matchmaker, a man with a curly black beard, a man with six
fingers, as people used to say. Seeing such guests, the rabbi,
Reb Zorach, grabbed his coat and put on his hat in such a
hurry that one of his earlocks was caught behind his ear, and
his skullcap stuck out from under his hat, and his cheeks
began to flame. We could see that something unusual was
about to happen. Lately Reb Sholom-Shachne the matchmaker had been coming to the *cheder* frequently and each
time he came he called the rabbi out of the room and there
through the doorway we could see them whispering together,

shrugging their shoulders, gesturing with their hands—ending up with a sigh.

"Well, it's the same old story. If it's to be, it will be. Regardless."

Now when these guests came in, the rabbi, Reb Zorach, was so confused he didn't know what to do or where to seat them. He grabbed hold of a low bench on which his wife used to salt the meat, and carried it around the room with him, till he finally put it down and sat on it himself. But he quickly jumped up and said to his guests, "Here is a bench. Won't you sit down?"

"That's all right, Reb Zorach," said my father. "We just came in for a minute. We'd like to hear my son recite something—out of the Bible." And he inclined his head toward Hershel Beltax.

"Surely, why not?" said the rabbi, and picking up the Bible he handed it to Hershel Beltax, with a look that said, "Here—do what you can with it."

Hershel Beltax took the Bible like a man who knew what he was doing, bent his head sideways, shut one eye, shuffled the pages and handed it to me open at the first paragraph of the *Song of Songs*.

"The *Song of Songs?*" said Reb Zorach with a smile, as though to say, "You couldn't find something harder?" "The *Song of Songs*," says Hershel Beltax, "is not as easy as you think. One has to understand it."

"That's not a lie," said Reb Sholom-Shachne, the matchmaker, with a laugh.

The rabbi beckons to me. I walk up to the table, and begin to chant in a loud voice, with a fine rhythm:

"The *Song of Songs!* A song above all other songs. Other songs have been sung by a prophet, but this song was sung by a prophet who was the son of a prophet. Other songs have been sung by a sage, but this was sung by a sage who was the son of a sage. Other songs have been sung by a king. This was sung by a king who was the son of a king."

While I sang I watched my examiners and saw on the

face of each of them a different expression. On my father's face I saw great pride and joy. On the rabbi's face was fear lest I make a mistake. His lips silently repeated each word. Hershel Beltax sat with his head bent sideways, his beard between his lips, one eye shut, and the other raised aloft, listening with a very knowing look. Reb Sholom-Shachne the matchmaker did not take his eyes off Hershel Beltax the whole time. He sat with his body bent forward, swaying back and forth along with me, interrupting me with a sound that was part exclamation, part laugh, part a cough, pointing his fingers at me:

"When I said he knew it I really meant he knew it."

A few weeks later plates were broken, and I became engaged to Hershel Beltax's daughter, Flesterl.

Sometimes it happens that a person ages more in one day than in ten years. When I became engaged I suddenly felt grown up—seemingly the same boy and yet not the same. From the smallest boy to the rabbi himself they all treated me with respect. After all, I was a young man engaged to be married—and I had a watch! No longer did my father scold me—and as for whippings—that was out of the question. How could you whip a young man who wore a gold watch? It would be a shame and a disgrace. Once a boy named Eli, who, like me, was engaged to be married, received a whipping in *cheder* because he was caught skating on the ice with some peasant boys. The whole town talked about it, and when his fiancée learned of the scandal she cried so long that her parents broke the engagement. And the young man, Eli, was so heartbroken and so ashamed that he wanted to throw himself into the river. Fortunately, the water was frozen over . . .

Such a calamity befell me, too, but not over a whipping, and not over skating on ice, but over a fiddle. And here is the story:

In our tavern we had a frequent guest, Tchetchek, the bandleader, whom we called Colonel. He was a strapping fellow, tall, with a large, round beard and sinister eyebrows. His speech was a mixture of several languages, and when he spoke he moved his eyebrows up and down. When he lowered his eyebrows his face became black as night, and when he raised them, his face glowed like the sun, because under those thick eyebrows were a pair of eyes that were bright blue and full of laughter. He wore a uniform with gold buttons and that was why we called him Colonel. He came to our tavern frequently—not because he was a heavy drinker, but because my father used to make a raisin wine—"the best —and rarest—Hungarian wine" that Tchetchek could hardly praise enough. He would put his enormous hand on my father's thin shoulder and roar in his queer mixed language:

"Herr Kellermeister, you have the best Hungarian wine in the world. There is no such wine even in Budapest, *predbozhe*."

Tchetchek was very friendly with me. He praised me for my stories and liked to ask questions like: "Who was Adam? Who was Isaac? Who was Joseph?"

"You mean—*Yosef?*" I would say.

"I mean Joseph."

"*Yosef*," I corrected him again.

"To us he is Joseph, to you he is *Yosef*," he would say and pinch my cheek. "Joseph or *Yosef, Yosef* or Joseph, it's all the same, all equal—*wszystko yedno*."

But when I became engaged Tchetchek's attitude also changed. Instead of treating me like a child he began to talk to me as to an equal, to tell me stories of the army and of musicians. (The Colonel had wonderful stories to tell but no one had time to listen except me.) Once, when he was talking about music, I questioned him, "What instrument does the Colonel play?"

"All instruments," he said, and raised his eyebrows.

"The fiddle too?" I asked, and his face became in my eyes the face of an angel.

"Come to my house some day," he said, "and I will play for you."

"I can only come on the Sabbath. But please, Colonel, no
one must know." *"Przed bohem,"* he said fervently and raised
his eyebrows.

Tchetchek lived far off beyond the town in a small white
cottage with small windows and brightly painted shutters,
surrounded by a garden full of bright, yellow sunflowers that
carried themselves as proudly as lilies or roses. They bent
their heads a little, swayed in the breeze and beckoned to
me, "Come to us, young man, come to us. Here is space,
here is freedom, here it is bright and fresh, warm and cheerful." And after the stench and heat and dust of the town,
the noise and turmoil of the crowded *cheder,* I was glad to
come, for here was space and freedom, here it was bright
and fresh, warm and cheerful. I felt like running, leaping,
yelling, singing, or like throwing myself on the ground with
my face deep in the fragrant grass. But that is not for you,
Jewish children. Yellow sunflowers, green grass, fresh air, the
clean earth, the clear sky, these are not for you . . .

When I came to the gate the first time, I was met by a
shaggy, black dog with fiery, red eyes, who jumped at me
with such force that I was almost knocked over. Luckily he
was tied to a rope. When Tchetchek heard me yell he came
running out of the house, without his uniform on, and told
the dog to be quiet. Then he took me by the hand and led
me up to the black dog. He told me not to be afraid. "Here,
pat him—he won't hurt you." And taking my hand he passed
it over the dog's fur, calling him odd names in a kindly
voice. The dog dropped his tail, licked himself all over and
gave me a look that said, "Lucky for you my master is standing here, or you would be leaving without a hand."

Having recovered from my fright, I entered the house
with the Colonel and there I was struck dumb: all the walls
were covered with guns, and on the floor lay a skin with
the head of a lion—or maybe a leopard—with fierce teeth.
The lion didn't bother me so much—he was dead. But those
guns—all those guns! I didn't enjoy the fresh plums and

juicy apples with which my host treated me. I couldn't keep my eyes away from the walls. But later, when Tchetchek took out of its red case a small round fiddle with an odd belly, spread over it his large round beard and placed on it his huge powerful hand and passed the bow over it a few times, and the first melody poured out, I forgot in one instant the black dog, the fierce lion and the loaded guns. I saw only Tchetchek's spreading beard, his overhanging eyebrows, I saw only a round fiddle with an odd belly, and fingers which danced over the strings with such speed that it was hard to imagine where so many fingers came from.

Then Tchetchek himself disappeared—with his spreading beard, his thick eyebrows, and his wonderful fingers—and I saw nothing in front of me. I only heard a singing, a sighing, a weeping, a sobbing, a talking, a roaring—all sorts of strange sounds that I had never heard in my life before. Sounds sweet as honey, smooth as oil, kept pouring without end straight into my heart, and my soul soared far far away into another world, into a paradise of pure sound.

"Would you like some tea?" calls out Tchetchek, putting down the fiddle and slapping me on the back.

I felt as though I had fallen from the seventh heaven down to earth again.

After that I visited Tchetchek every Saturday to listen to his playing. I went straight to the house, not afraid of anyone, and I even became so familiar with the black dog that he would wag his tail when he saw me, and try to lick my hand. But I wouldn't allow that. "Let's be friends at a distance," I said.

At home no one knew where I spent my Saturdays. No one stopped me. After all, I was not a child any more.

And they wouldn't have known until now if a fresh calamity had not occurred—a great calamity which I shall now describe.

Who should care if a young fellow takes a Sabbath walk

by himself a short distance out of town? Whose business is it? Apparently there are people who care, and one such person was Ephraim Klotz, a busybody who knew what was cooking in every pot. He made it his business to know. This man watched me closely, followed me, found out where I was going, and later swore with many pious oaths that he had seen me at the Colonel's house eating pork and smoking cigarettes on the Sabbath.

Every Saturday when I was on my way to Tchetchek's I would meet him on the bridge, walking along in a sleeveless, patched, summer coat that reached to his ankles. He walked with his arms folded behind him, his overcoat flapping, humming to himself in a thin voice.

"A good Sabbath," I would say to him.

"Good Sabbath," he would reply. "Where is the young man going?"

"Just for a walk," I said.

"For a walk? Alone?" he repeated, with a meaningful smile . . .

One afternoon when I was sitting with Tchetchek and drinking tea, we heard the dog barking and tearing at his rope. Looking out of the window, I thought I saw someone small and dark with short legs running out of sight. From his way of running I could swear it was Ephraim Klotz.

That night, when I got home, I saw Ephraim Klotz sitting at the table. He was talking with great animation and laughing his odd little laugh that sounded like dried peas pouring out of a dish. Seeing me, he fell silent and began to drum with his short fingers on the table. Opposite him sat my father, his face pale, twisting his beard and tearing hairs out one by one—a sign that he was angry.

"Where are you coming from?" asked my father, with a glance at Ephraim Klotz.

"Where should I be coming from?" I said.

"Where have you been all day?" said my father.

"Where should I be all day? In *shul.*"

"What did you do there all day?"

"What should I be doing there? Studying . . ."

"What were you studying?" said my father.

"What should I be studying? The *Gamorah* . . ."

"Which *Gamorah?*" said my father.

At this point Ephraim Klotz laughed his shrill laugh and my father could stand it no more. He rose from his seat and leaning over, gave me two resounding, fiery slaps in the face. My mother heard the commotion from the next room and came running in . . .

"Nochem," she cried, "God be with you! What are you doing? The boy is engaged to be married. Suppose his father-in-law hears of this?"

My mother was right. My future father-in-law heard the whole story. Ephraim repeated it to him himself. It was too good to keep.

The next day the engagement was broken and I was a privileged person no more. My father was so upset that he became ill and stayed in bed for days. He would not let me come near him, no matter how much my mother pleaded for me.

"The shame of it," he said. "The disgrace. That is worst of all."

"Forget about it," my mother begged. "God will send us another match. Our lives won't be ruined by this. Perhaps it was not his lot."

Among those who came to visit my father while he was ill was the bandmaster. When my father saw him, he took off his skullcap, sat up in bed, and extending an emaciated hand, said to him:

"Ah, Colonel, Colonel . . ."

More he could not say because his voice became choked with tears and he was seized with a fit of coughing. This was the first time in my life that I had seen my father cry. My heart ached and my soul went out to him. I stood staring out of the window, swallowing tears. How I regretted the trouble I had caused!

Silently I swore to myself never, never to disobey my father again, never to cause him such grief, never in this world.

No more fiddles.

THE DAY BEFORE
YOM KIPPUR

(Sketches of Disappearing Types)

1 NOAH-WOLF THE BUTCHER

If the day before *Yom Kippur* were three times as long as
it is, it would not be long enough for Noah-Wolf the
butcher to finish his work in time for the evening services.

And this is his work: he has to apologize to a townful of
people for his year's misdeeds. He has to go to all the customers who buy meat from him, all the neighbors who live
in the same street with him or have their shops near his, or
sit close to him in the butchers' synagogue.

There is not a person in our town with whom Noah-
Wolf has not had an argument at one time or another. Not
that Noah-Wolf is such an evil person, but he undoubtedly
has, as he himself says, an ugly temper. He simply has to
fight with people.

If you come into his shop for some meat, you are met
with a pailful of cold water. And he cannot even tell you
why.

A housewife comes in: "Reb Noah-Wolf, do you have any
fresh meat today?"

And he answers: "How should I have fresh meat? If you
want rotten meat, you can get it."

Or: "Noah-Wolf, give me a good portion."

"I'll give you just the kind of portion you deserve."

Or this: "What kind of carcass are you giving me, Noah-Wolf! Look at it!"

"What does a carcass like you know about carcasses?"

That is how Noah-Wolf treats his customers, the house-wives themselves. So how would you expect him to treat the servant girls? When one of them has to go to his shop, she curses her fate. She knows what a greeting she can expect. Either he will slap her across the face with a beef tongue, or he'll fit her marketbasket over her head, or he'll simply chase her out.

"Get out of here! Go to some other shop! There are enough butchers without me!"

Nevertheless one thing has nothing to do with another. Noah-Wolf the butcher may be stubborn and eccentric, and yet his customers won't go anywhere else, because they know that he is the most honorable butcher in town. They know that his scale is true and that he keeps his word. If he tells you that the meat was slaughtered yesterday, you know that it is so. And if he promises you some sweetbreads, or a piece of lung, or a neat's foot for Saturday, you can sleep in peace. The lung or the foot is as good as yours. Furthermore, he will never connive with your servant girl to rob you behind your back. And he won't combine with other butchers to raise their prices. That is why the servant girls slander him, and the other butchers would like to drown him in a spoon-ful of water. He sticks in their throats like a bone. He is a stubborn man. If he makes up his mind on anything, he's like an ox being dragged to slaughter. You can't make him budge.

And he even looks like an ox. He is tall and broad and red-faced, and his hands are enormous. When he raises his cleaver to split a side of meat he does it as ferociously as if the ox or cow had committed some crime and had been con-demned to be chopped to pieces by him in person.

"That man is a murderer!" they say in our town, and there are grown people who are actually afraid of him.

But if all year long he gets under your skin, he changes

with the coming of the New Year. Then you would hardly recognize him. He becomes someone else, pious, God-fearing, virtuous, and sees omens in everything. He stops fighting with the other butchers, becomes soft as butter toward his customers, is considerate to the servant girls, becomes so unctuous you could almost spread him over a boil. Even when he chops his meat now he does it differently, not murderously as before, but gently, mercifully. A different Noah-Wolf altogether.

The day before *Yom Kippur* he locks up very early (he had said his morning prayers when most of us were still asleep), puts on his holiday gabardine, and goes from house to house, to all his customers and neighbors, friends and acquaintances, to offer his apologies, to ask for pardon for the year's misdeeds.

"Good *yom-tev*," he says. "If anything I have said offended you, I want to apologize, and wish you a happy New Year."

And they say to him: "The same to you, Noah-Wolf. May God pardon us all."

And they invite him to sit down and they treat him to a piece of holiday torte.

2 EZRIEL THE FISHERMAN

Since the world was created, you have never seen as ill-tempered a creature as Ezriel the fisherman.

An ill-tempered man with angry eyes, thick eyebrows, bristling mustache, and a beard that looks as if it has been pasted on. And he wears a quilted jacket summer and winter, with the fringes of his *tallis-kot'n* sticking out underneath. And he smells of raw fish a mile away.

All week long you don't see him at all. But before every Sabbath and every holiday he appears in the marketplace with his wagon piled high with fish. On top of the wagon sits a girl with pockmarked face, watching the fish. And his wife, Maita, a heavy, swollen woman, stands alongside the wagon with a stick and watches the fish.

"Fish—fish—fresh and quivering! Women! Fish for Sabbath!"

That is the way Ezriel the fisherman announces his wares across the marketplace, in his loud, familiar chant, and he never takes an eye off the women who have already crowded around his wagon and laid siege to it from all sides, clutching the fish by the heads, peering under the gills, poking at the eyes or prodding at the bellies to see if the fish is fresh. These liberties Ezriel hates and despises like something un-*kosher,* and he chases the women away.

"Away from here! You've pawed over them long enough already!"

This he hurls at them in a quick undertone, and then, once more to the world at large, in his loud, clear chant:

"Fish—fish—fresh and quivering! Women! Fish for Sabbath!"

Every woman, whether a housewife or a servant girl, is treated alike by Ezriel the fisherman. He watches her like a hawk. He does not suspect anyone of being a thief, but he knows that when it comes to fish, you can never tell. The richest, most honorable, most charitable woman is frequently torn by the desire to make off with a good, fresh fish if no one is looking. "Fish," he says, "is a temptation that is hard for a woman to resist."

Every year at least one scandal takes place around Ezriel's wagon. He slaps some woman across the face with a wet and shiny pickerel. From all directions men and women come running up; there is noise and confusion. The crowd puts in a word for the woman, gives her advice, tells her to file a complaint with the Justice of the Peace, or have Ezriel dragged off to the rabbi. But since the pain is moral rather than physical, it soon wears off, and the whole affair comes to nothing.

Most of the women know him already. They would think

no more of edging too close to his fish than to the gold and precious stones under a king's guard.

"How much are your rubies and emeralds today?" a woman may ask, standing with her basket at some distance and pointing with her little finger at the wagon.

"I deal in fish, not rubies!" Ezriel answers proudly, without even condescending to give the woman a glance with his angry eyes. And once more he lets out his call to the world at large:

"Fish—fish—fresh and quivering! Women! Fish!"

"An apoplectic man!" the women say of him. They would much rather not have anything to do with him, but that is impossible. There is not another fisherman in town, so what can one do? Lie down on the ground and die? Or live through the Sabbath without fish? But that is even worse than dying, for if a woman dies she knows she is dead: it's all over. But if she comes home without fish for Saturday, then she has her husband's wrath to contend with. And that is worse than dying.

"I wish something terrible would happen to him!"

That is what the women say when *Yom Kippur* eve comes around and they rush off to the marketplace with their baskets, afraid that they might be too late, because the day before *Yom Kippur* Ezriel is in the habit of getting up so early that God himself is still in bed. And when other people are just getting ready for their morning prayers, Ezriel is through with everything and is all dressed up for the holiday. His heavy, quilted jacket has been put away and he wears the coarse, shiny, black gabardine that is seen only on the Sabbath and high holidays, but which nevertheless is saturated through and through with the odor of raw fish.

Ezriel begins his fast earlier than anyone. Earlier than anyone he comes to the synagogue that afternoon, takes his place close to the back wall, covers his head with his prayer shawl, and stands without rest for twenty-four hours. He won't sit down even for a minute. He prays quietly, so that no one can hear a word. He weeps a great deal, but no one can ever see a tear.

But that is in the evening. Before that, all day long, he goes around the town to his customers, bringing his apologies, asking their pardon.

"If anything I have said to you during the year offended you, I want to apologize, and wish you a happy New Year."

And they say to him:

"The same to you, Reb Ezriel. May God pardon us all."

And they invite him to sit down and they treat him to a piece of holiday torte.

3 GETZI THE GOVERNOR

Getzi the Governor—that is what we always called the *shammes,* the sexton, of the old synagogue.

Everywhere, in all the synagogues of the world, a *shammes* may be a *shammes.* But Getzi, the *shammes* of our old synagogue, is more like a member of the board of governors than a *shammes.* Did I say a member of the board? He acts like the president of the board!

Getzi does not permit any secular business in the synagogue. He says that a synagogue is a place of worship. If you want to talk business you can go to the marketplace. If you want to discuss politics there is a bath house. Under no conditions will he let you talk during an intermission or a recess. Getzi is a man who shows no respect for anyone. You can be the holder of a pew by the eastern wall, you can have seventeen silver stripes on your *tallis,* he won't debase himself before you. You can be the richest person in town, Reb Joshua Hershel himself, if you say a single word out loud, you hear his hand come pounding down on the table, and a cry of "Qui-et!" so loud that you are almost deafened.

Or try to take one of the sacred tomes from the synagogue

bookshelf, and forget to bring it back in time! You'll be put in your place soon enough.

Or if on the Sabbath you pledge a half pound of candles for the synagogue, or eighteen *kopeks* for the poor fund, and then forget to give it! You might as well go bankrupt, or leave everything behind and rush off to America!

Or try to send Getzi on an errand that has nothing to do with the synagogue. This is what you'll hear: "Do *you* have feet? Then go yourself!"

That's the kind of man Getzi is.

The only ones who dare to be impudent with Getzi are the small fry. Inquisitive youngsters, small boys barely learning their alphabet, mischief makers, pranksters of all kinds, these make life miserable for him. The things they do to him would make anyone shudder. They turn over the prayer stands when no one is looking, they let water out of the washbowl, tie knots in the towels, let tallow drip on all the holy books, and tear *Yekum Purkon* out of all the prayer books, so that no matter which one you open the prayer is missing.

These little troublemakers shortened Getzi's life, they taught him the terrors of Gehenna. He kept constant watch; maybe he would catch one of them in the act. And when he caught one, he evened accounts for everything the whole band had ever done. To emerge from his grasp with only a light bruise, a black eye, or an ear that was only partly pulled off, that was luck indeed. Getzi hated drawn-out affairs, worthless investigations and formal trials. No matter whom he caught, a rich man's child or an orphan in rags, it made no difference.

Getzi knows all about slapping. When you feel his hand you behold your grandfather in Paradise. A powerful man, from a family known for its strength, although to look at him you would have hesitated to give two broken *kopeks* for him. Lean, dried up, skin and bones. But his sidelocks were thick and black, and he himself was dark as a Tartar, with fierce, black eyes, hollow cheeks, a crooked nose, and black drooping mustache. All these things taken together made him look either as if he was about to sneeze but was trying not to, or as if he had something to tell you but was keeping it to himself, or simply as if he were an ill-tempered, evil man.

The most evil man in town, was what a lot of people called him. A worm-eaten, spiteful creature who knew no master and did whatever he pleased. If he wanted to open the synagogue, he opened it. If he wanted to shut it, he shut it. When winter came, you had to get down and beg him to start the fire. But when he did make up his mind to start it, you thought you were in a steam bath.

Let some wandering pauper beg with his last breath to be allowed to spend the night in the synagogue. "A synagogue is not a poorhouse," says Getzi, and drives the poor man out without a trace of pity.

And when the High Holidays come around, Getzi rules in the synagogue with a strong and ruthless hand. If he has conceived a dislike for you, you will never get his permission to let your son or son-in-law sit where you would like to have him. You can resign yourself to this: he will sit where Getzi wants him to. And if you go up to the trustees with your complaint, you'll get this answer: "Go to the governor."

And you know that what they mean is Getzi the *shammes*. To his face you will call him Getzi, but behind his back he is the Governor.

It's like that all the time. During *Succos,* if Getzi does not bring the *esrog* to you on time and you complain, he says: "You can wait a minute, can't you? I waited longer for you!"

So once more you bring your charges to the trustees. But this is the only answer you get:

"What can a person do with a governor?"

All year long it's the same. Getzi provides the materials for all the holidays, candles for *Hannukah,* noisemakers for *Purim, matzo* for Passover, and greens for *Shevuos.* Getzi runs the whole town, rules over it like a king. Like a king? Like a conqueror! All of us have to endure it. The only time when people dare to talk is on the Sabbath or a holiday, at dusk, when we sit and wait in the gathering darkness for the evening services. Then we can say something. For a few minutes we do not have to be afraid of the *shammes,* we can talk freely and openly. And no matter what we talk about, we come finally to the Getzi captivity, which seems worse to us than the Babylonian captivity we have heard about. We ask each other, "How long? Till when? How long will this captivity last?" And that is as far as we go. What else can we do? We Jews have suffered under so many evil kings and governors!

But there is one day of the year when Governor Getzi suspends his tyranny. Not a whole day, but a half day, really only a few hours. That is the day before *Yom Kippur,* right after the morning prayers, and before people start coming for the high services, when Getzi once more becomes king. But during those few hours he forgets that he is *shammes,* forgets he is governor. He is dressed in his holiday best, and he runs from house to house, stops everywhere, with these words:

"If anything I have said to you at any time offended you, forgive me. And may you have a happy New Year."

And he gets this reluctant answer: "You too, you too."

And they invite him to sit down and they give him a piece of holiday torte.

THREE LITTLE HEADS

I offer you a present for *Shevuos,* a picture of three little heads, three wonderfully fine heads of three poor, tattered, barefoot Jewish children. All three little heads are dark, with curly hair and eyes big and luminous that stare at you with wonder and always seem to ask the question: "Why?" You look back at them with wonder and a feeling of guilt as if somehow you are to blame for their having been created, three more superfluous creatures on the face of the earth.

The three little heads—Avremchik, Moisechik and Dvorka—are two brothers and their little sister. Avremchik and Moisechik—that was what their father, Peiseh the box-maker, called them, in the Russian manner. If he hadn't been afraid of what his wife would say, and if he weren't such a bitterly poor man, he'd have changed his own name too, from Peiseh the boxmaker to Piotr Pereplotchik. But since he was afraid of his wife, and since he was as poor as he could be, he remained, for the time being, Peiseh the box-maker, till the time should some day come, the happy time when everything would be different, as Bebel said and as Karl Marx said, and as all good and wise men say. But until that lucky time arrived, he would have to stand from morning till dark, cutting cardboard and pasting boxes and containers.

So Peiseh the boxmaker stands on his feet all day and cuts cardboard and puts together boxes, and sings songs, some of the old ones and some new ones, some Jewish songs and some not a bit Jewish—many of them not a bit Jewish—happy sad songs with a sad happy tune.

"Will you ever stop singing those outlandish songs? You must have fallen in love with them! Since you have come to the big city you are not a Jew any more."

The three—Avremchik, Moisechik and Dvorka—were born and grew up in the same place, between the wall and the oven in a single crowded room. Every day the three saw the same things before them: their jolly father who cut the cardboard, pasted boxes and sang songs; and their worried, exhausted mother, who cooked and baked, swept and scrubbed and was never finished. Both were always at work, the mother at the oven, the father at his boxes. Who would ever need so many boxes? What would they do with all these boxes? The whole world must be full of boxes. That's how it seemed to the three little heads, and they waited for their father to get so many boxes ready that he would have to pile them on his head, and fill both arms with them—maybe a hundred thousand boxes—and then go out with them. Later he came back without any boxes—with no boxes at all, but with a little money for their mother, and with oddly shaped buns, *beigel* and candy for the children.

How good their father was to them, how wonderfully good! Their mother was good too, but she was the one to scold them. Rushing between washtub and oven, she pushed them out of her way, gave their hands a slap, boxed an ear. She did not want them to upset things playing house. She did not want Avremchik to cut up the scraps of cardboard that fell from his father's work table, or Moisechik to steal paste from the pot, or Dvorka to make mud cakes. Their mother always wanted them to sit quietly and sedately. Their mother forgot that young heads worked all the time, that young spirits tore themselves, pulled with all their might, strained toward—toward what? Toward the outdoors, toward the light, toward the window—the window . . .

One window—that's all there was. One small window.

The three little heads try to reach the one small window—
and what can they see there? A wall, a high, broad, gray
damp wall, always damp, always dripping, even in summer.
Does the sun ever come in here at all? Of course the sun
comes in—sometimes. That is, not the sun itself, but a glim-
mering reflection of the sun. And when that happens it is a
time for rejoicing. The three little heads crowd against the
small window, look up, way up, and glimpse a long, narrow, blue strip, like a long blue ribbon.

"There, do you see that, children? That's the sky!"

That is Avremchik speaking. Avremchik knows. Avremchik goes to *cheder*. He is already studying the alphabet.
The *cheder* is not so far—two houses away, or rather, two
doors away. Oh, what stories Avremchik tells about *cheder!*
Avremchik says that he himself saw, on his word of honor,
a huge brick building covered with small windowpanes from
top to bottom. He swears that he saw with his own eyes, on
his word of honor, a chimney, a tall chimney reaching to the
sky, with smoke pouring out of it, and machines that run
by themselves without anybody operating them, and carts
that move without horses. And other such fabulous tales Avremchik brings back from his trips to *cheder,* and swears, as
his mother swears, on his word of honor. And Moisechik and
Dvorka listen to him and sigh with envy, because Avremchik knows everything—everything.

For instance, Avremchik knows that a tree grows. Of
course he himself has never seen a tree grow any more than
they have—there are no trees on their street—but he knows
(he heard it in *cheder*) that trees bear fruit. And that is why
when you eat fruit you say, "Blessed art thou, O Lord our
God, King of the universe, who createst the fruit of the
tree." Avremchik knows (what doesn't he know?) that potatoes, for instance, or cucumbers, or onions or garlic grow
on the ground. And that is why for these things you say,
"Blessed art thou, O Lord our God, King of the universe,
who createst the fruit of the earth." Avremchik knows
everything! But he doesn't know how or in what manner

these things grow either. For on their street there is no field, no garden, there are no trees, there's not a blade of grass—not one! On their street there are only tall buildings, gray walls, high chimneys pouring smoke, and every building is covered with windowpanes, thousands of little windowpanes, and inside the buildings are machines that run by themselves, and carts that move without horses. And aside from that there is nothing, nothing.

Even a bird is rarely seen. Sometimes a sparrow blunders into the neighborhood and the sparrow is as gray as the walls themselves. It pecks once or twice at the cobblestones, rises and flies away. And chickens, ducks, geese? Once in a great while they have a quarter of a chicken for Saturday, chicken with a pale scrawny leg. How many legs does a chicken have? Obviously four. Just like a horse. That is Avremchik's opinion, and Avremchik knows everything.

Sometimes their mother comes from market bringing a chicken's head with glazed filmy eyes. "It's dead," says the older Avremchik, and the three little heads look at each other with large dark eyes and sigh. Born and brought up in the great city, in the large buildings, in crowded quarters, the three children never had a chance to see anything alive—a hen, a cow, or any other creature except a cat. They have their own cat, a live one, a large cat, gray as the tall gray damp walls. The cat is their one joy. They play with it whenever they can. They tie a kerchief around its head and call it Auntie, and laugh uproariously.

But then their mother catches them at it and goes after them, slaps one's hands, boxes another's ears, sends them back to their place behind the oven. The oldest, Avremchik, begins to talk and the younger ones listen, look up wide-eyed at their older brother, and listen. Avremchik says that their mother is right. He says that you're not supposed to play with a cat, because a cat is an unclean thing, an evil spirit. Avremchik knows everything, everything. Is there anything in the world that he doesn't know?

Avremchik knows everything. He knows that there is a

land, a land far away, far, far away, that is called America,
There in America they have many friends and relatives.
There in America Jews have a better life and a happier one.
Next year, or the year after, if all is well and someone sends
them tickets from over there, they plan to go to America
too. Without tickets you can't go, because there is an ocean
you have to cross, and storms come up and toss the ship
about. Avremchik knows everything.

Everything . . . Even what goes on in the next world.
For instance, he knows that in the next world there is a
Paradise—for Jews, of course. In that Paradise you'll find the
most brilliant trees with all kinds of fruit, rivers flowing with
all good things. Diamonds and precious stones are scattered
over the streets; all you have to do is bend down and fill
your pockets with them. And pious Jews sit day and night
studying the holy books and enjoying the divine presence.

Avremchik tells them all these things, and the children's
eyes sparkle and they envy their brother, who knows everything—even what happens in heaven. Avremchik swears that
twice a year—one night of *Succos* and one night of *Shevuos*
—the skies split open. Of course he has never seen the
skies split open, because where they live you can't see the
sky. But some of his schoolmates saw it happen. They swore
that they saw it. And they wouldn't swear to a lie, would
they? That would be a sin. And to prove that the skies really
split open, Avremchik runs to his mother and pulls her
skirts.

"Mama, isn't it true that this *Shevuos* at midnight the
heavens will split open? Isn't it true?"

"Split open? My head is splitting open!" cries their
mother, pulling herself away from his grasp.

And getting only this answer from their mother, Avremchik waits for their father to come home. Their father has
gone to market with a stack of boxes.

"Children, what do you think he's going to bring us today?"

And the children begin to guess. They count on their fingers—everything that could possibly be at the market, everything that the eye could see and the heart could long for—all those oddly shaped buns and the *beigel* and the candy. But none of them guessed right, and I am afraid that none of you will guess it either. This time Peiseh the box-maker brought neither buns nor *beigel* nor candy. He brought grasses, a bagful of grasses, strange, long, green, sweet-smelling grasses.

And the three little heads, Avremchik, Moisechik and Dvorka, surrounded their father.

"Oh, what is it? What did you bring? What is it?"

"Greens. Can't you see?"

"What do you mean—greens?"

"Greens for the holidays. It's *Shevuos* tonight. All Jews need greens for *Shevuos*."

"Where do you get them?"

"Where do you get them? M-m-m . . . You buy them at the market."

And saying this, he scatters the green, fragrant grasses over the freshly swept floor. He keeps some of it in his hands and fingers it and sniffs at it joyfully.

"Isn't it wonderful?"

"Wonderful for you!" says their mother. "A wonderful litter. Something new for the children to mess with."

That's how their mother takes it, as she goes on with her work, always worried, always burdened, just the opposite of their father.

And the three little heads look at their mother, look at their father, look at each other. And when their parents' backs are turned for a moment, they throw themselves on the floor, bury their heads in the fragrant grasses, fondle and kiss the rough blades that are called greens, and that Jews must have for their holidays, and that you buy at the market.

Everything can be found at the market, even greens. Their father brings them everything. There are so many things that Jews must have, and they get them. Even greens . . . Even greens . . .

A COUNTRY PASSOVER

Let the winds blow. Let the storms rage. Let the world turn upside down. An old oak that has been standing since the beginning of time, whose roots have sunk deep into the earth, cares nothing about winds. He pays no heed to storms . . .

This old oak is not a symbol. It is a living person named Nachman Verebivker of Verebivka. He is tall and broad shouldered, a giant of a man. The whole town envies him his strength, and at the same time pokes fun at him. "How do you do?" they greet him. "How is your health today?" Nachman knows they are making fun of his height, so he bends his shoulders to make himself look smaller, a little less like a peasant. But it doesn't help. God has made him big.

Nachman is an old settler in Verebivka. The peasants who call him "Our Lachman" consider him a pretty good fellow, a man of intelligence, with whom they like to talk things over once in a while. They come to ask him what to do about their grain. "Lachman" has an almanac, so he ought to know if grain will be high or low this year. Sometimes they discuss affairs of the world. "Lachman" goes to town occasionally, he sees people, he knows what goes on outside of their village.

It is impossible to imagine Verebivka without Nachman Verebivker. Not only did his father Feitel Verebivker live and die there, but also his grandfather, Aryah, may he rest in peace. Aryah, a wise man and one who liked to play with words, used to boast that the town was named Verebivka because Aryah Verebivker lived there. Actually he had lived there long before the town was ever known by that name. And do you think he said this only to be talking? He was not that kind of a man. What he was referring to was the decrees against the Jews. Even in those days they spoke of driving the Jews out of the villages; and not only talked but actually drove them. All of them were driven out, that is, all but old Aryah Verebivker. It is said that the governor himself could do nothing about it, for Aryah proved that according to law he could not be forced out of Verebivka. He had lived there too long for that . . . . Oh, those men of old!

Naturally if one is such an exception as to be permitted to live in Verebivka, one has a right to feel secure, and can laugh at the whole world. Why does a man have to worry about decrees, proclamations or statutes? Why does he have to pay attention to the stories that the peasant Kurachka, his neighbor, is always bringing from the district office? Kurachka was a short, heavy-set man who wore a short, heavy jacket and tall boots and a large watch on a silver chain, like a landed proprietor. He was clerk in the district office and knew everyone's troubles. In addition he read all the choice newspapers that printed inflammatory stories against the Jews.

By nature Kurachka was not such a bad fellow. He was a neighbor of Nachman's and supposedly a good friend. When Kurachka had a toothache, "Lachman" gave him a remedy for it. When Kurachka's wife was having a baby, "Lachman's" wife acted as midwife. But for some time now, since he had started reading those choice newspapers, Kurachka had become a changed man. The spirit of Esau had entered into him. He was always coming with another piece of news: a new governor had been appointed, a new proclamation had been issued, a new decree had been announced about the Jews. And hearing this, the Jew Nachman felt heavy-hearted. A chill went through him, but he never let on that he was disturbed. He heard him out with a smile and showed him the palm of his hand, as though to say, "When hair grows on this hand, then I'll begin to worry."

Let governors change, let ministers issue proclamations. What did Nachman Verebivker of Verebivka care about that?

The living that Nachman Verebivker made was a fairly good one, though it did not compare to that of former years. When his grandfather Aryah was alive, times had been different. Ah, those times! Then all Verebivka, you might say, belonged to them. They owned a tavern, a store, a mill, a granary. They had everything they wanted. But that was long ago. Now they had lost all these things. No tavern, no store, no granary. Nothing, simply nothing. But if that was so, you ask, then why did he remain in Verebivka? Well, then, where else could he go? Should he go dig a hole for himself? If he sold his home he would not be a Verebivker any more. He would become an outcast, a stranger. This way, at least, he had a place he could call his own, a roof over his head, a home of his own. And behind his house he had a garden. His wife and daughters worked the garden themselves and all summer they had greens to eat and then potatoes for the whole winter and into spring. But you can't live on potatoes alone. You have to have bread, too, and bread there was none. So Nachman would take his stick and go through the countryside looking for something to buy. He never came back empty-handed. Whatever God sent his way he bought—some scrap metal, a basket of millet, an old sack, a hide. The hide he would stretch, air out, and take to Avrom-Eli the tanner in town. And from all these great transactions he either made a *ruble* or lost a *ruble*. That's what happens in business. *"Kupetz kak streletz,"* Nachman would say in Russian: "A businessman is like a hunter," and Avrom-Eli the tanner, a man with a bluish nose, and fingers that looked as though they had been dipped in ink, laughed at him for being so coarsened by country living that even his jokes were now of peasant origin.

Nachman agreed. He had become coarse. It was lucky that his grandfather could not see him now. What a man he had been! Also a giant of a man, but learned as well. He knew his prayers and all the Psalms by heart. Those men of old! And he, Nachman—what did he know? He could barely read his prayers; but that at least was something. His children would not know that much . . .

When he looked at his children, growing up big and burly like himself, and unable to read or write, also like himself, he grew sick at heart. And most of all was he saddened by the sight of his youngest child, his baby, a boy named Feitel, after his father, Feitel Verebivker. A fine, promising little boy, different from the others, smaller in build, more gentle and refined in appearance. A true child of Israel. And what a brain! Just one time, for the fun of it, they had shown him the letter *aleph* and the letter *beis* in a prayer book, and he never forgot which was which. And a child like that had to grow up in a village among calves and pigs, with Kurachka's son Pedka as his playmate. Feitel and Pedka rode a broomstick together, pretending it was a horse. Together they chased cats, dug caves, amused themselves as small children will. When Nachman saw his favorite child playing with the peasant boy, his heart was heavy within him.

Pedka was an alert child, too, the same age as Feitel, with a bright winning face and flaxen hair. They liked to be together and would do anything in the world for each other. All winter long they remained indoors, close to the oven, but they longed for each other and often stood by the window each hoping to see the other. But now the winter, the long dark winter, was past. The snow was gone. The sun shone. The wind had dried the earth. The grass sprouted.

And down below the hill the brook gurgled once more. The little calf spread its nostrils and took a deep breath. The rooster shut an eye and stood lost in thought. Everything was coming to life again everywhere. Everything was growing, rejoicing. It was Passover Eve. Neither Pedka nor Feitel could be kept at home any longer. They burst out into God's green world, took each other by the hand, and raced toward the hill which beckoned to them both, "Come, children, come." They leaped up toward the sunlight, which greeted them both, "Come, children, come." And when they grew tired of running and leaping they sat down on God's earth which knew neither Jew nor Gentile, but invited them both, equally: "Come to me, children, come . . ."

There was so much to talk about after not having seen each other all winter. Feitel boasted to his friend that he knew almost the whole alphabet by heart. And Pedka boasted about his new whip. Then Feitel said that they were having their Passover Feast that very night. They had baked *matzos* for the whole eight days and they had wine too. "Do you remember, Pedka, that *matzo* I brought you last year?" "*Matzo?*" said Pedka, and over his fair face there spread a broad smile, as he remembered. "Would you like to taste some *matzo* now, Pedka, fresh *matzo?*" What a question to ask. Would he like some *matzo!* "Then let's go there," said Feitel, pointing to the green hill that beckoned to them. They climbed up the hill and stood enchanted, looking between their outspread fingers at the rays of the sun, and then threw themselves on the earth, still damp but already fragrant with the coming growth. Feitel reached inside his shirt and pulled out a fresh round white *matzo* punctured with rows of tiny holes. He broke the *matzo* in half and divided it with his friend, "Well, what do you think about it?" he asked. But what could Pedka say with his mouth full of *matzo* that crackled between his teeth and melted on his tongue like snow? One more minute and the *matzo* was gone.

"Do you have any more?" asked Pedka, looking with his gray eyes into Feitel's shirt, and licking his lips like a cat that had swallowed the butter. "Would you like some more?" said Feitel, laughing and chewing his last crumbs, and looking at his friend out of mischievous black eyes. What a question! Would Pedka like more? "Then wait a while," said Feitel, "next year you'll get some more!" At this promise they both burst out laughing, and then without any signal, as if they had arranged it before, they threw themselves on the ground and rolled down hill faster and faster like two balls . . .

On the other side of the hill they stood up and watched the farming brook, which ran off to the left, and they themselves ran to the right farther and farther across the fields which were not yet green but gave promise of becoming green soon. They could not smell the grass itself yet, but there was an odor in the air of coming grass. They walked on and on without words, as though in a dream, over the soft, sweet-smelling earth under the kindly sun. They seemed to be flying rather than walking, flying together with the birds that soared overhead, dipping and rising in the open sky which God had created for all living creatures.

Now they had come to the mill—the mill that belonged to the village mayor. Once it had belonged to Nachman Verebivker, but now it belonged to the mayor, a shrewd and rich man. He had tricked Nachman out of the mill and also a store he had once owned in the village. Usually at this time of the year the mill was turning, but now it stood still. There was no wind. Strange to have no wind in the early spring. For the boys this was a piece of good luck. Now they could examine the mill. There was plenty to see. They looked closely at the stones, the wheels, and finally sat down and began to talk, one of those conversations that has no beginning and no end. Feitel told Pedka all the wonders of the city, where his father had taken him once. He had gone to market, had seen stores, not one store as in Vere-

bivka, but many stores. Then in the evening they had gone
to the synagogue, because it was the anniversary of his
grandfather's death. "Do you understand, Pedka, or don't
you?"

Perhaps Pedka understood, but he wasn't listening. Suddenly he dove in with a story of his own. He told Feitel how
last year he had seen a bird's nest high up in a tree, how he
had tried to climb the tree but couldn't, how he tried to
reach it with a stick, but it was too high and finally how he
had started to throw stones at the nest, and kept on throwing them until he knocked down two small bleeding birds.

"Were they dead?" asked Feitel, incredulous, frightened.

"But they were so small," Pedka defended himself.

"But you killed them?"

"They had no feathers yet, they were nothing but tiny birds
with yellow bills and round little bellies."

"But you killed them. You killed them."

It was quite late when the two young comrades saw by
the sun that it was time to go home. Feitel had forgotten all
about the holiday that night and he suddenly remembered
that his mother still had to wash his head and put new
clothes on him. He jumped up, with Pedka after him, and
together they started for home, running and leaping with
the same joy and eagerness with which they had started out
hours ago. And so that neither one should be left behind
they took each other by the hand like true comrades and
began to run toward the village as fast as they could. And
when they arrived this is what they saw.

Nachman Verebivker's house was surrounded by all the
people of the village. Kurachka, the clerk; Aponas, the
mayor; the constable; the inspector; the sheriff—all the officials were there. Everybody was talking at once. Nachman
and his wife stood in the middle of the crowd explaining,
defending themselves, making all sorts of motions with their
hands. Nachman stood with his shoulders bent, trying
to make himself less conspicuous, wiping the sweat from his

brow. Near by stood the older children with frightened faces.
Suddenly the whole picture changed. Someone pointed at the
two boys and the whole crowd—the clerk, the mayor, the
police officers, all stood open-mouthed. Only Nachman
looked over the crowd, straightened his broad shoulders,
cried out, "Well?" and burst out laughing. His wife clapped
her hands together and burst out crying.

The mayor, the constable, the inspector, the sheriff all
stepped out of the crowd and turned to the boys.

"Where were you all this time, you . . . you . . ."

"Where were we? We were at the mill, that's where we
were."

Both boys, Feitel and Pedka, got what they had coming
and neither understood why. Feitel's father gave him a good
beating so that he'd know better next time. But what should
he know next time? And apparently out of pity his mother
took him away from his father, gave him a few cuffs of her
own and quickly began to wash his head for the holiday.
Then she put on his new pants, his only new clothes for
Passover, and as she did so she sighed. Why did she sigh?
Feitel could not understand. But a little later he heard her
say to his father, "Ah, if *Pesach* were only over already. I
hope it goes by without trouble. For my part it could have
gone by before it started." Feitel racked his brain but he
could not understand why she wanted the holiday to be over
before it had started. He couldn't understand his father's
whipping or his mother's cuffs. What kind of Passover Eve
was this?

Pedka understood as little as Feitel did. First of all his father Kurachka had grabbed him by the hair, swung him
around savagely and given him a resounding slap for good
measure. Pedka accepted the slaps like a philosopher. He was
accustomed to them. A little later he heard his mother talking with the other peasant women. Such queer stories they

told! There was one about a child who had been lured into
a cellar by some Jews on the eve of Passover. They kept
him there a day and a night and were just about to begin
torturing him when people heard the screams of the child,
came running from all directions, and rescued him. His
body had already been pierced on four sides in the sign of
the cross. The woman who told the story was a heavy, red-
faced, blustering creature in a wide headdress. The other
women in their brightly colored kerchiefs, stood around her
in a circle, listening to the story, shaking their heads and
crossing themselves. "Poor child," they said, "Poor little
thing." And some of the women looked at him—at Pedka.
And Pedka couldn't understand why they looked at him so
strangely and what the story had to do with him and with
Feitel. He could not understand why his father Kurachka
had pulled him by the hair and slapped him in the bargain. He didn't enjoy hair pullings and slaps, but they didn't
bother him too much. What did bother him was the reason
for these things. Why—on this day of all days? Why?

"Well?" Feitel heard his father say joyfully to his mother
the morning after Passover, as though some great good fortune had come to him. "You were afraid, just like a woman.
Our Passover is gone, their Passover is gone, and nothing
has happened."

"God be thanked," his mother answered, and still Feitel
did not understand what his mother had been afraid of. And
why they were so happy that Passover was gone. Wouldn't it
have been much better if it had lasted and lasted? That
afternoon when Feitel met Pedka outdoors he blurted everything out. He told how they had celebrated Passover and
what good things they had to eat, and he described what all
the good Passover dishes tasted like, and how sweet the
wine was that they had drunk. Pedka listened solemnly, then
looked inside Feitel's blouse. He was still dreaming about
the *matzo* he had tasted the other day. Suddenly a shrill
voice was heard calling, "Hvedka—H-vedka!"

That was Pedka's mother calling him for dinner. But he was in no hurry. This time he wouldn't have his hair pulled. In the first place they were not at the mill. And in the second place it was "after Passover." After Passover they did not have to be afraid of the Jews. And he lay on the grass on his stomach with his flaxen head between his hands and opposite him lay Feitel also on his stomach with his dark head between his hands. The sky was blue, the sun was warm and a soft breeze played about their heads. The calf stood nearby and so did the rooster with all his wives. And the two young heads, the fair one and the dark one, were propped up facing each other and the boys talked and talked and talked . . .

Nachman was not at home. Early in the morning with his stick in his hand he had gone out over the countryside looking for something to buy. He stopped at every house. He greeted each peasant with a friendly good morning, calling each one by name, and talked about everything under the sun except what had happened the day before Passover and the terror that had lasted all through Passover. And before leaving he touched the peasant's wagon. "Do you have something you don't need, neighbor?"

"Nothing, Lachman."

"Some metal, millet, anything at all? A skin maybe?"

"Believe me, Lachman, I don't have a thing. Times are hard."

"Hard? You must have drunk everything up. A holiday like that."

"I—drink—on a holiday? These are hard times, I tell you."

The peasant sighed and Nachman sighed with him. Then they talked about other things so that it wouldn't look as if he had come to buy anything.

From this peasant's house he went to that of another and then to a third, till at last he found something, so that he shouldn't have to come home empty-handed.

Nachman Verebivker, loaded down and sweating, hurried home with his long strides and thought of only one thing: how much could he earn, how much could he lose . . .

He had completely forgotten the Passover incident. He had completely forgotten the Passover terror. And Kurachka and his governors and his decrees had fled his mind. He had forgotten about them completely.

Let the winds blow. Let the storms rage. Let the world turn upside down. An old oak that has been standing since the beginning of time whose roots are sunk deep in the earth cares nothing about winds. He pays no heed to storms . . .

THE LOTTERY TICKET

βenyomchik—that boy of mine—is a regular lottery ticket."

That is the way Yisroel, the *shammes* at the old synagogue, described his young son, Benjamin, who was known in our town as a promising lad when he was still a pupil in Yarachmiel-Moishe's *cheder*. Yarachmiel-Moishe could not praise him highly enough.

"Your youngster," he said to Yisroel the *shammes* one morning in the synagogue, "is one of the best boys I have. He is a hard worker—a very hard worker. And the understanding he has! The memory! Oh-ho!"

The "Oh-ho" Yarachmiel-Moishe sang out with such enthusiasm that Yisroel the *shammes* glowed with pride.

"May God grant you health and fortune for these words," Yisroel said to the teacher and helped him put away his *tallis* and *tfillin*. This he did out of gratitude for the teacher's praise of his son. For the lessons the boy received Yisroel paid the same amount that all the other parents did—two *rubles* a quarter besides the usual presents at *Hannukah* and *Purim*, although Yisroel supported his own family on little more than the *Hannukah* and *Purim* gifts that others gave him.

Afterwards, when Benyomchik had gone through all of Yarachmiel-Moishe's classes, Yisroel the *shammes* wanted

very much to send him to Eli-Maier, the *Gamorah* teacher,
but Eli-Maier would not take him. In the first place, his
school was already full. In the second place, Yisroel could
not begin to pay what the well-to-do householders did. So
Benyomchik did what many other boys do. If they have nothing to pay with, they study by themselves. That's what we
have a large synagogue for, with a lot of bookstands, and
candle-ends salvaged from memorials for the dead, and
books—all the books one needs: Bibles, the tracts and commentaries, and whatnot. If a person only wants to, he can
study anywhere, even in an attic. Do you know how many
great people, scholars of renown, grew up among us that
way, bent over tiny candle-ends in the synagogue? And how
many more we might have had by now—holy men of genius,
Talmudists and *Kabalists*—we cannot even guess.

But something happened: in the last forty or fifty years a
ray of worldly light has stolen into our corner of the earth
and has reached even into our very synagogues, even there
where the impoverished lads sat with their tomes. There you
found them secretly snatching their first taste of secular food,
some rhetoric as an appetizer, then swallowing—or choking
over—a Russian grammar, with maybe a few chapters of a
novel for dessert. From studies like these, naturally, no *Talmudic* scholars or famous rabbis emerged. Instead, Jewish
youths wandered off into the world and were ruined, became doctors, lawyers, writers of prose and verse, teachers
—and plain non-believers. Not a single rabbi who was worth
anything. That is, there were a number of rabbis. But what
kind? Crown rabbis wished onto us by the czar, whether we
wanted them or not. As if he had said, "Here is a loaded
bomb; hold on to it." But let us proceed . . .

Benyomchik did not study in the synagogue all alone. He
had two companions, penniless boys like himself, and that
was how the trouble started. One man by himself cannot do
wrong as easily as he can with others. It was always that
way. Look at Adam. So long as he walked in the Garden
alone, all was still and heavenly. But as soon as Mother Eve

appeared, all was changed. She talked him into eating of the fruit of the Tree of Knowledge, and who knows what more she would not have done if they had not been driven out in time?

It was the same with Benjamin. If Benjamin had sat alone in the synagogue, all would have been well. But he studied together with these comrades, boys as naked and barefoot, as hungry and thirsty as himself; and together they longed for the large, bright world, the world of wisdom and knowledge. They sat at the table, bent over the yellowed pages, but their thoughts were far away, among the great of the earth, among the learned ones, the fortunate ones. It pulled and dragged at them like a magnet—this outside world. So was it strange that one Saturday night three boys left their study table in the synagogue—Itzik, Yossil and Benyomchik—and disappeared? They were hunted everywhere, all over town, in every corner and hole, but they were gone without a trace. Well, the other two lads, Itzik and Yossil, were waifs, orphans without father or mother. Whom did they run away from? But Benyomchik! Yisroel the *shammes* turned the town upside down, searched everywhere, and calmed down only on the following day, when a letter came from the three boys, asking everybody not to worry; they were, bless the Lord, safe and sound. They had become aware (that is how they wrote) that here in the synagogue there was no future for them, and therefore they had gone off to attend a seminary, a *yeshiva*, in Vilna or Volozhin or Mir. They had cleverly listed all three seminaries so that no one should know where to go and look for them.

But all that was unnecessary. No one ran after them. The town itself was in fact happy about it. In the first place, it meant that there would be two or three fewer people to keep alive—you could not let them starve to death. And in the second place, it was such a fine thing to see poor boys who wanted to become educated. If all the others in the town could only have done it, they would have gone off somewhere too, rather than stay here and struggle for a living.

Whatever happened to the two other lads—Itzik and Yossil—no one knows, but after about six months Yisroel the *shammes* got a letter from Benyomchik—not from Volozhin, not from Vilna and not from Mir, but from another large city. He told them not to worry because at last he was on the right path, some day he would amount to something—if only, with the help of God, he succeeded in passing his examinations to enter the *gymnasium*. He wanted to prepare himself for the study of medicine and when he became a doctor he would be able to make a good living and could then support his father and mother in their old age. His father would not have to work so hard any more, being a *shammes,* and his mother a *shammeste.*

"And there is one thing, my dear and loyal parents," he wrote, "that you must never worry about. A person can have all the education there is and still remember his debt to God. I want you to know that I pray every day, that I use the *tfillin,* and wash before meals and say grace before and after I eat—that is, when there is something to eat. Usually we eat every other day, sometimes a piece of dry bread alone and sometimes dry bread with salt water. And when there is nothing at all, we suck a piece of sugar. Sugar is a remedy for hunger, it drives away the appetite. But there is something besides food, and that we have in plenty! Don't forget: we have four grammar texts to go through, and geography and history, and how many other things! Mathematics we won't even talk about. That is too simple. When we were still home we used to study algebra in the synagogue, and the rhetoric books we devoured in those days help us now when we have compositions to write. There is only one thing wrong: we have so far not been able to correct our accent altogether. But that will be done in time. So don't worry; everything will turn out all right. The important thing is not to become discouraged. We must have faith in the Eternal."

When Yisroel the *shammes* received this letter he went at once to Yarachmiel-Moishe the *melamed,* an old colleague, an honest man and a confidant.

"Do me a favor," he said. "Read this letter through and answer it. I could have written to him myself, but I am sure you can do it better."

Yarachmiel-Moishe the *melamed* knew very well that the *shammes* was telling a big lie, but you can't make it appear that you know. So he took out his glasses and put them on his nose—a strange pair of glasses, held together by a piece of wire and two pieces of string; lenses there were none— one frame was covered with a circular piece of tin and the other was empty, just a hole.

Yisroel could not resist asking, "What good are these glasses, Rabbi? Can you see anything with them?"

"They're better than nothing, and besides, I'm used to them," Yarachmiel-Moishe answered, and held the letter off at a distance, one eye (the one behind the tin) closed; and with the other he read like water going over a dam, in a loud clear voice, stopping every so often to look at Yisroel as if to say, "How is that for reading?" And Yisroel stood by, his head a little to one side, beaming with joy, as if to say, "And the letter itself—how is that for writing?"

And when Yarachmiel-Moishe took off his glasses and gave him the letter back again, Yisroel asked, "Well, Rabbi, what do you think of it?"

"What can I tell you? It's good. It's very good. He says that he prays every day, with his *tfillin* too. May it be no worse in the future."

"What I meant was that he is growing up. My Benyom-chik is becoming something," said Yisroel. At the tip of his tongue were other words but he was afraid to use them— words like *"gymnasium,"* "examinations," and finally "doc-tor" itself. So he said, "I'm wondering what to think about it. You said that he was studying to be a—doctor? What do you think of that? What is your opinion, Rabbi? You're a man of experience."

Yarachmiel-Moishe knows that he is a man of experience, but what can he say? Naturally, if it were up to him, he would not have let him study in the *gymnasium*. What does a man like Yisroel want to have a son in the *gymnasium* for? And studying to be a doctor! But he wants advice . . .

Yarachmiel-Moishe looks with glazed eyes at the wall and sighs. The *shammes* understands what the sigh means; he feels a little like that himself, he is not too well pleased with the *gymnasium*. If it were only a *yeshiva* . . . And yet, there was the other side too: his son, Benyomchik—a doctor!

"But, Rabbi, he says he is not forgetting. He prays every day. He is still one of us."

And then, after another pause: "Rabbi, I asked you to do me a favor. Won't you answer the letter? And another thing, Rabbi. You know our town. People love to talk. So I want to ask you: keep it to yourself. You understand?"

"I understand. Of course I understand," said Yarachmiel-Moishe, and once more saddling his nose with the strange glasses, he took a piece of paper, pen and ink, dipped the pen into the ink, and waited for the *shammes* to tell him what to write.

"Tell him this," says the *shammes,* and dictates:

"To my beloved son, Benjamin. To begin with I want to tell you that we are all, bless the Lord, in the best of health, and may we hear no worse from you now or in the future, Amen. And secondly, tell him that Simma, my wife, and I send our friendliest greetings and ask him to write to us frequently, let us know how he is getting along, and tell him that we wish him all the luck in the world and that he should succeed in his work, and tell him not to worry. God is our father. The main thing is that he should take care of himself, in his health and in his habits and in his prayers: he should remember that he is a Jew. That is the main thing, and tell him that I am sending him a *ruble,* a *ruble* I'm sending him" (here the *shammes* feels through all his pockets) "and tell him that I would have sent more if I had it, but right now conditions are very bad. I am not earning a thing; no one is dying and no one is getting married and no one is having children. And what else do I make a penny from? I don't remember when there has been a wedding, not one since Reb Hersh married off his youngest daughter. That is, a few weddings there have been, but I am speaking of *real* weddings, weddings worth mentioning . . ."

"Sh-h . . . don't rush like that," says the teacher. "You're pounding away like a post horse. I can't catch up to you . . . Mmmmmm. Well. What next?"

"And tell him further . . . that there is nothing to say. And tell him that I send him my friendliest regards, and Simma, his mother, sends her friendliest regards, and all his sisters too, Pessil and Sossil and Brochele. And remind him to be sure to remember that he is a Jew, not to forget the synagogue. That is the main thing. And when you're through, I'll sign my name to it."

When the teacher had written all this down, Yisroel the *shammes* rolled up his sleeve, took the pen carefully with two fingers and prepared himself for the delicate operation. He spelled out his own name carefully—Y-i-s-r-o-e-l—and the name of his father—N-a-f-t-o-l-i—and the family name —R-i-t-e-l-m-a-n. And while he wrote, his tongue moved from side to side, following his fingers from right to left and from left to right.

It is to be understood that it did not take long for people all over town to learn the secret, that Yisroel the *shammes'* young son was studying, or getting ready to study, to be a doctor. And this did not hurt Yisroel in the least, though there were some people who teased him:

"So you're going to have a doctor in the family—going around bareheaded? With brass buttons, maybe, like a state official? How will that look, Yisroel? I mean for you—like a hen that hatches ducklings . . ."

Yisroel the *shammes* let them talk, and himself said nothing. But deep in his heart he thought: "Laugh, laugh at my Benyomchik! He's still my lottery ticket!"

One day—it was Passover Eve—Simma the *shammeste* and her three daughters, Pessil, Sossil and Brochele, were cleaning up for the holiday, when the door opened, and in came a striking young man in a coat with white buttons and an odd-looking cap on his head. He fell on Simma's neck and then on the three girls, hugging and kissing and squeezing them.

The young man was Benjamin.

Simma was so happy she burst out crying. And Yisroel hurried in, frightened and out of breath. He shouted at his wife, "Stop crying, will you! Look how upset she is! Do you know what you're crying about?"

But when he himself had looked the boy over and seen how much he had grown and changed, he almost began to cry too. But a man does not do such things.

"When did you get here?" he asked his son. "Turn around, let me see what you look like from the back. What kind of suit is that? Take off your coat—why don't you take off your coat?"

And when Benjamin took off his coat and stood there in his blue uniform with silver buttons—his cheeks rosy and his eyes shining—he charmed not only the rest of the family, but everyone who saw him. "What do you think of Yisroel-the-*shammes'* son?" they said. "How he has grown! What a fine-looking boy he is!" And Mintzi, the neighbor's daughter, a girl of nineteen with black eyes and a heavy black braid tied with a red ribbon that suited her so well, came in to see if Simma had an extra pot that she could borrow, although she knew very well that in all her life Simma had never had an extra pot. But it gave her a chance to see Benjamin close up, to glance at him with her lively black eyes and to toss her head with the thick black braid and the bright red ribbon—it gave her a chance to turn around and run off, and a little later to come back again under another pretext, until Benjamin's three sisters looked at each other as if to say: "How do you like the way she runs in and out?"

In the meantime Benjamin called his mother aside. "Here

is something for *Pesach*," he said, and pushed some money
into her hand. Poor Simma! She had never held so much
money before in all her life! And for the girls he had
presents and presents—ribbons and combs and mirrors and
trinkets without number! And for his mother a silk shawl, a
yellow one with red and blue flowers. And once more
Simma the *shammeste* burst out crying.

And Yisroel asked with a laugh, "What's all this? How
did you ever get so much money, my boy?"

"Why shouldn't I have money?" asks Benjamin, proudly.
"I'm earning money now, bless the Lord. Eight *rubles* a
month. I'm a tutor. I have a few children to teach and I get
paid for it. I'm in the fifth class at the *gymnasium*. There are
eight classes altogether, so in three more years I'll be
through. And then—the university, to study medicine."

Benjamin talks and talks, and they all stand around him.
They can't take their eyes off him, and they think, "Can that
really be Benjamin? That barefoot Benyomchik who used to
spend all his time in the synagogue, studying? Eight *rubles*
a month . . . eight classes . . . a silk shawl . . . the university . . . doctor . . .

The Lord alone knows if anyone else had such a happy
Passover, such a cheerful *seder,* that year. And I am not talking about the wine, or the brandy, or the fish, or the dumplings, or the pudding. I am speaking now of the *Hagadah,*
the Passover ceremonial, that Yisroel and Benjamin both
chanted, one louder than the other. It was wonderful to listen
to! When they came to *"Rabbi Eleazer omer, minayin shekol
mako umako,"* and the men both began to sway with a new
vigor and struck up a louder tone, Simma, who had been
sitting all the time with her eyes on Benjamin, suddenly
began to pucker up her lips as if to cry, and the three sisters,
Pessil and Sossil and Brochele, seeing her, could control
themselves no longer and began to laugh; and seeing them,
the others began to laugh too, even Simma herself . . . Ah,
what a Passover that was! You can well imagine!

The next morning, the first day of Passover, when Ben-

jamin came to the synagogue, everybody gaped at the boy in
the student's uniform with the silver buttons as if he were
a strange animal from the jungle. The smallest boys, full of
mischief, crowded around him and pointed at him with their
fingers and laughed right in his face. But Benjamin stood all
the time with his small prayerbook in his hand and prayed.
And when he was called up to the *Torah* (Reb Monish, the
gabai, arranged it in order to please Yisroel) and Benjamin
recited the benediction in a loud clear tone with an accent
and an emphasis that one saved for the holidays, the whole
synagogue was agog with wonder: "What do you think about
Yisroel's young scholar?"

And when they were all ready to leave the synagogue, the
rich man of the village, Reb Hersh, turned to the *shammes.*
"Yisroel," Reb Hersh said broadly, as a rich man does when
he speaks to one of the lesser creatures, looking a little to
one side and clearing his throat and nose in a double cough,
"Yisroel, ah-h, come here, hm-m, with that young man of
yours. Let me—hm-m—take a look at him."

Hearing that Reb Hersh wanted to talk to Yisroel-the-
shammes' "young scholar" the crowd gathered around to hear
what the rich man would say and what the other would
answer. Benjamin approached Reb Hersh as if he were an
equal, not at all self-consciously, greeted him like an acquaintance of old, and Reb Hersh looked him over from
head to foot, not quite knowing how to start. Should he address him in the respectful plural—a child like that? That
would be showing too much respect for the son of the
shammes. And yet, to use the singular, to say *du,* as you
might say, "Hey, there . . ."—maybe that would not be right
either. After all, he was a *gymnasium* student with silver
buttons, he looked almost like a young prince . . . So at last
he spoke to him neither one way nor the other, but vaguely
and impersonally: "How are things? When did the visitor
come? When is he going back?"

Benjamin put his right foot forward. With one hand he
toyed with a button at his chest, with the other he stroked

his upper lip. And he answered every question—confidently, without any shame or hesitation. Reb Hersh liked it—and yet he did not like it. "Not a foolish lad at all, but he doesn't know his place." And he became involved in a broad discussion about his school: "How many classes are there? What is the significance of eight classes? Why not nine? And what is the difference between one class and another?"

And Benjamin thought: "He looks so important, and yet he is such an ox!" And he gave him to understand what the difference was between one class and another. Reb Hersh did not like this at all, having a child explaining things to him, and making it sound so simple that it needed no explanation. He said, "Why, everybody knows that. But what is the sense of having eight classes instead of nine?"

"Simply because if there were nine classes, you would say: Why should there be nine and not ten?"

At this the crowd begins to laugh, that is, everybody laughs except Reb Hersh. He thinks: "A tramp—that's all he is." And with his double cough he says, "Hm-m. It's time to go home. Hm-m . . ."

If you did not see Yisroel the *shammes* then, standing a little to one side, looking from one to the other and swallowing each word of Benjamin's, you have never seen a happy and fortunate man. He was waiting for Reb Hersh to stop questioning his son so he could take him home, where the women were waiting anxiously. On the table, the fresh crisp *matzos* were also waiting, and in the oven a delicious Passover borsht was simmering, and hot *kneidlach* with chicken fat, and maybe even a potato pudding! And at last when Reb Hersh had coughed his double cough again and gone off with a few of his close friends, Yisroel the *shammes* invited his one and only good friend and confidant, Yarachmiel-Moishe the teacher, to come along with them, as the others had gone with Reb Hersh, for a glass of wine. And when they arrived he poured out for the old teacher a glass of genuine raisin wine, and Simma brought in such wonderful *chremzlach* that it would have been hard even for an epicure to tell if there was more honey in them or more chicken fat, because they were so sugary and so rich that they stuck to the gums and ran down his beard. Yarachmiel-Moishe, a quiet man, who rarely said a word, now at the first glass of genuine raisin wine found his head whirling round and his tongue running loose and wild. He called Benjamin over to him, and put him through a quick but thorough examination of the Scriptures and commentaries that he had once studied in his *cheder.*

Benjamin remembered not only the Scriptures, but the commentaries as well, so thoroughly that Yisroel the *shammes'* heart almost burst with pleasure. He followed the teacher out through the door. "What do you think of him?" he asked.

"A perfect vessel—a saint!" answered Yarachmiel-Moishe, puckering his lips and shaking his head.

"But a Jew all the same? He hasn't forgotten that?" said the *shammes,* and watched the teacher's eyes for the answer.

"With God's help," said the teacher.

"A lottery ticket! A lottery ticket! Do you agree with me?"

At this Yarachmiel-Moishe tossed his head—it was hard to tell if it was a nod or a shake—blinked his eyes and made a gesture with his hands that meant that he thought the boy either was, or was not, a lottery ticket.

"A good day!" he cried, and once more kissed the *mazuza.* "May God keep us alive and well another year, and may we come to each other in joy—for your daughters' weddings and then your son's—and may the Jews have some relief from all their troubles, may there be good news for all of us, it's time that God had mercy on us, improved our lot, lightened our load . . . And may all things be good everywhere, and cheer in every heart. And—ah . . ."

Yarachmiel-Moishe himself did not know what more he wanted. It seemed as if he had already poured out everything that was on his mind. He stood with his tongue out, unable to say one thing or another . . . Yet how can a man go away like this, without a word of farewell of any kind? Fortunately he remembered one more thing:

"And may—may the Messiah come soon!"

"Amen!" answers Yisroel the *shammes,* and in his heart he thinks: First let my Benjamin graduate as a doctor. And *then* let the Messiah come.

As cheerful and bright as everything was at Yisroel the *shammes'* when Benjamin arrived, so was it dark and gloomy when he went away again.

And the three years passed, the three years before Benjamin could enter the university. It was not an easy time. Yisroel the *shammes* experienced one trouble after another at home, and his son Benjamin over there in the city. Many a night Yisroel could not fall asleep here, and Benjamin his son there. Yisroel could not sleep because he kept thinking of the difficult time Benjamin had, of all the hard work he had to do. And Benjamin could not sleep because he was getting ready for his examinations.

"If God helps me and I pass my examinations," Benjamin wrote home, "I'll come to see you again, my dear and faithful ones, and be with you all summer to rest my bones."

And Yisroel the *shammes* waited for the good news of the examination as a pious Jew waits for the Messiah.

At last summer came, but Benjamin did not. His letters began to come less and less often, and as time went on they became shorter and more gloomy. All he ever said was that on such and such a day he would have to take this or that examination.

"The next examination," wrote Benjamin in his last letter, "is my Day of Judgment, because if I get less than a ninety-four I shall not be able to get in, and if I can't get in now I shall have to stay over another year. And who knows what will happen next year? Maybe next year it will be even worse. What will I do then? What will happen to me? Why did I ever have to work so hard, wear myself out like this? Study so hard, starve day after day, freeze in unheated rooms and spend so many sleepless nights? I am not the only one to ask these questions. There are many others like me— Jewish boys—who stayed over from last year and can't get in because their average is not quite high enough. I don't know what I shall do . . ."

Yisroel the *shammes* went around in a daze. He could not understand why Benjamin's letters suddenly should have become so melancholy. He asked Yarachmiel-Moishe to write to Benjamin and ask him what he meant by "average" and "ninety-four." In short, he asked Benjamin to write and explain everything, and not to worry, but rely on the Eternal One who could do everything. And the main thing still was that he should remember he was a Jew, and if the Lord willed, all would be well . . .

But this letter was never answered, and neither were all the others that Yisroel sent later. But he kept writing and writing, until at last, ashamed to come again to Yarachmiel-Moishe, he gave up writing.

"What can be the matter?" Simma asked her husband. "There has been no letter for such a long time."

And she got an answer: "What do you expect? Is that all he has to do? Write letters? Wait a little. Let him finish his examinations, whatever they are, and then he'll write!"

But Yisroel himself went around with a heavy heart and low spirits. He could not find a place to turn. What went through his head during those days, may no other father ever know. And his dreams every night were frightful and horrible, with black canopies, black candles, everything black . . .

Have you ever heard of Lemel the *starosta?* Or is this the first time you have heard his name? In addition to being the *starosta,* the mayor, a man of substance and influence, what in plain Yiddish we refer to as a soup-ladle, right here in town, he was also a power of some sort in the provincial capital, knew all the important people, dealt with them, was intimate with them. Whenever he comes to the capital, he says, he never knows where to go first. Everybody wants to drag him off to himself. "*Pan* Lemel!" shout the Poles. "*Gospodin* Lemel!" plead the Russians. "*Reb* Lemel, you're ours!" say the Jews. He simply does not know what to do! And every time that he comes back from the capital he has news to bring, something startling to talk about for the next three months. A sensational bankruptcy, a terrible fire, a murder to make your hair stand on end. And although Lemel's bankruptcies took place too often, his fires and murders almost every week, it never occurred to anyone to contradict him. They knew he could not help it—he liked to talk, to tell stories, and if necessary, to make them up himself.

So you can imagine what a time our *starosta* had when an envelope came to his office from the provincial capital with a document instructing him to remove from the rolls of the Jewish community the name of Benjamin, son of Yisroel Ritelman, because of the fact that he had assumed another faith.

As soon as Lemel the *starosta* finished reading the message he forgot all his work and ran out into the street with the paper, stopped everyone he saw, whispered the secret into each one's ear, and soon had the story spread all over town.

No doubt you have heard of the halcyon days. The skies are clear, there is no breeze, not a drop of rain, everything is quiet, serene. The people are asleep, the town itself looks dead. Suddenly, no one knows how or where, something explodes, like a bomb from the sky, like an earthquake. The people awaken, start to run. They run this way and that. "What is it? Where? What happened?"

The story of Yisroel-the-*shammes*' son was like that bomb. It tore the town to pieces and woke up everybody. They were all as upset and excited as if this had to do with their own health or livelihood, as if this were the only thing they had to worry about. Some dropped their work, others left the table with their food untouched and went off to the marketplace to see what was going on. Around Reb Hersh's house there stood a whole ring of people, and Reb Hersh himself stood by the porch in a gabardine and skullcap, surrounded by his kinsmen, intimate friends, acquaintances, total strangers—men who catered to him, scraped and bowed and showed their respect for the man who might be able to do them a favor some time. Reb Hersh held forth and his followers echoed:

"Of course! Naturally! That's right, Reb Hersh!"

And Reb Hersh went on:

"A *shammes,* a ne'er-do-well, a pauper—and he wants to be better than anyone else! He has a son, so what does he have to become? A doctor. Nothing less. And if he became a *shammes* like his father, or, heaven spare us, a teacher, what would happen then? I'd like to hear what our *shammes* has to say now. Or maybe he doesn't know yet. I don't see him anywhere around? Where can he be?"

Where was he? There were some in the crowd who did not hesitate to hurry off to the synagogue to look for him. And some even went to his home, but they could not find him anywhere.

And the truth is that Yisroel knew nothing about it. At that moment, when all the town was in an uproar, Yisroel was sitting with his one and only good friend and confidant, Yarachmiel-Moishe the teacher. In the same mail that brought the document to the town hall there was a large envelope for Yisroel himself, and it was from his son. It was the longest letter that had ever come from Benjamin. With great difficulty he had read through a couple of pages, but had understood little more than a word here and there. So he took it to Yarachmiel-Moishe.

"It's here!" he shouted from the doorway, with joy.

"A letter from your son?"

"And what a letter! It's like a cushion!"

When he heard these words, Yarachmiel-Moishe told his pupils to take a rest, and he himself put on the glasses we had seen before, and began to read the letter in a loud, clear voice, almost a chant. At the start all was well, but soon he began to halt and stutter, as if he were walking over pointed rocks. He came upon hard, strange words he had never

seen before. He had to set his glasses straight, he held the
letter up to the window, shrugged his shoulders, chewed his
words, muttered, "Hm-m . . . What language is this? Na-
tion . . . emancipation . . . quota . . . he's beginning to
use strange words, that son of yours . . ."

Yisroel sat at the end of the table, holding his head in his
hands, and looked only at Yarachmiel-Moishe, listened to
every word, tried to catch the meaning—and made nothing
of it. He could not begin to understand why suddenly Benjamin should have to defend himself, try to justify himself,
insist with so many oaths that he was the same person as
before, that what he had done was out of greater love and
greater loyalty . . . Yisroel could not understand why he
should be any different now, and why he should ask his
forgiveness. What was there to forgive? "But it could not
have been otherwise," he wrote. "I have struggled so long
with myself. I know the pain I am giving you, but the fight
I have carried on since childhood for an education, my need,
my desire for learning has become so great, so strong, that I
finally yielded."

"What? What was that? Read it again, read it once more.
What did he say?"

Yarachmiel-Moishe adjusted his glasses to read it again,
but just then the door was pushed open and in came Bassya-
Hinda, the teacher's wife, a tall gaunt woman with a sallow
face, carrying a large market basket. In the basket were all
sorts of good things—potatoes and onions, two black radishes, a small piece of beef-lung that she had barely managed
to coax from the butcher, because there are always customers
by the hundred who want beef-lung. Women fight over it
as men do over the greatest honors at the synagogue, and
the reason is this: it costs so little and there are no bones in
it, and if you cook it with potatoes and onions and a lot of
pepper and it simmers long enough, it tastes quite well . . .

Coming in and seeing the *shammes* sitting with her husband and reading something, Bassya-Hinda took a quick
glance to see if the poor *shammes* knew already. But she

could not tell from their faces, so she put the basket down,
and while she wiped her face with her hand, winked at her
husband.

" 'Chmiel-Moishe, come here," she said, and he, seeing that
she wanted to say something to him, took off his glasses and
excused himself for a minute. And there on the other side of
the doorway, this conversation took place between husband
and wife:

She: Does he know?

He: Who?

She: The *shlimazl.*

He: Which *shlimazl?*

She: The *shammes.*

He: Know what?

She: About his son.

He: Which son?

She: Benjamin.

He: What about him?

She: The whole town is full of it.

He: Full of what?

She: His son.

He: But what about?

She: Oh, you make me tired!

The Lord knows how long this conversation would have
dragged on, if at this point the *shammes* himself had not
forced his way into the room and in a frightened voice,
asked, "What—what are you saying? What did you say Benjamin did? What?"

Bassya-Hinda did not know what to do now. Why should
she be the one to tell him? Better send him straight to
Lemel the *starosta,* let him take care of it himself.

"Nothing," she said, wiping her face again. "What do I
know? They say a paper came in. I don't know—something
about your son."

"What kind of paper?"

"Something. In the town hall."

"Who has it—the paper?"

"The *starosta*."

"What is it about?"

"Your Benjamin. Something."

"What's the matter with Benjamin?" he asked, this time angrily. "What happened to him?"

"I should know? Ask me! Go over there, go to Lemel. He's somewhere in the marketplace. He has the paper."

Paper . . . Lemel . . . the town hall . . . Benjamin . . . what did all this mean? Yisroel felt his cheeks grow hot and he heard a whistling in his ears. He pulled down his cap, bent over double, and stumbled out . . .

There are people who love to watch a person in agony, who stare at him when he weeps, look after him when he follows a corpse at a funeral, stand by when he wrings his hands. I do not care for such scenes. Say what you will, I don't like mournful pictures. My muse does not wear a black veil on her face. My muse is a poor—but cheerful one . . .

Where did Yisroel run? Whom did he see? What did he hear? What did he say? Do not ask, it will give you no joy to know. What will you have gained, for instance, when you have learned that there were people who finally lived to have revenge on Yisroel the *shammes*, who had gone around so long showing off his lottery ticket?

"He had it coming," said Reb Hersh, with his peculiar double-cough, and stroked his paunch comfortably. "It should be a lesson for people. A pauper should be careful how he jumps in your face. A doctor he had to have . . ."

Others, it is true, had pity on the *shammes*, "poor fellow" —and you know what that means. My grandfather Minda had a saying, "Look out for people who pity you, and God protect you from those who call you 'poor fellow.'"

So I won't tell you what Yisroel did or whom he saw, but it was dusk when he turned in at his cottage, looking like a ghost. Entering without a word, he sat down on the ground, took off his boots, tore his shirt at the heart as one does for the dead, and prepared to sit in mourning for an hour, as

one does at a time like that. Simma did the same, and so did
the three sisters. Together they sat on the ground, moaning
and weeping for the one they had lost.

Later, when Yarachmiel-Moishe the teacher came to offer
condolence, this is what he found: Yisroel sitting with his
head thrown forward between his knees, Simma with her
hands covering her face and Pessil, Sossil and Brochele sitting with red swollen eyes, each one looking with expression-
less face into a separate corner, as if in their shame and pain
they could not face each other openly.

He came into the house quietly without a greeting of any
kind, as one does in a house of mourning, and slowly lower-
ing himself to the edge of a bench at one side of the room,
sighed. That was all. He didn't say a word. A little later,
another sigh and again silence; and later still a sigh again.
It was only after a while that he looked around and decided
that it was not right to sit there and not say a word, he
ought to say something to comfort them. But what was there
to say? When a family is in mourning because a person has
died, you can come to sit with them for a while, and say,
"The Lord giveth and the Lord taketh away." Or, "Man is,
after all, like a fly." Or, "Death—that is something none of
us can escape." Or, "Vanity of vanities, all of us will die."
Or other such sayings that cannot make one especially happy,
but are still a comfort. If a person says something, gets it
off his chest, he feels a trifle better. But what can one say
at a time like this, when it is a living person they are
mourning for? Yarachmiel-Moishe turned a little on his
bench with a shy cough, wanted to say something, but the
words would not come. He tried a few different times, till
finally he started again and it worked. And now he was
unable to stop, he did not know where or how to end it.

"Ah, well, it's the same story as always. What can you call
it—a trial from heaven, from the Lord. For everything is
from Him; without Him nothing is done, nothing occurs,
not a finger here on earth is lifted. He is a real Master, let
us agree on that. Oh, what a Master! And we obey Him—

how we obey Him! . . . So it was decreed that this had to happen, exactly as it happened. And here is the proof: that if it did not have to happen this way, it would not have happened. But it did happen, so it must have been ordained. If He had wanted something else to happen, it would have happened the other way. It would have . . ."

Yarachmiel-Moishe began to feel that he did not know what he was saying, so he paused, took a pinch of snuff, lowered his head to one side, and heaved a deep sigh. He told himself that it was time to go, but talking about going is an easy matter. How are you going to do it, though, if you are glued to the bench? There is no visit that is worse than one to a house of mourning. You are supposed to leave without a word of parting, without a sign or a look. But how can you do it? Yarachmiel-Moishe sat waiting for a miracle to happen. If only they would doze off a little so he could leave while they slept. Or if something happened outside, a riot, a fire—anything—so he could escape in the excitement. He sat looking around at the ceiling, at the four walls, and then he said to himself: "It is time to think about going. The children will turn the *cheder* upside down . . ."

When the hour was up, Yisroel and his family rose from the floor, quietly, without talking, put on their shoes and crawled off each to his own corner, to his own work. Yisroel rushed through his late-afternoon prayers and hurried off to the synagogue to be in time for evening services. After all, he was the *shammes,* his time was not his own. He had to be where he was needed. Work—that was the only remedy, the means of chasing all worries away, of forgetting all troubles . . .

In the synagogue a few busybodies came up to him.

"What do you hear from your lottery ticket? How is your son getting along?"

"A son? Have I got a son?" answered Yisroel with a bitter little smile.

And seeing the bitterness and the ache in the smile, the

meddlers retreated. All they had to do was look at his face and they did not want to talk to him any more about his son.

What happened afterward? What became of Benjamin? Did he write any more letters? And what did he write? And did his father answer him? And if he answered, what did he say? Don't press me with questions. I shall not say a word. I'll tell you only that as far as Yisroel was concerned, there was no Benjamin any more anywhere. Benjamin was dead. In the lottery, Yisroel had drawn a blank.

THE MIRACLE OF
HASHONO RABO

The miracle of *Hashono Rabo*—that was what we called the train wreck that almost took place on *Hashono Rabo,* the day when our judgment is sealed in Heaven, and our fate decided. And it happened right in my home town of Heissin. That is, not in the town itself, but a few stations away, at a place called Sobolivka.

You who have ridden on the train in our region know what the service on the Straggler Special is like. When it reaches a station and stops, it forgets when to start again. According to the timetable, it has a definite schedule. For instance, at Zatkovitz it says that the train is supposed to stop exactly an hour and fifty-eight minutes; and at Sobolivka, the place I am now telling you about, not a second more than an hour and thirty-two minutes. But take my word for it, no matter where it stops—whether at Zatkovitz or at Sobolivka, it stands at least two, and sometimes more than three hours. It depends on how long the switching and fueling take, and what switching and fueling mean to a train like the Straggler Special, I don't have to tell you.

First of all the locomotive has to be uncoupled, and then the train crew—the conductor, the engineer and the fireman —sit down together with the stationmaster, the guard and the telegraph operator, and drink beer—one bottle after another.

And while these important operations, or maneuvers, are going on, what do the passengers do? You have seen what they do. They go crazy with boredom. Some yawn; some find themselves a corner and take a nap; and some walk back and forth on the platform, their hands clasped behind their backs, idly humming a tune.

On the day that I am telling you about, while the Straggler was waiting in the station of Sobolivka, a man was seen standing nearby, his hands clasped behind his back, watching. He was not a passenger, simply an inquisitive onlooker, a resident of Sobolivka. And what was a Sobolivka householder doing there? Nothing! It was *Hashono Rabo*—a half holiday; the man had been at the synagogue already, had eaten already, and as it was a half holiday and there was nothing for him to do at home, he took his walking stick and went out for a walk to the station, to meet the train.

Meeting the train, as you know, is an old custom in our part of the country. When the train is due, everyone who is not otherwise occupied, rushes off to the station. Maybe they'll see somebody there. See whom? See what? A man from Teplik? An old woman from Obodivka? A priest from Golovonievska? In Sobolivka that's great excitement—and you go. And especially since in those days the train was still a novelty, there was always something new to see, something strange to hear. Anyway, on that special *Hashono Rabo*, when the fate of all of us had been sealed already, as I told you before, there stood the train at the station, uncoupled and waiting; and watching it with a mild curiosity, in a half-holiday mood, stood a householder of Sobolivka with a stick under his arm.

Well, you may say, what of that? What if a resident of Sobolivka stands and looks at an uncoupled locomotive? Let him stand and look! But no. It had to happen that on this day, among the waiting passengers, was a priest from Golovonievska, a village not far from Heissin. Having nothing to do, the priest walked back and forth on the same platform, his hands also clasped behind his back, and he also stopped to look at the locomotive. Seeing nothing unusual, he turned to the Sobolivker and said, "Tell me, Yudko, what is there to stare at?"

The man answered crossly, "What do you mean—Yudko? My name is not Yudko. My name is Berko."

So the priest said, "Let it be Berko. Well, tell me then, Berko, what are you looking at so seriously?"

Without taking his eyes from the locomotive, the man answered, "I am standing here beholding the wonders of God. Think—a simple thing like that. You turn one screw this way, another screw that way, and this strange and terrifying machine moves off."

"How do you know that?" the priest asks him. "How do you know that if you turn one screw this way, another the other way, the machine will start?"

Answers the man from Sobolivka, "If I didn't know, would I have said so?"

Says the priest, "What do you know? How to eat potato pudding? But this is not a pudding."

At this the man becomes angry (the people of Sobolivka are famous for their tempers), and he says, "Well then, my Father, maybe you'd care to climb up into the locomotive with me and have me show you what makes these things move and what makes them stop?"

This did not sound so good to the priest. What was this little man trying to say? Was he going to tell *him* the principle whereby a locomotive moved or stood still? So he answered him sharply, "Go, Hershko. Climb up then."

As sharply the other corrected him, "My name is not Hershko. My name is Berko."

"All right," said the priest. "Let it be Berko. So climb up, Berko."

"What do you mean—climb up? Why should I climb up? You can go first, Father."

"You're the teacher this time—not I," says the priest, with some bitterness. "So lead the way."

They argued, they bickered; the debate became heated, but in the end they both climbed up, and the Sobolivka householder began to instruct the priest in the workings of modern machinery. Slowly he turned one handle, slowly, he turned another, and before they could say a single word, they were horrified to find that the locomotive had begun to move. And away it went!

Now this is the best time, I think, to leave the two good men to themselves in the roaring locomotive, while we pause and consider who is this man of Sobolivka who was so bold and so brave that he dared to climb together with the priest into the locomotive . . .

Berel Essigmacher—that was the name of the man I'm telling you about. And why did they call him Essigmacher? Because his business was that of making vinegar—*essig* in Yiddish—the very best vinegar in our corner of the world. The business he had inherited from his father, but he himself had invented a machine—so he says—that gave the vinegar its distinctive and superior quality. If he only had the time, he could make enough vinegar to provide for the needs of three whole provinces. But why should he? He didn't have to. He wasn't that greedy. That's the kind of man this Essigmacher was.

He had studied nowhere, and yet he could do the most delicate work you could imagine, and he understood the workings of all kinds of engines. How did this happen? Well, all you had to remember, he explained, was that the manufacture of vinegar had much in common with that of whisky. Both were made in a distillery; and a still had almost the same machinery as a locomotive. A still whistled, and so did a locomotive. What difference was there? The important thing—so said Berel himself and showed you what he meant with his hands—the important thing was the power that came from the heat. You started, he explained, by heating the boiler, and the boiler heated the water. The water turned to steam, the steam pushed a rod, and the rod turned the wheels. If you wanted to turn it right, you twisted the lever right, if you wanted to turn it left, you twisted it left. It was as plain as the nose on your face.

And now, having introduced you to this man of Sobolivka, I have at the same time no doubt answered many of the questions you had in mind. So we might as well go back to the wreck of the Straggler Special.

You can imagine the horror and dismay of the passengers when they saw the locomotive go off by itself, no one knew by what strange power. And besides that, the confusion that overwhelmed the crew itself. The first thing they did was to jump up and chase after the engine as if they thought they could catch up with it. But it did not take them long to realize that they were wasting their strength; and as if to tease them, the locomotive suddenly proved that it could develop speed. In fact it flew like mad. It was the first time that anyone had ever seen it move so fast. There was nothing to do but turn back, and this they did. And then, together with the guard and station master, they sat down and drew up a complete and detailed report; after which they sent off telegrams to every station along the line: BEWARE RUNAWAY LOCOMOTIVE. TAKE ACTION. WIRE REPLY.

What a panic this telegram created you can well imagine. What does this mean: Beware runaway locomotive? How does a locomotive run away? And what was this: Take action? What action could they take—besides sending telegrams? And so once more telegrams began to fly back and forth, forth and back, from one end of the line to the other. The instruments clicked and clattered as if they were possessed. Every station wired every other station, and the frightful news spread fast, till every town and every hamlet knew all the tragic details. In our town, for instance, in Heissin, we knew the exact number of people killed and injured. So violent a death! Such innocent victims! And when did it happen? On what day? Exactly on *Hashono Rabo,* when the tickets of our fate are made out, inscribed and sealed high up in Heaven! Apparently Heaven wanted it thus . . .

That is what people said in Heissin and all the nearby towns, and it is impossible to describe the agony and the suffering that we all endured. But how did that compare with the suffering of the poor passengers themselves, who were stranded in the station at Sobolivka without a locomotive, like sheep without a shepherd? What could they do? It was *Hashono Rabo.* Where could they go? Celebrate the holiday in a strange town? And they all huddled together in a corner and began to discuss their plight and to speculate about what had happened to the Fugitive, as they had now named the vanished locomotive. Who knew what might happen to a *shlimazl* like that? Just think of it—a monster like that careening down the track! How could it keep from colliding somewhere along the way with its sister train creeping from Heissin through Zatkovitz on its way to Sobolivka? What would happen to the passengers in the other train? In their imagination they saw the collision—a frightful catastrophe with all its gory details. They saw it before their eyes—overturned carriages, shattered wheels, severed heads, broken legs and arms, battered satchels and suitcases spattered with blood! And suddenly—another telegram! A telegram from Zatkovitz. And what did it say? Here it is:

THIS INSTANT LOCOMOTIVE FLEW PAST ZATKOVITZ WITH BLINDING SPEED CARRYING TWO PASSENGERS ONE A PRIEST. BOTH WAVED THEIR HANDS POINTED. CAN'T SAY WHAT THEY MEANT. NOW ON WAY TO HEISSIN.

What do you think of that? Two men in a runaway locomotive—and one of them a priest? Where were they going —and why—and who could the other man be? Asking here and there they finally found out that it was a resident of Sobolivka. But who? Did anyone know? What a question! Of course they knew! Berel Essigmacher of Sobolivka! How did they know? How does anyone ever know? They knew!

Some neighbors of his swore they had seen him and the priest from a distance standing together near the unhitched locomotive, gesturing with their hands. What did that mean? Why should a vinegar maker be standing with a priest near a locomotive, gesturing with his hands?

The talking and the shouting went on so long that soon the story reached Sobolivka, and though the town is only a short distance from the tracks, still by the time the story was relayed from one person to another it had been altered so much, assumed so many different forms, that by the time it reached Berel's home the story was so fantastic that Berel's wife fainted at least ten times and they had to bring a doctor. And all Sobolivka came pouring into the station. The place became so crowded, the noise so deafening, that the stationmaster instructed the guard to clear the platform.

If so, what are we doing there? Let's be off and see what happened to our friend the vinegar maker and the priest on the Fugitive, the runaway locomotive.

It is very easy to talk about seeing what happened in the runaway locomotive, but we'll have to take Mr. Essigmacher's word for it. The stories he tells about his adventure are so remarkable that if only half of them were true, it would be enough! And from what I know of him he doesn't seem to be the sort of person who makes up stories.

At first—this is Essigmacher's version—when the locomotive began to move, he scarcely knew what was happening. Not that he was alarmed; he was simply upset by the fact that the locomotive would not behave as it should. According to logic, he said, it should have stopped dead at the second turn of the lever. Instead, it went faster than ever, as if ten thousand evil spirits were pushing it down the tracks. It flew with such speed that the telegraph poles shimmered and flickered in front of his eyes like the spots you see when you're dizzy. A little later, when he came back to his senses, he remembered that a locomotive had brakes that could slow it down or stop it altogether. There should be brakes somewhere—hand brakes—air brakes—a wheel that you gave a good turn and it came pressing down on the rims of the wheels and they stopped turning . . . How could he ever have forgotten a simple thing like that! And he made a leap for the wheel, was going to give it a turn, when suddenly someone grabbed him by the arm and yelled, "Stop!"

Who was it? The priest, pale as a sheet. "What are you trying to do?" he asked. "Nothing," said Berel. "I'm just trying to stop the engine." "May God help you," cries the priest, "if you ever touch anything on that machine again! If you do, I'll pick you up by the collar and throw you out of here so fast that you'll forget your name was ever Moshko!" "Not Moshko," Berel corrects him. "My name is Berko." And he tries to explain what is meant by a wheel that's called a brake. But the priest won't let him. He was a stubborn man!

"You've turned enough things here already, and look where your turning got us! If you touch that wheel, I'll touch *you!* You'll wish you'd broken your neck before you ever saw me!"

"But, Father!" pleaded Berel. "Don't you think that my life means as much to me as yours does to you?"

"Your life!" snorted the priest bitterly. "What good is your life? A dog like you . . ."

At this Berel became angry and he turned upon the priest with a fury that will not soon be forgotten. "In the first place," he pointed out, "even if I were a dog you ought to feel sorry for me. According to our law even a dog mustn't be harmed. It's a living thing. And in the second place, in the eyes of the Almighty, in what way is my life any less important than any other life? Are we not alike? Do we not all have the same pedigree? Are we not all descended from the same man—Adam? And are all of us not going to the same identical place—the rich, black earth? And thirdly, Father, look at the difference between you and me. I am doing everything I can to make the locomotive stop, that is.

I have the welfare of both of us in mind; while you are ready to throw me out of here, that is, to murder a human being!"

That and many other fine things he told him. There in the flying locomotive he delivered a sermon complete with quotations and examples, until the poor, helpless priest was ready to collapse. And in the midst of the lofty discourse the station of Zatkovitz suddenly came into view, with the stationmaster and the guard straining themselves at the edge of the platform. Berel and the priest tried to signal to them; they yelled and waved their arms, but nobody knew what they were trying to say. The station flew past, and the locomotive was on its way to the next town—Heissin. As they went farther on, the priest became more friendly, but on one thing he still insisted. Berel must not touch the machine. But he did say this much:

"Tell me, Leibko . . ."

"My name," corrected Berel, "is not Leibko. It's Berko."

"All right," said the priest, "let it be Berko. Tell me, Berko, would you be willing to jump off this locomotive together with me?"

"What for?" asked Berel. "Just to get ourselves killed?"

To this the priest answered, "We're going to get killed anyway."

Said Berel, "Where was that decided? What proof do you have? If God wants to—Oh, Father, what He can do!"

Says the priest, "What do you think He'll do?"

Says Berel, "That depends on Him. Listen, Father, I'll tell you something. Today we Jews have a sort of holiday—*Hashono Rabo*. Today up in Heaven, every human being, every living thing, gets a certificate that's signed and sealed, a certificate of life or death. So, Father, if God marked me down for death, there's nothing I can do. What difference does it make to me if I'm killed jumping off the locomotive or standing *in* the locomotive? As a matter of fact, I can be walking along the street, and can't I slip and get killed? But on the other hand, if it was inscribed that I should go on living, then why should I jump?"

This is the way the vinegar maker of Sobolivka tells the story, and he swears that every word is true. He does not remember how it happened or when he first became aware that something had happened. It was somewhere close to Heissin; they could see the chimney on the station. Berel looked at the priest and the priest looked at Berel. What was this? The locomotive was slowing down. Little by little its speed decreased. Soon it was barely crawling. Now it paused, then moved a few feet farther, then thought it over and stopped completely.

What had happened? He suddenly remembered: the fire must have gone out. And when the fire in a locomotive goes out, the water stops boiling, and when the water stops boiling—well, you don't have to be a vinegar maker in Sobolivka to know that the wheels stop turning. And that's all there is to it.

And naturally, being Berel, he turned to the priest right then and there. "Well, Father, what did I tell you?" he said. "If God Almighty had not decided this morning in Heaven that I should go on living here on earth, who knows how much longer the fire might have continued to burn, and how much farther we might have gone by now?"

The priest said nothing. He stood where he was, with his head down, silent. What was there to say? But later, when it came time to part, he came up to Berel and held out his hand. "Goodbye, Itzko," he said. And Berel answered, "My name is not Itzko. It's Berko."

"Let it be Berko," said the priest. "I never knew you were such a . . ." And that was the last he heard. For rolling up the skirts of his cassock, the priest had started off with long strides back to his home in Golovonievska.

Berel himself went on to Heissin and there he had a real holiday. Like the good Jew that he was, he offered up thanks for his deliverance, and then he told his story from start to finish to everyone he saw, each time with new incidents and new miracles.

And everybody wanted the vinegar maker of Sobolivka to come home with him, spend the night with him, and tell him in person the story of the Miracle of *Hashono Rabo*.

And what a celebration we had that night! What a *Simchas Torah* that was! What a *Simchas Torah!*

HODEL

You look, Mr. Sholom Aleichem, as though you were surprised that you hadn't seen me for such a long time . . . You're thinking that Tevye has aged all at once, his hair has turned gray . . .

Ah, well, if you only knew the troubles and heartaches he has endured of late! How is it written in our Holy Books? "Man comes from dust, and to dust he returns." Man is weaker than a fly, and stronger than iron. Whatever plague there is, whatever trouble, whatever misfortune—it never misses me. Why does it happen that way? Maybe because I am a simple soul who believes everything that everyone says. Tevye forgets that our wise men have told us a thousand times: "Beware of dogs . . ."

But I ask you, what can I do if that's my nature? I am, as you know, a trusting person, and I never question God's ways. Whatever He ordains is good. Besides, if you do complain, will it do you any good? That's what I always tell my wife. "Golde," I say, "you're sinning. We have a *Medresh* . . ."

"What do I care about a *Medresh?*" she says. "We have a daughter to marry off. And after her are two more almost ready. And after these two—three more—may the Evil Eye spare them!"

"Tut," I say. "What's that? Don't you know, Golde, that our sages have thought of that also? There is a *Medresh* for that, too . . ."

But she doesn't let me finish. "Daughters to be married off," she says, "are a stiff *Medresh* in themselves."

So try to explain something to a woman!

Where does that leave us? Oh, yes, with a houseful of daughters, bless the Lord. Each one prettier than the next. It may not be proper for me to praise my own children, but I can't help hearing what the whole world calls them, can I? Beauties, every one of them! And especially Hodel, the one that comes after Tzeitl, who, you remember, fell in love with the tailor. And is this Hodel beautiful . . . How can I describe her to you? Like Esther in the Bible, "of beautiful form and fair to look upon." And as if that weren't bad enough, she has to have brains, too. She can write and she can read—Yiddish and Russian both. And books—she swallows like dumplings. You may be wondering how a daughter of Tevye happens to be reading books, when her father deals in butter and cheese? That's what I'd like to know myself . . .

But that's the way it is these days. Look at these lads who haven't got a pair of pants to their name, and still they want to study! Ask them, "What are you studying? Why are you studying?" They can't tell you. It's their nature, just as it's a goat's nature to jump into gardens. Especially since they aren't even allowed in the schools. "Keep off the grass!" read all the signs as far as they're concerned. And yet you ought to see how they go after it! And who are they? Workers' children. Tailors' and cobblers', so help me God! They go away to Yehupetz or to Odessa, sleep in garrets, eat what Pharaoh ate during the plagues—frogs and vermin—and for months on end do not see a piece of meat before their eyes. Six of them can make a banquet on a loaf of bread and a herring. Eat, drink and be merry! That's the life!

Well, so one of that band had to lose himself in our corner of the world. I used to know his father—he was a cigarette-maker, and as poor as a man could be. But that is nothing against the young fellow. For if Rabbi Jochanan wasn't too proud to mend boots, what is wrong with having a father who makes cigarettes? There is only one thing I can't understand: why should a pauper like that be so anxious to study? True, to give the devil his due, the boy has a good head on his shoulders, an excellent head. Pertschik, his name was, but we called him "Feferel"—"Peppercorn." And he looked like a peppercorn, little, dark, dried up and homely, but full of confidence and with a quick, sharp tongue.

Well, one day I was driving home from Boiberik where I had got rid of my load of milk and butter and cheese, and as usual I sat lost in thought, dreaming of many things, of this and that, and of the rich people of Yehupetz who had everything their own way while Tevye, the *shlimazl*, and his wretched little horse slaved and hungered all their days. It was summer, the sun was hot, the flies were biting, on all sides the world stretched endlessly. I felt like spreading out my arms and flying!

I lift up my eyes, and there on the road ahead of me I see a young man trudging along with a package under his arm, sweating and panting. "Rise, O Yokel the son of Flekel, as we say in the synagogue," I called out to him. "Climb into my wagon and I'll give you a ride. I have plenty of room. How is it written? 'If you see the ass of him that hateth thee lying under its burden, thou shalt forebear to pass it by.' Then how about a human being?"

At this the *shlimazl* laughs, and climbs into the wagon. "Where might the young gentleman be coming from?" I ask.

"From Yehupetz."

"And what might a young gentleman like you be doing in Yehupetz?" I ask.

"A young gentleman like me is getting ready for his examinations."

"And what might a young gentleman like you be studying?"

"I only wish I knew!"

"Then why does a young gentleman like you bother his head for nothing?"

"Don't worry, Reb Tevye. A young gentleman like me knows what he's doing."

"So—if you know who *I* am, tell me who *you* are!"

"Who am I? I'm a man."

"I can see that you're not a horse. I mean, as we Jews say, *whose* are you?"

"Whose should I be but God's?"

"I know that you're God's. It is written, 'All living things are His.' I mean, whom are you descended from? Are you from around here, or from Lithuania?"

"I am *descended*," he says, "from Adam, our father. I *come* from right around here. You know who we are."

"Well then, who is your father? Come, tell me."

"My father," he says, "was called Pertschik."

I spat with disgust. "Did you have to torture me like this all that time? Then you must be Pertschik the cigarette-maker's son!"

"Yes, that's who I am. Pertschik the cigarette-maker's son."

"And you go to the universtiy?"

"Yes—the university."

"Well," I said, "I'm glad to hear it. Man and fish and fowl —you're all trying to better yourselves! But tell me, my lad, what do you live on, for instance?"

"I live on what I eat."

"That's good," I say. "And what do you eat?"

"I eat anything I can get."

"I understand," I say. "You're not particular. If there is something to eat, you eat. If not, you bite your lip and go to bed hungry. But it's all worthwhile as long as you can attend the university. You're comparing yourself to those rich people of Yehupetz . . ."

At these words Pertschik bursts out, "Don't you dare compare me to them! They can go to hell as far as I care!"

"You seem to be somewhat prejudiced against the rich,"

I say. "Did they divide your father's inheritance among themselves?"

"Let me tell you," says he, "it may well be that you and I and all the rest of us have no small share in *their* inheritance."

"Listen to me," I answer. "Let your enemies talk like that. But one thing I can see: you're not a bashful lad. You know what a tongue is for. If you have the time, stop at my house tonight and we'll talk a little more. And if you come early, you can have supper with us, too."

Our young friend didn't have to be asked twice. He arrived at the right moment—when the borsht was on the table and the *knishes* were baking in the oven. "Just in time!" I said. "Sit down. You can say grace or not, just as you please. I'm not God's watchman; I won't be punished for your sins." And as I talk to him I feel myself drawn to the fellow somehow; I don't know why. Maybe it's because I like a person one can talk to, a person who can understand a quotation and follow an argument about philosophy or this or that or something else . . . That's the kind of person I am.

And from that evening on our young friend began coming to our house almost every day. He had a few private students and when he was through giving his lessons he'd come to our house to rest up and visit for a while. What the poor fellow got for his lessons you can imagine for yourself, if I tell you that the very richest people used to pay their tutors three *rubles* a month; and besides their regular duties they were expected to read telegrams for them, write out addresses, and even run errands at times. Why not? As the passage says, "If you eat bread you have to earn it." It was lucky for him that most of the time he used to eat with us. For this he used to give my daughters lessons, too. One good turn deserves another. And in this way he became almost a member of the family. The girls saw to it that he had enough to eat and my wife kept his shirts clean and his socks mended. And it was at this time that we changed his Russian name of Pertschik to Feferel. And it can truthfully be said that we all came to love him as though he were one of us, for by nature he was a likable young man, simple, straightforward, generous. Whatever he had he shared with us.

There was only one thing I didn't like about him, and that was the way he had of suddenly disappearing. Without warning he would get up and go off; we looked around, and there was no Feferel. When he came back I would ask, "Where were you, my fine-feathered friend?" And he wouldn't say a word. I don't know how you are, but as for me, I dislike a person with secrets. I like a person to be willing to tell what he's been up to. But you can say this for him: when he did start talking, you couldn't stop him. He poured out everything. What a tongue he had! "Against the Lord and against His anointed; let us break their bands asunder." And the main thing was to break the bands . . . He had the wildest notions, the most peculiar ideas. Everything was upside down, topsy-turvy. For instance, according to his way of thinking, a poor man was far more important than a rich one, and if he happened to be a worker too, then he was really the brightest jewel in the diadem! He who toiled with his hands stood first in his estimation.

"That's good," I say, "but will that get you any money?"

At this he becomes very angry and tries to tell me that money is the root of all evil. Money, he says, is the source of all falsehood, and as long as money amounts to something nothing will ever be done in this world in the spirit of justice. And he gives me thousands of examples and illustrations that make no sense whatever.

"According to your crazy notions," I tell him, "there is no justice in the fact that my cow gives milk and my horse draws a load." I didn't let him get away with anything. That's the kind of man Tevye is . . .

But my Feferel can argue too. And how he can argue! If there is something on his mind, he comes right out with it. One evening we were sitting on my stoop talking things over—discussing philosophic matters—when he suddenly said, "Do you know, Reb Tevye, you have very fine daughters."

"Is that so?" said I. "Thanks for telling me. After all, they have someone to take after."

"The oldest one especially is a very bright girl," said he. "She's all there!"

"I know without your telling me," said I. "The apple never falls very far from the tree."

And I glowed with pride. What father isn't happy when his children are praised? How should I have known that from such an innocent remark would grow such fiery love?

Well, one summer twilight I was driving through Boiberik, going from *datcha* to *datcha* with my goods, when someone stopped me. I looked up and saw that it was Ephraim the matchmaker. And Ephraim, like all matchmakers, was concerned with only one thing—arranging marriages. So when he sees me here in Boiberik he stops me and says, "Excuse me, Reb Tevye, I'd like to tell you something."

"Go ahead," I say, stopping my horse, "as long as it's good news."

"You have," says he, "a daughter."

"I have," I answer, "seven daughters."

"I know," says he. "I have seven, too."

"Then together," I tell him, "we have fourteen."

"But joking aside," he says, "here is what I have to tell you. As you know, I am a matchmaker; and I have a young man for you to consider, the very best there is, a regular prince. There's not another like him anywhere."

"Well," I say, "that sounds good enough to me. But what do you consider a prince? If he's a tailor or a shoemaker or a teacher, you can keep him. I'll find my equal or I won't have anything. As the *Medresh* says . . ."

"Ah, Reb Tevye," says he, "you're beginning with your quotations already! If a person wants to talk to you he has to study up first . . . But better listen to the sort of match Ephraim has to offer you. Just listen and be quiet."

And then he begins to rattle off all his client's virtues.
And it really sounds like something . . . First of all, he
comes from a very fine family. And that is very important
to me, for I am not just a nobody either. In our family you
will find all sorts of people—spotted, striped and speckled,
as the Bible says. There are plain, ordinary people, there are
workers, and there are property owners . . . Secondly, he is
a learned man who can read small print as well as large; he
knows all the Commentaries by heart. And that is certainly
not a small thing, either, for an ignorant man I hate even
worse than pork itself. To me an unlettered man is worse—
a thousand times worse—than a hoodlum. You can go around
bareheaded, you can even walk on your head if you like, but
if you know what Rashi and the others have said, you are a
man after my own heart . . . And on top of everything,
Ephraim tells me, this man of his is rich as can be. He has
his own carriage drawn by two horses so spirited that you
can see a vapor rising from them. And that I don't object to,
either. Better a rich man than a poor one! God Himself must
hate a poor man, for if He did not, would He had made
him poor?

"Well," I ask, "what more do you have to say?"

"What more can I say? He wants me to arrange a match
with you. He is dying, he's so eager. Not for you, naturally,
but for your daughter. He wants a pretty girl."

"He is dying?" I say. "Then let him keep dying . . . And
who is this treasure of yours? What is he? A bachelor? A
widower? Is he divorced? What's wrong with him"

"He is a bachelor," says Ephraim. "Not so young any more,
but he's never been married."

"And what is his name, may I ask?"

But this he wouldn't tell me. "Bring the girl to Boiberik,"
he says, "and then I'll tell you."

"Bring her?" says I. "That's the way one talks about a
horse or a cow that's being brought to market. Not a girl!"

Well, you know what these matchmakers are. They can
talk a stone wall into moving. So we agreed that early next

week I would bring my daughter to Boiberik. And driving home, all sorts of wonderful thoughts came to me, and I imagined my Hodel riding in a carriage drawn by spirited horses. The whole world envied me, not so much for the carriage and horses as for the good deeds I accomplished through my wealthy daughter. I helped the needy with money—let this one have twenty-five *rubles,* that one fifty, another a hundred. How do we say it? "Other people have to live too . . ." That's what I think to myself as I ride home in the evening, and I whip my horse and talk to him in his own language.

"Hurry, my little horse," I say, "move your legs a little faster and you'll get your oats that much sooner. As the Bible says, 'If you don't work, you don't eat' . . ."

Suddenly I see two people coming out of the woods—a man and a woman. Their heads are close together and they are whispering to each other. Who could they be, I wonder, and I look at them through the dazzling rays of the setting sun. I could swear the man was Feferel. But whom was he walking with so late in the day? I put my hand up and shield my eyes and look closely. Who was the damsel? Could it be Hodel? Yes, that's who it was! Hodel! So? So that's how they'd been studying their grammar and reading their books together? Oh, Tevye, what a fool you are . . .

I stop the horse and call out:

"Good evening! And what's the latest news of the war? How do you happen to be out here this time of the day? What are you looking for—the day before yesterday?"

At this the couple stops, not knowing what to do or say. They stand there, awkward and blushing, with their eyes lowered. Then they look up at me, I look at them, and they look at each other . . .

"Well," I say, "you look as if you hadn't seen me in a long time. I am the same Tevye as ever, I haven't changed by a hair."

I speak to them half angrily, half jokingly. Then my daughter, blushing harder than ever, speaks up:

"Father, you can congratulate us."

"Congratulate you?" I say. "What's happened? Did you find a treasure buried in the woods? Or were you just saved from some terrible danger?"

"Congratulate us," says Feferel this time. "We're engaged."

"What do you mean—engaged?"

"Don't you know what engaged means?" says Feferel, looking me straight in the eye. "It means that I'm going to marry her and she's going to marry me."

I look him back in the eye and say, "When was the contract signed? And why didn't you invite me to the ceremony? Don't you think I have a slight interest in the matter?" I joke with them and yet my heart is breaking. But Tevye is not a weakling. He wants to hear everything out. "Getting married," I say, "without matchmakers, without an engagement feast?"

"What do we need matchmakers for?" says Feferel. "We arranged it between ourselves."

"So?" I say. "That's one of God's wonders! But why were you so silent about it?"

"What was there to shout about?" says he. "We wouldn't have told you now, either, but since we have to part soon, we decided to have the wedding first."

This really hurt. How do they say it? It hurt to the quick. Becoming engaged without my knowledge—that was bad enough, but I could stand it. He loves her; she loves him—that I'm glad to hear. But getting married? That was too much for me . . .

The young man seemed to realize that I wasn't too well pleased with the news. "You see, Reb Tevye," he offered, "this is the reason: I am about to go away."

"When are you going?"

"Very soon."

"And where are you going?"

"That I can't tell you. It's a secret."

What do you think of that? A secret! A young man

named Feferel comes into our lives—small, dark, homely, disguises himself as a bridegroom, wants to marry my daughter and then leave her—and he won't even say where he's going! Isn't that enough to drive you crazy?

"All right," I say. "A secret is a secret. Everything you do seems to be a secret. But explain this to me, my friend. You are a man of such—what do you call it?—integrity; you wallow in justice. So tell me, how does it happen that you suddenly marry Tevye's daughter and then leave her? Is that integrity? Is that justice? It's lucky that you didn't decide to rob me or burn my house down!"

"Father," says Hodel, "you don't know how happy we are now that we've told you our secret. It's like a weight off our chests. Come, Father, kiss me."

And they both grab hold of me, she on one side, he on the other, and they begin to kiss and embrace me, and I to kiss them in return. And in their great excitement they begin to kiss each other. It was like going to a play. "Well," I say at last, "maybe you've done enough kissing already? It's time to talk about practical things."

"What, for instance?" they ask.

"For instance," I say, "the dowry, clothes, wedding expenses, this, that and the other . . ."

"We don't need a thing," they tell me. "We don't need anything. No this, no that, no other."

"Well then, what do you need?" I ask.

"Only the wedding ceremony," they tell me.

What do you think of that! . . . Well, to make a long story short, nothing I said did any good. They went ahead and had their wedding, if you want to call it a wedding. Naturally it wasn't the sort that I would have liked. A quiet little wedding—no fun at all. And besides, there was a wife I had to do something about. She kept plaguing me: what were they in such a hurry about? Go try to explain their haste to a woman. But don't worry. I invented a story— "great, powerful and marvelous," as the Bible says, about a rich aunt in Yehupetz, an inheritance, all sorts of foolishness.

And a couple of hours after this wonderful wedding I hitched up my horse and wagon and the three of us got in, that is, my daughter, my son-in-law and I, and off we went to the station at Boiberik. Sitting in the wagon, I steal a look at the young couple, and I think to myself: what a great and powerful Lord we have and how cleverly He rules the world. What strange and fantastic beings He has created. Here you have a new young couple, just hatched; he is going off, the Good Lord alone knows where, and is leaving her behind— and do you see either one of them shed a tear, even for appearance's sake? But never mind; Tevye is not a curious old woman. He can wait. He can watch and see . . .

At the station I see a couple of young fellows, shabbily dressed, down-at-the-heels, coming to see my happy bridegroom off. One of them is dressed like a peasant with his blouse worn like a smock over his trousers. The two whisper together mysteriously for several minutes. Look out, Tevye, I say to myself. You have fallen among a band of horse thieves, pickpockets, housebreakers or counterfeiters.

Coming home from Boiderik I can't keep still any longer and tell Hodel what I suspect. She bursts out laughing and tries to assure me that they were very honest young men, honorable men, whose whole life was devoted to the welfare of humanity; their own private welfare meant nothing to them. For instance, the one with his blouse over his trousers was a rich man's son. He had left his parents in Yehupetz and wouldn't take a penny from them.

"Oh," said I, "that's just wonderful. An excellent young man! All he needs, now that he has his blouse over his trousers and wears his hair long, is a harmonica, or a dog to follow him, and then he would really be a beautiful sight!" I thought I was getting even with her for the pain she and this new husband of hers had caused me; but did she care? Not at all! She pretended not to understand what I was saying. I talked to her about Feferel and she answered me with "the cause of humanity" and "workers" and other such talk.

"What good is your humanity and your workers," I say, "if it's all a secret? There is a proverb: 'Where there are secrets, there is knavery.' But tell me the truth now. Where did he go, and why?"

"I'll tell you anything," she says, "but not that. Better don't ask. Believe me, you'll find out yourself in good time. You'll hear the news—and maybe very soon—and good news at that."

"Amen," I say. "From your mouth into God's ears! But may our enemies understand as little about it as I do."

"That," says she, "is the whole trouble. You'll never understand."

"Why not?" say I. "Is it so complicated? It seems to me that I can understand even more difficult things."

"These things you can't understand with your brain alone," she says. "You have to feel them, you have to feel them in your heart."

And when she said this to me, you should have seen how her face shone and her eyes burned. Ah, those daughters of mine! They don't do anything halfway. When they become involved in anything it's with their hearts and minds, their bodies and souls.

Well, a week passed, then two weeks—five—six—seven . . . and we heard nothing. There was no letter, no news of any kind. "Feferel is gone for good," I said, and glanced over at Hodel. There wasn't a trace of color in her face. And at the same time she didn't rest at all; she found something to do every minute of the day, as though trying to forget her troubles. And she never once mentioned his name, as if there never had been a Feferel in the world!

But one day when I came home from work I found Hodel going about with her eyes swollen from weeping. I made a few inquiries and found out that someone had been to see her, a long-haired young man who had taken her aside and talked to her for some time. Ah! That must have been the young fellow who had disowned his rich parents and pulled his blouse down over his trousers. Without further delay I called Hodel out into the yard and bluntly asked her:

"Tell me, daughter, have you heard from him?"

"Yes."

"Where is he—your predestined one?"

"He is far away."

"What is he doing there?"

"He is serving time."

"Serving time?"

"Yes."

"Why? What did he do?"

She doesn't answer me. She looks me straight in the eyes and doesn't say a word.

"Tell me, my dear daughter," I say, "according to what I can understand, he is not serving for a theft. So if he is neither a thief nor a swindler, why is he serving? For what good deeds?"

She doesn't answer. So I think to myself, "If you don't want to, you don't have to. He is your headache, not mine." But my heart aches for her. No matter what you say, I'm still her father . . .

Well, it was the evening of *Hashono Rabo*. On a holiday I'm in the habit of resting and my horse rests too. As it is written in the Bible: "Thou shalt rest from thy labors and so shall thy wife and thine ass . . ." Besides, by that time of the year there is very little for me to do in Boiberik. As soon as the holidays come and the *shofar* sounds, all the summer *datchas* close down and Boiberik becomes a desert. At that season I like to sit at home on my own stoop. To me it is the finest time of the year. Each day is a gift from heaven. The sun no longer bakes like an oven, but caresses with a heavenly softness. The woods are still green, the pines give out a pungent smell. In my yard stands the *succah* —the booth I have built for the holiday, covered with branches, and around me the forest looks like a huge *succah* designed for God Himself. Here, I think, God celebrates His *Succos,* here and not in town, in the noise and tumult where people run this way and that panting for breath as they chase after a small crust of bread and all you hear is money, money, money . . .

As I said, it is the evening of *Hashono Rabo.* The sky is a deep blue and myriads of stars twinkle and shine and blink. From time to time a star falls through the sky, leaving behind it a long green band of light. This means that someone's luck has fallen . . . I hope it isn't my star that is falling, and somehow Hodel comes to mind. She has changed in the last few days, has come to life again. Someone, it seems, has brought her a letter from him, from over there. I wish I knew what he had written, but I won't ask. If she won't speak, I won't either. Tevye is not a curious old woman. Tevye can wait.

And as I sit thinking of Hodel, she comes out of the house and sits down near me on the stoop. She looks cautiously around and then whispers, "I have something to tell you, Father. I have to say goodbye to you, and I think it's for always."

She spoke so softly that I could barely hear her, and she looked at me in a way that I shall never forget.

"What do you mean—goodbye for always?" I say to her, and turn my face aside.

"I mean I am going away early tomorrow morning, and we shall possibly never see each other again."

"Where are you going, if I may be so bold as to ask?"

"I am going to him."

"To him? And where is he?"

"He is still serving, but soon they'll be sending him away."

"And you're going there to say goodbye to him?" I ask, pretending not to understand.

"No. I am going to follow him," she says. "Over there."

"There? Where is that? What do they call the place?"

"We don't know the exact name of the place, but we know that it's far—terribly, terribly far."

And she speaks, it seems to me, with great joy and pride, as though he had done something for which he deserved a medal. What can I say to her? Most fathers would scold a child for such talk, punish her, even beat her maybe. But Tevye is not a fool. To my way of thinking anger doesn't get you anywhere. So I tell her a story.

"I see, my daughter, as the Bible says, 'Therefore shalt thou leave thy father and mother'—for a Feferel you are ready to forsake your parents and go off to a strange land, to some desert across the frozen wastes, where Alexander of Macedon, as I once read in a story book, once found himself stranded among savages . . ."

I speak to her half in fun and half in anger, and all the time my heart weeps. But Tevye is no weakling; I control myself. And Hodel doesn't lose her dignity either; she answers me word for word, speaking quietly and thoughtfully. And Tevye's daughters can talk.

And though my head is lowered and my eyes are shut, still I seem to see her—her face is pale and lifeless like the moon, but her voice trembles . . . Shall I fall on her neck and plead with her not to go? I know it won't help. Those daughters of mine—when they fall in love with somebody, it is with their heads and hearts, their bodies and souls.

Well, we sat on the doorstep a long time—maybe all night. Most of the time we were silent, and when we did speak it was in snatches, a word here, a word there. I said to her, "I want to ask you only one thing: did you ever hear of a girl marrying a man so that she could follow him to the ends of the earth?" And she answered, "With him I'd go anywhere." I pointed out how foolish that was. And she said, "Father, you will never understand." So I told her a little fable—about a hen that hatched some ducklings. As soon as the ducklings could move they took to the water and swam, and the poor hen stood on shore, clucking and clucking.

"What do you say to that, my daughter?"

"What can I say?" she answered. "I am sorry for the poor

hen; but just because she stood there clucking, should the ducklings have stopped swimming?"

There is an answer for you. She's not stupid, that daughter of mine.

But time does not stand still. It was beginning to get light already, and from within the house my old woman was muttering. More than once she had called out that it was time to go to bed, but seeing that it didn't help she stuck her head out of the window and said to me—with her usual benediction, "Tevye, what's keeping you?"

"Be quiet, Golde," I answered. "Remember what the Psalm says, 'Why are the nations in an uproar, and why do the peoples mutter in vain?' Have you forgotten that it's *Hashono Rabo* tonight? Tonight all our fates are decided and the verdict is sealed. We stay up tonight . . . Listen to me, Golde, you light the samovar and make some tea while I go to get the horse and wagon ready. I am taking Hodel to the station in the morning." And once more I make up a story about how she has to go to Yehupetz, and from there farther on, because of that same old inheritance. It is possible, I say, that she may have to stay there through the winter and maybe the summer too, and maybe even another winter; and so we ought to give her something to take along—some linen, a dress, a couple of pillows, some pillow slips, and things like that.

And as I give these orders I tell her not to cry. "It's *Hashono Rabo* and on *Hashono Rabo* one mustn't weep. It's a law." But naturally they don't pay any attention to me, and when the times comes to say goodbye they all start weeping —their mother, the children and even Hodel herself. And when she came to say goodbye to her older sister Tzeitl (Tzeitl and her husband spend their holidays with us) they fell on each other's necks and you could hardly tear them apart.

I was the only one who did not break down. I was firm as steel—though inside I was more like a boiling samovar.

All the way to Boiberik we were silent, and when we came near the station I asked her for the last time to tell me what it was that Feferel had really done. If they were send‑ ing him away, there must have been a reason. At this she became angry and swore by all that was holy that he was innocent. He was a man, she insisted, who cared nothing about himself. Everything he did was for humanity at large, especially for those who toiled with their hands—that is, the workers. That made no sense to me. "So he worries about the world" I told her. "Why doesn't the world worry a little about him? Nevertheless, give him my regards, that Alexan‑ der of Macedon of yours, and tell him I rely on his honor (For he is a man of honor, isn't he?) to treat my daughter well. And write to your old father some times."

When I finish talking she falls on my neck and begins to weep. "Goodbye, Father," she cries. "Goodbye! God alone knows when we shall see each other again."

Well, that was too much for me. I remembered this Hodel when she was still a baby and I carried her in my arms, I carried her in my arms . . . Forgive me, Mr. Sholom Aleichem, for acting like an old woman. If you only knew what a daughter she is. If you could only see the letters she writes. Oh, what a daughter . . .

And now, let's talk about more cheerful things. Tell me, what news is there about the cholera in Odessa?

A DAUGHTER'S GRAVE

You're on your way to the Fair, and we're coming home from the Fair, I have done my weeping already, and you're still going to weep . . . So let me make room for you, Here, move a little closer. You'll be more comfortable."

"There, that's good!"

Thus spoke two passengers sitting behind me in the train. That is, one of them spoke, and the other threw in a word like an echo, from time to time.

"We were both there together, my old woman and I," said the first. "There she is over there, sleeping on the floor. Poor thing, she's all worn out. She's done enough weeping for all of us, there at the cemetery. She fell face down on the grave—and you couldn't drag her away! I begged her, 'Isn't that enough? Your tears won't bring her back to life again!' Did she listen to me? But what do you expect? Such a tragedy! An only daughter. A treasure. Gifted and beautiful and clever. A high school graduate . . . It's two years now since she died. Maybe you think it was consumption? Not at all! She was strong and healthy. She did it herself—took her own life . . ."

"Is that a fact!"

From their conversation I understood the kind of Fair they were talking about. I recalled that it was September, the

season of mourning, dear to the hearts of Jews. All over
the Pale, during those weeks before *Rosh Hashono,* Jews
travel from one town to another, paying their respects to the
remains of mothers and fathers, sisters and brothers, children
and other relatives. Bereaved mothers, orphaned daughters,
lonely sisters and just unfortunate women throw themselves
on the dear hallowed graves, shed a few tears, pour out their
grief, ease their tortured souls . . .

I can tell you: this isn't the first year I've been a traveling
man, but I can't remember when we've had such a good
crop of mourners as this September. The railroads, bless the
Lord, will make money. The carriages are packed. They are
full of long-faced men and women with swollen red eyes
and shiny noses. Some are on the way *to* the Fair, and others
are coming home *from* the Fair . . . Outside you can smell
early autumn. In your heart you feel autumn. And you're
longing, you're longing for home . . .

I can't help but overhear the rest of the conversation.

"Maybe you think it was one of today's tragedies? Black
smocks, red flags, Siberia? Heaven forbid! That much, at
least, God has spared me. I saw to that! After all, I had a
reason to. An only daughter. Such a gifted girl. So beautiful and clever. And a high school graduate!

"I did everything I could. I watched where she went and
whom she talked with, and what she said and what books
she read. 'Daughter, darling,' I said. 'If you want to read
books, go right ahead! But I have to know,' I said, 'what
you're reading.' It's true I don't know too much about
such things, but I have a certain intuition, an inner feeling.
Me—all I have to do is look into a book—even if it's in
French—and I can tell you right away what it smacks of!"

"Imagine that!"

"I didn't want my child to play with fire. I was afraid . . .
But don't think I resorted to trickery or force. On the con-
trary, I was gentle. All I did was remind her of a proverb.
'Daughter, darling,' I said. 'Let the wheel turn as it will.
Neither you nor I can stop it . . .' That's the way I talked

to her. And what did she say? Not a thing! An angel. Quiet
as a dove! . . . And what does God do? The bad times pass.
We live through all the troubles . . . Revolutions! Con-
stitutions! Black smocks, red flags, shorn hair, bombs and the
devil knows what else! All these things are gone. Although
before those times passed, you can understand, I almost
lost my wits. After all, didn't I have a right to? There was
plenty to be afraid of. An only child. Gifted and beautiful.
A high school graduate!"

"So! What happened?"

"To make a long story short . . . Praise the Lord! We
lived through those terrible times. Now, with God's help,
we could start thinking about marrying her off. A dowry?
That's the least of my worries. Let the Lord only send the
right man along! And the merry-go-round began. Matches,
matchmakers, prospects, suitors! And my daughter shows no
interest. You think maybe she doesn't want to get married?
Who knows? . . . What then? I'll tell you. I began to look,
to check up, and I find something. She's been reading a
book—in secret! And not alone. Three of them were reading
it together. She, and a friend of hers, our cantor's daughter
—a smart girl, too, a high school graduate—and a third. Who
is that? A nobody. A good-for-nothing, with a round face
full of pimples and weak eyes without lashes, and gold-
rimmed glasses to make him look still handsomer. A repulsive creature. And on top of it all, persistent. You couldn't
get rid of him. He crawled after them—like a worm! Why
do I call him a worm? I'll explain it to you. There are all
kinds of people in the world. Some are oxen. Some are
horses. Some are dogs. There are some who are pigs. And
this one was a worm. Now do you understand?"

"Of course!"

"How did this worm ever find his way into my house?
Through the cantor's daughter. He's a cousin of hers. He was
studying to become a druggist—or a lawyer—or a dentist—
the devil alone knows what! All I know is that to me he
was the Angel of Death. I didn't like him from the very

beginning. I even said so to my wife. But she said to me, 'What foolish notions you have!' Still, I keep an eye on them. I keep my ears open, and I'm not at all pleased with the way the three of them are always reading together, and the way they talk together, getting all wrought up and feverish . . .

"So I say to her one time, 'Daughter, darling, what's this book the three of you are so worked up about?'

" 'Nothing,' she says. 'It's just a book.'

" 'I see it's a book,' I tell her, 'but what kind of a book?'

" 'And if I told you,' says she, 'would you know?'

" 'Why shouldn't I know?' says I. And she laughs and tells me, 'It isn't what you're afraid of. It's just an ordinary book. It's name is *Sanni*. A novel by Archie Bashe's.'

" 'Archie Bashe's?' I say to her. 'Why, that was a blind teacher we had in this town. He died a long time ago.'

"Again she laughs, and I say to myself, 'Ah-ha, my daughter! You laugh, and your poor father is bleeding inwardly!' Here is what I thought: the old troubles were beginning again . . . And do you think I didn't get hold of that book and read it myself?"

"My goodness! Really!"

"Not exactly myself . . . But I got somebody to read it for me. A young man who works for me, a clerk in my shop. A very smart young fellow. Reads Russian like a professor . . . So one evening I sneaked the book away from my daughter's room, gave it to this clerk of mine, and said, 'Here, Berel, take it and read it through. And tomorrow you'll tell me what it's all about.' I barely lived through that night. The next morning, as soon as he came to work, I grabbed hold of him. '*Nu*, Berel,' I said. 'What about the book?' And he says, 'What a book!' And his eyes are about ready to pop out of his head. 'All night long,' he tells me, 'I couldn't sleep. I couldn't tear myself away!'

" 'Is that so?' I ask. 'Well, then, tell me more! Let me in on it too!' And my Berel tells me a story . . . How can I describe it to you? It just made no sense. Listen to this:

"It's about a big, strong Russian named Sanni who was always drinking whisky and eating sour pickles! And he had a sister whose name was Lida, and she was madly in love with a doctor, but she had an affair with an army officer and became pregnant. And there was a student named Yura who was head-over-heels in love with a girl, a school teacher, named Krasavitza. And this girl went out for a boat ride one evening—do you think she went with her boy friend? Not at all! She went out with that drunkard, Sanni!

" 'Is that all?' I asked.

" 'Wait a minute,' he tells me. 'That isn't all. There's another teacher too, a man named Ivan, and one day he goes with this drunkard to watch some naked girls bathing . . .'

" 'Come, come,' I say. 'What does it all lead up to? What's the point of it?'

" 'The point of it is this,' he tells me. 'This drunkard, Sanni, has a habit—he brays like a stallion and one time he comes home to his own sister Lida and he . . .'

" 'Go to the devil!' I tell him. 'That's enough about that drunkard. Tell me what happens! What is it all about? How does it end?'

" 'Oh,' he says, 'it ends like this. The army officer shoots himself, and the student shoots himself too, and Krasavitza takes poison, and a Jew—there's a Jew in the book too, Soloveitchik, hangs himself.'

"I lose my patience. 'Go!' I say. 'Go hang yourself together with him!' And he says 'Why do you talk to me like that? Is it my fault?' And I say, 'No not yours. I mean this Archie Bashe's.' That's what I tell Berel, but in my mind I'm thinking of that repulsive young fellow, the devil take him! And do you suppose one day I didn't catch him alone and take him to one side . . ."

"You did!"

"Of course! And I said to him, 'Look here! Where on earth did you ever pick up that trash?'

" 'What trash?' says he, flashing his gold-rimmed glasses at me.

" 'This story of Archie Bashe's,' I say, 'with that drunkard in it—Sanni.'

" 'Sanni,' he tells me seriously, 'is not a drunkard.'

" 'What else is he?' I want to know.

" 'Sanni,' he tells me, 'is a Hero!'

" 'And what makes him a Hero?' I ask. 'The fact that he drinks brandy out of a tea glass, eats sour pickles, and brays like a stallion?'

"The young fellow becomes furious. He takes off his glasses and looks at me with his red-rimmed eyes. 'You've heard the tune, Uncle,' he says to me, 'but you don't know the words. Sanni,' he says, pointing his finger up in the air, 'Sanni is a Man of Nature—a Free Man! He says what he means and does what he wants!' And he goes on and on, he doesn't stop. Freedom, and love, and again freedom, and once more love . . . And he puffs out his small pigeon's chest, makes gestures with his hands, and rants like a visiting preacher.

"I stand there looking at him, and think to myself, 'Heavenly Father, what is this repulsive thing talking about? How would it be if I took him by the collar and threw him out of doors so hard he would have to stop and pick up all his teeth?' But then I think it over: still, would it be better if he talked about bombs? Well, go be smart and foresee that there are things worse than bombs, and on account of trash like that I would lose my child, my only one, the apple of my eye, and that my wife would very nearly go out of her head, and that I myself out of shame and agony would have to give up my business and sell my home and go to live in another town! But I am getting ahead of myself. Let me tell you exactly how it came about and what started it.

"It started during the agrarian riots. When these riots started we naturally feared that it would end in another pogrom, as such things always do, and we lived in a state of terror. But if the Lord wishes, miracles happen, and from evil good comes out. How so? From the provincial capital authorities sent down a platoon of soldiers, and it became

quiet and peaceful again. And besides, because of the soldiers, the whole town came to life, business flourished. For
what can be better for any small town than a company of
soldiers with doctors and officers and corporals and com-
manders and I don't know what else they call them?"

"Why, naturally!"

"But go be smart and foresee that the cantor's daughter
would fall in love with an officer and declare that she was
willing to be converted in order to marry him? You can
imagine what went on in our town! But don't worry. The
cantor's daughter was *not* converted and she did *not* marry
the officer; because as soon as the agrarian riots ended the
troops were sent back where they came from, and in his
great hurry the officer even forgot to say goodbye to his beloved . . . But the girl did not forget. And woe to her parents! You can imagine what they went through. The whole
town seethed. Everywhere, from every mouth: 'The cantor's
daughter, the cantor's daughter.' Evil tongues were busy.
Someone sent a midwife to the girl. Someone else asked the
cantor what they were going to name the child. Though
actually it was very possible that the whole story was a lie.
You know what damage a few long tongues can do in a
small town!"

"How well I know!"

"Oh, what a pitiful sight they were! I mean the cantor
and his wife . . . We could hardly stand it. Because after
all—were they to blame? But at the same time I warned
my daughter, once for all, no matter how friendly they had
been before, from that day on she must have nothing to do
with the cantor's daughter. And with me—when I say something, there is nothing more to be said. She may be an only
daughter, but a father has to be respected! How was I to
know that my daughter would keep on seeing her in secret?
But when did I find that out? When it was too late. When
it was all over . . ."

Suddenly behind my back I heard someone cough and sigh
in her sleep, and the man who was telling the story became

silent. He waited a few minutes and then continued in a lower tone than before.

"It was the midnight services a week before *Rosh Hashono*. I remember it as if it happened yesterday. You should have seen our poor cantor as he led the services. It was pitiful to hear him. His sobbing was real, his groans were genuine. It was enough to melt a stone. And nobody knew what he was living through the way I did. These modern children! You can pity their parents . . . Well, the very next morning, I came home early from the synagogue, had a bite to eat, took my keys and went to the marketplace. I opened my shop and waited for Berel to come. I waited a half-hour. I waited an hour. No clerk, no Berel. At last I look up and there he is. 'Berel, why so late?' And he tells me, 'I was at the cantor's.' 'Why all of a sudden at the cantor's?' And he tells me, 'Why, haven't you heard what happened to Haika?' 'What happened to Haika?' I ask. 'Why, she poisoned herself . . .' "

"Think of that!"

"As soon as I heard that I ran straight home. My first thought was: what would Etka say? (That was my daughter, you know.) I come into the house and ask my wife, 'Where is Etka?' 'Etka is still in bed. Why, what's the matter?' 'What's the matter?' I say, 'Why, Haika just took poison.' When she heard this my wife threw her hands over her head and began to weep and wail. 'What's the matter?' I ask. 'Why,' she says, 'only last night Etka was with her. They went walking together—for about two hours!' 'Etka—with Haika?' I say. 'What are you talking about? How could that happen?' 'Oh,' she moaned. 'Don't ask me. I had to let her do it. She begged me not to tell you that she saw her every day. Something terrible has happened! I know it! I hope it's not true!' And with these words my wife runs into Etka's room and falls down on the floor in a faint. I come after her, run to the bed, screaming, 'Etka!' Etka? Did I say Etka? There is no Etka . . ."

"No Etka?"

"She was dead. Face down across the bed—dead. On her table was a bottle, and near it a note, in Yiddish, in her own hand. She used to write the most beautiful Yiddish; it was a pleasure to read it. 'My dear, faithful parents,' she had written. 'Forgive me for having caused you this grief and shame. Forgive me. Forgive me. We promised each other that we'd do it—Haika and I. On the same day, at the same hour, by the same means; because without each other we could not live. I know,' she wrote, 'dear parents, that I am committing a great wrong. I fought with myself for a long time, but it had to be. There is only one thing I ask of you, my dear ones, and that is that you bury me together with Haika, in a grave next to hers. Be well, and forget—forget that you ever had a daughter Etka . . .'

"Can you imagine that! To expect us to forget that we ever had a daughter Etka!"

Behind my back I heard a shuffle, the sound of steps, a sigh, and then a woman's voice, stifled and still sleepy:

"Avrom! Avrom!"

"Yes, Gitka—what is it? Did you sleep? Maybe you want some tea . . . Just a minute, we're coming to a station. I'll get some hot water. Where is the teakettle? Where is the tea and sugar?"

CNARDS

Nowadays a game of cards is an everyday affair.

Where don't we play cards nowadays? *When* don't we play cards? And *who* doesn't play cards nowadays?

There was a time, if you know what I mean, when we used to play cards only once a year—at *Hannukah.*

That is, if you want the whole truth, people used to get together for a game in those days too—a real game, a hot game! But where? In a secret chamber, behind locked doors.

In winter, in *cheder,* between the late-afternoon and evening prayers, when the rabbi was at the synagogue warming himself by the stove and we were left alone; or in summer, in a dark corner of the stable, near a thin crack in the wall; or at other times of the year when we bribed Getzel, the *shammes,* and locked ourselves up in the synagogue, high up in the women's balcony, turned a lectern face down for a table, and dealt out a hand of *Starshy Kozir* or Thirty-one or Turtle-myrtle.

One day Riva-Leah, the *gabai's* wife, of blessed memory (she has gone to her rest these many years) found a strange object in her lectern and almost fainted dead away. Who could have planted a thing like that—in her lectern?

Aghast, she ran out of the synagogue into the street, shouting at the top of her voice:

"Help, fellow Jews! Help! A misfortune has come to pass!
A calamity! A plot! Come with me and I'll show you!"

What was the calamity and what kind of a plot? You
couldn't get any answer from Riva-Leah. Only this: "Come,
come with me and I'll show you"

And before long she had drawn around her a fine assem-
blage, consisting of the rabbi, the *shochet,* a few of the
elders, and the cantor, together with a liberal sprinkling of
our secular aristocracy.

Naturally, when the rest of the people saw Riva-Leah
proceeding up the street followed by the rabbi, the *shochet,*
a few of the elders and the cantor and so many of our leading citizens, they joined the procession too. And then the
women and boys, and the little children, torn by curiosity,
fell in behind, and together they marched into the synagogue. At the head, came Riva-Leah, and behind her, the
townspeople.

You can imagine what a terror gripped the town. People
thought—it must be something serious. Either someone had
left a foundling, or some poor wretch had been found hanging from the rafters, or, God forbid, someone had been murdered.

Worried and frightened, they clattered up to the women's
balcony—Riva-Leah first, followed by the rabbi, the *shochet,*
the cantor, with the rest of the town after them.

"Where—where is it?" the crowd asked Riva-Leah, and
listened for the cry of the foundling and looked for the
hanging body or the trail of blood leading to the corpse that
some unknown enemy had left there to bring trouble on our
town.

And then imagine how astounded they all were when, instead of a foundling or a bleeding corpse, they found this
strange and ominous object in Riva-Leah's lectern: a picture
of a bearded man—obviously a Russian Orthodox priest—
with an odd black cross at his side. And not just one priest,
but two priests and two crosses, one priest upright, and the
other one standing on his head . . .

They all bent down and peered into Riva-Leah's lectern: first the rabbi, then the *shammes,* then the *shochet* and the elders and the cantor; then the leading citizens; then the common people. They looked and drew away. For to touch the thing with their hands—for that no one was bold enough. That is, no one except one man, Velvel Ramshevitch, the cantor's son-in-law.

When Velvel Ramshevitch looked and saw what it was his face lit up, and then with a laugh, he cried, "It's nothing! What's there to get excited about? It's just the king of clubs!"

"And what is the king of clubs?"

"A card. A card—that you play with."

"How did it get here?" they wanted to know. "In the lectern of Riva-Leah, the *gabai's* wife, in the women's balcony of the synagogue? That's one thing. And the other is, how does it happen that you, the cantor's son-in-law, know what a card is, and that it's called the king of clubs? And that it's a game that people play?"

At this our Velvel realized that he had fallen into a trap. And he turned every color imaginable and began to babble and to bleat, make sounds like a sheep or a goat, sounds that no one could understand, no human being, at any rate . . .

But that is not the story I started to tell. It is only an introduction to our tale about cnards. I merely wanted to show you what a forbidden thing cards used to be and how carefully we had to hide our knowledge of them.

There was only one lucky week in the year when we could play cards freely and openly.

That was the week of *Hannukah.*

And freely and openly we gathered that week at Velvel Ramshevitch's house. He was a free soul even then: he had shaved his beard and sidelocks, smoked on Saturdays on his front porch where all could see, and ate pork sausage— even on fast days! And he dared anyone to criticize him.

And his wife, Chayela, the cantor's daughter, imitating

him, threw away the wig that all respectable married women
wore in those days and went about in her own yellow hair;
sprinkled powder over her pockmarked face and spent all
her time with a gay young crowd, laughing and making
merry—showing everybody her large, stained teeth.

The Chapel—that was what we all called Ramshevitch's
house—was open to all the young people in town. There we
could read a newspaper or a secular book, there we could
smoke a cigarette on the Sabbath, nibble at sausage on fast
days, and—most important of all—play a game of cards.

They both loved a good game of cards, and if anything she
loved it even more than he did. She could hardly keep away
from the table. It was even rumored that they made their
living that way, for it was obvious that she was always winning. No matter who dealt she always had trumps. She beat
everybody. There was nothing we could do about it.

As you remember, in those days many young men were
supported by their fathers-in-law while they themselves went
on with their holy studies. And in our town, because of this
same Chayela with the blond hair and pockmarked face, more
than one such son-in-law gambled away his entire dowry and
his wife's pearls, and even drove his father-in-law into bankruptcy.

With one such son-in-law, in fact, she once played through
a whole winter, and before she was through with him he had
divorced his wife, a wonderful girl, a beauty, and come to
live with the Ramshevitches. No use telling you what a scandal it made in our town. Everybody was horrified.

But that is still not the story of cnards that I started to
tell. It is only the introduction to the scene of the story
which took place in the Chapel I have mentioned—the
Ramshevitch home—on the first night of *Hannukah*.

As I was saying, it was the first night of *Hannukah*. We
were all sitting in the Chapel, playing our favorite Jewish
card game, a real *kosher* game of Okeh.

And we played, as usual, in shifts. One group finished a

game and the next group sat down to play. It was that way all the time. One group played in the morning, another in the afternoon, and a third at night. And one of the Ramshevitches played with each group. Either he—or she—or both. At night, if he was sleeping, she played; and if she was asleep, then he played. And sometimes it happened that one night passed, and two nights, and three nights, and neither of them slept. They both played. Except for a half-hour or so when one of them dropped out between games and took a nap.

That was something all of us learned to do. Whenever we got too tired to play, we found something to lean against and dozed off.

It was the same with eating. On the table there was always a bottle and a small glass, herring and sausage. And when you were hungry you took a few minutes off and ate.

Naturally, you understand, we paid for all this. At each game part of the winnings were taken out for "the maid," though in the Chapel there never had been a maid. The Ramshevitches did not need a maid. There was no cooking to do, no beds to make—and no house to clean. There was no time for these things. So what did they need a maid for? Nevertheless with every hand the few cents were put aside and all of us knew that this went for rent and heat, for new decks of cards, and for food. Human beings must eat. And this I can say: there was as much to eat and drink as any of us ever wished for.

And it was the same with cigarettes. Whole boxes full of cigarettes. And whoever wanted to reached for one. And the Ramshevitches smoked more than anybody; and she smoked more than he did. I cannot imagine Chayela Ramshevitch without a cigarette in her mouth. Add to this the powdered pockmarked face and the uncombed blond hair, with the tired, puffy eyes. And the rooms thick with smoke, and the noise and the tumult. Think of all these together and you can picture to yourself what the Chapel looked like at *Hannukah,* when we could play cards openly and freely and we did not have to hide ourselves, or worry about being seen by any of the good people of the town.

That day—I am now coming to the story of the cnards—I was on the third shift. That is, I was one of the group that sat down to play in the evening, when the second candle was lit, and didn't get up until it was time for the third candle the next evening.

It was not the host—Velvel Ramshevitch—who lit the *Hannukah* candles that evening, but one of the guests, an elegant specimen—Eli Rafalski, one of those sons-in-law I mentioned earlier, who loved a card game more than almost anything else in the world, but who, nevertheless, had not strayed from the path in matters of Godliness. That was one thing you could say about the Ramshevitches: they didn't ask you what you were. You could be as pious as you wanted to be: so long as you had something in your pocket, and you played Okeh, and there was room at the table for another hand, you were welcome to sit down with us and were an honored guest! May my enemies have as many plagues and I as many lucky years as the number of times we played with people five nights and five days in succession, and then broke up without ever knowing who they were or what they were or where they had come from. A game of cards is not a marriage contract. You can play a very good game without knowing your opponent or his pedigree.

Well, there we were, sitting around the table, so absorbed in our work that we did not notice that two strangers had come in, men so unusual and odd in appearance that when we heard their "Good evening," and looked up at them, we were struck motionless and dumb.

Perhaps you want to know what they looked like to have frightened us so? I'll describe them to you as well as I can, and briefly.

One of them was a tall man—long and thin—in a long, black silken coat; earlocks—long and narrow, curly, reaching almost to his belt; a fur cap on his head; and a long beard and a pair of whiskers so thick and black that if you had met this man on a dark night on a deserted road, you'd want to say your prayers.

The other was just the opposite: short and round, also with earlocks and with a strange beard and whiskers, but not quite as overgrown as the other. In one hand he held a lantern and in the other a kerchief full of money.

Noticing the effect they had on us, the tall, thin one with the curly earlocks smiled at us gently through his whiskers, and repeated, "Good evening, my dear people. We have come here to greet you in honor of *Hannukah*."

And as he spoke he looked around at the *Hannukah* candles at the far end of the room, then at the table with the cards, and heaved a deep sigh. His companion, the short, round one, sighed also. Both of them sought with their eyes for a place to sit down.

Luckily the host, Ramshevitch, remembered that it was his duty to be polite, so he got up from the table and shook hands with the newcomers and asked them to sit down. And the rest of us followed suit, each one separately, some of us shaking hands with them and others just nodding from a distance.

The two sat down, looked at each other again, and gave another deep sigh. And once more the host remembered his manners.

"What's your name?" he asked, as one always should. "Where are you from? Have you been here long? Where are you going to?"

It was the tall, thin one who answered, in a tone as sweet as honey. Speaking slowly, one word at a time and with a delicate sweet smile that came out of his thick and frightful whiskers (he did not even seem to be talking to us, but looked rather as if he were deep in prayer, in humble communion with the Lord), he said:

"My dear friends, I am the grandchild of the *Bal-Shem-Tov*, the founder of Chassidism. I have but one duty, to wander about the world and collect money for the *yeshivas,* the holy seminaries, both here and in the Holy Land of our fathers."

And he sighed again. "And this is my companion who goes with me everywhere and who guards the contributions." With his eyes he indicated the fat one, and this time both of them sighed deeply. "We have devoted our whole life to the *yeshivas,* in order that God's Law may not be forgotten.

"And so, my friends," he continued, with another sigh, "give us a contribution—whatever you are able. One," he said, nodding his head as if in prayer, "can give more, and another can give less."

And his companion, rolling his eyes aloft, added, "And all who give more, will receive more from Heaven."

And he laid his kerchief full of money on the table with a clang. A corner came open and we could see the glint of silver and gold.

Money, they say, attracts money. Seeing all the money already in the kerchief, we had no choice but to add more from our own pockets, and as we did it each one of us thought (I am sure of it): "Ah, if I had the money in that kerchief! What couldn't I do with it . . ."

Our hostess, Chayela Ramshevitch, could not conceal her excitement. Her eyes fairly blazed. We were all aware of it, even the *Bal-Shem-Tov's* grandchild and his companion, who was in no apparent hurry to remove the kerchief from her sight. The two continued to sit there with their eyes on the cards scattered around the table, and we could see that this was the first time in their lives that either one of them had seen such a thing.

At last the *Bal-Shem-Tov's* grandchild raised his eyes. "I hope I am not disturbing you, but I'd like to ask a question," he said in his unctuous voice and with his soft, sweet smile, pointing with an extended little finger at one card after another. "What sort of thing is this—on the table here?"

"Why, cards," answered our host and hostess together, with

a glance at us that seemed to say, "So there are still people on earth so uncivilized that they don't even know what cards are!"

The *Bal-Shem-Tov's* grandchild shut an eye, wrinkled up his nose and forehead, turned his face toward his companion, and with an unearthly sigh, repeated: "Cnards?"

And his companion, with a sigh of his own, repeated after him, "Cnards."

"No, that's wrong," Chayela Ramshevitch undertook to correct them, without once taking her eyes off the kerchief full of money. "Not cnards—cards!"

Naturally they did not say a word to her, nor did they turn their soft, smiling, clever eyes upon her. They were holy men, and such men, you understand, never glance at a female.

But turning to their host, Velvel himself, the *Bal-Shem-Tov's* grandchild said, "I don't want to disturb you, but tell me—what are these things—these cnards? What are they good for? That is, what do you do with them?"

"You play with them," answered Ramshevitch. "Don't you know? When *Hannukah* comes, people play cards."

Again the *Bal-Shem-Tov's* grandchild shut an eye, and turning his face slowly toward his companion, said:

"When *Hannukah* comes—they play cnards."

"Imagine that," echoed his companion.

"But what does that mean?" asked the *Bal-Shem-Tov's* grandchild, slowly, unctuously. "How does one play with these—cnards? And why? What for?"

"For money," answered Ramshevitch, looking from us to the kerchief on the table.

Apparently this answer sounded wild and meaningless to both of them, for they turned upon each other with such a strange, bewildered expression that all of us burst out laughing.

But our hostess come to their defense. "What is there to laugh at?" she demanded, and lit a cigarette to hide her own laughter. And Ramshevitch helped her out by explain-

ing to them briefly and clearly the meaning and the use of
cards; concluding with the observation that cards were both
a diversion and a vocation. In short, you could say that cards
were a trade. A trade like any other.

And saying this, Velvel the cantor's son-in-law picked up
the cards again with a quick glance at all of us to see if we
were ready, and to show the meddlers that we were busy
and that time was short. Let them stop bothering us; it was
time for them to get up and be on their way.

But that was apparently not their intention. On the contrary, they edged still closer to the table and stared at our
host who was now shuffling the cards. Their eyes grew large
as though they were expecting something to pop out at any
minute.

"I hope I am not disturbing you," said the *Bal-Shem-Tov's*
grandchild again in his unctuous tone and with his fine
sweet smile . . .

"Do you want to watch us play?" Ramshevitch interrupted.
"Then go ahead and watch. You can't do us any harm. Well,
children! Let's get to work! Time doesn't stand still! Whose
deal is it now?"

And the interrupted work was resumed with a new vigor,
a new warmth, with skill and cunning; as they say in society, with *éclat*.

And the visitors looked on, listened to every word we
said, and studied our hands. And every time that one of us
cautiously looked at our covered card, our two guests bent
and turned and twisted until they could see the card too, and
made such strange faces that it was all we could do to keep
from splitting with laughter. It was lucky we were all so absorbed in the game that nothing less than an earthquake
could have disturbed us.

I am afraid that I was the only one who really kept an eye
on them. From time to time I looked up and I began to
think that to them we must look even stranger than they did
to us. We and not they were peculiar, involved in a strange
pursuit, speaking a wild language and conducting ourselves

in general like savages: sitting bareheaded, inhaling smoke, exchanging little squares of paper, throwing money into a plate, and talking to each other in a language that might have been Turkish or Greek. For who could understand the meaning of *pass, deuce, pair, flush, jack, queen, king, ace,* and other such words that belong to the language of cards?

I can swear to you that we had forgotten all about the two holy men in our midst, when suddenly a pale white hand came slapping down on the deck of cards, and we heard these words:

"There! Now we understand it! We've caught on to it! It's a temptation, I tell you! A terrible temptation! The work of the devil himself and all the evil spirits! Do us a favor, please! Give us some too! Oh, what a diabolic invention! I hope the Lord will pardon us. Man is sinful. I beg you, give us some! We want to feel the taste of these cnards too!"

It was the *Bal-Shem-Tov's* grandchild who said this. He said it in such a trembling voice, with such fire and feeling, almost with tears in his eyes, that it almost tore our hearts out. And to our sympathy was added the sight of the kerchief full of gold and silver . . . Each one of us, I am afraid, would have liked the kerchief and what was in it to become his personal property. You should have seen our Chayela Ramshevitch. Her eyes were aflame and her cheeks were flushed, and she said to her husband and to the rest of us:

"They are asking us a favor. Why shouldn't we let them? After all, it's *Hannukah.*" And her eyes were on the kerchief with the money which the *Bal-Shem-Tov's* grandchild had now drawn close to him, and from which with trembling fingers he was taking out coin after coin, one for himself and one for his companion, making two even piles of silver, one for each of them. At the same time he murmured to himself apologetically:

"Never mind! We have a great and powerful God! If we win, the *yeshivas* will have more money. And if we should lose, then the Lord will pardon us. He is long-suffering, as Jeremiah so truthfully said."

Thus he spoke, with a glance aloft, and his companion fol-lowed him, also with an upward glance and with these holy words:

"Long-suffering and full of kindness and truth."

All of this happened so suddenly, so unexpectedly, that not one of us had time even to be surprised. It seemed as natural as could be. And in addition I must confess that our minds were playing with the kerchief of money and our eyes were fixed on the two piles of silver.

There was only one thing left to decide: which of us should drop out. With two new players added, the question now was, which of us should make room for them. You understand, of course, that none of us was anxious to retire when the rare opportunity presented itself of playing with the grandchild of so holy a man as the *Bal-Shem-Tov*, especially when he had been so thoughtful as to have brought with him a kerchief full of money. And the argument began.

"You go take a rest." "No, you." "Why should I?" "You look tired."

The first to be sacrificed on the altar of hospitality was the pampered son-in-law I have already told you about, Eli Rafalski, the one who a little earlier in the evening had lit the *Hannukah* candles for us. And it was our hostess, Chayela Ramshevitch, who decided that. She insisted that it was time for him to go home. It was late, his wife's parents would complain; they might even create a scandal, and it would get them all into trouble.

That was her excuse, but all of us knew the truth. Eli had lost all he had and no one wanted to let him have any more. In the midst of a game no one loans out money.

That took care of one. For the second we drew lots. And then we went to work. Little by little the two fresh even stacks of silver disappeared, the kerchief became lighter and lighter, while in front of each of us now appeared the funds

once destined for the *yeshivas* of all the world. Soon the
kerchief was almost empty and it began to look as if the
Bal-Shem-Tov's grandchild would be lucky if he still had his
gabardine to go away in. We were beginning to wonder
what would happen if we took their last *kopek* away. What
would the town say? What would the whole world say?

But all of you who play the game know the mysterious
quality that cards possess. One minute you're flat on the
ground, ready to be carried out in a blanket, and suddenly
your luck changes—you don't know yourself how it happened! That's just what happened to our visitors. They began to win hand after hand, especially when the *Bal-Shem-
Tov's* grandchild began to deal.

"They are possessed by the devil. Let me have them," he
said, taking the cards and beginning to deal them out, at
first clumsily and inaccurately, with trembling, inexperienced
hands, and eyes that followed each card until it landed.
Looking at him we could not suppress our laughter. But as
time went on he began to do it faster and faster until the
cards sped from his hands in an endless stream. And everything went his way. No matter what cards you had, he had
better ones. If you had three jacks, he had three queens. If
you had kings, he had aces. If you had aces, he had a flush.
And if you became frightened and dropped out with an un-
promising pair, he had nothing at all! Until, with a start, he
pushed his chair back, sprang to his feet, and stretched himself.

"*Raboisi!*" he cried, gathering up his winnings and stuffing them not into the kerchief but into his own pockets.
And then with a glance aloft he sighed, and his companion
followed him with the same upward glance and the same
sigh, and finished the quotation from the Passover services
which the other had started:

"*Masters, the time has come to say the morning prayers!*"

Stunned and sleepy, hungry and depressed, sulking as los-
ers always do, we remained sitting a while, unable to move.
Then gradually one by one we got up and went up to the

table for a drink and a bite to eat. That is, all except our two guests, who were ready to take their leave, and coming to the doorway did not forget to kiss the *mazuza*.

But suddenly our host, Velvel Ramshevitch, jumped in front of them, and spreading out his arms, blocked their way with these words:

"Oh, no! You can't go away from here without taking a bite to eat!"

Velvel could not have imagined a vengeance more complete. Our poor guests stood as though trapped, looking at each other as if we were forcing them to empty their pockets of all their winnings. The first to recover his speech was the *Bal-Shem-Tov's* grandchild, who addressed us once more with his unctuous tone and his sweet little smile:

"We thank you wholeheartedly for your kindness. Hospitality to wayfarers is, according to our Law, one of the greatest of all acts of virtue. But you must not forget that my companion and I are careful about what meat we allow to touch our lips. No doubt it's *kosher,* but . . ."

That was too much for us. "Oh, so you can't eat our food!" we cried. "You're afraid it isn't *kosher* enough for you, but our cards were *kosher* enough? To take our money away was proper enough? No, we won't let you get away with that! You tasted our hospitality at the card table; now you must taste some sausage too!"

Crestfallen, they looked at each other. Then the *Bal-Shem-Tov's* grandchild let out a deep sigh, almost a groan, and said to us. "Just as you say, my friends. After all, we are in a Jewish home, and we must never be suspicious of our own people. And what if the food, heaven forbid, is not as *kosher* as it might be? Our Lord is a great and mighty One . . ."

And murmuring a prayer that none of us could make out, he turned humbly toward the table where our hostess was preparing sardines, herring and sausages. Picking up a glass he turned to us. "Your health, my friends. I drink your health," he said, and lifted the glass and barely moistened his lips. Then, with a trembling hand he took a bite of herring, and then a thin slice of sausage. His companion followed him, and together they struggled with their food, almost choking on it. And only when they were through did Velvel take his full revenge. Without a trace of pity, he addressed them in these words:

"Do you know what you have just eaten? It was not Jewish food at all. Do you know what kind of sausage that was? Do you know what it was made of? Gentlemen, you have just been eating real, genuine . . ."

Before he could finish the sentence our two visitors clutched their heads in terror, opened their mouths wide as if to spit everything out, and then with a bitter groan sprang for the door and swept out of the house like a cyclone.

Our vengeance was so complete that we almost forgot how much we had lost that night, forgot the depths to which we had sunk, and looking at each other we laughed and laughed and laughed. We thought we would never stop laughing, but we did—and suddenly too—when from the table where we had been playing we heard a shriek that was barely human.

"Quick! Quick! Come here! Oh, may lightning strike me! I can't bear it!"

It was Chayela Ramshevitch. We had not even noticed that as soon as she had finished eating she had gone back to the table to clean things up. First, as always, she gathered up the cards we had played with; they could still be sold or traded for new decks. And in sorting out the cards she had noticed something strange. There were too many aces—far too many. Six or seven to the deck.

We grabbed up the rest of the cards and discovered not only aces but a wealth of everything else as well: kings and queens and jacks, in fact everything! And many of them! Well, we didn't go home to rest as we had planned. Instead, we made a pilgrimage. We went to every synagogue in town, visited every chapel and prayer house. We looked everywhere, searched everywhere, asked everywhere. But no one had seen the *Bal-Shem-Tov's* grandchild and his companion. No one had even heard of them.

Unsuccessful, dejected, we decided to try the railroad station. There we searched everywhere. We went through the station itself, through every carriage in the waiting train. Not a sign of the grandchild or his companion. The earth must have swallowed them both!

It was after the third bell had rung, the last whistle had blown, that we heard a familiar voice from one of the carriages.

"Cnards!"

We sprang toward the carriage from which the word had come. From an open window of a second-class carriage, two strange men were watching us with interest and amusement. One was tall and thin, the other short and fat. Both were clean-shaven, both wore short tailored jackets and derby hats. And yet they were familiar. Not so much the faces as the eyes—soft, smiling, shrewd little eyes.

The first to recognize them was the pampered son-in-law, Eli Rafalski. As soon as he saw their smiling faces he pointed straight at them:

"There they are!" he cried. "There they are! The two cnard players—as sure as my name is Rafalski!"

But the train was already moving. The wheels had just begun to turn. And slowly passing us by, the two men looked at us once more with their soft, smiling shrewd eyes. And for Eli Rafalski, who had been so acute as to recognize them, they had a special farewell.

Together they raised their thumbs to their noses, and made a broad arc with their outstretched fingers.

GLOSSARY*

Al-kein n'Kvach l'cho (*Al-ken ne Kave lecho*): The beginning of the second part of the prayer *Alenu:* "Therefore we hope . . ."

Bar Mitzvah: A thirteen-year-old Jewish boy who is confirmed; the confirmation ceremony itself.

beigel (*bagel*): Hard circular roll with hole in the center like a doughnut.

blintzes: Cheese or *kasha* rolled in thin dough and fried.

bris: Circumcision ceremony.

Bubi-Kama (*Baba Kama*): "First Gate," a Talmudic treatise on compensation for damages.

chad gadyo (*Had Gadya*): "One Kid," an Aramaic nursery song sung at the conclusion of the *Seder* home service on Passover.

Chassidim: Plural of *chassid;* members of a mythical sect founded in the middle of the 18th Century by Rabbi *Bal-Shem.*

cheder: Old-style orthodox Hebrew school.

* Many of the spellings of Hebrew words used in these stories are rendered phonetically as they occurred in popular usage. In such cases, throughout the glossary, the correct transliterated spelling is given in parentheses.

cholent: Potted meat and vegetables cooked on Friday and simmered overnight for Sabbath eating.

chremzlach: Fried *matzo* pancakes, usually served with jelly or sprinkled with powdered sugar.

datcha: Summer cottage in the country.

dreidel (from the German *drehen,* "to turn"): A small top, spun with the fingers, and played with by children on *Hannukah* in East European countries.

dybbuk (same as *gilgul*): A soul condemned to wander for a time in this world. To escape the perpetual torments from evil spirits it seeks refuge in the body of a pious man or woman over whom the demons have no power.

eirev (*erub*): The law limiting the movements of the pious and the carrying of objects on the Sabbath, hence also the rope used to define the area of free movement.

esrog (*ethrog*): A large sweet-smelling citrus-fruit of the lemon family waved together with palm, myrtle and willow branches in the synagogue procession during the Feast of Tabernacles.

fisnoga: Comical combination of the Yiddish *fis* (feet) and the Russian *noga* (feet).

gabai: Synagogue treasurer.

Gamorah (*Gemara*): The Aramaic name for the *Talmud,* i.e. to learn. (See *Talmud*).

gilgul (see *dybbuk*).

gospoda (Russian): Term of address, "Gentlemen!"

gragar: A noisemaking toy used by Jewish children during the *Purim* festival; a rasping chatterbox.

gribbenes: Small crisp pieces left from rendered poultry fat, eaten as a delicacy.

grivnye: Silver coin worth ten *kopeks.*

groschen: Small German silver coin whose old value was about two cents.

gulden: An Austrian silver florin worth about forty-eight cents.

Hagadah: The book containing the Passover home service, consisting in large part of the narrative of the Jewish Exodus from Egypt.

hamantash: A triangular pocket of dough filled with poppy seed or prunes and eaten on *Purim.*

Hannukah (Channukah): Described variously as "The Festival of Lights," "The Feast of Dedication," and "The Feast of the Maccabees." It is celebrated for eight days from the 25th day of *Kislev* (December). It was instituted by Judas Maccabeus and the elders of Israel in 165 B.C. to commemorate the rout of the invader Antiochus Ephinanes, and the purification of the Temple sanctuary.

haroses: A mixture of nuts and apples to symbolize the clay which the children of Israel worked into bricks as slaves in Egypt. Eaten at the *Seder* services on Passover.

Hashono Rabo (Hoshana Rabbah): The seventh day of *Succoth* (Feast of Booths).

Kabala (Cabala): Called "the hidden wisdom," mystical, esoteric knowledge that, beginning with the 13th Century, arose in opposition to the rationalism of the *Talmud.*

kaddish: The mourner's prayer recited in synagogue twice daily for one year by the immediate male relatives, above thirteen years, of the deceased.

kasha: Groats.

Kazatsky (Kazatske): A lively Russian dance.

kneidlach: Balls of boiled matzo meal cooked in chicken soup.

knishes: Potato or *kasha* dumpling, fried or baked.

kopek: A small copper coin; there are 100 *kopeks* in a *ruble.*

kosher: Food that is permitted to be eaten and prepared according to the Jewish dietary laws.

kreplach: Small pockets of dough filled with chopped meat, usually boiled and eaten with chicken soup.

kugel: Noodle or bread suet pudding, frequently cooked with raisins.

mah nishtano: Literally, "What is the difference?" The first words in the opening "Four Questions" of the Passover *Hagadah,* traditionally asked by the youngest child in the household at the *Seder* service. (See *Seder*).

matzos: Unleavened bread eaten exclusively during Passover to recall the Jewish Exodus from Egypt.

mazl-tov: Good luck!

mazuza *(mezuzah):* Small rectangular piece of parchment inscribed with the passages Deut. VI. 4-9 and XI. 13-21, and written in 22 lines. The parchment is rolled up and inserted in a wooden or metal case and nailed in a slanting position to the right-hand doorpost of every orthodox Jewish residence as a talisman against evil.

Megila (Megillah); Literally, "a roll," referring to the *Book of Esther* which is read aloud in the synagogue on *Purim*.

Medresh (Midrash): A body of exegetical literature, devotional and ethical in character, which attempts to illuminate the litcral text of the Bible with its inner meanings. The *Midrash* is constantly cited by pious and learned Jews in Scriptural and Talmudic disputation.

melamed: Old style orthodox Hebrew teacher.

Mishnayos (The *Mishna):* A compilation of oral laws and Rabbinic teachings, edited by Judah ha-Nasi in the early 3rd Century A.D., which forms the text of the *Talmud.* It is obligatory for pious Jews to study it constantly.

Mohel: The religious functionary who performs circumcisions.

nogid: A rich man, leading secular citizen of a community.

nu: Exclamatory question, i.e. "Well? So what?"

Oleinu (Alenu): Literally, "it is our duty," the last prayer in the daily Jewish liturgy.

Pesach: Passover, the festival commemorating the liberation of the Jews from their bondage in Egypt. It lasts seven days, beginning with the 15th of *Nisan* (March-April).

Perek: A chapter of the *Talmud.*

piatekas: Five-*kopek* piece.

Pupik: Navel; a term of teasing endearment.

Purim: Festival of Lots, celebrating the deliverance of the Jews from Haman's plot to exterminate them, as recounted in the *Book of Esther.* It is celebrated on the 14th and 15th of *Adar,* the 12th Jewish lunar month (March).

Rabbiner: A crown rabbi, chosen by election at the requirement of the Czar, to be an official functionary. Generally unpopular in old Russia.

Raboisi (*Raboisai*): Respectful Hebrew term of address used in Talmudic disputation, saying grace after meals, etc. Literally, "my masters."

Rambam: Popular name for Rabbi Moses ben Maimon (Maimonides) eminent, Spanish-Jewish philosopher and physician (1135-1204).

Reb: Mister.

Rosh Hashono (*Rosh Hashanah*): The Jewish New Year, celebrated on the 1st of *Tishri* (in September), is the most solemn day next to *Yom Kippur* (Day of Atonement).

Rov: Rabbi.

schnorrer: A shameless beggar.

seder: The home service performed on the first two nights of Passover (see *Hagadah*).

Shabbes: Sabbath (Saturday).

shadchan: Marriage-broker.

Shahu notch shomayem (bastardized Russian-Hebrew): Walk at night under the heavens.

shammes (pl. *shamosim*): Sexton.

sheigetz (pl. *shkotzim*): A Gentile youth.

sheitel: A wig worn by ultra-orthodox married women.

Shevuos (*Shabuot*): Variously known as "The Festival of Weeks" and "Pentecost." It originally was a harvest festival and is celebrated seven weeks after Passover.

shi-shi (*shishi*): Sixth part of the Scriptural portion for the week read aloud on the Sabbath in the synagogue, and regarded as a great honor for the reader.

shkotzim: Plural of *sheigetz*.

shlimazl: An incompetent person, one who has perpetual bad luck. Everything happens to him.

Shma Koleinu (*Shema Koleinu*): "Hear our voices!" The first words of a Day of Atonement hymn; a popular idiom meaning: "idiot."

Shma Yisroel (*Shema Yisroel*): The first words in the confession of the Jewish faith: "Hear, O Israel: the Lord our God the Lord is One!"

Shmin-esra (*Shemoneh 'Esreh*): Eighteen (actually nineteen) benedictions, forming the most important part of the daily prayers, recited silently, standing up, by the worshipper.

shochet (pl. *shochtim*): Ritual slaughterer.

shofar: Ram's horn blown in the synagogue at services on *Rosh Hashanah* and *Yom Kippur.*

Sholom Aleichem: Peace be unto you.

shul: Synagogue.

Simchas Torah: "Rejoicing over the Torah," the last day of *Succoth* (Feast of Tabernacles), celebrating the completion of the reading of the Torah.

starosta: Village elder or "mayor" in Czarist Russia.

succah: A booth made of fresh green branches in which pious Jews celebrate the Feast of Tabernacles. This is done symbolically to recall the forty years' wandering—"that your generations may know that I made the children of Israel to dwell in booths, when I brought them out of the land of Egypt."

Succos (*Succoth*): The Feast of Tabernacles, survival of the ancient festival on which male Jews were required to go on a pilgrimage to the Temple in Jerusalem. Lasts nine days and begins on the 15th day of the seventh lunar month of *Tishri* (September-October).

tallis (*tallith*): Prayer-shawl.

tallis-kot'n (*tallith katon*): "Small *tallis,*" a four-cornered fringed undergarment worn by male orthodox Jews in pursuance of the Biblical commandment to wear a garment with fringes.

Talmud: The Corpus Juris of the Jews, a compilation of the religious, ethical and legal teachings and decisions interpreting the Bible; finished c. A.D. 500.

tfillin: Phylacteries.

T'hilim: Psalms of David.

Torah: "Doctrine" or "law"; the name is applied to the five books of Moses, i.e. the Pentateuch.

Troika: A Russian sleigh drawn by three horses.

tzimmes: Dessert made of sweetened carrots or noodles.

vareniki: Fried dough filled with cheese or jelly.

verst: A Russian measure of distance, equal to about ⅔ of an English mile.

vertutin: Cheese or cooked cherries rolled in dough.

Yekum Perkon (*Yekum Purkan*): Aramaic prayer in the Sabbath service.

yeshiva: Talmudic college.

Yom Kippur: Day of Atonement; the most important Jewish religious holiday; a fast day, spent in solemn prayer, self-searching of heart and confession of sins by the individual in direct communion with God. It takes place on the tenth day of *Tishri,* eight days after Rosh Hashanah (New Year).

yom-tev (*yom-tov*): Holiday.